Thorpe Regis

by

Frances Mary Peard

Thorpe Regis
by Frances Mary Peard

Copyright © 2023

All Rights reserved.

ISBN: 978-93-59957-93-7

Published by

DOUBLE 9 BOOKS

2/13-B, Ansari Road
Daryaganj, New Delhi – 110002
info@double9books.com
www.double9books.com
Tel. 011-40042856

ABOUT THE AUTHOR

Between 1867 and 1909, Frances Mary Peard wrote more than 40 story books for kids and adults. She was born on May 16, 1835, and died on October 5, 1923. Most of them were books or collections of short stories set in the United States. Many of them were historical and took place abroad. Commander George Shuldham Peard (1793-1837), a navy officer who went to the Arctic to look for Sir John Franklin, and Frances Cooke (née Ellicombe, 1805-1895) had five children; two of them died young. She was born in Exminster, Devon. Joshua Peard was her grandpa, and John Whitehead Peard was her uncle. Her brother George Shuldham Peard (1829-1918), who was also an artist, had served in the Crimean War. Since she comes from a family of famous soldiers and sailors, it's not a surprise that fights and military themes show up a lot in her stories. She seems to have traveled a lot, maybe even as far as India. But in her later years, she lived with her mother in Torquay, Devon. French author Frances Peard wrote books for kids of all ages, including fiction for adults. She got ideas for her books from her trips, especially in France and India.

CONTENTS

Chapter One

Nowadays the word "change," when applied to a place, seems so naturally to carry in itself the ideas of growth, enlargement, and progress, that we find a certain difficulty in adopting the word in its retrograde sense, or of recognising other steps than those which we are in the habit of looking upon as advancement. And yet, if it be true that, under the pressure of an ever-increasing population, hamlets have become towns and fishing-villages seaports, it is no less certain that the great march leaves behind it, or pushes out of its way, many stragglers too sick, too feeble, or too weary for its ranks. Thorpe Regis was such a straggler. Not to speak of those ancient days, the glories of which only its name now kept in faint remembrance, there had been a time when the great high road to London ran through its length. Twice a week the London coach lumbered up to the door of the Red Lion, changed horses, let out its stiff and cramped passengers to stretch their limbs in the paved space before the door, or refresh themselves with a tankard of foaming ale in the stuffy little bar; and then lumbered off again out of the midst of a gaping knot of ostlers and stable-men. Twice a week came the London coach back, bringing with it a stir of life and importance, the latest messenger from the great world unknown to Thorpe except through its medium,—more peremptory, more consequential, and more exacting. There was not a boy or man about the place but felt a sense of interested proprietorship in the Defiance and the Highflyer, and a pride in their respective performances. From the tiny hamlets round, lying in their green seclusions of elm-trees and apple orchards, the rustics used to make muddy pilgrimages to Thorpe, to carry an occasional letter to its post-office, and to watch the coach with steaming leaders swinging down the hill. That was the moment of triumph. A few little half-fledged boys, who were sure to be on the lookout, would hurrah feebly and set off running as fast as their legs could carry them, and a woman or two was generally at hand to cast up her eyes and exclaim at the pace; but the majority preserved a stolid, satisfied silence. That Thorpe Regis was theirs and the London coach must stop there were facts as undeniable as the Church, the Squire's house, and the Red lion itself, and needed no comment.

Even facts, however, come to an end sometimes. There arrived a day when the railway, which had gradually been drawing nearer and nearer, reached Underham, a little out-of-the-world village about five miles west of Thorpe, which had hitherto looked humbly up to its more important neighbour, and without a murmur had carried its little tribute of weekly budgets to deposit at the door of the Red Lion. So readily does human nature accommodate itself to added greatness, that Underham was the first to claim from Thorpe the homage which all these years it had yielded ungrudgingly, and beyond a doubt it gave additional sharpness to the stings of humiliation endured by the fallen village, to know that its sudden depression had been caused by the prosperity of its rival.

For a short time the two coaches continued to run. The Highflyer was the first to succumb, while the Defiance, acting in accordance with its name, struggled on for another six months as best it could. But—although there might be something heroic in so unequal a warfare, and a certain dogged obstinacy in the refusal to accept defeat, which appeals forcibly to our English sympathies—the result could not possibly be averted. The old people who held railway travelling to be a tempting of Providence, and would fain have clung to the old ways to the end of their days, were too few in number, and too seldom travellers at the best, to support any means of conveyance whatever. Their journeys were rare events, and the last journey of all was not far off. So gradually the struggle came to an end. Underham built, paved, started a High Street, and gathered into itself all the traffic of the district. A company was formed to cut a canal and unite the railway with the river; and there were timber-yards, black coal-wharves, and all the busy tokens of prosperity, where, in former times, thatched cottages stood in the midst of their gardens, and bees sucked the wild blossoms of the honeysuckle.

Thorpe had long ago given up competing with its neighbouring rival. The old generation which resented the passing of its glories had passed away itself; only here and there an old man, leaning against his gate, would point with trembling finger up the hill, and in a cracked and feeble voice would tell his grandchildren how the London coach once brought the news that Nelson had beaten Bony at Trafalgar, and he, as a little lad, had clipped his hands and cheered with the rest. "They doan't get news like that thyur down to Under'm, not they," he would end, shaking his head scornfully. But, as a rule, it was only the old people whose memories pertinaciously resented the fallen fortunes of Thorpe. To others it was, as it had always been, a pretty old-fashioned village, set in the midst of green pastures at the foot of a tolerably steep hill, with a tangled network of lanes about it, and glimpses above the high hedges of a distant purple moorland. The cottages—broken by great outer chimneys running up like buttresses—were whitewashed, with many stages of descent between the first dazzling glaze of cleanliness and the last tumble-down exposure of the red-brown cob; while the thatch, beautiful in one season of its existence, presented as many gradations as the plaster, from its crude freshness to the time when withies were bound on it to prevent the wind from ripping it off, or the rain from dropping, as it often dropped, into the low bedroom of the family. Other houses there were of a more ambitious class. A few shops kept up a struggling existence, for although, except Weeks the butcher, no Thorpe person was rash enough to depend upon a single trade, there were combinations which developed a by no means contemptible ingenuity. Draperies and groceries were disposed from the same counter, with only an occasional inconvenience resulting from homely odours of tea or candles clinging to the materials with which they had long rested in closest neighbourhood. And a triple establishment at the corner, opposite the Red Lion, where the shoemaker kept the post-office and his wife instructed the Thorpe children in a back kitchen, was sometimes treated as the centre round which the village revolved.

Looking towards the hill which had been both the glory and the ruin of Thorpe Regis, since the flatter ground about Underham had led the surveyors for the railway to report more favourably upon its situation, the church with its red stone tower lay to the right, a little way up a lane, which in the hottest weather was hardly ever known to be dry; and the Vicarage might be entered either through the churchyard, or more directly from the village by an iron gate and drive. At the time of which I am writing, the vicar was the Rev. William Miles, whose family consisted of his wife, his son, and his daughter; and the squire of the place was old Mr Chester of Hardlands.

Returning through the village and walking straight forward, instead of taking the road to Underham, a tall, ugly brick house, with a gravel sweep before it and a delightful old garden at the back, would soon be reached. It was inhabited by two brothers called Mannering, who had once been well-known London lawyers. Entering the house by three steps, a low and old-fashioned hall presented itself in singular contrast to the tastes of the day; a staircase with oak banisters fronted the door, to the left was the dining-room, and a door beyond led you into the study, where, about the hour of noon, it was very probable that the two brothers would be found together. At any rate it was so on the morning on which my story opens.

The room was one of those comfortable dens which man, without the aid of feminine taste and adornments, is occasionally so fortunate as to construct for himself. It was low and square, and had neither chintz nor flowers to relieve the dark furniture; but the Turkey carpet, although somewhat faded, had lost little of the richness of its finely blended colours; the books which lined the walls were bound with a care and finish which hinted at something approaching to bibliomania on the part of their owners;

the pictures, though few, were choice, and the chairs were deep and inviting. Moreover, a summer noonday brightened whatever sombreness remained: sunshine came broadly in through a deep oriel-window, and the scent of flowers and newly mown grass mingled pleasantly with that of Russia leather and old morocco. The room was a cheerful room, although the cheerfulness might be of a subdued and old-world character; and the writing-table, while conveying certain suspicions of business transactions in the form of sundry bundles of papers docketed and tied with red tape, bore also a proof of more voluntary studies in a magnificently bound edition of Homer lying open upon the blotting-pad.

Mr Mannering, who had but just pushed his chair away from the table, was standing upon some low steps in the act of drawing another volume from his amply filled book-shelves, and turning round as he did so to answer a remark of his brother Robert's. His slim figure was dressed with scrupulous neatness; he had slender hands, — one of which now rested on the top step, straight from the wrist, and, if one might draw an illustration from another member, as it were on tiptoe; his shoulders were a little stooping, his head bent and turned inquiringly; and his quiet voice and smile contained something of quaint humour, and were noticeable at once.

"My dear Robert," he was saying, "can there be any use in my giving an opinion? So far as I understand the matter, you are blaming Stokes for not understanding the different natures of Gesnera elliptica and Gesnera elongata. How can I, who until this moment was ignorant of the existence in the world of any Gesnera at all, be an equitable arbiter?"

"Wrong, Charles, wrong. That is not the question; in fact, that has nothing whatever to do with the question," said Mr Robert, resuming his hasty march up and down the room. "Stokes is a fool, and, as he never was anything else, I suppose he can't help himself. I don't complain of that. What I complain of is, that he should attempt to be more than a fool. Haven't I told you fifty times," he continued, stopping suddenly before the delinquent, "that your business is to mind my orders, and not to think that or think this, as if you were setting up for having a head on your shoulders? Haven't I told you that, eh? — answer me, sir."

"'Tain't no fault of mine," rejoined the gardener, slowly and doggedly. "If this here Gehesnear had had a quiet time and no worriting of charcoal and korkynit and such itemy nonsense, you wouldn't ha' seen a mossel of dry-rot in the bulb. That's what I says, and what Mr Anthony says, too."

"Confound your impudence, and Mr Anthony's with it. So you have been taking him into consultation? No wonder my Gesnera has come to a bad end between your two wise heads. Charles, do you hear?"

"Mr Anthony has mastered horticulture, has he?" said Mr Mannering, turning his back upon the combatants, whose wrath was rapidly subsiding. "If the boy goes on in this fashion there must be a new science created for his benefit ere long. Well, Robert, science has always had its martyrs, and you should submit with a good grace to your Gesnera being among them. When did Mr Anthony come back?"

"Tuesday night, sir. He comed up here yesterday, but you was to Under'am."

"I forbid his going within ten yards of the stove plants," cried Mr Robert, hastily. "If I find him trying experiments in my hot-houses, you shall be packed off, Stokes, as surely as I have put up with your inconceivable ignorance for seven years. I've not forgotten what Anthony Miles's experiments are like. Didn't he nearly blow up Underham with the chemicals he got hold of when that idiot Salter's back was turned? Didn't he bribe the doctor's assistant, and half poison poor old Miss Philippa with learning how to mix medicines, forsooth? Didn't he upset his mother, and frighten her out of the few wits she possesses, by trying a new fashion of harnessing? And now, as if all this were not enough, my poor plants are to be the victims. I forbid his coming within the great gate,—I forbid your speaking to him while he is possessed with this mania,—I forbid his looking at my Farleyense—"

"He've a seen that, sir," said Stokes, with his stolid features relaxing into a grin.

"O, he has seen that, has he?" said Mr Robert, struggling between indignation and gratified pride. "Do you hear that, Charles? Actually, before I've had time to give my orders. And, pray, what had Mr Anthony to say of my Farleyense?"

"He said," replied the gardener, doling out the sentences to his impatient master with irritating slowness, "as how he had comed through Lunnon, and been to one o' they big flower-shows they talk so much about. And he said as there were a Farlyensy there—"

"Well, well?"

"As belonged to a dook—"

"Yes,—well, what did he say? Can't you speak?"

"As warn't fit to hold a candle to owers," burst out Stokes triumphantly, slapping his leg with an emphasis which made Mr Mannering, who had returned to his seat at the writing-table, start and look round in, mild expostulation. His brother was rubbing his hands, and beaming in every feature of his round face.

"To be sure, to be sure," he said in a tone of supreme satisfaction. "Just what one would have expected. But I am glad Anthony happened to be up there just at this time, and I will say for the lad that he makes better use of his eyes than three parts of the young fellows one meets with. So it was an inferior sort of article, was it?—with fronds half the size, I'll lay a wager. You hear, Charles, don't you? Well, Stokes, you have been exceedingly careful to treat that Farleyense in the manner I showed you,—I knew it would answer,—here, man, here's half a sovereign for you, and mind the earth doesn't get too dry."

"Thank ye, sir, thank ye," said Stokes, prudently abstaining from the contradiction in which at another time he might have indulged.

"And, Stokes—"

"Yes, Mr Robert."

"If Mr Anthony comes up again, just let me know. I should wish him to see one or two of the other things in the house, but I prefer showing them to him myself."

"It's most likely he'll be up again to-day, sir. He wants Miss Winifred to have a look at the plant."

"Certainly, certainly. You can send in word when they come. And, Stokes—"

Stokes, who by this time had his hand upon the door, having tucked the luckless Gesnera out of sight, turned obediently.

"No experiments, mind, no experiments."

"No, Mr Robert 'Specially korkynit," added the gardener in an audible whisper, as he went out. Whether or not Mr Robert heard him, it is impossible to say. Something like a red flush rose in his face, and he looked hurriedly at his brother; but Mr Mannering was sitting back in his deep chair, his elbows on its arms, his fingers joined at the tips, his eyes fixed upon the volume before him, and if the shadow of a smile just hovered about his lips, it might have been excited by some touch of subtle humour in the pages which apparently absorbed his attention. The younger brother fidgeted, went to the window, altered a slight crookedness about the blind, stood there in his favourite attitude, with his hands behind his back, and at length returned to the writing-table, and took up one of the bundles of papers which were lying upon it.

"You have written to Thompson about the mortgage, I suppose?" he said in a business-like tone which contrasted oddly with his previous bustling excitement.

"Really, Robert," said Mr Mannering, looking up, and speaking apologetically, "I believe I have done nothing of the kind. Upon my word, I do not know where my memory is going. I had the pen in my hand to begin the letter, and something must have put the matter out of my head."

"Never mind. If you can make room I'll sit down at once, and give the fellow a summary of what he has to do."

But Mr Mannering was evidently annoyed with himself.

"I am growing old, that is the truth," he said despondingly.

"Old?—pooh! Go and look in the glass, Charles, before you talk of getting old to a man that is but three years your junior. Old?—why, there isn't a Mannering that comes to his prime before seventy. I expect to grow younger every day, and to have a game of leap-frog with you before many years are past;—do you recollect the leap-frog in the play-ground of the Grammar school?—why, it seems but yesterday that great lout of a fellow, Hunt, went flying over my head, and struck out with his hob-nailed shoes, and caught me just across the knuckles. I can feel the sting yet. There, glance over this, and see if it will do for Thompson. I wonder where old Hunt is now."

"I met him in the city the other day with a grandson on either side."

"I dare say. He was always too much of a blundering blockhead to understand that the way to grow old is to have a tribe of children treading on your heels. You and I know better. Here we live, as snug a pair of cronies as is to be met with for twenty miles round, without any such sharp contrasts disturbing our equanimity."

In answer to his brother's cheery words, and the hand which grasped his as they were spoken, Mr Mannering shook his head a little sadly.

"Things might have been different—for you, Robert, especially. Do you think I have forgotten Margaret Hare?"

"Why should you forget, or I either? Things might have been different, as you say, but it does not follow they would have been better. Look here, Charles; we have not spoken much of Margaret Hare of late years. I don't forget her, though I am an old blustering fellow, I don't forget her, but I can look back and say God bless her, and thank him, too, that things are as they are. I don't want any change, and I have never repented."

"It does my heart good to hear you say that, Robert."

"Well, there, it's said and done with. Are you going to Underham to-day?"

"I promised Bennett to look in. He wants me to dine with him to-morrow."

"That's very well for young fellows like you, but don't accept for me. If I go off the premises we shall be having Anthony Miles up here with an infallible compound for destroying caterpillars and all the plants into the bargain. I shall administer a lecture to-day, when he brings Miss Winifred."

"Get her to do it."

"I'm half afraid she does it too much already. It seems to me that love-making is more altered than leap-frog since our day, Charles,—Well, well, some things don't change, and luckily luncheon is a permanent institution. Come, and spare Mrs Jones's feelings."

"I am losing my appetite," said Mr Mannering, sighing.

"Come in, at all events." And, with a little show of reluctance on the part of the elder, the brothers walked off to the long dining-room lying on one side of the library, and looking out upon the cheerful and sunny garden which had somehow caught the spirit of Robert Mannering's kindliness.

Chapter Two

"So many worlds, so much to do,
So little done, such things to be."

In Memoriam.

The path from Thorpe Regis to Hardlands lay across two or three of those green fields which ran in and out of the village and gave it the air of deep retirement remarked by the few visitors who jogged in a fly from the nearest town to see the thatched cottages, the red church, the apple orchards, and the great myrtles which grew boldly up to the very eaves of the houses. You might reach Hardlands in a more dignified and deliberate fashion by driving along the old London road, and turning into a short lane, when the iron gate would soon appear in sight; but the most sociable and habitual means of approach was that which led through the fields to a narrow shrubbery path, emerging from which the long white house, with a green veranda stretching half-way across its front, became pleasantly visible at once.

Between Hardlands and the Vicarage a very brisk communication was kept up. The Squire and the Vicar had not indeed been friends beyond the term of Mr Miles's residence at Thorpe, but that had now reached a period of fifteen years; and although fifteen years at their time of life will not balance an earlier friendship of but five, and although there was neither similarity nor natural sympathy between the two men, yet neighbourhood and a certain amount of isolation had formed a bond which either of the two would have found it painful to break. Mr Chester, moreover, had lost his wife while the Mileses were yet fresh comers, and with two motherless girls left upon his hands it became a natural thing to apply in his perplexity to Mrs Miles, a woman in whom, whatever else might lack strength, it was not the sweet tenderness of motherly instincts. Winifred and little Bessie were at least as much in the Vicarage nursery as their own, sharing all things with Marion and Anthony; and if, as they grew older, a half-unconscious change took place in their relationships, it had not been the means of loosening the intimacy, or diminishing the number of mutual visits. Bessie and her father had that morning looked in at the Vicarage, and in the late afternoon Marion and Anthony walked across the fields by the familiar path along which they could have gone blindfold, towards Hardlands.

The day was one of those exhilarating days of early summer, before any languor of great beat has stolen into its heart, and while the freshness of spring still leaps up in breezy flutterings of leaf and bough. Hay-making was going on vigorously, and the air was laden with the grateful scent. There were fields yet green with cool depths of waving grass, and others where keen shadows fell upon the smoothly shaven turf. Here and there a foxglove reared itself upwards in the hedges, here and there dog-roses unfolded innocent little pink and white buds. Without any striking beauty in the landscape about Thorpe, a certain pastoral and homely charm in the thatched cottages, the fields, the blossoming orchards, and even in such unromantic details as the shallow duck-pond under Widow Andrews's wall, made a more exacting demand upon the affections of those who lived among them than could altogether be understood by such as only looked upon them from the outside. Anthony Miles, as he walked along with his head a little thrown back, switching the grass with a laurel rod confiscated from Widow Andrews's little grandson, who had been caught by the brother and sister, as they passed, using it as an instrument of torture upon a smaller and weaker companion, was not thinking of the familiar objects with any conscious sense of admiration, and yet they were affecting him pleasantly; so that, although he might have said many other places were filling his heart at this time,—for there is an age with both men and women when place has even more power than people,—it is likely that, had he known the truth about himself, he would, after all, have found Thorpe in the warmest corner; old sleepy stupid Thorpe with its hay-ricks, its bad farming, and its broad hedges cumbering the land, against which he was at this moment inveighing to Marion.

"Did you ever see anything cut up like these half-dozen acres? There's one slice taken out, and here's another; a hedge six foot across at the bottom if it's an inch, and a row of useless elms sucking all the goodness out of the ground. I don't believe there's a richer bit of soil in all England, and they can do no more than get a three-cornered mouthful of pasture out of it for one old cow."

"O Anthony, why can't you let things alone, when they don't concern you? My father has allowed you to have your own way about the paddock, and you surely need not tease Mr Chester to death over his hedges."

"That is so like a woman, who can never see anything beyond her own shadow. Can't you understand that it would be for the good of Thorpe if the ground that feeds people's mouths were better drained and if there were more of it?"

"So this is to be the next hobby, is it?"

"Farming? Hum, I don't know. If I could induce old Chester to go in for a few experiments, it might be worth while, perhaps, to get up the subject. But everything is on such an absurdly small scale here, that it would be hardly possible to do anything satisfactory."

"And you really mean that you would be willing for all your schemes to resolve themselves into the miserable mediocrity of settling down at Thorpe and improving the hedges of the district!" said Marion indignantly.

"One might do a good deal in that way," Anthony answered, with a mischievous twinkle in his eyes as he looked at his sister. Any one who had seen him at that moment must have been struck with the extreme boyishness of his appearance. It might have been the curly light brown hair, or, more likely, the slight figure and sloping shoulders, but something there was which had changed but little for the last ten years, and kept him a boy still. Marion looked years older. He was always irritating her by his quick changes, his enthusiasm, his projects for the good of other people. So long as he might have his own way in the doing, there was nothing that he would not have done.

Marion had small sympathy for such notions; she clung to what was her own with a passion and a wilfulness which made her blind to what she would not see, but she did not care to go out of that circle. Yet people said that the brother and sister were alike, and to a certain extent the world's judgments were correct, as the world's judgments often are, only that a hundred little things too subtle for so large a beholder made a gulf between the two. He provoked her constantly as he was provoking her now.

"I sometimes think you will end in doing nothing," she said, walking on quickly.

"So do I, a dozen times a day. Who's this coming?—isn't it that fellow Stephens? I've a bone to pick with him, I can tell him. What do you suppose he's after now? He wants Maddox to let him have that bit of ground close by the school to build a chapel upon. I think I see it! Stokes gave me a hint of it, and I've been bullying Maddox all the morning, and pretty well got his word for it at last. The canting methodistical rascal! I wish I could see him kicked out of the place."

Anthony was speaking with great energy. He and Marion were walking through the cool meadows, beyond which lay the softly swelling hills. To the left, a little in front of them, the Hardlands shrubbery gate led into a thin belt of fir-trees, but the path continued through the meadows, until it crossed a small stream, and reached a lane branching from the high road. People liked to turn away from the hard dust and get into these pretty fields, where soft shadows fell gently and the delicate cuckoo flowers grew; and Mr Chester had tacitly suffered a right of way to be established, though he inveighed against it on every occasion. It was a grievance with which he would not have parted for the world, even if his own natural kind-heartedness had not been entirely on the side of the tired wayfarers, and nobody took any notice of it. So that even Anthony's indignation did not extend itself to the fact that David Stephens was coming towards them along the narrow track.

"I shall go on: Winifred will be wondering what has become of us," said Marion, who had not sufficiently forgiven her brother to be ready to take his side in the contest. He stood still with his hand on the gate, waiting for Stephens to pass, so determinedly, that the man as he reached the spot stopped at once.

He was much shorter than Anthony, as short, indeed, as an ordinary-sized boy of fourteen, and there was an actual though not very prominent deformity of figure. Yet this warp of nature seldom struck those who fronted him, for the head and face were so powerful and remarkable that they irresistibly seized the attention. Even Anthony, who was as enthusiastic in his prejudices as in his other feelings, was conscious of something in the eyes which checked his first flow of resentment. He would have preferred beginning with a more trenchant opening than—

"Hallo, Stephens, you're the person I wanted to see."

"Did you, sir? Well, this is the second time I've been to Thorpe to-day."

"Yes, I know that," said Anthony, recovering himself, and feeling the words come to him. "I've seen Maddox, he's just been at our house, and what you're after won't do at all. Do you suppose my father would stand one of your ranting places stuck up just under his nose? You'd better take yourself off a few miles, for, let me tell you, Thorpe doesn't want to see you, and you may find it a little hotter residence than you have any fancy for."

"I am not afraid of threats, sir," said Stephens quietly.

Anthony had been speaking in an authoritative tone, as if his decision quite set the matter at rest, and opposition irritated him as usual.

"I simply tell you what will happen if you come where you're not wanted," he said, raising his voice. "And as to the chapel, we'll take care that is never built. You may call it a threat if you please, but it's one that will find itself a fact."

"Mr Miles, the word of God has borne down fiercer things than you are like to hold over me, and it will do so yet again. I am sorry to go against you, but I must either do that or against the inward conviction."

"Cant," muttered Anthony wrathfully. "And so you suppose you're to have that field?"

"Mr Maddox has as good as promised it, sir."

"You'll find him in a different mind now."

"He'll not go against his word!"

For the first time during the interview Stephens's quietness was broken by a touch of passion. His eyes, lit up by a sudden fire, fastened themselves anxiously upon Anthony. Anthony, who had hitherto been the angry one of the two, felt a contemptuous satisfaction at having raised this wrath.

"His word! Things are not done quite so easily as all that. You had better turn and go back again, for all the good you'll get by going on."

"I should be glad of a direct answer, sir," said David, restraining himself with an effort. "Has Mr Maddox told you downright that he will not let us have the field?"

"Yes, he has."

Stephens's face had lost its red flush, but his eyes still held their deep fire.

"Then God forgive you!" he said in a low passionate voice, opening out his hands slightly, and walking away with quick steps. Anthony did not look after him; he turned into the little path, and began to whistle with a certain sense of pleasure in his victory which was not checked by any pitiful misgivings.

Chapter Three

"God Almighty first planted a garden; and indeed it is the purest of human pleasures."
Bacon's *Essays*.

As Anthony emerged from the little path under the fir-trees, he saw that Winifred and Marion were in the garden, and that Winifred was gardening, her gown drawn up, gauntleted gloves on her hands, and a trowel held with which she was at work.

"We shall be ready in a minute," she called out, nodding to him. "I am so glad you are come, for I thought you might have forgotten our walk."

"It was too hot before," said Anthony, strolling towards them, and stretching himself lazily upon the grass.

"And I have done no end of work. You see those bare places in the beds, over which you were so unmerciful, are quite filled. Luckily Thomas had a great many surplus plants this year."

As she stood up, a great clump of flowering shrubs—guelder roses, pink thorn, azaleas—made a pretty and variegated background. She had drawn off her big gloves, and was beating the earth from them as she spoke, and smiling down upon him with bright pleasantness. Anthony looked at her, and a satisfied expression deepened in his eyes. He had hold of one of the ribbons of her dress, and was fingering it.

"Why don't you always wear lilac?" was his somewhat irrelevant answer.

"You don't attend to what I am saying," said Winifred, a little impatiently. "I want to know what you think of the flowers, and not of my dress."

"Why should I not talk about that as well? You have at least as much to do with the one as the other."

"It is not what I have to do with it, but how it looks when it is done. Marion, can't you prevent Anthony from being frivolous?"

"Don't ask Marion," said Anthony, biting a bit of grass. "She has been falling foul of me all the way here, though neither of us can exactly say what it has been about. My ruffled feathers want smoothing down, if you please, Winifred."

"You don't look ruffled a bit."

"That is my extraordinary amiability."

"Marion did very well to scold you, I am sure."

"And that is the way women jump at conclusions."

"I shall jump at the conclusion presently that you mean to go to sleep on the grass, and leave us to walk to the Red House alone."

"I? I am ready to start this moment, and the time you have supposed to be wasted I have spent in making up my mind that a mass of amaranthus ought to replace the verbenas in that bed."

"Amaranthus! O Anthony, they would be so gloomy."

"Just the effect you want, when everything is too flaming."

"No, no," said Winifred, resolutely holding her ground. "You must find your relief at the back, for the flowers themselves can't be too bright."

"Now, Winifred, there are certain principles," began Anthony, sitting upright and speaking energetically, "principles of contrast, by means of which you get a great deal more out of your brilliancy than when you run one colour into the other. I wish you would let me explain them to you."

"Understanding the principles would never make me doubt my eyes. No, indeed, I am very sorry, but I could not sacrifice those splendid verbenas after watering them for so many evenings."

"You should not water at all."

Winifred looked at him, laughed, and shook her head.

"I don't mean to give way to these horrible new theories. To begin with, they would break Thomas's heart."

"O, very well," said Anthony, getting up, affronted. "Did you say you were ready to start? Marion! We are waiting."

He marched before them in evident displeasure; Winifred, who knew that his discontent would not last long, looking at him with a little amusement. They skirted the field where the haymakers had been at work all day, and the sweet dry grass lay tossed about in fragrant swathes as the forks had dropped it. Across, between the elm-trees, the sun shone upon the canal and the Underham houses, while, beyond again, lay meadows and wooded hills, and the soft western moorland. On the other side of the nearest field was a figure on an old bay cob, with a dog standing by his side, and a man pointing. This was the Squire, too deep in consultation over some boundary annoyances to notice the little party scrambling over their stiles, and waving every now and then to attract his attention.

"Which of you are going to dine at the Bennetts' to-morrow?"

"Papa, Anthony, and I."

"And is Marmaduke to be there?"

"I suppose so. It depends on the trains."

"And Mr Mannering, of course. Marion, did you ever hear that there is a romantic story about those brothers?"

"What's that?" said Anthony, stopping and looking round.

"It was Miss Philippa who told me," Winifred explained, "and she was not at all clear about it; but it seems that one of them was engaged to a lady, when his brother fell into a bad state of health, requiring great care for a long while, and the other gave up everything, devoted himself, nursed, prevented people from finding out how incapable he had become, and was really the means of saving his life, or his reason, or whatever was in danger. But then comes the sad part. The lady grew tired of waiting, and married some one else."

"It is rather a complicated story. And which is the hero?"

"Mr Mannering," Marion said, promptly.

"I believe it to have been Mr Robert," said Anthony, in a tone of decision.

"So do I," said Winifred, looking brightly at him, happy in fulfilling a longing against which she not infrequently fought more steadily, from thinking that it was not well for him to carry matters altogether as he liked.

Anthony smiled, and fell back a little with his good-humour restored. After all, it was a pleasant thing to be walking through the Thorpe fields with Winifred, who had a certain charm about her, harmonising with what surrounded them. In a crowded room she might have passed with little notice; but here, in the open air, with an evening breeze sweeping up from the sea, six miles distant, and fresh cool scents just touching it, the buoyancy of her step, the clearness of her voice, and the frank honesty of her eyes, were all in agreement with the country life in which she had grown to womanhood, and the outer influences of which work in proportion as we admit them. That day, also, had been full of light-hearted happiness. Anthony had returned from an absence of some months, which he had spent in travelling. He and she were in excellent accord in spite of their little passage at arms, and they were just in an easy social position towards each other, which made it seem scarcely possible that they should not always go on as smoothly. It was when they were together in what is called society that little storms arose, that Winifred's eyes would suddenly flash, and some quick speech descend upon Anthony, in abrupt contrast to the sugared politeness which had been flowing in pleasant streams. It was natural that he should resent it. With an older experience she might have treated him differently; but her very eager longing that he should rise above what she herself despised made her impatient that he did not rise at once. It is no untrue assertion that too close knowledge is an obstacle to love. When a boy and girl grow up together, the light beats too strongly for those delicate and shadowy enchantments, those delicious surprises, those tender awakenings, by which others are led on all unconsciously. It may, now and then, lose no particle of strength because of this, but such cases are at least rare. Winifred had a hundred misgivings for Anthony, who had none for himself. It seemed to him as if nothing were out of his reach, as if neither time, nor opportunity, nor success could fail. Was he not twenty-four, with a lifetime before him? Had he not gained the Chancellor's gold medal? He had, moreover, that sense of fellowship, which more than any other gift heartens a man for work among his kind; he was full of enthusiasm for doing good, for upholding right, for beating down wrong,—he would be an author, a reformer, a politician,—he would raise Thorpe by penny readings,—he would improve the Hardlands property by inducing the Squire to sweep away his hedges,—the church singing should be converted into harmony, ignorance into intelligence, wrong into right,— are there any limits or misgivings which trouble these young champions who leap into the arena, and believe a hundred eyes are upon them? It was Winifred who looked at him and trembled.

Mr Robert Mannering met them inside the gates.

"I saw you coming," he said. "Well, Anthony, and so you are back from your travels, and your father says you have not yet made up your mind what new worlds you shall conquer. I congratulate you. Only, my dear boy, don't make Stokes your prime minister. Leave pottering about amongst leaf-mould and bell-glasses to superannuated old fellows like me. Miss Winifred, I am proud to hear that you are come to see my Farleyense."

"Anthony says it is such a fine plant."

"It is a fine plant. It might be almost anything," said Anthony. "I told Stokes that if I were he I should treat it differently. I wish he would let me have a turn at it for a fortnight." Mr Mannering gave a quick gasp, and stood still to look at the speaker.

"I shall keep the key in my pocket until he is out of the place. Miss Winifred, Miss Marion,—we are old friends,—detain him at the Vicarage, at Hardlands, find some innocent occupation for him which shall not harrow old gentlemen's pet hobbies. Set him to cure Miss Philippa's rheumatism,—I don't wish to be uncharitable, but by her own account it can't be worse than it is, whereas my Farleyense—Good Heavens, I shall not sleep for a week for thinking of the peril it is in."

"Of course, there must be a certain amount of risk," said Anthony coolly; "but, after all, the experience gained for others is worth more than the thing itself. That always seems to me the only object in gardening. However, if you don't care about it, sir,—that's enough. I'm going to hunt up the tortoise."

"Do, do, by all means. The fellow's shell is thick enough to protect him. This way, Miss Winifred. I hope you don't mind a few steps. You are judicious in your time, for I always think this soft late light is more becoming than any other to the plants. There,—a picture, isn't it? I almost wish Anthony had come down after all."

"He is too full of projects to be a safe visitor just at present," said Winifred, shaking her head, but secretly proud in her heart.

"I'll defy him to find a finer Farleyense anywhere, at any rate," said Mr Mannering valiantly. He was looking at Winifred as he spoke, and thinking that Thorpe had other pretty things to show Anthony. There was a soft gloom in the house, out of which seemed to spring the delicate green feathery ferns full of still strange life, and Winifred, standing among them, had a sweet light in her eyes and a half-smile on her lips. It was not very often that people agreed she was pretty, and then they were probably thinking of the fresh colouring, the bright hair, and that indescribable fairness of youth which, even without other claim to beauty, carries with it so great a charm; but the true attraction in her face consisted in a certain nobility of expression, of which the delight would but deepen as the more fleeting fairness departed.

"Here is an exquisite little Cystopteris, Miss Marion," said Mr Robert, beginning to bustle about, "and that is the finest hare's-foot in the county. I want to have a look at your oak fern, but I must go into Underham to-morrow. Miss Philippa has a quarterly paper which requires signing at least five times every year."

"Marmaduke comes to-morrow," said Marion, who had been silent. "Can't he sign his aunt's papers?"

"No, I am sorry to tell you that the law makes a distinction between a man and a magistrate. So Marmaduke comes to-morrow? And he and Anthony, I have no doubt, will chalk out a fresh career for every day in the week when they get together."

"There is not much room for what you call a career in poor Marmaduke's case," said Marion, drawing her gloves tightly through her hands, and keeping her head turned away, so that only a sharply cut profile could be seen. "A clerk in a merchant's office does not look forward to anything very brilliant."

"Unless he wins the heart of the daughter of the principal partner, and you have been so hardhearted as to cut that chance of promotion from under his feet. Well, these are the contrarieties of life, but they tumble into shape somehow at the end, so keep a good heart, my dear."

He said it with an odd quaver in the cheery voice, although neither of the two noticed it. They were thinking of themselves with the unconscious egotism of youth. There were all sorts of tender visions flitting about among the soft shadowy ferns, and some not less tender than the rest that they were dim with age and years. Marion went on after a momentary pause:—

"I suppose his best chance lies with Mr Tregennas."

"Yes and no, and no more than yes, I take it. If Marmaduke will stick to his business and not allow imaginary prospects to unsettle him, they may do him no harm. But it's ill waiting for dead men's shoes, especially if you do not step into them at the last. There is nothing so likely to sour a man's life."

"There cannot be doubt when he has promised," Marion said, turning towards him with a movement which was abrupt enough to betray a little anxiety in the words.

"He has, has he?"

"Yes, indeed. Marmaduke has often told me how much Mr Tregennas said, and no one, no one could be so cruel as not to keep to his word in such a matter!"

"Not intentionally,—at least, not many men. But, my dear Miss Marion, you never will be an old lawyer, and so I don't promise that you will ever find out how much of what we hear depends upon what we think, or how much of what we say depends upon what we believe we ought to have said. Now, you have not gone into such ecstasies as I expected over my Farleyense, but by to-morrow my imagination will have supplied all your deficiencies, and yours will make you ready to swear that you were as prettily enthusiastic as the occasion demanded."

"I beg your pardon," said Marion, smiling.

"Don't do that. Have I not just explained to you the recipe for harmonising the minor discords of one's life? There is some happy stuff in our composition—vanity, if you will—which fills up what is wanting."

"Are you there? Shall I come down?" said Anthony's voice from the top of the steps.

"No, no, wait a moment; we are coming, we are coming this instant," said Mr Mannering, hurriedly. "Take care of the wet, Miss Winifred,—here we are; thank you, yes, I prefer to lock the house for the night. And how did you find the tortoise, and what did you do to him, Anthony?"

"Do to him? I did nothing,—at least, I only moved him to the sunny side of the wall, where he will be a good deal better off."

They were strolling towards the road, Mr Mannering with his hands locked behind his back, and a twinkle of amusement about eyes and mouth.

"Thank you, my dear boy, thank you," he said, gravely. "But I should be a good fourteen stone to carry, and, to tell the truth, I would rather stay where I am."

"What do you mean?" said Anthony, puzzled. "Was I talking to myself? I beg your pardon,—it was the oddest idea,—do you know, just for a moment I had a feeling at the back of my neck as if I were the tortoise."

Chapter Four

"I did but chide in jest: the best loves use it
Sometimes; it sets an edge upon affection:
When we invite our best friends to a feast,
'Tis not all sweetmeat that we set before 'em;
There's something sharp and salt, both to whet appetite
And make 'em taste their wine well."

Middleton.

From what has been said of the resources of Thorpe Regis, it will be easily understood that it did not possess any public vehicle capable of conveying its inhabitants to dinner-parties or other solemnities. When such a conveyance became an absolute necessity, there was sent from Underham a fly which had a remarkable capacity for adapting itself to different occasions. A pair of white gloves for the driver and a grey horse presented at once the festive appearance considered desirable for a wedding, while the lugubrious respectability demanded by an English funeral was attained by the substitution of black for white, and by a flowing hat-band which almost enveloped the little driver. Its natural appearance, divested of any special grandeur, was that of a roomy, heavily built, and some what battered vehicle, which upon pressure would hold one or two beyond the conventional four, and carry the Thorpe world to the evening gayeties of the neighbourhood with no greater amount of shaking and bumping than habit had led them to consider an almost indispensable preparation to a dinner with their friends.

On the evening of Mr Bennett's party, the Underham fly might have been seen drawn up in front of the Vicarage porch, a snug little excrescence on the south side of the house, and scarcely a dozen yards from the church. The dinner-hour was half past six, and it was a three quarters of an hour's drive to Underham, so that the sun was still slanting brightly upon the old house, green with creepers of long years' growth; upon the narrow border of sweet, old-fashioned flowers that ran along the front, edged with box, and separated from the grass-plot by a little gravel walk; upon the fine young cedar half-way between the house and the road, the tall tritonias, and the cluster rose that had clambered until it festooned two ilex-trees with its pure white blossoms. Some charm of summer made the homeliness beautiful,— the repose of the last daylight hours, the cheerfulness of children's laughter in the village, the midges dancing in the quiet air, the shadows on the grass where pink-tipped daisies folded themselves serenely. Even the wrinkled face of Job White, the one-eyed driver, had caught something of glow from the sunshine, as he sat and conversed affably from his box with Faith, the parlour-maid at the Vicarage, a rosy-faced girl, not disposed, as Job expressed it, "to turn agin her mate because it warn't pudden." Job himself was one of the characters of the neighbourhood, a good-humoured patron of such of the gentry round as he considered respectable, and intensely conservative in his opinions. He had begun life as a Thorpe baby, and, although professional exigencies afterwards led to his settling at Underham, he did not attempt to disguise his contempt for the new-fangled notions prevalent in that place. One of his peculiarities led him to decline accepting as correct all time which could not be proved to agree with the church clock at Thorpe. The country alteration to what was called railway time which took place some twenty or five-and-twenty years ago he could not speak of except in terms of contemptuous bitterness; and, had it been practicable, he would have insisted upon remaining twenty minutes behind the rest of the world to the end of his days; but as his calling rendered this an impossibility, he contented himself with utterly ignoring the station clock, and obliging all those he drove to accommodate their hours to those of Thorpe. "He've been up thaes foorty years, and he ain't likely to be wrong now," was his invariable answer to remonstrances; and perhaps there could be no stronger testimony to the old west-world prejudices that, in spite of changes, yet clung about Underham, than the fact that with these opinions for his guide Job White still drove the Milman Arms fly.

At the moment when Faith, shading her eyes from the sun, was looking brightly up with instinctive coquetry, Job was settling in his waistcoat fob the globular silver watch which he had duly compared with his oracle in the tower. It was so bulky that it required a peculiar twist of his body to get it into the pocket at all, and wheft that difficulty was surmounted it formed an odd sort of protuberance, apt to impress beholders with a sympathetic sense of discomfort Faith, however, regarded it with due respect.

"True to a minit," Job said in a tone of contented self-satisfaction. "Now, Faith, my dear, suppose you wos just to step in and tell Miss Marion that, without she's pretty sharp, we sha'n't get to Under'm by half past six, nor nothing like it."

"She's on the stairs now," said Faith, reconnoitring, "and if there isn't Sarah come out of the kitchen to see her drest! I'm sure it is a wonder if she can stand there for a minute and not say something sharp. It wants the patience of a saint to live with Sarah."

"And that doesn't come to everybody as it do to me,—with their name," said Job. "She's a woman who isn't tried with a hitch in her tongue, but she's a neat figure for a cook."

"Well, I'm sure!" said Faith, pouting a little. "I never could see nothing in Sarah's figure,—but you'd better get down and open the door, Mr White."

With so great a scarcity of conveyances, combinations were matters of necessity in Thorpe, and the fly had already driven to the Red House in order to pick up Mr Mannering. The delay in starting had been caused at least as much by the Vicar's desire to hear his opinion upon a certain pamphlet which, when sought for, turned out to be missing, as by Marion's lingering doubts between the respective merits of two white muslins; but the truth was that punctuality did not exist at the Vicarage, and the church bell on Sundays stretched itself indefinitely, until the Vicar himself looked out from the vestry door and nodded for it to stop. Mr Mannering, having, on the contrary, a lawyer's respect for time, had for the last ten minutes been sitting upon thorns, taking out his watch, and regarding the door with as much uneasiness as a courteous attention to Mrs Miles's household difficulties would permit. Anthony had walked into Underham to meet Marmaduke Lee, and Mr Mannering fell uninterruptedly to Mrs Miles's care, until the Vicar opened the door and informed him that they were ready, with the really serious conviction common to unpunctual people that his visitor was the person for whom they had all been waiting.

They were in the hall and out in the little porch at last: the Vicar with his broad shoulders and plain face, Mrs Miles coming softly down to see them off, and pulling out Marion's skirts with a little motherly anxiety. They were all talking and laughing, and the sun still shone bravely on Marion's pretty gown and the roses she had twisted into her dark hair, and the jessamine which clambered to the topmost windows. Sniff, the Skye terrier, was dancing round the old grey horse, and barking wildly. Outside, in the little wet lane, brown sweet-breathed cows were plodding slowly back to their farm, and stopping now and then to contemplate the green lawn of the Vicarage, until Sniff, catching sight of an intruding head, became frantic with a new excitement, and, scrambling to the top of the hedge, was last seen as the fly turned out of the gate, a ball of flying hair in pursuit of a retreating enemy.

It was through a curious tangle of lanes that Job jolted his load, a little more unmercifully than usual, lest the time which had been lost should be laid to the account of the Thorpe clock by unbelievers at Underham. The hedge-rows were so high that the sun at this hour of the day shone only upon the tops of the blackthorn and nut bushes which crowned them, shone with a keen yellow light contrasting strongly with the dim shadows falling underneath upon the long grass and moss. But every now and then a break in the hedge, or a gate leading into the fields, revealed a sweet homelike view,—with no bold glory of form or colour, but tender with subtle harmonies of tints melting one into the other, a haze of blue, white smoke curling upwards, straw-thatched barns, with quiet apple orchards lying round them, where the grass grew long and cool about the stalks of the old trees, and the young fruit mellowed through the kindly summer nights. By and by the lanes widened, they passed an old mill, half hidden by ash-trees, drove between flat meadows, crossed a bridge, and reached the outskirts of Underham. Mr Mannering and the Vicar had fallen into a discussion upon a new edition of Sophocles, and Marion looked out of the window with a happy glow upon her face, not understanding how the two men should bury themselves in those old-world interests, when life was rushing on, full of charm, of pain, of wonderment. After all, it is but a world of new editions. Sophocles was no further removed from them than the hundred hopes and fears with which she and Marmaduke beguiled the time until they should meet again, touch each other's hands, look into each other's eyes. But Marion had not learnt this yet.

The Bennetts' house stood directly against the road, and the wall along which for some distance the footpath ran was the wall of their garden; the Underham boys holding fabulous views of the fruit that ripened on its innermost side, where green geometrical lines were marked out upon the warm brick. Mr Bennett was a lawyer, and having no children, he and his wife had adopted the daughter of a sister of Mrs Bennett's, treating her in every respect as though she were their own child. Miss Lovell was smiling up at Anthony when the Vicarage party arrived, and Mr Chester, who was always a little loud and peremptory in his voice, was holding forth to Mr Bennett upon a local election.

"I should be the last person in the world to wish to influence anybody," he was saying, "but you'll not deny, I suppose, that the other men are a pair of fools."

"Still, one doesn't altogether like to go against North,—he as good as belongs to Underham."

"Don't see the value of that," said the Squire, with a little roughness; and then dinner was announced, and they all trooped down. Anthony sat between an elderly lady and Miss Lovell, the Bennetts' niece, Marmaduke had Marion, and Winifred's neighbour was the son of Sir James Milman, the member. Anthony was always popular in society, so that to secure him was almost a pledge to the host and hostess that things would go brightly;

moreover, he had but just returned from his travels, and an added charm of novelty hung about him. Even Mrs Featherly, next to whom he was sitting, the wife of the rector of Underham, and one of those excellent women whom people all blamed themselves for disliking, began to look as if the fault-finding on which she rested as the moral backbone of her character was yielding to Anthony's pleasantness.

"You have seen a great deal since you left home, Mr Anthony, of one kind and another, and I hope you will make good use of it," she said graciously.

"He earned his holiday," said Mr Bennett, nodding his head. "After such great things at Cambridge, a man can't do better than take a run and let his brain have a little rest. I'm never for overwork."

"Only I do hope you have written some more beautiful poetry," Miss Lovell put in on the other side. She was a pretty girl, fair, with a long soft curl falling on her shoulder, and a voice which had a little imploring emphasis in it. "And not in Latin this time, or you really must send us a translation."

There was a good deal said in the same strain, to which Anthony made laughing disclaimers, liking the incense all the while. He was conscious of exaggerations, but it is not difficult to forgive exaggerations which lead along so pleasant a path, and his was a nature to grow warmly responsive under kindly treatment, so that his conversation became brighter and more entertaining, until even Mrs Bennett, who was contentedly eating strawberries, made the effort of inquiring at what they were laughing.

"Mr Miles is telling us such amusing things," said Miss Lovell, with unmistakable admiration in her tone.

"Amusing things!" repeated the Squire; "I never hear anything worth listening to of any sort. Bless you, they talk nineteen to the dozen in these days, but there's no making head nor tail of it when all's said. It's speechifying and argufying, and nothing done. That's what made half the mischief in the Crimea. We sha'n't get anything again like the old times, when there were no railways, nor confounded telegraphs pulling up the generals for every step they took, or making them believe there'd be a pack of men at their heels to pull them out of any holes they were fools enough to blunder into."

In his youth the Squire had been in the Dragoons, and no one at Underham was bold enough to question his authority as a military man. Mrs Bennett only said placidly,—

"Dear me, was it not a little inconvenient?"

"It's a good deal more inconvenient, ma'am, to have a heap of lies talked by people who don't know what they're talking about. Letters were letters in those days, and you didn't get pestered by every tradesman who wants to puff off his twopenny halfpenny foolery. When they came they had something in them. My mother, now. I've heard my father say that when news from Spain came in, and the old Highflyer was so hung about and set at, all the way down from London, that it was twelve o'clock at night before she got into Thorpe, as soon as my mother heard the wheels far off on the road, no matter what the weather was, rain or shine, moon or no moon, she would go out into the hall and put on her hood and cloak, and away she would trudge across the fields to the Red Lion to see if there might be a letter from poor Jack. My father was crippled at the time, and there wasn't one she'd let go in her stead. Poor old mother!" said the Squire, with an involuntary softening.

"I remember your mother, Squire," said old Mr Featherly.

"Then you remember as good a woman as ever breathed," said Mr Chester, strongly again.

"Well, she was, she was. People called her a little high, but no one found her so when they were in trouble. And a fine woman, too, as upright as a dart, going straight to her point, whatever it was, with as pretty an ankle and as clean a heel as any one in the country. Miss Winifred reminds me of her in many ways."

The Squire had pushed his chair a little back, and was looking at the glass of port he was fingering on the table with a pleased smile. But he shook his head at the old clergyman's last remark.

"Winifred's not so tall by half an inch or more as my mother was when she died."

"She carries her head in the same fashion, though," persisted Mr Featherly. "And there's something that reminds me."

It was certainly true that Winifred was at this moment holding her head with a little touch of stateliness. She had heard a good many of the flattering words which had been poured upon Anthony, and perhaps valued them at even less than they were worth, and it vexed her to see their effect upon him. Something in his nature courted the pleasant popularity and the spoiling. Is it women only who care for such pretty things? He might have told you that he despised them, but the truth was that they made a sunshine in which he liked to bask, a delight which was not without its influence. Winifred, who saw the weakness, was not merciful: she was a woman, with, perhaps, a grain of jealousy sharpening her perceptions, and rendering them sufficiently keen to probe the feminine flatteries which fell so sweetly upon him, and it is probable that, although a woman who loves—even unconsciously—sets herself, often unconsciously too, to study the character of the man she loves with a closeness of purpose, and an almost unerring instinct, swift to unravel its inmost workings, Winifred did not at this time rightly understand him. What she condemned as vanity was rather an almost womanish sensitiveness, to which the sunshine of applause might be said to have been needful. If it was withdrawn, he might either shrink or become bitter and morose. Perhaps there are two sides even to faults, and the people who love us best are sometimes our most severe judges: no one there thought hardly of Anthony, except Winifred, who would have had none of these little flaws, and sat, carrying her shapely head a little scornfully, as Mr Featherly had noticed. Anthony, on his part, was not long in discovering her displeasure, although unconscious of the cause. It provoked him, and he would not look in her face when the ladies went out of the dining-room.

Marion had drawn her into the balcony to pour out some of her hopes and fears about Marmaduke, and the two were talking eagerly when Ada Lovell came out, followed by such of the gentlemen as had come up stairs.

"I have been envying your good fortune to Mr Miles," she said, with an innocent air of admiration. "Of course you can see all his poetry whenever you like. It must be so delightful."

"Only I never do," said Winifred, standing upright. "I don't care for poetry unless it is the very best."

Woman like, she felt a pang in her own heart the instant she had sent forth her shaft. She glanced quickly and almost imploringly at Anthony, to see how sharply he was hit. If he had looked at her he might have known that she had flung down her weapons, and was waiting to make amends. But he would not look. He saw nothing of the involuntary grace of her attitude, as she stood in the glow of the sweet evening light, a little shamefaced and sorry, with a tender rosy softness in her face. He only felt that she had tried to wound him, and was angry with her for the second time that evening. Ada Lovell, looking up at him with admiring awe, had no such pricks with which to make him wince, and, perhaps, it was to be expected that he should devote himself to her for the remainder of the time. Winifred made no more advances. She stood leaning against the railing, looking gravely down upon the tall white lilies that by degrees grew and glimmered out of the dusk, until Mr Milman joined her. Marion and Marmaduke talked in a low voice at one end. People came out now and then, declared the dew was falling, and made a little compromise by sitting round the window, past which the bats flitted softly. Mr Mannering was telling clever stories, and making every one laugh. The Squire called his daughter at last. He disliked being kept waiting, and she went hurriedly, but as she passed Anthony she made a little pause to say gently, —

"Good-night, Anthony."

"Good-night."

There are some things which rest in our minds with quite a disproportionate sense of heaviness. Winifred knew that she should see Anthony the next day, by which time he would have forgotten her offence, but she seemed to have lost some of the confidence which ordinarily grew out of such a knowledge, for she could neither forgive herself nor forget the sound of his cold good-night.

Chapter Five

> "'Yet what is love, good shepherd, sayn?'
> 'It is a sunshine mixt with rain.'"

Sir Walter Raleigh.

Places like Underham offer peculiar attractions to maiden ladies, who find in them equal protection from the solitude of the country and relief from the somewhat dreary desolateness of a great town. It might have been an old friendship for Mrs Miles which first brought Miss Philippa Lee into the neighbourhood, but she firmly resisted all attempts to decoy her nearer to Thorpe. She took a small house not far from the Featherlys, and there devoted herself to the care of her orphan nephew with that pathetic self-renunciation which we see in not a few women's lives. She pinched herself to send him to a public school, and would gladly have supported him at college, but even had this been practicable for such straitened means, there were circumstances which prevented more than a secret sighing on her part. Marmaduke had, on his mother's side, a great-uncle who was the one rich man in a poor family, and who if not actually childless was so by his own assertion to all intents and purposes, his daughter having mortally offended him by a marriage against his will. She was the Margaret Hare of whom we have heard Mr Mannering speak, for it was not until after her marriage that her father, upon an access of fortune, changed his name to "Tregennas," and a little later, perhaps in a fit of desolation, took for his second wife and made miserable until her death an aunt of Mr Miles, the Vicar of Thorpe. The connection, although scarcely deserving of the name, was sufficient to form an additional link between the families, and Marmaduke read with the Vicar, and won Marion's love while they were little more than girl or boy.

To Mr Tregennas—who, it must be allowed, took a certain interest in his great-nephew, if interest is proved by occasional gifts of sovereigns and somewhat arbitrary advice on the subject of his education—Marmaduke meanwhile looked as the maker of his fortunes. He was careful from the first to withhold Miss Philippa from contradicting him, as, to tell the truth, she was not disinclined to do. Odd little shoots of jealousy crop up even in the most loving. Add to this that Mr Tregennas strongly opposed her favourite college scheme, and it will not be surprising that more than once Miss Philippa would very willingly, as she expressed it, have put her foot to the ground, if only Marmaduke had not knocked that very ground from under her, by adopting his uncle's views. And he was possessed of a certain languid self-will with which he invariably carried his point, even at the time when he appeared to yield, so that people were sometimes puzzled to reconcile cause and effect. Nevertheless, it was no doubt a severe disappointment when Mr Tregennas, instead of assisting him to enter a profession, advised his seeking employment in one of the great manufacturing firms of the north, and indeed actually applied to the heads before he had received an answer to his suggestion. Whether his will was the strongest, or his nephew's philosophy overcame dislike, his plan was carried out, and Marmaduke had been for two years engaged in the most distasteful occupation that could have been provided for him. It was, perhaps, this very sense of ill-usage which rooted the more firmly his belief that he was to be his uncle's heir. A grievance quickly excites the idea of compensation, and Marmaduke welded the two together so persistently that the one stood on nearly the same level as the other. The force, however, which prevented his throwing up his work had never proved sufficient to conquer his repugnance towards it, and the fact of feeling himself a victim, while it seemed to give him a right to feed upon future hopes, made it also a duty to seek alleviations in the present; so that a trifling vexation, or other change of mood, not infrequently brought about a flying visit to Thorpe and a drain upon Miss Lee's slender resources.

He had told Marion at the dinner-party that he must see her alone the next day, and, accordingly, when he walked to the Vicarage, at a time when Mr Miles and John were likely to be absent, Marion was waiting eagerly for him. Mrs Miles, who was in the room, was made more uneasy by his increasing thinness than by her daughter's determination to go out with him, for although no open engagement existed between the two, it was one of those events which might be expected to fell into shape at some future time, and which, if it were connected with Marion's will, it was hopeless for her mother to resist, even had she been disinclined towards it. But Marmaduke had a gentle ease of manner pleasant to those with whom he was thrown into contact, and Mrs Miles really loved and pitied him, and was grieved at his looks.

"Does your Aunt Philippa give you porter jelly, Marmaduke?" she asked anxiously. "I wish she would. I am sure it is the very best thing. Sarah shall heat some beef-tea for you in a moment, if you will only take it."

"Nothing will do me good while I have to work in that hole," said Marmaduke, with a dreary intonation in his voice. "Life is simply existence. And to think that I have had two years of it already!"

Marion, who had looked at him as he spoke, did not say a word until they were out of the house, and in the deep lane, fresh with a cool beauty of water and shining cresses. Then, as they walked on, Sniff paddling beside them, she asked quietly,—"Is anything the matter?"

There was noticeable in her manner to him—at all times—a difference from her usual fashion of speaking. The abruptness, something even of the brightness, was gone, and in its place seemed to have grown a soft care, a tenderness almost like protection. And at this moment their natures might have been transposed, for Marmaduke turned upon her with an impetuosity unlike himself.

"Anything! I tell you, Marion, that what I go through is unendurable. You might know better than to ask such a question as that."

"But why—what is it?" she persisted, with a vague trouble lest something more than she had heard was to be unfolded to her. Her loyalty to Marmaduke made her always ready to feed his self-pity, but she was afraid that he had taken some rash step.

"What good can a man do with work that he loathes?"

"You must remember to what the work will lead," she said, relieved.

"When?—how? It is absolute folly to dream that matters going on as they are going now can ever lead to anything satisfactory. How much do you suppose that I can squeeze out of a paltry hundred and fifty a year? Even Anthony acknowledges it to be absurd, and Anthony is Utopian enough to believe that everything grows out of nothing. That may do very well for him, who will never need to prove it," added Marmaduke, bitterly.

They were both leaning against a stile, and looking towards the cloudy distance of the moors. Marion slipped her hand softly into his.

"Surely we all heard when you went there that it would bring better things in a few years?"

"You talk of years as if they were days," he said in the same tone. "Nobody denies it. When I have drudged at that disgustingly low business for half a dozen years, I shall probably be fifty pounds a year better off than I am now, and by the time we are both too old to take pleasure in life we shall be able to marry, and this seems to content you perfectly."

Marion caught away her hand with a sudden movement. It made him turn to look at her, and the hurt anger in her eyes brought back his usual gentleness of manner at once. He was desirous to bind all her feelings on his side, and he knew her well enough to be aware that his shortest means of doing this was to revert to the wretchedness of his position.

"Forgive me, dearest," he said; "you don't know what a poor wretch a man becomes when he grinds along in one eternal round of small miseries. It is such a horrible separation from you all. And what is the good of being old Tregenna's's heir, if he can't put his hand into his pocket and let me live like a gentleman?"

"He promised that, did he not, Marmaduke?"

"It depends upon what you call promising. He is not the man to say out honestly, 'Marmaduke Lee, you're my heir, and I'll give you a fit allowance till you come into the property.' If he had, I should not be as I am. But he said quite enough. Of course I am his heir. There isn't a Jew in the country but would lend me a few thousands on the chance. Of course I am his heir. I wish you would make your father understand, and then he might allow us to consider ourselves engaged; at present it's like dropping a poor wretch into a pit, and blocking up his one glimpse of blue sky. I tell you, Marion, again, I cannot endure this state of things any longer. I've not got it in me to toil on in that dirty hole without so much as an atom of hope to cheer one."

They were both silent for an instant, and then Marion cried out passionately, "Toil! I would toil day and night for the joy of earning a sixpence which I could lay aside and say, 'This is ours.'" There was such a swift leaping out of the love of her heart in word and eyes, that it seemed fire which must needs kindle whatever it touched, if only for a moment. But no answering glow passed across his pale face. He looked away again as if what she said had not any relation to his thoughts, and she presently continued more timidly. "Surely it would be the height of imprudence to give up your work? And you know that if you did so my father would be less than ever likely to consent to our engagement, than now when you are at least on the road to independence."

"I can't go on as I am," he said, a little doggedly. "Mr Miles must give me something to hold by, or I shall throw up the whole concern. I have nearly done so a dozen times already."

"Is there no way of influencing Mr Tregennas?" asked Marion, after a minute's troubled thought.

"That's what I wanted to speak to you about. As I said before, it isn't fair that he should leave me in such a position. It's not as if I should have to work for my bread all the days of my life, like some poor devils. By and by I shall step into as pretty a place as you'll find anywhere, and why I should have to do compensation now by sitting on a high stool and addling my brain over ledgers is more than I can see. If he'd only say something definite one would know what one had to go upon. But—"

"But what?"

"O, you must understand, Marion, that I can't very well go to him and say this sort of thing!"

"Why not?"

"Why not? Well, women are queer about such matters, but I should think you might guess it's not the way to make yourself agreeable to an old fellow who has you in his power."

"It is only justice," said Marion, whose cheek had flushed under the presence of an absorbing pity for Marmaduke which swept her away like a flood. "I wish I could tell him what I think."

"You can do something better," said Marmaduke, seeing she had reached the point to which he had been leading.

"What? Only tell me."

"Get your father to interfere."

She shook her head, moving her hands nervously. "You know he will not. He is so scrupulous about such matters. Over and over again I have heard him say he would never ask a favour of his uncle."

"A favour! But I am not demanding an allowance of a thousand a year. All I want to know is how I stand. And if Mr Miles sees in black and white that I am his heir, he will no longer object to an engagement. I tell you plainly, I can't work unless I see some end before me. Besides, one must go step by step, and if he would acknowledge my position straightforwardly, by and by other things would follow. No one is so well entitled to ask as your father. Marion, you don't want to keep me in this misery?"

She was at no time insensible to these appeals, and perhaps less than ever on such a morning as this, when things about her were shining, dancing, singing in a burst of happy life, could she endure any weight of gloom for the man she loved best in the world. To some of us every echo of a happiness which does not at the same time fill our own souls with its music seems only discord. We cry out against it with voices that clash and jar and sadden themselves with the dissonance, when if we would be but content to listen in patience, some tender vibrations of an eternal harmony should reach us from afar, and satisfy us with their beauty. To Marion it was a positive wrong that the skylark high in the air was singing joyously; that the fresh breeze stirred into brightness the little stream which ran along the meadows; that the sound of the scythe and the chatter of the hay-making folk rose now and then with cheerful distinctness above lesser summer sounds; that Sniff was yelping with delight after the birds he was vainly chasing. Marion told him sharply to be quiet, but he only stopped for a moment, and looked at her with his head on one side at an angle of consideration, before he was off again, his little red tongue hanging out, his brown eyes on fire with excitement. Marmaduke, who was leaning moodily against the gate, waiting for Marion to speak, said at last, —

"Anthony is a lucky dog, with the world before him, and no one to please but himself. But I don't know that such sharp contrasts are the most encouraging reflections in the world."

The languor and depression of his voice pierced the girl's heart like a thorn. She exclaimed impetuously, —

"Something must be done, — my father shall write, — nothing can be so bad as that you should suffer in this way."

She put out her hand again, and he took it in his, and began to thank her in the gently caressing tones which fell easily from his lips. Her resolution, indeed, carried a greater relief to him than seemed to be contained in it. It was not only that he wanted to escape from the irksomeness of his duly toil, and believed the acknowledgment of his position the first step towards it, but he was also fretted by a wearing anxiety lest the position might never be his, and the very assumption of a certain claim on his part by Mr Miles might have a good effect, and remove a vague uneasiness, for which he could not account, of Anthony as a possible rival. Poor Marion thought it to be love for her which urged him; but although he did love her after a fashion, she was only one of the pleasant things he wanted to sweep into his net. He was full of satisfaction at the promise she had given.

"Who are these — by the watercourse?" he said. "One of them looks like Anthony."

"And the other is Mr Chester," said Marion, abstractedly. "Come."

"Yes, it is the Squire. I can see his red face, and that little flourish of his stick which he gives when he is angry. They see us by this time, and we may as well hear the battle-royal, if there is one. Listen."

Mr Chester's loud voice came up well before him.

"I tell you, sir, I tell you your father will live to see you a carping radical yet. When a young fellow gets this sort of notions into his head, we all know what'll be the end of it. Everything respectable goes out by the heels, and he makes a fool of himself over balloting and universal suffrage, and a heap of rascally French republicanisms. How d'ye do, Marion, how d'ye do? Glad to see you, Marmaduke. Hope you're not infected with any of this modern rubbish?"

"No, sir, I'm a Conservative. A Liberal-Conservative," added the young man under his breath, not expecting to be heard. But the Squire's quick ears caught the word.

"Don't be half anything. There's nothing I think so poorly of as a man that can't make up his mind. He says this on one side and that on another, till he knows no more than a teetotum where his spinning will lead him. I should have twice the opinion of Anthony if he could say straight out what he means, instead of calling himself one thing and talking himself into another." There was a good deal of truth in the Squire's accusation, and the clash was not one for which he had any sympathy. Anthony himself was too young not to be sore upon the charge of inconsistency. He said hotly, —

"Really, sir, I don't know what hedges and draining have to do with the ballot. I have not been the one to say anything about it."

"I'm only showing what these ideas lead to," said Mr Chester, enjoying his adversary's irritation. "I'm content to take my land as it came to me. That's good theology, ain't it, Marion? By the way, I forgot to tell you that young Frank Orde comes to-morrow. Come up to dinner, all of you, will you? I dare say he's as bad as the rest, but you'll not make me believe my father hadn't as good common-sense as the young fellows that find fault with his farming."

Sometimes, by talking loudly enough, a man becomes impressed with so confident a sense of triumph, that the sound of his own voice is like the salvo of guns over a victory. It was so now with the Squire, who remained in high good-humour during the rest of the walk, and gave Anthony to understand that he looked upon him as crushed and annihilated by an overwhelming weight of argument.

Chapter Six

Marion was not the person to delay the doing of anything which she had made up her mind should be done, nor had she the faculty instinctive in many women, of approaching a critical subject with that deliberate and delicate touch of preparation which smooths the way for a more open attack. Whatever was uppermost in her mind was apt to take possession of her with so great an intensity that she had no longer the mastery of herself required for this method of handling. She did not trouble herself to join in the family conversation at luncheon, and when her father went into his study,—a small room choked with a heterogeneous collection of books and pamphlets, heaped here and thrown there in utter carelessness to dust and disorder,—Marion followed him and said abruptly,—

"Papa, something must be done to improve Marmaduke's position. Will you write to Mr Tregennas, and point this out?"

"Write to Mr Tregennas!" said Mr Miles sharply, turning round from the papers on his table.

"What do you mean? Is Marmaduke dismissed? No? Then there cannot be anything much amiss." He said this with a relieved air, going back to his papers. "Marion, I wish you'd just see whether that last hospital report is up stairs. Mannering tells me I've been down on the committee for a twelvemonth, but I cannot credit it."

"Marmaduke has been at that hateful place for two years," said Marion, unheeding. "It is quite unfit for him, and some one ought to point it out to his uncle."

"What is the matter with the place?" Mr Miles asked, still searching. "Really, your mother must speak to the maids; I cannot allow them to disturb everything under pretence of tidying. I am confident I left that report on this table."

Marion was trembling with impatience. "Papa," she said, "you might think a little more about poor Marmaduke's happiness."

"Happiness? Humph! He is too young to be talking about happiness. Let him take what comes to him, and be thankful for it—" The Vicar turned suddenly round with a quick, clumsy movement, "He has not been talking nonsense to you, has he?"

The girl was standing with her back to the door, so that a clear light fell upon her. As her father spoke, a soft beautiful change came over her face, tender brightness shone in the dark eyes, the curve of the mouth was touched with tremulous joy, a faint glow on her cheek gave an indescribable look of youth, and her head bent gently with the perfection of womanly grace.

Mr Miles, who had spoken sharply, could not but be moved by this strange magic, — this mute answer, — so unlike Marion that it affected him the more. He did not know what to say; he wished he had not ceased speaking, had not looked at her, and so become aware of what — in its contrast to her usual expression — was almost a revelation. Hitherto, although he had vaguely listened to what they told him, it had been but a feeble attention he paid, considering that the children must necessarily pass through certain stages of existence, the boys going to school, running wild over cricket, coming home to snowballing, having the whooping-cough, every now and then requiring a thrashing, teasing Marion, quarrelling with her, and at last by the same law, as he imagined, falling in love with her. When Miss Philippa solemnly told him that Marmaduke had confided to her his affection, and Mrs Miles complained that Marion had lost her appetite, the Vicar half laughed at himself for so far treating it seriously as to tell Marmaduke that he was in no position to talk to his daughter of love, and, contenting himself with this prudent command, dismissed the matter from his thoughts. He had, indeed, a mind which did not occupy itself freely with many subjects at once. Those which ceased to interest him he would lay on the shelf, and forget altogether, until they would sometimes start from their unwatched seclusion in a form so grown, so changed, so great with life, that the shock gave him a sudden blow. Such a blow came now. For, looking at her so standing, with the sweet flush of girlish triumph vanquishing for the moment all care and fret, and softening the harsher lines in her face with its happy touch, the father's awakening brought sharp remorse for his former blindness. It was not possible for him to reproach her when he felt as though reproach might so justly fall upon himself, and if she had been thinking of him at that moment she might have noticed a wistfulness in his eyes, a faltering change in his voice, as strange perhaps as that other revelation.

"How long has this been?" he said at last, not that he would have chosen the words, but that they seemed to force themselves out.

"How long have we cared for each other, do you mean?" she answered directly. "I think — always."

He shook his head at this. That which was so new to himself in his own child must, he believed, be new-born.

"Children like you do not know your own minds," he said, but faintly, and with a want of confidence which Marion was shrewd enough to note.

"Papa," she said, going closer to him, "we are not children. We are not asking for anything foolish. I would give up all in the world for Marmaduke. I would bear anything for him. I should feel it my richest joy to be with him, at his side, however poor and struggling he was. But of course I understand that could not be. It would not do for him to be hampered with a wife while he can scarcely make his miserable means support himself." As she spoke with a growing impetuosity, her father, who had been holding her hand in his, and looking into her face, turned slightly away, still holding her hand, and leaned a little backwards against the writing-table.

"We know all that," she went on. "I have not said a word against it. But now that I have seen him, and understand how miserable he is, chained to work utterly distasteful to him, and without even the most meagre of hopes, I cannot bear it any longer, I cannot, indeed. Why should we not be engaged?"

Hearing that she paused for a reply, Mr Miles, after pausing also for a moment, said, —

"You are thinking only of him."

"And of whom should I think?" she asked, vehemently.

"Perhaps I have been in error: I think I have been in error," said Mr Miles, speaking with a strange humility. "One has no right to live with one's eyes shut. But, Marion, if this be so, I cannot make wrong more wrong. Marmaduke has no prospect of being able to marry for a considerable number of years, unless, indeed, this shadowy hope to which he clings of Mr Tregennas—"

"It ought not to be shadowy. It is disgraceful that he should not say more. Papa, you must write and press this upon him."

"I!"

"Yes, indeed! There is no one else."

"This is simply absurd, Marion," said Mr Miles with some anger.

But he had given her an advantage, which she was resolved to use even to ungenerosity.

"You said you had been unjust to Marmaduke—"

"Not to him, Marion."

"He and I are one in such a matter, papa."

Ah, there was the strangeness of it! His child's life had seemed to him no more than an undeveloped bud, some day to expand, but as yet folded securely within its sheath, and suddenly it had shot apart from, was almost opposed to them all. It was a thing so strange that the father, looking at the woman, thought only of the child, and took to his own blindness greater blame than it deserved.

"Well," he said, sighing, "it is possible, as you say, that I have not acted in the best way for Marmaduke, or indeed for any one."

"And you will write?"

"To tell the man he is to make Marmaduke his heir!"

"O, he has said it already. Tell him that he must be kinder to him, poor fellow!—that he is thrown away in his present position—"

"I cannot say that," said the Vicar, with a wavering smile at the childishness of the proposition. And as the idea struck him, he looked keenly at her again. "Child, is this really what you suppose it? Do you care so much for Marmaduke that you are prepared to be his wife? You have been thrown together, you have no experience to guide you, you have seen nothing of the world. I ought to take you about and show you other places," he added in grave bewilderment.

Marion, who had been going to the door, turned round and laughed.

"It is too late now, papa."

Too late! And he had been thinking of her life as a smooth, untrodden meadow!

Outside, in a spot of cool shade under the cedar, Mrs Miles was sitting and working placidly at some little white squares, which never seemed to grow nearer their completion. The Vicar, after looking at her for a moment from his window, went out into the hall, through the porch, and across the grass-plot to her side. It was very rarely that he carried any problems to his wife; but it now appeared to him that there were certain complications, such as the white intricacies lying upon her lap, which it might be given only to a feminine understanding to disentangle. He sat down gravely by her side, looking with abstraction at the sunshine falling pleasantly on the house and the fine old tower beyond, and listening, perhaps, to the hum of the bees, or the rough rhythm which came from a saw-pit in the lane. Mrs Miles only looked up and smiled, and went on with her knitting, believing the Vicar to be absorbed in the Sunday sermons which she held to be the great events of Thorpe life. These, although never weak, ran a risk of being considered by a critic as rather dry and lengthy, but loyal wifehood excited a most earnest admiration in Mrs Miles. She knitted softly, therefore, lest the click of her needles should interfere with the roll of his ideas, and in the hush of the sweet summer afternoon a pleasant drowsiness was creeping over her, when her husband startled her by asking abruptly,—

"Wife, how old is Marion?"

"Marion, my dear?" said Mrs Miles, with a perplexed conviction that the Vicar must have meant some other person more nearly connected with his sermon,—"Marion was twenty last month. Don't you remember we had a junket on her birthday, and it was the first time Sarah quite succeeded in it?"

"Twenty!" repeated Mr Miles with a little groan. "I believed her to have been sixteen."

"My dear! And dining out as she does, and so admired."

"Well, well," said the Vicar in a moment or two, "it is no fault of yours or hers. But tell me whether you understood that Marmaduke was serious in his attachment to her?"

"Why not?" asked Mrs Miles, a little motherly indignation making itself heard in her voice.

"Why not?" repeated her husband, standing up and looking down on her, impatiently. "They are both children."

"I never could think of Marion as a child at all," said the mother, with a little sigh. "She has always been so much older than her years. And as for Marmaduke, poor fellow, I am sure he can't have proper food at his lodgings. I have told Sarah to make some jelly for him to take away with him. Of course it is natural that the separation should be a trial to him, but I dare say it will all come right by and by."

"But—good heavens, what a marriage for Marion!" cried the Vicar, beginning to walk hastily up and down under, the cedar, and crushing the daisies that peeped up through the not too carefully trimmed grass.

"My dear," said Mrs Miles, knitting calmly, "Marion is a girl who would be miserable unless she had her own way. With all his strong will, Anthony would be more likely to listen to reason."

"Anthony!" exclaimed her husband, stopping before her. "There is nothing of the sort going on with Anthony?"

"It has not come to the same point, of course, but it is easy to see that he has a fancy for Winifred. I am sure I should be very glad if you could persuade him to make up his mind as to what he will be, and get him out of the place."

"I don't see why," said the Vicar, amazed at his wife's penetration. "I have never thought of what you have just put before me, but it appears to me that Anthony would be fortunate to secure so good a girl as Winifred Chester."

"Fortunate, Mr Miles!" said his wife, laying down her work, and speaking with unusual irritation. "Why, Anthony, with his good looks, his cleverness, and his fortune, might marry any girl in the county. I have never seen any one good enough for him, that is the worst of it; and as for Winifred, what you can see in her that you should call him fortunate, I am sure I cannot conceive. She will be a very lucky girl that gets our Anthony."

The Vicar said, "Pooh, pooh!" but he had a humiliating sense of being baffled by his women. He went away, without further words, across the lawn and past the mignonettes and sweet-peas into his study. There he pulled down the blind to shut out the sun, in a fit of absence tore up a carefully arranged table of parish accounts which he had just prepared for Mr Mannering to audit, flung it into the waste-paper basket, and sat down to write a letter to old Mr Tregennas.

Chapter Seven

Sunday was rather a gay day at the Vicarage. The Hardlands party were in the habit of spending a good deal of time there, Winifred, indeed, remaining for the early dinner, so as to be in her place in the school before the afternoon service; and there were further elements of friendliness in the two Mr Mannerings, who would drop in for a chat with the Vicar when his work was over.

On this particular Sunday, the people of Thorpe had undergone one of those disturbances of routine which they were uncertain whether to resent as an injury or to hail as a welcome variety. One of the neighbouring clergy had been taken ill suddenly the day before, and Mr Miles had ridden over to supply his place, while Mr and Mrs Featherly were jolted from Underham by Job White to undertake the services at Thorpe. Lest it should be supposed that the plural number has been used unadvisedly, it must be explained that many persons who had fair means of forming an opinion held it to be no less than a moral impossibility that the rector of Underham should accomplish any act in his ministerial or private life without his wife's support, and believed that if her head, crowned with marabouts, were withdrawn from the seat immediately below the pulpit, the sermon would collapse in some fatal and irretrievable manner. The influence, whatever it was, was in no way connected with criticism, since Mrs Featherly, as the rector's wife, considered herself released from the necessity of seeking benefit from any preaching whatever, and it probably depended upon that subtle link of habit by which all persons are in some degree bound, and which, in her own case, led her almost mechanically to count the heads of the congregation, and to store in her memory, with unerring acuteness, the names of those offenders who should have been and were not present.

So powerful in her, indeed, was this almost instinct, that as they drove painfully between the high hedges of the lanes, Mrs Featherly, with her head out of the window, reckoned the members of the different families they passed, and kept up a running commentary upon their numbers.

"I am convinced I have seen that woman in the red shawl at Underham. I believe her to be the farmer's wife who supplies Langford's dairy, and if so, I should like to know where her husband is? And there are the Crockers, and the daughter who is home from service not with them. Really, Mr Featherly, you ought to make a point of giving Mr Miles a hint. When people once take to neglecting their parish church I have the worst possible opinion of them."

The consciousness of so much wrong-doing imparted quite a judicial severity to Mrs Featherly's countenance, as she descended heavily at the Vicarage porch, just as the bells were chiming merrily and the people clustering in knots outside the church. There had been rain in the early morning, and large clouds were still coming up, but the sun was shining after the shower, and the wet on grass and roof only gave a touch of additional brightness. The boys who were too big to go to school lounged up in little companies, too shamefaced to venture alone, and putting on an appearance of great boldness and explosive mirth, to cover their actual bashfulness. The girls generally tossed their heads, walking on demurely without taking any notice of their contemporaries, but a ruddy-cheeked young farmer or two, who had come from the outskirts of the village, received such smiling glances from the same damsels as to bring down an occasional sharp remark from one of the elder women.

"You'll a lost yere eyes as well as yere bonnet before iver you gets into choorch, Emma," said one of these matrons, with a satirical look at the red rose that crowned its wearer's last effort at millinery.

Emma, who was blue-eyed and literal-minded, gave an anxious pull to assure herself of the safety of the structure, before she answered good-humouredly, —

"You see, Mrs Anders, Susan gits a new shape for me into Under'm now and then, and I'm sure, if Polly wanted wan—"

"My Polly!" began Mrs Andrews, in so high a staccato of indignation that her husband, who was standing nearer the porch, looked round and said, in a deprecating tone, —

"Stiddy, missus, stiddy. Hyur's the new parson coming oop to t' choorch."

"Ees, fay, so it be," said another man. "Hers so smarl us can sceerce see un."

"I can find him a tex for his sermond," retorted Mrs Andrews, lowering her voice a little, but looking at Emma with wrathful contempt, "'The pompses and vanities of this wicked wordel.' That's a tex as might agree with some as is not so far off at this minit, and doan't know how to be'ave themselves afor their betters."

"That bain't no tex, though," said old Araunah Stokes, slowly shaking his head. "That's noa moor than watt godfaythers and godmoothers have got to doo in t' catechiz. Noa, noa, thicky thyur bain't noan of the Scripter texes."

"And I'd be glad to know, Mr Stokes," replied the irate Mrs Andrews, unfolding her prayer-book from its pocket-handkerchief as if with the intention of appealing to written authority, "I'd be glad to know whether Scripter and the catechiz bain't wan? P'raps you'll be holding next as the Ten Commandmints bain't in the Bible, becos they'm put down in the catechiz?—nor the Blief, nor my dooty towaeds my nayber as I was bound to say wann I wor a little maaed, till it slipped aff my tongue so faest as pays owt of a barrel, nayther? If any wan have a right to spake abeowt the catechiz, it's me, though you doo caest it up to me, Mr Stokes, as I doan't know texes when I see 'em."

"Cloack's strook, fayther," said Jeremiah Stokes, interposing feebly in the character of peacemaker. Old Araunah, however, only hobbled off to where two or three other old men were standing, looking apathetically into a little newly dug child's grave.

"Cloack's strook, as you say, lad, but a woman's tongue 'ull diffen cloacks and bells, and arl t' rest o' um. Ees, yer moother gived me a bet o' 'sperience that way. An' so that's fur little Rose Tucker's little un? Whay, I minds her moother wann her warn't noa begger, and us wor—"

But here an unexpected interruption occurred. Mr Featherly, unconscious of the ordinary arrangements by which the Vicar caused the ringers to accommodate themselves to his own erratic time, had, punctually as the clock struck, appeared in the reading-desk. The ringers, unprepared for such a movement, did not even cast a look in that direction, and, engaged in cheerful conversation, only became aware when the exhortation had been with some difficulty concluded, that the service had actually begun. The consequence was a sudden stoppage of the bells, instead of the ordinary change for three minutes to a single toll, which gave time for the loiterers in the churchyard to present themselves; and it was not until one of the ringers had come out and related what had happened, that the men were able to persuade themselves that the single bell was not yet to be rung. Mrs Featherly was terribly scandalised by the unseemly stamping and scuffling that followed, and the male part of the congregation, naturally incensed at being placed so unexpectedly in the wrong, looked a little hot and sulky throughout the remainder of the service.

A larger number than usual turned into the Vicarage garden afterwards. Frank Orde, the Squire's nephew, had arrived the day before, and old Mr Wood, of the Grange, had walked over to the Red House, not, certainly, with the expectation of finding Mrs Featherly installed at Thorpe, nor with any satisfaction at the fact.

"Why on earth didn't you get rid of the woman?" he growled sharply, under his breath. "She says as many disagreeable things as if she were a relation."

"Charles manages her admirably," said Mr Robert, laughing. "His excessive politeness is just what she cannot meet with her usual weapons. Not that I believe there's harm in her, except when compassion for Featherly is too strong for one's justice."

"Compassion! If a man cuts his throat it's his own doing," said Mr Wood. "There! the very dogs have more sense."

Sniff, indeed, showed a rooted dislike to Mrs Featherly, a feeling which was fully returned; on this occasion, however, she so far unbent as to call him in a gracious tone, "Dog, dog," an indignity which Sniff as naturally resented, as we should resent being addressed in the abstract as "man," and marked his displeasure by turning a deaf ear to her endearments.

"And there, the Squire is falling foul of Anthony again," said Mr Robert, hurrying on with a good-humoured design to act as peacemaker.

"Red's red, I suppose," Mr Chester was loudly asserting, "without a chimney-sweep standing up beside it. Give me a good old-fashioned garden, with rose de Meaux and gilliflowers, and that sort. I hate that talk about contrasts and backgrounds and rubbish."

"Never mind these young fellows, Squire," said Mr Robert, interposing before Anthony had time to answer. "There are a certain set of theories they are bound to run through before they settle into good sound stuff like you and me."

The Squire, who was easily propitiated, but unwilling to allow it, walked away with a grunt.

Since this last home-coming of Anthony's, it seemed as if there were always some little contest springing up between the Squire and him; the things were almost too trivial to deserve notice, but there was a pervading spirit of antagonism Anthony probably enjoyed it, for he provoked it at least as much as Mr Chester, though there were times, as on this occasion, when his opponent's bristles rubbed a sore spot, and when the sense of restraint was galling. He drew Winifred on one side, and she went willingly, for there had been a little shadow between them ever since the dinner at the Bennetts', and she accused herself of having been in fault, and longed to hold out her little olive-branch. There was a sweet hush and serenity in the day itself. The homely garden, which vexed Mr Robert by its disorder, was fresh and fragrant, daisies held open their rosy-tipped cups, soft little wafts of air just rustled the lighter branches, and made tremulous shadows on the grass: she was glad to move away from the others, and to stroll along a broad path bordered with stiff hollyhocks, which led towards a mulberry-tree standing in its own square of turf.

It is one of the privileges of old friendship—at least to us taciturn island folk—that there may be silence between two people without any feeling of awkwardness marring its pleasantness. Under its influence Anthony's wrath subsided quickly, but there was still a touch of irritation in the voice in which he said at last,—

"Your father finds fault with everything I do."

"He doesn't mean it,—or he doesn't mean it seriously," said Winifred, correcting herself. "He has been accustomed so long to us girls, that he can't understand anything that seems like contradiction."

"I never contradict him."

"O no, you only disagree. Only the two things are so dreadfully alike, Anthony, that no wonder he is puzzled," said Winifred, with a quick look of fun.

"Living with you ought to have broken him in to difference of opinion."

"O, I can't afford to waste my contradictions on papa. I keep them for my friends."

They glanced at each other and laughed, and walked on again silently side by side. Both were too easy in their companionship to be thinking about love, but they were very happy and contented to be together. Her influence tightened its hold upon his heart all imperceptibly, like so many threads which did not let themselves be known for fetters. There is a peril in those little threads, woven by habit, by proximity, by opportunities,—not a peril of their breaking, but of their untried strength being all unguessed, of some blast of passion, some storm of resentment, even some petty gust of pique, seeming for the moment to sweep them off, and free the heart of them forever,—until, as the rush dies away and the calm comes back, too late, perhaps, we learn that not a thread has snapt, that the work has been a work of desolation, that the small cords bind us still, like unyielding links of iron, and that the freedom we fancied we had gained is no more than a double bondage. Winifred said presently, in a questioning tone,—

"Anthony, I cannot make out what is the matter with Marion."

"She is uneasy about Marmaduke. She has persuaded my father to write to old Tregennas. It's the last thing I would have done myself; however, it's his business, not mine."

"I should long so much more for everything to go smoothly with them, if I felt more sure about Marmaduke. I wish you would tell me if you really like him," said Winifred eagerly, "or whether it is the having been old playfellows that prejudices you towards him."

"Of course I like him," said Anthony, a little indignantly. "He's the best fellow in the world. Talk of prejudices, you women keep fresh relays which come in every week, and last about as long. Here's a poor fellow eating his heart out over work which he detests, and just because he's down in the world, you must all set your faces against him. I wish there were a better chance of things coming right than I see at present."

The speech ended more mildly than it began, for Anthony was suddenly struck with the golden threads which the sunshine brought out in Winifred's hair. They were standing at this moment close to the mulberry-tree. And then he rushed off to point out to her the spot which David Stephens had intended to appropriate for the chapel. But he returned presently to the subject.

"I wonder you do not feel more for him. It must be horribly hard to know so much is against one. I'm not sure that I could stand it myself."

"I don't know that you could," said Winifred, composedly.

"What makes you say so? Aren't you ashamed of yourself, Winifred, just come from church, and going to teach those wretched little victims, with uncharitableness written on every hair of your head. Poor Marmaduke! Well, he gets on with your father better than I do."

"I don't know that, really. Only you and papa have each your own hobby-horses, and instead of trotting comfortably along, you must go full tilt at each other. I am sure he was very proud when he heard you had won the Chancellor's medal. How nice it was of you, Anthony!"

"You could not have cared much about it."

"Why not?" asked Winifred, who knew what was coming.

"You do not care for any poetry but the very best, you know."

"That need not stand in the way," said Winifred, smiling, and holding out her olive-branch magnanimously, "and besides—"

"Well?"

"I was rather cross that night, Anthony."

"At what?"

"O, I don't know! How can one know what makes one cross? I think Mr Milman bored me. Were you bored, too?"

"I don't believe I was. That Miss Lovell is pleasant enough."

"Do you think so? She worries me by drawling the last word of every sentence, and it is all so very commonplace."

"Well, perhaps it is commonplace, but one doesn't expect to find anything else."

"If you like it, there is nothing to be said against it," said Winifred carelessly, still playing with the mulberry leaves. "Shall we go back? There is something I want to tell Bessie."

"Wait a moment," said Anthony, not thinking much of what had been said. "Tell me, why did you say just now that you did not think I could stand being down in the world?"

Winifred was silent.

"Tell me," he urged, trying to look in her face. "I don't mean to go down. My belief is that circumstances are much more under our own control than we allow. Still, I should like to know why you made the assertion."

"I suppose it is owing to that very belief you have just stated, and to your having such terrible faith in your own powers," said Winifred, speaking with a kind of sweet strength. "You think you are sure to get what you aim at because it is good and great. I have an idea that, the higher one aims, the less one will be satisfied with what is reached, and then it is called failure, and that seems to discourage some people utterly."

"And you think I should be discouraged?" said Anthony. "It is better not to dream about failures. They generally belong to half-heartedness, so far as I can see."

"Not all," said Winifred softly.

They did not speak again, and she walked along the grass that bordered the path, smelling a dewy cabbage rose which he had given her, and humming under her breath one of the old version psalms. Sometimes, in the midst of all our familiar knowledge of another, there is a sudden impression cut deep into our memory. We can give no definite reason for it, but it is there, and there forever. Anthony and Winifred had walked a hundred times as they were walking then: no change had come over the old Vicarage, which stood up to their left with fluttering shadows on the grey stones, and house-martins flashing in and out under the eaves; no new charm belonged, to the bright freshness of the garden, the quiet of the day, nor indeed was he conscious of any peculiar force about the little picture which should so impress it on his mind, and yet — he never afterwards forgot it, it never faded into dull outline, or lost its delicacy of colour; there always, not to be cast out, grew into life the quaint trim hollyhocks, the busy martins, the daisies in the grass, and brown-haired Winifred walking along with a quiet grace, singing the old psalm tune, and laying the cool rose against her cheek.

Chapter Eight

"O Life and Love! O happy throng
Of thoughts, whose only speech is song!
O heart of man! canst thou not be
Blithe as the air is, and as free?"

Longfellow.

Mr Tregennas's answer to the Vicar's letter was a little unsatisfactory and perplexing. Answer, indeed, it could hardly be called, since it touched upon no subject which Mr Miles had introduced, but it contained an unexpected invitation for himself and Anthony to start at once, and pass a few days at Trenance.

Probably at no other time within the last ten years would such an invitation have been treated by the Vicar with more consideration than a hasty reply in the negative, and a speedy forgetfulness that it had been given. A man who has all his life hated change, and that uprooting of habit which even the absence of a day will effect, becomes at last a positive slave to the feeling. Nothing could be more distasteful to Mr Miles than the prospect of leaving behind him his familiar every-day life, of having the trouble of accommodating himself to new forms, and of moving, in feet, out of a world in which instinct had grown to serve him almost as well as the deliberate exercise of will. When, added to this, arose a consideration of Mr Tregennas and his uncongenial society, it was perhaps natural that on ordinary occasions he should have thrown aside the letter without so much as giving its contents a second thought.

But now there was a change. Ever since Marion's appeal in the study, a close observer might have traced an almost wistful uneasiness in her father, would have noticed that his eyes followed her, that his voice was modulated into unusual gentleness in addressing her, and that once or twice in a discussion with Anthony he had sided with her, taking her part, indeed, with a sharpness which seemed uncalled for. His heart smote him for the blindness which, after all, had caused little or no mischief. But we are all inclined to suppose that we might have averted evil had we only seen it coming. It seemed to him as if his girl's determination were something against which he should have watched and prayed. Not that he had any cause of complaint to make him object to Marmaduke personally as her husband, but that his poverty and present position held out no prospect of marriage, and he keenly felt what the bitterness of a long waiting would be to her. It made him long to do something that should atone for his failure of care. He called Marion into the study, put the letter into her hand, and waited silently.

"Of course you will accept, papa," Marion said, looking up. "To-morrow will be a very good day."

"He says nothing of Marmaduke," Mr Miles observed slowly.

"But it means that he will listen to you."

"I suppose I must," said the Vicar, looking round his room with a sigh. "But I don't know about to-morrow. Anthony may not be able to start so soon."

"Anthony! Why should he go?" said Marion, in a tone of dissatisfaction.

"We are asked together; I could not go without him."

No more was said, and it may have been that the greatness of the sacrifice he was about to make in some measure appeared to the Vicar to compensate for his mistakes, for he did not attempt to disguise his misery at the prospect before him, and Marion breathed more freely when she saw him seated with Anthony in the little pony-carriage, of which James and a portmanteau shared the back seat. Even when they had started, her anxiety was not ended, for twice, to Sniffs extreme disgust, the fat pony came tugging round the corner again, once to leave a message for a farmer, and once to say that Tom Lear must wait to be married until the Vicar's return. At last they were fairly off. The children ran out to courtesy; the women speculated as to the meaning of the portmanteau.

"Mr Anthony's gwoin' agaen," said old Araunah, shaking his head. "Thyur's a dale of comin' and gwoin' nowadays. Us used to think twice afore us car'd ower legs dree or fowter miles out o' t' pleace, us did, and 'twarn't wi'out there wor a good rason for't, a peg to sell, or a bet o' sense like that. But thyur's a dale of comin' and gwoin' nowadays."

"I shall never believe they are gone until they are back again, I am sure," said Mrs Miles, coming into the porch with tearful eyes. "It is three years since the Vicar slept out of the house, and that was to preach, and it does seem so unnatural he should have left his sermon book behind him. But there is really one good thing about it, and that is that we can have the kitchen chimney swept quite comfortably. Marion my dear, you'll not mind cold—"

But Marion had escaped. She wanted some vent for the excitement which was apt to rise even to the verge of pain in its passionate impetuosity. The little shrubbery path was as oppressive to her as the four walls of the house, and almost mechanically she opened the gate and crossed the road towards the Hardlands meadows.

The Squire and Bessie were just starting for a ride when Marion reached the house, and Winifred was with them at the door, indulging the pony and the roan cob with lumps of sugar. Bessie was a pretty bright-eyed girl of sixteen, a good deal spoilt by her father, whose special pride it was that she displayed a keener talent for housekeeping than Winifred had ever developed, and who, in consequence, aided and abetted her attempts to gain the upper hand in that department. The Squire was in high good-humour over the result of his hay-making, and it was not lessened by the triumph with which he compared his own success with the less favourable crop secured on the Vicar's glebe.

"Good morning, Marion, good morning," he began in his loud hearty voice, "what does your father say now to my waiting a good fortnight after my neighbours? Tell him to come up and have a look at the ricks, if he's not convinced yet. I suppose he was wanting to jump with Master Anthony's theories, eh? He'll lead you all a pretty dance yet, if you don't look out."

"That's a shame, papa," said Bessie, promptly, "for Anthony was not at home when they cut their hay at the Vicarage."

"I don't know, I don't know, I'm sure. Anthony has a finger in every pie that I can see. Where's he off now? Who's this old Tregennas? Well, Bessie, you and I had better be jogging, or Winifred's fine cook will be spoiling the luncheon, and swearing it's our fault."

With Marion's feverish longing for the open air, she would not allow Winifred to go into the house, but insisted upon her walking to the end of the garden and crossing one of the newly mown fields, which led up to a crowning circle of firs commanding the widest view in the neighbourhood. There she poured out a torrent of hopes and fears, all Marmaduke's wrongs, and all she had determined Mr Tregennas should do. It struck Winifred at times as a little strange that Marion could speak so readily of things which her own instinct, more delicate and more proud, would have guarded like a treasure in a casket, but she put the thought aside. Marion was lying on the grass, rolling the short blades into balls, while Winifred sat up and looked straight before her over the gently sloping fields, the apple orchards, Underham with its white houses and black wharves, the river winding and broadening between red wooded banks, until it lost itself in a distant dimly glimmering sea. All the colours blended into each other with a sweet fair freshness. There was just that subtile charm of warmth which brings life, not languor. Sounds reached them, softened, but vigorous. Vessels were discernible in the river, coming up with spread sails before the breeze, and timber or coal on board for those same black wharves. It might have been a blank to Marion, whose mind was too self-absorbed to be affected by the outer world, but Winifred was at all times open to these external influences, and they contrasted strangely with Marion's impetuous complaints of misery.

"If I could be only at Trenance!" she ended.

"Dear Marion, Anthony will be there,—he will do his best. Old Mr Tregennas is sure to like him."

"Anthony!" said Marion, with a hard little laugh. "Anthony will fell into one of his fevers. He will find the estate at sixes and sevens, and imagine it to be his mission to set it to rights. Besides, it is Marmaduke, not Anthony, whom it is of consequence that Mr Tregennas should like."

Winifred hardly knew what to say. Her sympathies were so active that a strongly expressed idea such as Marion's was apt to carry her away, even in spite of her better judgment, and yet her mind was healthfully constituted, and repelled by what was morbid or strained. Surely there was no such absence of hope in Marmaduke's lot that it should be bewailed as unbearable. Surely Mr Miles had painfully uprooted himself, and Anthony agreed to a distasteful journey for his sake. And meanwhile the sun was shining, and the larks singing, and a sea-breeze sweeping along the water up to the fir-crowned height. She must have sung, too, if it had not been for the risk of hurting Marion's feelings. As it was, her foot was beating on the short grass, and her eyes danced in spite of all her efforts to feel concerned.

"What are you thinking about?" asked Marion discontentedly.

"Of what we shall wear as your bridesmaids. If you don't let me choose for myself, I will never forgive you."

"How silly you are! If things go on as they are going now, I shall be too old to have any bridesmaids at all, by the time we are married."

"Well, I don't know how things could go much faster, but I believe you would like to be married in a whirlwind. Now, it seems to me it would have been quite dreadful if you had not had these little hitches and impediments. Why should you be different from other people?"

"I hope you will have them yourself, and then you will know they are not so agreeable."

"But I did not say they were agreeable," said Winifred, her voice taking a changed tone. "Only that they are such small things in comparison—"

"In comparison with what? I don't understand,—I don't think you understand yourself," Marion exclaimed impatiently.

"O yes, I do," Winifred said confidently, but without further explanation. Marion was not the person to whom she could have breathed a word of the little visions that trooped up softly as she spoke,—innocent womanly visions, coming and going with a tender grace. She only looked out towards the shining streak of sea and smiled.

Somebody opened the gate at the bottom of the field, waved his hat, and began to clamber lazily towards the two girls,—a big man, with long limbs and high shoulders. Winifred jumped up with a little relief when she saw him, and nodded and beckoned at once as if he needed to be shown where they were.

"How did you find us, Frank?" she called out.

"Parker told me you were somewhere about. Women always give themselves so much trouble before they can do anything comfortable, that I knew I should find you at the highest point of the place."

He came straggling up, and stretched himself on the grass with an air of contentment. The lark had finished its song, and dropped silently into the grass; the wind was freshening, blowing back Winifred's hair, and stirring her face into colour;—everything was full of delicious, strong beauty. Winifred looked down at her cousin and smiled, perhaps at the sight of his brown, good-tempered eyes.

"Now that you are come, you shall tell us what you have been doing," she said, not sorry to lead Marion's thoughts away from the road of unavailing regrets.

"Doing? I have been walking through the mud. That is what you all do here always, isn't it? I met an old woman who told me a great deal more about cider than I ever knew before, and a man—O, by the way, Winifred, that is what I wanted to ask you—who is a short man, rather deformed, with a powerful face, and strong religious opinions?"

"It must have been David Stephens, Anthony's bugbear," said Winifred.

Other people's bugbears often strike one curiously in an opposite light. Frank repeated the word a little wonderingly.

"He is a dissenter," said Marion, beginning to listen. "He actually wanted to build a chapel in Thorpe, and had almost got that stupid old Maddox to let him have the field by the church. Luckily Anthony found it out, and stopped it. I dare say he hates him for it."

"Poor fellow!" said Frank kindly, while Marion stared at him. "One can soon see he is a dissenter. There is nothing very original in his opinions, either, so far as they go: he has got hold of the usual distortion of facts. But it was the intensity of the man's convictions which impressed me. In these days it is something even to be a fanatic."

"Every one says he is a most mischievous agitator," persisted Marion, eagerly. "We are quite unhappy because our maid—Faith Stokes—has allowed herself to be engaged to him. Her father is gardener at the Red House. All her family dislike it."

"She will stick to him," asserted Captain Orde. "He is the very man to get a hold over a woman. Unless he himself gives her up. If I don't mistake him, he would neither let his own happiness nor another person's stand in the way of what he imagined to be his work,—perhaps not even his own conscience."

"How could you talk to him?" Marion said reproachfully. "He must be very unsafe."

"Unsafe? Unsafe as a powder-train. But I don't know that it is altogether his fault. He has been cramped and goaded and sat upon, and no one has taken the trouble to do anything but run counter to his opinions."

"Because they are so wrong."

"Not altogether wrong. They may get mixed up with no end of mistakes, but there are some which seem to me a little beyond our improving. He believes he may help some poor men and women up towards God," said Captain Orde, speaking with tender reverence. "There is that, at all events."

Winifred, who had been listening silently, turned round quickly and clasped her hands.

"O yes, we cannot judge him," she said earnestly, "when we have never tried to do anything for him! I am so glad you have told us, Frank."

All her feelings had been stirred and touched somehow that morning. We cannot explain how it is that very often this is so when there seems no particular reason for it, it may be a chance word that awakens a chain of ideas, or reaches springs which are sealed at other times when we take more trouble to get at them. The happy sunshine about her, the thoughts which had grown into life, quickened Winifreds sympathies into generous glow. Frank was looking at her, at the flush on her cheek, the eager kindness of her eyes, with a strange thrill in his heart that his words should have so moved her. He could have very easily forgotten David Stephens, if Marion had not said coldly,—

"Anthony will not be much obliged to you, Winifred."

"O, Anthony will understand!" said Winifred, speaking with quick conviction. "It was natural that he should be annoyed about the chapel. That is another thing. But if Frank convinces him that the poor fellow is in earnest, Anthony will respect him, however much they may differ. I am sure he will try to help him."

Frank Orde did not say any more. His eyes had an odd, wistful look in them, as if some discord had suddenly jarred; but Winifred was quite blind to the look. Perhaps this very want of self-consciousness, which dulled the perception of things that touched herself, was one secret of her power of influence. People who forget themselves seldom fail to impress others.

Chapter Nine

The Vicar's departure caused a few lively gleams of astonishment among the Thorpe people, especially as it was not a call to preach that had taken him away; but no one would have dreamed of finding fault with him if he had locked up the church, carried the keys with him, and condemned the village to virtual excommunication until his return. Tom Lear and his young woman meekly submitted to the postponement of their bridal. George Tucker, who had wanted a certificate signed, said the parson was away, and there was an end of it. There is often something pathetically touching in this mute acceptance by the poor of the little hardships for which we should impatiently seek remedies; but in this case it was Mr Miles's true kindness of heart and courtesy of manner that made his people treat with a forbearance at least as refined the inconveniences to which his absent-mindedness and forgetfulness exposed them.

Then, as events strangely multiply themselves, the village awakened to another agitation, for an old woman declared that an attempt to rob her had been made in the night, and Mr Robert Mannering, summoned to the cottage in his magisterial character, was seen by attentive watchers to turn towards the Vicarage, and walk briskly up the drive towards the door. There also he was observed to knock, two little urchins having been sent to run down the Church Lane, and report whether or not he entered the house.

The knock outside was answered by Sniff within by a series of short sharp barks, which only increased in energy until the door being opened by Faith disclosed a friend. A dog of weaker character would at once have acknowledged his mistake by a sudden change of attitude, and a hospitable greeting to the new-comer. Sniff knew better. With infinite presence of mind, and without a moment's hesitation, he rushed past Mr Mannering as if he had nothing in the world to do with the matter, and, planting himself in the middle of the drive, barked long and loudly at an imaginary enemy, after which he subsided into an amiable calm, returned leisurely to the house, went up stairs, scratched open the drawing-room, door, and advanced to Mr Mannering with the most friendly of brown eyes.

"Then there was nothing really amiss?" Mrs Miles was saying.

"Nothing whatever. When does the Vicar return to put an end to these panics?" said Mr Robert, patting Sniff.

"I'm sure I don't know," said Mrs Miles, shaking her head. "I do hope he will write and tell us how he gets on with old Mr Tregennas. It makes me quite uncomfortable to think of their being there, when I remember how miserable William's poor aunt was."

Mr Mannering looked up quickly, checked himself, and said hesitatingly,—

"He once lived in Yorkshire, I believe?"

"Yes, indeed," said Mrs Miles, "Yorkshire was just where he did live. That was before he changed his name. Do you know about him? Do tell us what you know."

"He had daughters, I think."

"One daughter,—Margaret. But there is quite a sad story about her, for Mr Tregennas disapproved of her marriage, and never forgave her. He must be so terribly unforgiving," concluded Mrs Miles, with a sigh.

"I heard," said Mr Mannering, still slowly, "that her father objected to her choice, and that she and her husband went to Australia. But I heard also,—I hope it is so,"—he went on with a little agitation, "that Mrs Harford was a happy woman?"

"I don't know, I'm sure. Poor thing, she is dead now, and as for the child, of course it is for Marmaduke's interests that Mr Tregennas should hold out, but still—it does seem hard, doesn't it, Marion?"

"Mamma, what is the use of reviving that old story!" said Marion, impatiently. "Mr Tregennas is not likely to change his mind."

"No, my dear, no, to be sure not; indeed, one could not wish it. Only it does seem a little hard, for there was nothing against him that we could ever hear, and it was only that she was too fond of him to give him up. Don't you feel sorry for her, Mr Mannering?"

"Sorry! Good heavens, madam!" he said, jumping up with a sudden impetuosity which startled Mrs Miles, and made him beg her pardon hastily. "I knew Miss Hare in old days," he explained, "and, as you say, it strikes one as something horrible that her father should never have softened towards her. There is a child, isn't there?"

"Yes, a little girl; and how she may be brought up since the poor mother's death, I am sure nobody knows. William's poor aunt did all in her power to make Mr Tregennas think more kindly; but, dear me, she used to say one might as well talk to a stone-wall, and then Mr Harford was nearly as bad, so there was really no bringing them together."

"Things can't be forced," Marion put in again. "I dare say Mr Harford is a great deal better off staying out there and keeping his daughter to himself. His position is not half so trying as Marmaduke's, who is the last person considered."

"My dear, don't say so. I am sure I have been quite uncomfortable about him, poor boy, ever since he was here, and I do wish he had taken a hamper of vegetables with him. Still, one may be sorry for two people as well as one."

"Sixteen—seventeen—the child must be seventeen by this time," said Mr Robert meditatively.

"Only think of your remembering so well!"

"Yes, only think!" repeated Mr Mannering, with his old cheery voice returning as he rose to go. "Miss Marion, I give you warning that I shall not be able to come to the Vicarage much more if you allow my poor roses to fall into such a miserable condition. There's a Devoniensis at the porch, which it goes to my heart to see. Good by, Mrs Miles; you need not trouble your head about the robber, but if you or Marion will go and sit with her for an hour, I can't conceive any greater enjoyment to the poor old soul than to tell you the history from beginning to end."

"I am glad he is gone," said Marion, feverishly, as the door shut him out.

There were other little strings pulling to the same tune, and setting hearts throbbing at the Vicarage just then, while the sweet summer days blossomed and faded. David Stephens met Faith that very evening, as she came back from her father's cottage. Perhaps there could not have been a more favourable moment for him, for old Araunah, who was the most inveterate of the family against the preacher, had been inveighing loudly and angrily upon his granddaughter's infatuation, and her mother had joined in a weak, irritating sort of way, which had raised Faith's indignation on behalf of her lover.

"A poor crooked feller like that there David! It do vex me so to think o't, Faith, that I can't give my mind to my meat, an' if I doan't kep abowt an' do my niffles, I doan't know watt iver'll come to the house nor fayther. If he wor a fine, hearty young man, now, there'd be somethin' to say for 'ee."

"Handsome is as handsome does," said Faith, flushing. She was not very much in love with David, but this disparagement created a natural desire to set him a little higher than she might otherwise have done. "There was crowds to hear him last Sunday, and the people so taken up with him, they're ready to cut off their hands if he told them to."

"Likely enough," said old Araunah, with vast acorn. "You'll find more fules than wise, my gal, wheriver you goes. For my peart, I doan't see as this hyur ground grows much beside."

Faith had come away in the very thick of the battle, and as she suddenly turned a corner upon David, the feeling of championship excited on his behalf had not had time to cool. She showed him more plainly than usual that she was glad to see him, and the perception of this brought an immediate change in his pale face.

"You're looking tired, David," she said tenderly. "You've been tramping about too much, as you're always doing. Why can't you take a little rest? Nobody works so hard as you, I do believe; there's father at it all day, but when he comes home, there he sits comfortable, and you're only off to something else."

"Your father works for time, and I have to work against it, that's the difference. If you saw those poor souls looking up at you with hungry eyes you wouldn't know where to stop. Not but what the Devil is very keen in his temptations. He sets it before me again and again that there's more thrust on my hands by the Lord than one man can do, and he's not content with that, without raising up difficulties and hindrances on either side so as to make the work seem pretty nigh impossible at times. But in spite of all, there's a great stirring of hearts in those that hear."

"John Moore told me you'd more than ever last Sunday."

"Yes, there were plenty that had never been before, and perhaps they were more moved than those that have had the Gospel put before them longer. And many told me they should bring more the next time. It's the truth at work."

"And your preaching, David," said Faith, a little jealously. "They say they like to listen to you, because you never want for words, and that you are the finest preacher the Wesleyans have ever had here."

"It isn't that," said David, with a grave earnestness in his voice. "It never can be the instruments that do the work. I couldn't say ten words if I believed they were my own words that I was speaking. There's nothing in it, but that I tell them what the Gospel says to them, without letting man's devices come in between us."

"I don't know," said Faith, shaking her head incredulously; "I think it's the way you put it mostly that pleases them. There's old Mary Potter wanting to hear you, but she can never get in all the way to Underham. And grandfather's that angry when he hears them talk of a chapel in Thorpe!"

David sighed, but it was at the first part of the girls speech rather than the latter, which only acted upon him as a challenge to battle acts upon a brave man. He loved Faith with an intensity which often pained him, conscious as he was of a want of agreement between her nature and his own, conscious also that her theological views were rather adopted from an interest in himself, than from any firm persuasion on one side or the other. The truth lay before him in one narrow groove, out of which there was no turning a hair's-breadth to the left hand or right. It followed necessarily that a conviction would force itself upon him, — when he had the courage to face it, — that Faith had as yet no part or share in the salvation which he preached as altogether a matter of faith, and the further conviction which lurked behind the other, but which he never yet had ventured boldly to drag into the light, would have forced him to cast away his love, as the eye or hand which needed to be destroyed. It does not require the same conclusions to be aware that what to David Stephens was actually a matter of conscience there was danger in temporising with. He told himself that the sin was at least all his own, and suffered expediency to suggest the hope that Faith would by and by become other than she was. The unacknowledged scourge of anxiety which he felt made him the more zealous for the building of a chapel in Thorpe: he had then the promise of becoming its minister, and he was aware that the position held out charms to Faith, who had some sort of idea that it would raise her almost to a level with Mrs Miles herself. David told himself fiercely that once he had Faith for his own, he should have removed her from the teaching which he held to be utterly antagonistic to the truth, and that his prayers and his love must win her to his side for eternity. He had fully believed himself to have succeeded with old Maddox, — who, having lived a life of indifference, was beginning to find it less easy now that death was in view, and caught at any teaching which held out a promise of security, — when Anthony Miles had overthrown his hopes. He did not, however, yet despair, nor must it be imagined that it was the thought of Faith which even chiefly incited him in his efforts. Had she been lost to him that very day, his convictions were so earnest, his yearning to save souls so strong, that he would have toiled as perseveringly as ever: but she was the human spur which, almost unconsciously, gave a feverish anxiety to his endeavours, and excited at all events a strong personal persuasion that Anthony, in opposing him, was siding with the great enemy of all good, against whom David daily wrestled and prayed.

"Your grandfather may think different one day, Faith, but if he doesn't, we mustn't let the words of those that are dearest to us keep us back from the plough." David said this with a throb of anguish in his own heart, but he contrived to steady his voice, and it only gave it one of those singular thrills which added not a little to the influence it had upon his hearers. Faith was impressed with it just as her own thoughts had strayed off to picturing herself as minister's wife, sitting in the chapel arrayed in a silk gown, and she looked hurriedly in his face with a sensation partly pride and partly discomfort. The plough was not in her thoughts, but she acknowledged it to be David's duty to talk about it, and her little head had an idea that by becoming his wife she might both be good by proxy, and also share in the admiration which she heard largely expressed of his talents as a preacher. On the whole, she had seldom felt more kindly towards David than at this moment; while he, poor fellow, took it as a hopeful sign of grace, that she did not urge any of those arguments against his doctrines which she brought forward when she fancied they interfered with his advancement. He held her hand in his with a strong grasp as they parted, and the colour which rose in her cheek under his gaze gave him a glad thrill of exultation. It seemed to him as if he were borne on the top of an irresistible wave, which was sweeping triumphant spoil from the very grasp of the enemy. And now the soul dearer to him than his own was being drawn slowly but surely towards him, while to come to him must, as he believed, lead it onwards towards his God.

Chapter Ten

These few days of waiting were intolerable to Marion, who hated all delays, and from her earliest childhood objected to hear reason, as the old nurse used to say. Whatever was hanging over her head, good, bad, or indifferent, she would have come down at once, and let the crash be over. Poor Mrs Miles had too little in common with her daughter to know what to say or do. Every morning she was sure that a letter would come by that post, and as sure when the hour had passed that it was more natural that it should not arrive until the next day. Such little securities win their triumphs at last. On Saturday morning a few lines from Anthony announced their intended return in the afternoon.

It struck Marion at once that her father was depressed, although there was evident gladness at getting back to his home. After he had kissed her, and before turning to his letters, he looked for a moment into her face with a touch of the wistfulness which his talk with her in the study seemed to have brought into his eyes. She determined to find Anthony, who had gone off to the stables to see the pony nibbed down, and whose whereabouts were easily discoverable through Sniffs bark of delight. Hearing his sister's call, he crossed the yard.

"Hallo, Marion, what have you been doing with yourself? You look as if you wanted fresh air badly. Put on your hat, and come up to Hardlands with me."

"Hardlands! Anthony, you and papa are as cruel as can be to keep me in this horrible suspense. O Anthony, dear, do tell me,—what did he say?—what is Marmaduke to do?"

"I think it's pretty nearly right, or on the way to be right," said Anthony, digging his hands into his pockets, "though I don't exactly know what Marmaduke expects."

"To be his heir," said Marion quickly. "It was a promise."

"I think Marmaduke must have made a mistake there," began Anthony, but she interrupted him at once.

"He did not, indeed."

Anthony was silenced, and began to whistle, not knowing in the least what to say. His father had begged him to tell Marion no more than was absolutely necessary, and there was an uncomfortable and unacknowledged impression upon the two that she would not be satisfied with their tidings. Mr Tregennas would not admit anything definite. "Sha'n't forget the lad, I tell you. If you want to know for your daughter's sake, he'll have enough to live upon, and she, too, unless you've brought her up in these new-fangled fashions." This was what he had said, and of course it was something, Mr Miles would have said it was a good deal, if there had not been that uneasy consciousness of Marmaduke's expectations, and it was quite certain that it did not satisfy Marion. It was sufficient, however, to give her a further ground on which to urge her father to admit of their engagement. If the Vicar had felt himself as free as usual to follow his own judgment, he would, probably, for some time yet, have refused his consent; but he was in the position of a man who, having failed to see what all the time lay close at hand, feels a nervous distrust of himself, and, moreover, his life had fallen too completely into a matter of routine for him to meet an unexpected call for decision as firmly as he would have met it years ago. He would have willingly let the matter drift to the shore as the tide of circumstances carried it. But Marion was too well aware of the advantage she had gained not to push it farther; Mr Tregennas had rather encouraged than opposed the engagement, and Mrs Miles shook her head over Marion's loss of colour and brightness. The Vicar was inclined to believe implicitly in his wife at this moment, Marion had one of those temperaments which in their many changes act rapidly upon people's looks, and her father could not meet her heavy eyes and live his own life any more in peace.

So she had her way; the engagement was allowed, Marmaduke was to spend his approaching leave at Thorpe, and Anthony and he were to go for a week to Trenance.

Here again the poor Vicar was aware of perplexity. Mr Tregennas had shown an inconveniently strong liking for Anthony, whom nobody wanted him to like. His energy and brightness seemed to have such an attraction for him, that the old man, now with little more left of his old nigged self-will than a certain feeble captiousness, would sit and watch him by the hour from under his big eyebrows. The Vicar, who had become aware of this, was almost provoked at his son's unconsciousness. Anthony was at all times disposed to take it for granted that things would be as he thought best, and it seemed to him that Marmaduke was really as sure of his inheritance as if it had all been plainly set down in black and white. Even if the idea of his becoming his friend's rival had ever entered his head, the prospect of heirship would have had little fascination for him. He had some money of his own, which made him independent of his father. Trenance was but a dull country place, and he was too young and too sanguine to care much for money and possessions. He wanted power, but not of that sort, and how to gain it he had not yet resolved, but there was a swing of energy about the young fellow which made all things seem possible. If his self-confidence were too buoyant, too ready to rush blindfold, it was a danger which he would be the last to discover for himself; if, later in life, his character were likely to develop just a touch of arrogance, it was for the present concealed by his brightness and boyish gaiety of heart. At any rate he could never be covetous. Trenance was nothing to him, and thinking of Marmaduke it was with a little real compassion for a life which was to be bounded by so many acres, a mine or two, and the little church town. His own dreams reached far beyond those limits.

Already he had taken a step in one of the paths which lay before him, and seemed to invite him into smiling depths. He had written a pamphlet upon certain branches of reform, and it had been noticed with some commendation by an influential paper, to Mrs Miles's great delight. The notice was a good deal more dear to her than the pamphlet, and she would go up to her son's room and read out little bits, although with a sharp criticism of its shortcomings.

"There are only two quotations, and so much that people would have liked to read! And why should they say you are a young author? I am sure there is nothing your father might not have written so far as age is concerned."

"They must criticise, you know."

"Well," said Mrs Miles, doubtfully, "if they did not find a little fault, I suppose others would be jealous. But they could not deny that it is excellent."

She got up as she spoke, and went softly about the room, putting some tidying touches which Faith had neglected. The summer sun was shining in and discovering dust in little out-of-the-way corners where things were heaped. There was a faded sketch of Hardlands by Winifred stuck over the chimney-piece.

"It is a pity those people don't know who you are," Mrs Miles continued. "I wish you would write and tell them, Anthony; I am sure they would be pleased. My dear, you would find a better picture than this in the portfolio down stairs."

"It does very well," said Anthony sleepily.

Mrs Miles went on with her work, but presently began again.

"My dear, it is a long time since you called at Deanscourt, and Sir James Milman has always been so civil that it does not seem quite right. Suppose you were to ride over there this afternoon."

"I don't believe they've come down yet."

"Lady and Miss Milman are at home, I know," asserted Mrs Miles gravely, "for she wrote the other day to ask for Ellen Harding's character. Miss Milman seems a very sweet girl."

"Oh!"

"And very pretty, I'm sure."

"She's not my style," said Anthony, with an air of having disposed of her.

"My dear, I think you would find her so, if only you knew her better," interposed Mrs Miles earnestly, "and Mrs Featherly tells me—"

"What?"

"That all those girls have money."

"Well, mother, I'm too shy to venture there by myself, but, if you like, I'll drive you over in the pony-carriage."

"Thank you, I'm sure, my dear, it would be very nice," said Mrs Miles, whose pleasure in driving with her son was mixed with several pet perturbations of her own; "but are you sure the pony is not too fresh?"

"Fresh? He wants a little work, of course, but it's nothing on earth but play that makes him caper. I'll see he does no harm."

"My dear, I can't help wishing he would play in the stables, where he really has nothing else to do, but if you think he's quite safe—"

"As safe as any old cart-horse. Come, mother, if he should upset us, I'll give you leave to call me all the bad names you can think of."

"O dear, but that will not make it any better," said Mrs Miles, shaking her head. "I don't see how you can help it if he takes it into his head to play, as you call it. However, my dear, you really ought to go to Deanscourt, so I will be quite ready by four o'clock, and now I must go and speak to Faith about the dust in this room."

"You don't mean to say, mother, that you've let Faith engage herself to that dissenting fellow, Stephens," said Anthony, beginning to speak energetically.

"I could not prevent it," said Mrs Miles, giving her head a mournful shake by way of protest. "I don't know what the world is coming to, but servants are not at all what they were."

"We ought to have stopped it, though. How was he ever allowed to hang about the house? Faith is too good a little thing for a humbugging rascal like that. You wouldn't believe how he has worked upon that old idiot Maddox; if I hadn't gone into it, my father would have had a meeting-house stuck under his very nose, ay, and he'll have it still, unless I keep a sharp lookout. But, upon my word, it is a great deal too bad that he should get hold of Faith."

Anthony was handling a tool as he spoke, and punching a hole in a bit of wood with as much force as if it had been Stephens's head. Mrs Miles never liked to see her son "put out;" his face was quick to reflect his feelings, and he certainly did not look pleasantly upon what galled him. It was quite true that David was his present bugbear, and that he gave him credit for no motives except the lowest: his feelings had so much heat in them, that they deprived him in a great measure of the power of sympathy with that with which he had no agreement, and were always easily excited into prejudice.

Chapter Eleven

"Like, but unlike, the sun that shone,
The waves that beat the shore,
The words we said, the songs we sung,
Like, unlike, evermore."

A.F.C.K.

The summer was passing at Thorpe very much as other summers had passed, and yet with the difference that dogs our footsteps whether we will or no. The grass waves, the forget-me-nots look up from the brink of cool brown streams, the roses are as sweet as ever,—we wonder as we touch them how there can be a change and what it is, but we know in our hearts that it has come, and that things can never more be what they once have been.

As for Anthony, all things considered, he seemed to be leading a pleasant life enough. There was bright, settled weather, and the neighbourhood had taken one of those sudden freaks of gaiety with which such neighbourhoods are occasionally seized; dinners and picnics and cricket-matches succeeded one another rapidly, people came to stay with each other, glad to escape from the heat of London to these pretty country-places, where they could lie under the shadow of great elms, and pick dewy fruit in old-fashioned gardens. It was an easy, charming existence, with a busy idleness about it, which had an indescribable delight so long as the sun would shine. Anthony was wanted for all the little festivities, he was asked to stay here, to dine there; the Milmans, the Hunters, the Bennetts, the Davieses, had each some attraction to offer, and young ladies who were ready to encourage Mr Miles's attentions. By and by little echoes of rumours began to be heard. At one picnic he had talked to no one but Miss Lovell, at another dinner-party he had devoted himself for the whole evening to Miss Milman. Winifred had been there, and had seen it for herself, and, indeed, Anthony, when he indulged in these flirtations, generally contrived to be near Winifred. Not that a spirit of mischief prompted him on such occasions, or anything beyond a light-hearted enjoyment of the present moment. He liked the pretty flatteries of manner, the little attentions, which the young girls were not unwilling to lavish upon him,—liked to feel himself courted and appealed to,—liked also, or something more than liked, that Winifred should be near him, that he might look at her, listen to her at the very moment he was turning away, touch something she had touched, unconsciously compare her with her companions. Unconsciously, I repeat, for, although many problems were puzzling him at this moment, he was thinking least of all about his own heart. He did very much what he liked, and if it pleased him to talk to Miss Milman and to sit near Winifred, he talked and he sat. That was all.

That was all, and no one could have said a word against it if it had been always so. He had no intention of neglecting Winifred; but to a girl who loves, unintentional neglect is more cruelly wounding than any other. Each day worked with a sort of slow torture upon her, the more so that her cheeks burnt with shame, when she even acknowledged it to herself. She was in high spirits,—or so it seemed. She fancied herself that all sweetness and gentleness had died out of her heart, leaving bitter ashes behind. When she spoke to Anthony it was laughingly and lightly, only every now and then there would descend a sharp cut, or one that she thought sharp, poor child, and would repeat over to herself with a dreary satisfaction, while she invented other sayings more terrible, which the time never came for uttering. After all, they were not so severe as she intended, for such weapons did not belong to her by nature, and she used them as tremblingly as a woman will fire off a gun that she expects to explode in her hands. As often as not, Anthony did not notice these little attacks; he noticed more what she did not say, the pleasant things which fell so trippingly from others' lips, to Winifred's disdain. Feeling as if Anthony were slipping away altogether from the pleasant, familiar intercourse which had been enough to satisfy her while it lasted, and which, therefore, she fancied would have satisfied her forever, these sweet summer days, in which all the world was making holiday, were to her full of restless misery, to which she dared neither give a name nor a cause, and over which she shed the bitterest tears that her life as yet had known.

No one saw the struggle. It would have added tenfold to her suffering if they had done so, for she had too much of her grandmothers undaunted spirit not to be at times fierce and impatient with herself, and her very prayers were not so often that she might be loved again, as that she might cease to love, and so have done with the pain. She had no mother. The Squire, when he was in his most jovial moods, would strike Anthony on the back and ask who was the last flame, but his own daughter's name had never occurred to him. Mrs Miles was distracted between hopes and fears, represented by Miss Milman and Miss Davies. Marion was taken up with Marmaduke, who was at Thorpe, and who for his part was absorbed in thoughts of Mr Tregennas and Trenance. After this one step had been gained, he was greedy for a clearer declaration of the old man's intentions, and waited restlessly for a repetition of the invitation to himself and Anthony. Yet when it arrived, he said jealously to Marion,—

"Why should Anthony go? What has he to do with it? Is he trying to come over the old man?"

Even she flamed a little. "You should know him better. There was never any one in the world who cared less for money," she said angrily.

One wonders sometimes how many misjudgments will rise up and face us one day. Anthony was so far from thinking the thoughts that Marmaduke put into his head, that he was a good deal vexed at the summons which took him away from the pleasant little round into which he had fallen. But he consoled himself with grumbling, and the Milmans insisted upon putting off their picnic until his return.

"They'll turn the boy's head between them," said Mr Robert Mannering wrathfully to himself. He was in his garden, alternately attending to some newly budded roses, and doing his utmost to discomfit the imperturbable Stokes. The little ugly red-faced man guessed better than other people what was going on, and perhaps saw more clearly. "Confound those women!" he said ungallantly. "They do their best to spoil any man they take a fancy to! Stokes, I presume you suppose these unhappy buds are to undo their own bandages? I should like to tie you up for a week, and see how you'd feel at the end of it. And those seedling carnations are in a disgraceful condition."

"There bain't wan o' them worth the soil he grows in," asserted Stokes with round emphasis.

"Not worth! Pray do you know where the seed came from, and how much I gave for it?"

"I shouldn't be surprised but what you might ha' given anything they asked of you. I can't help that, Mr Robert. There's a lot of impostors in gardining like as there is in anything else, unless you looks pretty sharp. And they thyur caernations is rubbish."

"That's your ignorance. I should like to know how much you knew about gardening until I taught you."

"I knowed rubbish—always," said Stokes, with an air of decision which fairly drove Mr Robert off the field. He walked towards the house across the short fine turf, all unlike the Vicarage lawn with its intruding daisies and dandelions, smiling a little to himself over his own discomfiture.

"They are worthless, I believe," he said, "only I didn't think the fellow would have the wit to find it out. Who are these coming in at the gate? The Chesters, if I'm not mistaken." And away hurried Mr Robert to receive his visitors.

"The girls got hold of me, and would make me walk over with them," said the Squire, pulling Bessie's hair, and talking loudly. "What are you doing in the garden, eh? Your hobby, ain't it, Mannering? I'll lay sixpence, though, you don't show me a finer dish of peas than we had for dinner yesterday. What were they called, Bessie? Bessie's the one for remembering all the fine names."

"Come and dine with us one day, and I'll see what we can do. Will you say Thursday?—unless Miss Winifred has some engagement."

"No," said Winifred, with a little weariness in her voice, which Mr Mannering detected at once. "The Milmans were to have had a picnic on that day, but it is to wait."

"Because Anthony is going away," put in Bessie in an aggrieved tone.

"They want young Miles to marry the girl Milman, and so they can't make enough of him," said the Squire. "That's the long and short of it."

"Ah, I don't believe he has any such notion in his head," replied Mr Robert, manfully. "He'll not be marrying just yet, though other people will marry him a dozen times over."

"Perhaps not, perhaps not; I don't know that I should expect to see him do anything so sensible. Old Milman isn't over-troubled with brains, but they carry him along very fairly, and he's as sound a Tory as any man in the county. It might be the making of the young fellow to marry into a good steady holdfast family like that, and get some of his harebrained notions knocked out of him," said the Squire, who was becoming very sore with Anthony's arguments.

"O, his notions will come all right by and by!" said Mr Robert pacifically. "People can't all think and live in just the same grooves."

"More's the pity. I don't see that the new grooves are any the better."

"Well, perhaps sometimes they're not so much worse as we think them. And how does Bessie get on without Miss Palmer?"

"Why, she plagues us all," said the Squire, with great satisfaction. "She's always running out into the fields after me, when she ought to be at her lessons, or her sampler, I tell her. Winifred's got no end of trouble with her. And now she's bothering my life out to go into Aunecester twice a week, to the School of Art I suppose she must go, but who's to take her, I should like to know?"

"You, papa, of course," said Bessie decidedly. "You are always as glad as you can be to go to Aunecester."

"There, you hear. That's how she serves her father," said Mr Chester, chuckling, and pulling her hair again. "No, thank you, we'll not come in, Henderson's waiting to speak to me about his farm. Where's Mannering?"

"He's driven over to dine at the Hunters'."

"What a man he is for society."

"Yes, he likes it, and it does him good," said Mr Robert quietly.

"That's what people always say about things that please them. I tried it for a good bit upon salmon, but it didn't do. Had to give it up. Well, girls, now you've had your say, I hope you're satisfied, and will let me go home in peace. You're a lucky man, Mannering, to have your own way without being plagued for it. Here's Bessie, now: a fellow will have a pretty handful that gets her,—bless you, she'll not let him say his soul's his own," added the Squire, in high good-humour, making signs behind his youngest daughter's back.

"How is the Farleyense, Mr Mannering?" asked Winifred, lingering.

"I really think that, if possible, it is in more perfect condition than when you did it the honour to come to look at it."

"And Stokes has not tried any experiments?"

"He knows that if he did it would cost him his place. No, Miss Winifred, there is a point behind which even the easiest master must intrench himself."

The girl sighed a little. Her father and sister were strolling along the lane outside the gates, and the Squire's loud laugh came to them scarcely softened by the short distance. The rich fulness of August seemed to weigh somewhat heavily in the air; the hedge-row elms stood in thick unenlightened masses against the sky; the garden was a little parched and exhausted by its very profusion of flowers, the scent of the jessamine was almost oppressive in its richness; it was one of those days in which, without any perceptible change, the knowledge forces itself upon us that the change is there, and that something is gone from us.

"And do you still carry the key in your pocket?" said Winifred, with a faint smile.

"No, no, the house is open. Will you come and see it again?"

"Winifred!" called the Squire from the other side of the wall.

"Not now, thank you. I mustn't keep my father."

She spoke hurriedly, but walked lingeringly towards the gate, and Mr Mannering remained stationary for some moments after she had disappeared. "I wonder what is making her take such an interest in the Farleyense," he said to himself. "The plant is a picture, to be sure, but still — when I think of it—and why should I keep the key in my pocket?—Why — what an old fool I am!—I had forgotten all about Anthony, and no doubt the poor girl wanted to hear a word or two more about him. He's off somewhere to-day, I dare say, and going into Cornwall to-morrow,—the best place for him, too, if he doesn't know what's good for him; and there she is fretting over all these confounded reports, and thinking I could have said a word or two to comfort her. I've a great mind not to look at the Farleyense for a week. However, perhaps I'd better just go and give it a glance, to make sure that Stokes hasn't been meddling."

Chapter Twelve

"Brave spirits are a balsam to themselves:
There is a nobleness of mind, that heals
Wounds beyond salves."

Cartwright.

The two young men found time hang on their hands at Trenance somewhat heavily. The old shadowy house stood at the foot of a hill, by the river's side; the river was there, making silvery gleams between the trees; it was all cool, green, and dull for these energetic lives, but Marmaduke looked forward to the sweets of ownership, and found it more endurable than his companion. And yet Anthony was the most kind to the old man.

"Poor old fellow!" he said one day, as they locked the door of the boat-house, where the water was lapping drearily among the piles, and climbed the bank towards the house. "There must be a queer sort of feeling in looking at the man who is waiting to step into one's shoes. I am not sure we should stand it so well as he does."

"He has had his day."

"Well, I don't know that having had dinner one day makes one wish to go without it the next, if that's what you mean."

"You wouldn't care for dinner if you had lost your appetite," said Marmaduke.

"You mightn't care, though, much to see other people eat."

"Pray do you suggest my starving myself for company?"

"I wasn't thinking of you, I was thinking of him," said Anthony, stopping to cut down an ungainly bramble. "Everybody knows it's the course of nature, and all that. Still, I say it can't be altogether easy to be pleasant under those circumstances,—particularly when it's not your own son that's to follow."

"That's not my fault," said Marmaduke, who seemed to put himself upon the defensive.

"No, it's your luck, old fellow," said Anthony kindly. "Don't be crusty. Do you suppose I'm not glad from the bottom of my heart there don't happen to be a Mrs Tregennas and half a dozen young Tregennases to keep you out of Trenance? Though, by all the much-abused laws of justice and equity, I don't know that you ought to be here now."

"Why not?" said Marmaduke, turning hastily.

"Because there's nearer blood."

"Mrs Harford is dead."

"Of course she is. But her daughter isn't, so far as we know," said Anthony, finishing his bramble.

"She's well out of the way in Australia, at any rate."

"O, she's far enough off. And her grandfather seems to care little enough what becomes of her. If I were you, Marmaduke, I'd say a good word for her. My father tried, but he wouldn't listen."

"Thank you," said Marmaduke, curtly. They were near the house, and he turned abruptly into one of the side paths and walked off by himself. Anthony, whose temper was none of the sweetest, felt a little indignant at his manner. Marmaduke was not like the boy he remembered, a change seemed to have come over him; Anthony, perhaps, had not yet learned how many-sided we all may be, how as one front and then another comes forward, it needs a golden cord to draw us into the beauty of harmony, or a false mask to make pretence of it. Marmaduke had not either at this time. There were things surging up in him which were all at war; he was torn and distracted between them. He knew Anthony well, and yet he had lost faith in his own knowledge. The idea that had once taken root grew hatefully into form and haunting prominence, and there was not a look of old Mr Tregennas, or a word from the young man, but he caught at greedily, and with it fed the lurking fear. He was forever watching, and, as he called it to himself, countermining. Anthony's natural ease and brightness of manner became, in his sight, deliberate pitfalls spread to entrap the old man; so that although he did contrive to disguise his feelings with a facility which was becoming dangerous, he was restless and uneasy when Anthony was out of his sight, especially when he suspected him of being by Mr Tregennas's side. His disquiet was the more unaccountable that Mr Tregennas rather fell foul of the world in a peevishly discontented fashion, which had taken the place of his former ungracious doggedness, than showed any especial marks of favour on that side or on this. He snubbed Anthony quite as much as he snubbed Marmaduke, on the whole perhaps rather more, Anthony being less careful not to disagree with him, and having taken up a crusade about some labourers' cottages on the estate, a suggestion to improve which was popularly considered to have the same effect upon the master as the shaking of a red rag has upon a bull. Anthony used to talk to the men, and invite them to complain to the steward, and then come back and tell Mr Tregennas what he had done.

"What d'ye mean by that, sir?" the old man would growl in a rage. "What d'ye mean by stirring these rascals up?"

"They're in the right, sir, indeed they are. You can't get down to see the place, and White doesn't choose to tell you what the people say, but it's a shame that any one should have to live in such holes."

"You'll live in them yourself one of these days, if you go on in this confounded fashion of yours."

"Then I hope you'll have them set in order at once, sir," said Anthony, with a promptitude over which old Tregennas chuckled.

In about a fortnight he let them go. Anthony was so conscious of the sacrifice he had made upon the altar of friendship, that he was the more irritated at the change which had become perceptible in Marmaduke. It seemed at times as if he scarcely cared to conceal his repulsion, and at other moments as though he were studiously forcing himself to wear the old dress of pleasant companionship. Anthony's nature was one which very quickly took the tone which others exhibited towards him; he was apt to fall aloof at the first symptom of drawing back, and to feel more anger than sorrow at the loss of good-will. In this case, however, the thought of Marion prevented the alteration in their relations to one another becoming so marked as it might otherwise have been, and, indeed, Marmaduke was kept closely at his distasteful duties during the following autumn and winter months.

Anthony himself was not uninterruptedly at the Vicarage. He had a feeling as if this choice of a profession which lay before him were a crisis in his life; perhaps a little pleasant sense of self-importance gave it even undue gravity in his eyes. It was possible to debate upon it without that goad of necessity behind him by which men are often driven into the decisions of life, and his mind travelled after many projects in the paths which stretched to this and that summit in the horizon of the future. At one time he would be a barrister,—until he went to London and was talked out of it by one of the profession; at another he would travel with a pupil, an idea unconsciously crushed by Sir James Milman's energy in offering him the charge of a shock-headed lad whose irreproachable heaviness would have driven Anthony out of his senses by the end of a week; finally, his longest and favourite dream was that of literature, the gates of which were to fly open as all gates are to open before these young knights. Meanwhile his life was much what it had been in the summer, energetic in everything, whether shooting or flirting or dancing or writing, splendidly young, as Mr Robert once said. As to his relations with Winifred Chester, the barrier between them, doubtless, still existed, and caused a fret on either side, he telling himself that Winifred was changeable and unsympathetic, and she accusing him of giving up old friendships for new, yet neither the one nor the other so entirely believing in their own reproaches as to have lost the idea that some day things would go back to what once had been. Meanwhile, if the old familiar life did not flow on with the pleasant smoothness of former days, — and, indeed, the Squire's manner with Anthony must be allowed in some measure to have prevented this, — Winifred was less tired in the winter than in the gay brightness of the summer days, and it was less sharp to dream of his sitting by Miss Milman's side than to be actually there to feel herself neglected. Moreover, she was struggling with all her might to prove herself — even to herself — indifferent. It was balm to her sore heart, ashamed of its own weakness and attempting to ignore it, to keep away from the Vicarage when Anthony was there, to avoid the roads in which she was likely to meet him, to turn the conversation when it drew near the subject which was dearest, to remain in her own room when he came to Hardlands. Every such act was a triumph, but what a triumph! For Anthony was not likely to bear his treatment with good-humoured indifference. It galled him. He was inclined to retaliate, and he laid all the blame of their altered relations at Winifred's door. Now and then there came a faint return of what once had been, but there was no doubt that the last few months had developed a certain easiness to take offence, which had never before seemed to belong to the girl's nature, so that often even after a momentary relaxation she pulled herself up with a sharp and uncomfortable check. It is indeed a little difficult for a woman in her position to strike the just balance between self-respect and pride.

If she could not altogether deceive herself, she unconsciously contrived to mystify others: the men said she had refused young Miles, the women that she had tried in vain to marry him, even shrewd Mr Robert was puzzled. There was no one so loving, so tender, so observant, that they weighed the trifles which might have betrayed her, no swiftness of motherhood to read what was passing. So far as human sympathy was concerned, she bore her burden, without a finger being stretched to help her; but there is a Hand from whose loving touch the sorest heart never shrinks, and from out of the very depths it draws us gently.

Her self-containing puzzled even herself. There comes a time in most strong lives when the mysterious power of repression becomes an experience to them and grows into a wonder. It fills the world with a keener interest than when all things seemed open in the page of the great book. Face, heart, nature, — what is hidden beyond our sight? — what does the mask cover? — of what tremendous powers are we unconscious that lie beside us and round our very hearth? Now and then the crust heaves, and we see a flash, but the very working of our own hearts is often hidden from us, and it is only by slow degrees that we learn those forces in ourselves which teach us to reverence our brother's soul.

Chapter Thirteen

"He that wrongs his friend
Wrongs himself more, and ever bears about
A silent court of justice in his breast."

Tennyson.

Marmaduke came down in April, and it was evident enough to any one that he wanted change, or rest, or some other means of renewing health. His face was thin, his eyes unquiet; there was a sort of suspicious watchfulness in his manner unlike his old languor, which nobody could make out, but which they all noticed, except the Vicar and Marion. It made Winifred so uncomfortable that she could not help asking Marion whether anything were the matter.

"Everything is the matter," said the girl in her eager way. She could not get out of her head that each day that passed was defrauding them of that perfect bliss for which she waited impatiently. She looked with a little contempt at Winifred, who seemed not to understand this impetuous demand for happiness. Poor Winifred! It was impossible for her not to contrast Marion's position with her own, and to wonder that it should bring so little contentment. Once when Marion was pouring forth her complaints and longings, she said gravely, — "You don't know what worse than nonsense you are talking;" and yet, as she said it, her eyes were full of tender depth. Her moods were not very settled at this time, sometimes she was resentful, abrupt; but she said these words so strangely that they startled Marion, who was accustomed on the strength of her engagement to look down upon her friend as from a height of experience. She did not know that there were other springs of experience of which she could not fathom the depths, nay, that there is something far more divine and profound than experience itself, out of the strength of which came Winifred's quiet words. Yet something in them made her wonder. It was a spring afternoon, one of those days in which sudden surprises of shade and brightness alternate with each other. Now and then an intensity of light flashed out from a break in the grey hurrying clouds, and the young green of the larches and the tender pink blossoms of the elms grew vivid and sparkling under its touch; now and then it all faded into sober tints. A line of heavy blue marked the distant moorland; between a thinly clothed network of branches might be traced a crowd of small fields, patches of red soil crossed by sombre lines of hedges, brown nests in the rookery swaying in the wind, a pear-tree standing up in ghostly whiteness before the rent clouds. Winifred was leaning against a window of the Vicarage drawing-room, and looking out, her steadfast eyes grave with a sweet seriousness. Marion, who was watching her, said suddenly,—

"Winifred, you have grown older!"

She smiled, but gave no answer.

"But it is you who do not know. Wait until you are engaged yourself," continued Marion, falling back upon her old point of superiority, and yet anxious to induce Winifred to agree.

"It is possible to see, although one is outside,—besides, it has nothing to do with feelings."

This was said slowly, and Marion cried out at once,—

"Nothing to do with feelings!"

"The right or the wrong can't be affected by them, I mean," Winifred went on, still slowly, turning her face towards the grey clouds broken with white depths that were driven from the west. "There is something more secure for us to rest upon than even the love you hold to be so strong, Marion, or else—"

"Else what?" said Marion impatiently. But Winifred would not answer. She came from the window, and took up her hat which was lying on the sofa.

"I must go, or I shall be caught in the rain. Take care of your cold."

"O, I am taking care!" said Marion discontentedly. "Marmaduke was obliged to go into Underham on some stupid business of Miss Philippa's. Old people are so selfish. Anthony comes back to-morrow. Ask Bessie to bring the last magazines. But you don't know what you were talking about, Winifred, really."

Winifred laughed and went away.

Marmaduke had gone to Underham, as she said, doing what he had done a hundred times before, walking in through the narrow lanes, white with the blossom of the blackthorn, and past the farm orchards to the little ugly improving town, with its bustle, its grimy coal-wharves, and its rows of stiff houses run up quickly by the sides of the street. Marmaduke transacted

Miss Philippa's business, and stood talking for a while to Mr Featherly. He particularly disliked meeting Mr Featherly, because the old clergyman had a fashion of inquiring whether he were still at work in the north, with an expression which Marmaduke chose to interpret as astonishment, although his questioner only intended to prove his interest in the little lad whom he remembered running about with the Miles children in the days when he was a younger man, and rode out to Thorpe now and then when ordered forth by Mrs Featherly to take a constitutional Marmaduke, however, imagined that his words implied that wonder from which we are inclined to wince when it professes to be excited in our behalf, a wonder that Mr Tregennas had not done more for the nephew who was popularly looked upon as his heir, and he was careful to avoid the old clergyman whenever it was practicable. On this day his efforts had been in vain, and Mr Featherly kept him for an unusual length of time to tell him the story of some local event, which his wife permitted no one but herself to relate in her presence, and which Mr Featherly therefore hailed the opportunity of producing. Afterwards, Marmaduke, who had not Anthony's many-sided interests, and found time a wearisome weight, sauntered round by the canal, watched a coal-barge dragged up to her moorings, and then strolled towards the post-office, it being the custom at Thorpe for any responsible inhabitant who happened to be at Underham after the arrival of the mail train, to call for the letters due by the second delivery to the Vicarage, the Red House, and Hardlands. He was not, however, sure whether the train had come in, and stopped David Stephens, who was passing him, to ask the question.

His own feelings towards David were rather favourable than otherwise; not that his nature was sufficiently large to have a more just view of the real intensity of the man's longings, or, indeed, that he could have sympathised with any desires which were merely spiritual, and therefore to his mind unreal, but that he knew that Anthony was opposing David with all his might, and something within him inclined him to rank himself in every matter on the side against Anthony. He had not a very clear idea of what position David held amongst the dissenters, or of the points at variance between him and Anthony, and he was not sorry for the opportunity of putting one or two leading questions, which should at all events let David see that he was not offending all the family by his open warfare. He said in a conciliatory tone, —

"I heard something of your trying to get into the post-office, Stephens. Have you succeeded?"

"I hardly know as yet, sir. I have not many friends among those who have the disposal of the place; a dissenter seems necessarily to bring a large amount of ill-will about his head."

"Not necessarily, I should suppose. It is hard to believe that any man could be persecuted in these days for holding his own religious opinions."

"There are many hard things that are true," said David bitterly. "One would say that it is hard that so much as standing room should be denied to those who would worship God as they believe right, and yet you know, Mr Lee, whether that is true or not, and who has done it."

"Mr Anthony does not think much of the feelings of those who oppose him," said Marmaduke, slowly lighting a cigar. "I am afraid it is of no use for me to say anything, Stephens. You had better give it up, unless you really see a chance of succeeding in spite of him."

"Until to-day I had hopes, sir, but I find he has been more inveterate than I could have supposed. Mr Maddox has gone back from his word altogether; the fear of man has been too strong for him to battle against, even with the fear of another world before him. I thank you, sir, however, for your kindness."

He went on quickly, as if he were afraid of adding more, and Marmaduke strolled leisurely after him to the post-office, where the clerk handed him three letters for Mr Mannering, one for Hardlands, and none for the Vicarage. Setting off to walk homewards, however, he heard steps behind, and Stephens, overtaking him, said,—

"Mr Tucker overlooked one letter, sir."

"Thank you, Stephens. Are you going this way?"

"I am making haste to a cottage where they want me, and I have to be back at the office by an hour's time. Good day, sir."

For the second time they parted, and Marmaduke looked at the letter. He saw at a glance that it was for the Vicarage, and for Anthony, but he saw at the same moment something which brought a red flush into his face. The letter was for Anthony, and it came from Mr Tregennas.

To ordinary persons it might have seemed a not unnatural thing for Mr Tregennas to have written to Anthony, who had once or twice been his guest; but to Marmaduke the sight of the handwriting broke down the barriers which had hitherto stemmed in his slowly accumulating suspicions, and let loose a very torrent. The thoughts could not have leapt to life in that moment, but they leapt from their hiding-places. In those few feebly written words he saw revealed a very network of treachery, and walked on mechanically, looking at the letter as he walked with a kind of dumb rage. What did it conceal from him? What plot was weaving round him its web of ruin? How had Anthony toiled and dug, and how much had he gained?

Gained away from him,—his own as he had thought it, and called it, and counted upon it! How had he been so blind? Jealousies that hitherto had been vague and unacknowledged took shape and rose up in fierce array. He said to himself that Anthony had seemed abstracted of late, and called himself a fool as he recollected that just before he went to London a week ago he had noticed a letter in his hand, the address upon which stirred him with a half-memory. As he walked quickly on, shut in by green lanes, he lashed himself by a hundred evidences into the conviction that Anthony was a traitor, and that in his hand he carried the letter which held the key to this treachery.

In his hand.

It was a strange power. To his excited imagination the thought dawned like the beginning of retribution. How many chances were there not against its thus coming into his possession! Had justice so guided it that he, of all others, should be the one to whose care it was delivered? Had Anthony's absence and Miss Philippa's fancies all worked for this end? He looked at the letter as if there, hidden only by a slender cover, lay the means of confounding his enemies, at first with a kind of angry triumph that so much at least had been gained. The letter was in his hands, and that was the first step.

After all, however, he became soon aware that it was only a step. To himself it might be conclusive proof, but that was not sufficient, and he felt irritated and baffled. In what shape did the danger threaten, and would it be yet impossible for him to turn its tide? He had thought of giving Anthony Miles the letter, and so openly accusing him as to force from him a confession of his shamelessness; but, with a passionate impotence, he acknowledged this to be a vain manner of confronting the blow. He was not in the position to make good his claim. He must meet his enemy with all the subtlety of self-defence. But what had he to meet? How should he know what lay before him, from which side the thrusts should be parried, in what shape grew the threat? The questions beat in his brain with recurrent strokes, as if a hammer were smiting dull iron. All the keenness of suspicion could do no more than bring a shadowy uncertainty before him; nothing could solve the problem except the letter, with its poor feeble failing writing, which he held in his hand.

For there, to be sure, lay the certainty; there was hid the proof or the acquittal, as the case might be. He began to look at it as though Anthony were the prisoner on trial before him, while he himself was the person who possessed the clew, and could determine the guilt. To his distorted reasoning it became almost a sin against Anthony not at once to decide the question, when, after all, he might be innocent, and surely it would be better that this innocence should be placed beyond the power of doubt, than that so cruel a suspicion should divide two friends. For Anthony's own sake it seemed to Marmaduke a duty to determine the truth forever. The letter had been given to him for some purpose, he argued, as a man will argue, himself clothing the temptation in the strong armour with which it comes to meet him at last, mighty and irresistible. It needed only one look to convince himself, a look which could not harm Anthony Miles in any way, only put Marmaduke on his guard, and show him how to defend his rights. One look—nothing more—at the letter which was in his hands.

He opened it. And as he did so, out of some background of old associations, there rushed upon him such an intolerable loathing for his own action that for a few moments his eyes refused to see its contents. The false pleading with which he had covered it was no longer to be called up, could never any more be called up. It was with a sense of desperate degradation that he forced himself to master the writing, pathetic in its feebleness, confused and indistinct. "I think it is all coming to an end at last," it said, with a forlornness which might have touched him at another time, "and that my successor will soon be free of my shoes, such as they are. I don't talk about repenting, but somehow my girl's face comes before me night and day,—I might have been more patient with her, though I did no more than I told her to look for. Your father seems a just man; people call me a hard old fellow, but I have still a feeble belief in human nature, and I believe in him. If you choose you may place a decision in his hands, and if he tells me the thing should be done, I will make an alteration in my will, half the money shall go as it is now settled, and half to Ellen Harford, Margaret's child. But should he think the change unnecessary, I do not wish to be pestered by replies or arguments. Silence will answer me fully. I shall understand that he thinks my proposal unadvisable, and I shall never break it by an allusion."

And this was the letter which Marmaduke must deliver.

For a quarter of an hour he stood motionless with it in his hand. Over his head was the sweet changeable April sky, and on either side of the road a little green copse in which the birds were chirping and twittering. He looked up at last, with a fierce gesture of impatience at their glad piping, at the tender sunshine; a sudden storm, a wild rending of all these pretty gentle things, would have been more congenial to him just then than the burden of their joy. Two men jogged by him in a cart, and looked at him curiously as he stood by the roadside. It raised a quick fear that they might discover his secret, and he began to walk slowly on again, reading and rereading the letter in obedience to some mechanical impulse, for the first sight had burned the words into his brain. It was remarkable that he had no longer any fear of Anthony as a rival, probably from his own frame of mind being such that it was impossible for him to realise a sane man putting such a choice into the hands of his heir, and conceiving the idea of his exercising it in any way but one. It was only a robbery of himself which was revealed to him; an iniquitous deprival of half of his inheritance. For he needed no assurance of what Mr Miles's decision would be. He had a half-uncomfortable, half-slighting contempt for the Vicar's notions, which he classed with other antiquated forms of thought belonging to the old world. Anthony's words came back to him with a sting which they had not at the time they were spoken, when he believed them to be powerless, and he knew that half of those good things on which he had so long counted would go out of his grasp forever as soon as this letter was delivered. As soon as it was delivered,—but the question immediately forced itself on his thought of why such a letter should exist at all to harrow them with its sentence of deprivation. Was not the Vicar himself concerned, Marion's interests being equally involved with his own? And it was for the sake of a girl who knew nothing, hoped nothing, and whose father was as equally averse to a reconciliation as Mr Tregennas had been. Then he thought angrily that the decision, if there were one, should have been offered to himself. Indeed, fate said the same thing, and, resenting the injustice, gave him the needed opportunity. If he did not embrace it, he was yielding his own property, and sealing a gross injustice. The thought grew, it rang in his brain as he walked along,—alas, no song of birds could drown it!

He tore the letter across and across without a renewal of those accusing feelings which had rushed upon him when first he opened it, having wrought himself into a condition in which right and wrong became mere accidents dependent on his own will. He set his teeth and tore it into a hundred fragments, dropping them, as he walked, upon the grass by the side of the lane, and almost taking a pleasure, as it seemed, in their symmetrical destruction. No sense of pity touched him for the failing life that had there made its last vain effort, and the notion that he was baffling an act of injustice he was able by a strong and concentrated pressure of conscience to keep uppermost in the place it had usurped.

A little farther along the lane he once more met David Stephens, letting him pass this time without comment, and congratulating himself that the man had not timed his return earlier. It was, however, noticeable that, having delivered himself from his previous haunting suspicions of Anthony's rivalship, he should, nevertheless, immediately decide that he would in some hidden manner assist Stephens, thinking that the fortune which was to come into his hands would enable him to do this, and siding more strongly than even an hour ago with any attempt to oppose Anthony's influence.

David himself, accustomed to observe keenly, was aware of some disturbance in Marmaduke's face as he passed him, wondering, too, at his having gone so short a distance since they parted. It is possible that the surprise made him quick to notice trifles, for the tiny atoms which had fluttered on the grass would naturally have escaped his observation. As it was, he stooped and gathered some of them into his hand. They were torn so closely as to make it almost a matter of impossibility to fit one piece with another, unless he had bestowed long attention upon the work, and no impulse moved him to do this. But a scrap of the envelope, which Marmaduke had destroyed with less care, showed enough of the postmark for Polmear to be distinguishable, and Polmear had been stamped on the letter which Stephens had handed to Mr Lee. One or two other half-words there were, which, his curiosity being a little excited, he tried to put together as he went along, but for the most part they were illegible. Something, however, gave him an uneasy feeling as he hurried on to the post-office to hear whether his application had been successful.

Chapter Fourteen

"Our life is but a chain of many deaths."

Young.

For a few days things went on to all outward intents as if the letter which Marmaduke destroyed had never existed. Once or twice he had a feeling as if it were indeed nothing more than a dream through which he had passed, for the act struck himself as so unlike his usual languid easy-going nature, that even to him there was an unreality mingled with it, and he was inclined at all events to compassionate himself for the crisis which had forced anything so repugnant upon him. On the sixth day there arrived a telegram announcing Mr Tregennas's death.

Mr Miles, Anthony, and Marmaduke started at once. A sort of restraint had grown up between the two young men, which was, perhaps, although it began only by reflection, more perceptible in Anthony's manner than in that of Marmaduke, for the former was at all times quickly conscious of the feelings of others towards himself, and apt to throw them back. He was sensitive, moreover, to external influences; there was heavy rain falling, a damp chill in the air, and, as they drove down the road towards Trenance through woods in which the wild garlic was beginning to scent the air, the mournfully heavy drip of the rain through scantily clothed trees, the coarse sodden grass, the dreary moss-grown little paths that led away as it seemed into some dismal wilderness, the house with its shut and blinded windows lying under a pall of low clouds, deepened the disturbed expression of his face. No one spoke after they left the station. The carriage that had been sent for them, with its old moth-eaten cushions, rolled slowly along, the coachman not thinking very kindly of his load: a probable heir can scarcely expect a welcome from old servants who have grown fat and masterful under the weakened hands of age. The place had always seemed oppressed with a weight of silence, but now, as they drove up, the very wheels jarred upon the excessive stillness, broken only by the ceaseless dripping of the rain. Nevertheless, Marmaduke's spirits rose as soon as he found himself in the house; and while Anthony, with a pale and troubled face, flung himself down in the dreary drawing-room, which looked uglier and more uninviting than ever, he went about from room to room, only avoiding that which an awful Presence guarded. It was Mr Miles who went there first, and when he came down again he held a little miniature in his hand.

"It was found under his pillow," he said. "There is Margaret Hare, as she must have been in the old days before the unhappy quarrel. It makes me hope that he may, after all, have remembered her child."

"I shall go up to him," said Anthony, starting up. He had a shrinking from the sight of death and all painful things, but at this moment he could only remember the old man who had been kind to him after his fashion. "Marmaduke, will you come?"

"No," said Marmaduke carelessly, "it can do no good now. You can tell me if anything has to be arranged, and I will see about it."

He spoke with an easy assumption of authority, which stirred Anthony's anger. All that Marmaduke said or did seemed to jar upon him, upon the time, the quiet, the sadness; for, after all, although there is not so much to stir our sympathy, perhaps no death can be so sad as that of a forlorn and unlovely old age.

There were no relations to come to the house; all the orders were given by Mr Pitt, Mr Tregennas's lawyer, a little withered red-faced man with shrewd eyes, who was there when they arrived, and who kept himself in the library, away from them all, until the day of the funeral. Perhaps a more silent four could hardly have been found than the men who were gathered in the old damp house, although with Marmaduke the silence was rather compulsion than choice. Anthony was very grave and subdued. When the funeral came they were all together almost for the first time, rumbling along the desolate overgrown road, with two or three empty carriages crawling behind them, which had been sent by the neighbours with a vague belief that it was an easy method of doing honour to the dead. The rain was falling still as they all rumbled back again, and gathered in the library to hear Mr Pitt read the will. It was soon done. A few annuities were bequeathed to the old servants, five thousand pounds free of legacy duty to his great-nephew, Marmaduke Lee, and the remainder, half in entail and half unreservedly, to the great-nephew of his second wife, Anthony Miles. William Miles, clerk, was appointed executor.

Mr Pitt's monotonous reading was interrupted by Marmaduke Lee, with a white, quivering face, —

"I protest against such a will as a fraud. I can prove it to be a fraud," he cried, lifting his hand and letting it fall tremulously on the table.

Anthony neither turned towards him nor moved. Mr Miles said, a little hurriedly,—

"When Mr Pitt has finished, my son has something to say."

The lawyer, looking quietly from one to the other, took up his sing-song again, and went on as if there had been no break. Marmaduke had shrunk into his chair like a man who had received a heavy blow, his very passion was too weak to support him at this crisis, he scarcely heard the formal words running on in set rounded phrases: what he did hear at last was Mr Miles asking,—

"Is there no mention whatever of Miss Harford in the will?"

"There is nothing more than you have heard me read," said Mr Pitt, in his dry voice.

The name seemed to recall Marmaduke's senses, and a rush of rage stimulated him to burst out again,—

"It is false, and a lie! Anthony has taken advantage of his dotage. I will dispute every word of it."

Anthony looked at him with a contemptuous darkness in his face, which it was not pleasant to see, but he held his voice under repression as he bent forward, folding his arms on the table, and saying slowly,—

"Dr Evans is the person to testify whether or not Mr Tregennas was in the full possession of his senses. It was only a fortnight before his death that I received a hint of his intentions, which were as unwelcome to me as to Lee. I had fixed this very day for coming here to urge my objections. No one could have thought it would all have ended so soon," said the young fellow, with his lips quivering. "All that I can do is to make over to Lee that part of the property which is at my own disposal,—not because of his words, but because he has a better right to it than I."

Sometimes people get small thanks for large acts of generosity, and in this case it is possible that Marmaduke was too stupefied or too sullen for gratitude, Mr Pitt might have said something, but he only glanced at Anthony with his shrewd eyes, and gathered and tied up his packets silently. There was a chill about the whole business which struck keenly on Anthony, who liked to be generous, but who also liked acknowledgments, warm words, and hearty looks: he got up quickly and went out of the room, leaving his father to settle what remained.

As for Marmaduke, it was not easy for his mind at that moment to grasp the fact that things were not so crushing as he had dreaded. What might have seemed much to him at another time now seemed nothing, and he hated Anthony so much that his gift was an intolerable load. Was it for this that he had done the wrong? For, after all, however cunningly a man may disguise his sin beforehand, the disguise is but a poor helpless thing that falls off when it has served the Devil's turn, and leaves what it covered hideous. It was only before he opened the letter that he had tried to deceive himself with dreams of fairness to Anthony. Ever since it had been scourging him. And now a fierce rage was uppermost.

He went back to Thorpe the next morning alone, Mr Miles and his son finding it necessary to remain and set matters in train, and before he went he forced himself to say some ungracious words to Anthony about his gift. Perhaps it would have been better had he gone away in silence, for the words were not likely to do much towards healing the breach: they were said, however, and the Vicar and Anthony stood at the door and watched the carriage toiling away up the drive. The sky was a soft dazzle of blue, everything was shooting and sprouting after the rain, colours seemed full of light, there were young creatures leaping and running, a spring glory brightening the ugly old house.

"It is almost a pity that it should be let," said Mr Miles, standing on the steps with his hands behind him.

"I could not live here," Anthony answered, shrugging his shoulders.

There was a little silence. The Vicar was looking after the carriage, and not really thinking much about the house. He said at last, slowly, —

"I don't much like the spirit he has shown."

"It can't be helped," said Anthony, without much cordiality. "I don't suppose he can do me any particular harm."

"Harm!" repeated Mr Miles, startled. Then, as his son did not reply, he said, sighing, "I am thinking of poor Marion."

"She can be married now as soon as she likes, I suppose," said Anthony shortly, turning away and going into the house. He was not feeling much of that sweet sense of satisfaction which is held up to us as bringing a quick reward for our good actions: he had behaved more generously towards his cousin than ninety-nine men out of a hundred might have done, but his generosity did not tend to make him ignorant of this fact, and he had expected a certain reward which had not come. Mr Pitt's manner had chilled him as much as Marmaduke's. He would have resented the imputation that he was dependent upon external influences, yet there was a certain side of his character which seemed almost at their mercy, and a fortress is no stronger than its weakest point. If he made over the fortune to Marmaduke as an act of justice, it is certain that his mode of receiving it should have made no difference in Anthony's determination; nevertheless, at this moment he half repented, and perhaps would have undone it if he could.

Mr Miles stood where his son had left him, looking sadly up the road along which Marmaduke had but now driven. Something, which was so indefinable that only a woman might have noticed it, seemed to have changed his face and his whole bearing ever since the day in which he had spoken to Marion in his study: the shadow of a shade had now and then, as it were, just touched him and passed, but during the last few days it had rested longer. He was conscious of it himself, yet it was so little beyond a vague something that he was inclined to smile at his own fancifulness. Rousing himself at last, although with another sigh, he went slowly down the steps and round to the front of the house, instead of going into the library, where there were papers and accounts to be looked over. Anthony was right. Marion might marry if she pleased, now that there was enough money to make things easy to them. And yet with the thought the shadow deepened.

For two days, however, he said nothing. But one evening when Anthony, who had cast off some of his vexation, was planning changes in the estate before it passed into the hands of tenants, his father remarked slowly,—

"I think I shall go home to-morrow. Something ails me, and I don't know what it is. Perhaps your mother will find out."

"Do you mean that you feel ill?" Anthony asked, looking up hastily.

"No, I don't mean anything of the sort I have no more to say about it than just what I have said, so you need not alarm yourself. But I shall go, and you can either remain behind or run down again next week."

"My mother will set you to rights, sir," said Anthony cheerfully.

"Yes. And Marion. And Marion," repeated the Vicar with a little absence of manner.

"I'll go back with you, and come down again, as you suggest," his son went on. "I should like to put two or three things straight before the place is let. There must be a clean sweep of a good deal."

"Yes, yes," said Mr Miles, half impatient, half smiling, "your young man's idea of a reformer is a Briareus with a broom in each hand. It's lucky we don't all get treated in that fashion. Well, let me see your plans."

Father and son went home the next day, as the Vicar desired, and the shadow passed,—or so it seemed. It might have been Mrs Miles's little doctorings, or the return to the old routine of habit, which had grown into a second self; at any rate, the Vicar was apparently as well as he had been during the long years of his residence at Thorpe Regis, nor was there anything to distract his wife's interest from Marion's wedding when that took place a little later. No one could give any reason for delay strong enough to weigh down the girl's impetuous demand; that her father and Anthony felt a vague uneasiness was not sufficient to do more than perhaps excite her to a determined attitude of defiance. To outward eyes there was everything that a wedding should have, youth and love, sunshine, roses in the old garden, smiles, brightness. Yet it was not all smooth. Marmaduke was restless, and his easy temper every now and then broke down in fits of irritation, while there was a visible restraint between himself and Anthony. Mr Miles was grave and sad throughout the day. After it was over, and Anthony had walked up to Hardlands to dinner, taking with him the few Vicarage guests, his father stood in the drawing-room in a manner altogether unlike himself, and looked wistfully at his wife.

"We have been happy together, Hannah," he said slowly.

Mrs Miles's eyes filled with tears at this sudden appeal.

"Very happy, William."

"You have been a good wife,—it would be better perhaps if poor Marion were more like you. Somehow, I don't feel so sure about things now,—I forget—"

"Forget? I am always forgetting," said Mrs Miles consolingly. "I am sure you don't lose your spectacles half so often as I do, and where they are now is more than I can really say. But it has all gone off as well as possible."

"I wish I knew Marmaduke better."

"My dear, when you have seen him since he was no higher than the table!"

"Poor Marion! Poor child!"

"She is quite happy," said the mother, nodding her head sagaciously. "I only warned her to take care that he has plenty of beef-tea, for he is sadly thin."

The door was pushed open, and Sniff came running in, looking for Marion. Somebody had tied a white favour round his neck, of which nothing was left but a little ragged strip of ribbon. He had followed Anthony to Hardlands, and not finding Marion there or here, flung himself exhausted at Mr Miles's feet, with a piteous look of entreaty in his faithful eyes. The Vicar stooped and patted him.

"Is she gone, poor fellow—" he said.

What stopped the words?—What spring of life suddenly failed?—Was it the shadow, after all, no longer shadowy, but a presence, a reality? Mrs

Miles, running to him with a cry, caught him in her faithful arms, and held him by an almost supernatural strength from falling forward on his face.

"William, William!"

The servants in the kitchen heard the cry though he did not, and flocked in, Anthony was sent for, another messenger despatched to Underham for the doctor. All the doctors in the world could do him no good, but Mrs Miles would not believe it as she sat by the bed where he was lying.

"He was so well, Anthony, all the morning. And I think Marion's wedding made him remember our own, for do you know what he said just before? 'We have been very happy together, Hannah,' he said. I must tell him when he is better that I did not say half enough."

I think the words have been told by this time like so many other of those unspoken words which wait for our utterance, but he did not hear them then. No more sounds apparently reached his ear where he lay silent and motionless while the days passed slowly by, carrying his moments with them, until the last came, when they scarcely expected it, as quiet and gentle as his life had been throughout.

Chapter Fifteen

When death brings other departures besides the one that is greatest, a hundred pangs may be added to its sadness. There is the leaving the old home, the uprooting of old ties,—a shock meets you at every turn. Mrs Miles felt so sharply the fear of these added troubles, that she implored Anthony with a wistful entreaty he could not resist to let her remain at Thorpe, and to move, at least for the present, into a house they called "the cottage," about half a mile from the Vicarage. He agreed reluctantly, and because it seemed cruelty to his mother to oppose her at such a time. He himself disliked staying in the place, with their home no longer theirs; and his sorrow for his father was so great that he had almost an impatient longing to escape from a neighbourhood which was absolutely made up of associations. The Squire forgot all his little animosities with Anthony Miles, while the awe of standing by his old friends grave was fresh in his mind; but Anthony shrank from his homely attempts at consolation, as a man shrinks from the reopening of a wound. Even Winifred, whose sympathy was at once strong and delicate, found it difficult to show it. The little barrier which had reared itself between them did not fall away at her kind, womanly touch. Anthony was inclined to reject an attempt to share his sorrow,—almost to resent it. He wanted to escape, to try his wings, to make a career, and Mrs Miles promised to go with him to London; but her heart failed her, poor thing, whenever the time came, and he gave way to her wishes, meaning his own to have their way by and by.

So one by one the new things which had seemed so strange subsided into ordinary life. Marmaduke and Marion were living in one of the midland counties. A new vicar came to Thorpe,—a short, bustling man, in all respects a contrast to Mr Miles. But it was a peculiarity of the place that even change seemed to lose its characteristics in the quiet little village; a certain dogged custom was too strong for it, or the climate was too sleepy. Little by little Mr Brent laid down his arms, accepted this anomaly, that habit, and things went on in much the same groove as in Mr Miles's time, although Mr Brent was red-haired and energetic.

In the winter a visitor came to Hardlands, an old friend of the Squire's, and no less a person than Mr Pitt, Mr Tregennas's lawyer. It took Anthony by surprise to meet him one day walking with the Squire, and the young man, who had been chafed by a certain dry, unsympathetic manner in the old lawyer, was not very cordial in his greeting.

"So you knew Anthony Miles before?" said Mr Chester when they had parted. "Oh! ay! to be sure! I forgot you had to do with that queer affair of his uncle, or grandfather, or whoever he was, that died the other day."

"Who told you it was a queer affair?" said Mr Pitt, stopping short.

"Who? Why, my own common-sense could do so much, I suppose. I always thought the boy a romantic young idiot, and it's just the sort of thing I should have expected him to do," replied the Squire with great pride.

"Humph!"

"I'll say this for him, he hasn't got any of those low mercantile notions half the young men of the present day bring out of their pockets cut and dried for use. They'll be the ruin of the country, sir. Don't talk to me about reductions and rotten administrations, and all the rest of it; the other's the real evil, take my word."

"And you consider young Miles free from the prevailing passion?"

"I consider he hasn't that miserable, pettifogging spirit at his back, if that's what you mean. You must have seen it for yourself. You haven't many clients, I should say, that would knock off half a fortune to put things right, have you?"

"No," said Mr Pitt, thrusting his stick into a lump of red mud. "Certainly not many."

"There, that's what I said. Generally there is some spur in the background before they do that sort of thing."

"Squire, you deserve to have been a lawyer."

"Ay, ay," said Mr Chester, rubbing his hands in high glee, "that's the way with you fellows; you think no one can see an inch before his nose, except he's one of yourselves. The worst of your trade is the confounded low opinion you get of human nature. I dare say the best you would say for young Miles was that he was a fool for his pains."

"Certainly not," said Mr Pitt dryly. "A fool is the last thing I should have called him."

"Eh, what?" said Mr Chester, stopping suddenly, and looking at his companion with an expression of bewilderment. "What do you mean? Can't you speak out? What on earth would you call him?"

"A very prudent—scoundrel would be nearer the mark."

The effect upon the Squire was electrical. His face became crimson with anger.

"Do you know what you are talking about, sir? Anthony Miles a scoundrel! Why, you'll be saying I'm a scoundrel next! Anthony Miles!—a young fellow I've known since he was that high! It's an insult, an insult to us all.—Are you mad, Pitt?" said the Squire, pulling himself up with a sudden attempt at self-control which nearly choked him.

"No, I'm not mad, and I know all you have to say against it; but there are such unfortunate things as facts which outweigh everything else in the way of evidence. I've known you longer than you've known him, remember, and I've spoken out because I've heard a rumour that Mr Anthony Miles is desirous of marrying your daughter."

Mr Chester stared at him incredulously, and then burst into a laugh.

"O, that's one of your facts too, I suppose! Anthony many Winifred! Mercy on us, man, what cock-and-bull stories have you been picking up? Winifred and Anthony? They've played like brother and sister pretty nearly all their lives, and that's enough for the gossips, no doubt. You'd better ask Winifred, and see what she'll say."

"It is new to you, then?"

"New to me? Ay, as new as it is to them, I'll be bound. I'll tell you what, Pitt, you'd better not let it out, but some sly rascal has been housing you, and done it neatly, too, uncommon neatly. Come, come, isn't there a little more as good to tell me?" And the Squire, with all his good-humour restored, walked on, nodding to the children who came running up to make their courtesies.

"Well, if that part of my information isn't true, I'm glad of it," said Mr Pitt, coolly. "I told you, if you recollect, that it was no more than a rumour. But as to my opinion of young Miles, I am sorry to say it does not rest upon anything so doubtful."

"You had better speak out," said Mr Chester, fuming again, and striding on savagely. It was a very different matter to fall foul of the young man himself, and to hear this said of him in sober earnest, especially when he thought of a grave by which they had stood side by side not very long ago.

"I intend to speak out, now I have said so much. All my relations with Mr Anthony Miles date only from one time—"

"When he behaved as few young fellows would have behaved," interrupted the Squire warmly.

"I hope so, I am sure," said Mr Pitt, pointedly misapplying the words. "You are acquainted with the external features of the case, the bequest to the young man and his own subsequent division of the property?"

"I am proud to say I am."

"You are also probably aware that there is a granddaughter of Mr Tregennas living, or presumed to be living, for whom he had refused to make any provision whatever?"

"To Anthony's excessive regret," said Mr Chester, marching on bravely.

"Those are your words, not mine."

"Well, are you going to say they are a lie?" broke out the Squire in a white heat again. "His father told me with his own lips that they had done their utmost with the old curmudgeon, and he was the truest-hearted gentleman that ever breathed, sir!"

"Did his father tell you that, a week before his death, Mr Tregennas wrote to Anthony Miles, asking whether the Vicar would agree to half the fortune being made over to the grandchild, and—mark this—desiring him if he would not consent to take no notice of the letter?"

"Well?" said the Squire, stopping.

"Well."

"Can't you do anything but repeat one's words?" growled Mr Chester with something else between his teeth.

"That is all."

"What is all?"

"What I say. Mr Tregennas wrote that letter, and there the matter ended."

"Ended! Do you pretend to tell me there was no answer from Anthony?"

"Never a word more. And that was enough for Mr Tregennas. It had been all I could do to work him up so far, and I confess,—though I was a fool not to know the world better at my time of life,—I confess I hoped there was a chance for poor Margaret's girl when we had got him to that point."

"A chance!" stammered Mr Chester, as red and discomfited as if he had been the person accused. "Anthony would have jumped to give it to her, as I've told you already."

"So it seemed," said the lawyer, dryly.

"Confound you, man, but I tell you he would!"

"I can only answer you by the facts of the case."

"But—I'll ask him—you don't know what you're saying—my word for it, he never had that letter."

"I posted it myself. Besides, where is it? If there had been a non-delivery we should have heard by this time from the Dead-Letter Office. Pooh, pooh, Chester, the temptation was a little too strong, that's the long and short of it, and, after all, no one pretends that there was any fraud. Mr Tregennas put the choice into his hands, and he had no doubt an absolute right to choose."

The Squire, who had thrust his hands into his pockets, was striding on at a pace with which his friend found it difficult to keep up. He gave a sort of groan when Mr Pitt finished his deliberate speech, and then stopped and turned suddenly upon him.

"I tell you what, Pitt," he said, setting his teeth. "If you weren't who you are, I should like to—to—"

"To kick me," said the lawyer, coolly finishing the sentence. "I should not wonder. But considering who I am, and considering that I have certainly no personal animus against the young man,—what can you make of the story?"

"Do you want me to say I think my old friend's lad a villain? Good heavens, sir, and he was so proud of him!"

Mr Pitt's manner changed a little, losing some of the hard ease with which he had talked, as he began to understand the pain it cost the loyal-hearted Squire to receive his impressions. He said earnestly,—

"You think too harshly of it, Chester, and perhaps I spoke too strongly. There is no villainy in the matter. Few young men would have had strength of moral purpose sufficient to resist such a temptation, and give up half a valuable property."

"But that is exactly what he has done," broke in Mr Chester, quickly. "We're forgetting all that. He has voluntarily disposed of half. It is sheer nonsense, Pitt. How can you account for such an act?"

"Well, it has gone to his sister, which is a different business from losing it altogether. But I own to you that my own convictions point to a certain pressure having been brought to bear. I suspect that the secret was scented, and that this was the price of silence,—in fact, I may say that I put a question or two to young Lee, which proved pretty decidedly that he was acquainted with the contents of the letter. No other theory would explain his manner of receiving the gift, for he absolutely expressed no gratitude whatever."

It was evident that Mr Pitt's quiet persistence was producing the effect it usually does produce upon violent people. The Squire looked like a man who has received a blow. He walked on silently for some time, then stopping at a gate, said, —

"I think I'll go across to Sanders's farm; there's a little business I want to speak to him about. You can't miss Mannering's house if you go straight forward." He turned away as he spoke, but had not gone many paces before he strode back. "The boy's father did not know a word of the matter, sir; of that I'll stake my existence," he said positively, and went off again without giving Mr Pitt time to answer.

As the lawyer walked thoughtfully on towards the Red House, he acknowledged to himself that this conviction of the Squire's was probably well grounded. Even to the eyes of a suspicious man, and Mr Pitt was partly from nature and partly from profession suspicious, the Vicar had carried that about him which made it very difficult to doubt his honour. It was quite possible that the contents of the letter had been withheld from him. But the other affair had resolved itself almost into certainty. When Mr Tregennas read to him the words he had just written, Mr Pitt had felt that it was putting human virtue to too severe a test; he half smiled at himself now for having been such a fool as to cherish a hope that the young man would be generous to Margaret Hare's child at his own expense.

Chapter Sixteen

"A very pitiful lady, very young,
Exceeding rich in human sympathies."

Rosetti's *Dante*.

The Squire was more utterly cast down by Mr Pitt's communication than those would have thought possible who knew that Anthony Miles had never been a favourite of his. Perhaps a little touch of jealousy had given the first warp when he looked at the Vicar's son and his own daughters, and had made him always hard upon the young fellow; but it was not a jealousy which could take pleasure in such a discovery as this. He was so cross and miserable throughout the day that Winifred felt sure something was the matter. Mr Pitt had left them; the evening was cold and stormy, a southwest gale was blowing, and the wind tore at the windows and howled drearily round the house. Winifred only waited until Bessie had gone to bed—a concession to years of half an hour against which that young lady nightly rebelled—before she asked her father what had happened, and whether Mr Pitt had brought any bad news.

"Yes, he has," said the Squire doggedly; "very bad news. It's well the poor old Vicar should be dead and gone."

And then he told her.

As he went bluntly through Mr Pitt's account he once or twice looked curiously at her, for, in spite of his disclaimer, he could not help remembering that other hint which the lawyer had let drop, that Winifred was dear to Anthony. "If it is so, she'll have hysterics or something; that's how girls always show it."

To his relief, however, Winifred did not so much as utter an exclamation. If he had been quick to notice, he might have observed a little proud up-drawing of her head, and a sudden light in her eyes; but we are all apt to read only those signs for which we are on the lookout, and the Squire drew a long breath of relief.

"What do you think of this?" he said, when he had finished.

"Did Mr Pitt really tell you such an absurd story?" said Winifred, smiling.

Her treating the matter lightly was unfortunate, for her father had been made so wretched all day that it irritated him to have it supposed that he was throwing away his sympathies; and his love of contradiction was such that every instinct of his nature arrayed him on the side that was assailed, so that he began at once to adopt Mr Pitt's opinion as his own, to hasten to its defence, to run his thoughts more keenly over its possibilities. He flustered a little directly.

"It's very well for you to laugh, since you don't understand anything at all about it. Is Pitt a likely man to concoct a bundle of lies?"

"I don't know, I am sure," she said, looking at him with astonishment. "But you do not mean that anything he could say would make you believe such a story of Anthony?"

"Well, explain it, explain it," said the Squire grimly, "that's all."

Winifred sat forward, and began to speak with more impetuosity.

"That Anthony should—" she began, and then suddenly broke off and laughed outright. "It is so very ridiculous!" she said.

"I don't see the absurdity," growled Mr Chester. "I don't see how Pitt can be mistaken, or how Anthony can get over the thing. You women run away with your own opinions, without ever stopping to hear reason; but other people will put two and two together. It is a very bad business."

"It is exceedingly wrong of Mr Pitt to have dared to say such a thing," said Winifred, standing up quickly, and looking very tall and stately; "but it can hurt Anthony no more than—than it could hurt you. He could explain it, of course, but I hope he will never hear that anything so cruel and untrue has been suggested. Good-night, papa. I am glad there is nothing really the matter."

She walked out of the room with the smile still on her lips and the backward curve of her slender throat a little more apparent. But those few words of opposition had done Anthony's cause no good with the Squire. He repeated to himself that women were so obstinate there was no dealing with them, and while he fancied himself as grieved as ever, in his heart, I think there lurked a secret hope that Winifred might be forced to acknowledge herself in the wrong. He was not in the least aware of the petty obstacle which had turned the current, nor indeed would he have acknowledged that the current had been turned at all, but, no doubt, as he went over the array of presumptive evidence against Anthony, he weighted it in a manner which he had not done until this moment.

As for Winifred, the smile died out of her face before she reached her own room. A bright fire was burning; she went to the window, threw back the shutter, and stood looking out into the wild darkness. There were furious gusts, strange depths of blackness, lights gleaming and vanishing in the direction of Underham, a sawing of branches one against the other, now and then distant and mysterious sounds, as if the rush and roar of the great sea itself were swelling the tumult. Nothing but fancy could have brought such a sound, but Winifred caught at it, and would not let it go. The swoop of the wind upon the water, the jagged tossed waves hurling themselves against the sandy bar, the wild shrieks of the night, the blackness, the confusion, here and there, perhaps, a concentration of the horror, lives going out in a last cry... she pressed her face against the panes, shuddering and praying for the poor souls. All this while there was something nearer to her which she was shutting out and trying to overwhelm by a more terrible distress. It was the strongest of the two, after all. She softly closed the shutters, turning away from the window with pitiful compunction in her heart, as if she were leaving poor drowning men out in the cold, and came and sat before the fire to think of Anthony. For, though she might smile at her father's story, and a little smile again stole over the sweet grave face as she thought of the accusation, she knew Anthony well enough to dread the idea of its reaching his ears. There was no room now in her heart for pride, or for anything except a kind tenderness. That he did not care for her any longer, if indeed he had ever cared, she felt assured, and at this moment it seemed to her that she would not have had him care in such a sense, so long as they might be friends. Perhaps the very storm and darkness had something to do with this persuasion. When skies were soft, and the sun shining, and things bright about her, she too might have cried out for some share in the brightness and softness; but the grim earnestness of the night, a night for wrecks and disasters, and big with struggle and suffering, utterly shut out such joy of fair visions.

She could not but reflect what such a report would cost Anthony if it should reach him, and how he, of all men, would suffer and writhe under it. Kindliness, love, and praise seemed so completely his natural food, that if they were withdrawn it was certain that he would droop and flag. With the thought, her first impression came strongly back that the accusation should at any cost be kept from his knowledge, but her own nature was too brave and high-minded for such an impression to linger. Better the open wound than the secret calamity; better that he should taste the sharpness even of disappointment than be dogged by a suspicion to which he could give no tangible shape; better, a hundred times better, know, and meet, and repel.

But who should tell him?

As she put the question to herself, she trembled a little with a perception that the answer was fall of personal pain. Names floated before her, — her father, the Mannerings, Mrs Miles, — but each suggestion carried a negative with it, although she paused longest at the thought of Mr Robert. He was kind-heartedness itself; at the same time, she felt as if such a telling required more delicate care than he would give — who would give it? — who would give it except herself? Winifred shrank and flushed Pride put out its prickles; but, after all, there was something so much stronger than pride in her heart, that it failed to conquer. The little impalpable bar that had sprung up between them was the harder to pass for its very impalpability, yet — if she could help him, only as his friend, with no touch of love to mar it, as she thought, unconscious that it was the highest and most divine love which she was offering, then pain of her own should not withhold her, nor even the added estrangement which her words might cause.

The next morning she awoke with her determination unweakened. She would seek an opportunity, and tell him what slander he had to kill.

Chapter Seventeen

"When adversities flow
Then love ebbs; but friendship standeth stiffly
In storms."

Lilly.

People, women especially, make resolutions sometimes with no more to back them up than a vague hope that they will be able to carry them out in some haphazard fashion. Winifred had almost offended Mrs Miles by the slackness of her visits to the cottage, and hardly knew whether Anthony were in Thorpe or not. She persuaded Bessie, however, to ride with her father, and, putting on her red cloak, went across the meadows, making a little spot of brightness in the midst of the quiet winter colouring.

She walked through the village, lingering a little at the post-office, and afterwards going on towards Underham, simply from not knowing where else to turn. The rain had reduced the roads to thick mud, and strewn them with little twigs and branches, whipped from the trees by the violence of the storm. But, as not infrequently happens after these fierce gales, there was an exquisite beauty shining where lately the hurly-burly had raged. Instinctively Winifred stopped at a gate in the hedge to look at what was generally dull and uninteresting enough, a long stretch of flat meadows with low hills beyond. But the meadow was transfigured with a depth of colour; there were rich patches of indigo and russet, poplars lighting up the sober background with streaks of brown light, breadths of freshly turned earth, infinite traceries springing from dark stems, a delicate sky broken by soft shadows and round masses of living light, little pools of shining beautiful water left by the rains, hedges ruddy with crimson berries, a white horse, an old man leaning on his stick, — the picture was full of simple, homely grace.

She was still looking at it when some one came along the road behind her. It was Mr Robert Mannering, and his first words connected themselves with her own purpose.

"Have you seen Anthony Miles?" he asked. "He was to come down by this train, and I am particularly desirous to meet him." Something that he saw in Winifred's face made him add immediately, "So you have heard it, too?"

"Does Anthony know?" asked the girl, without answering directly.

Mr Robert's kindly face looked grave and worried. He began to brush imaginary dust from his coat-sleeve,—an action in which he always took refuge under any annoyance.

"If you mean the report," he said, laying a little stress upon the last word, "I imagine that he does not. To tell you the truth, that is why I am here; for his father's sake I am inclined to let him hear what is said."

Winifred flushed a little.

"I do not know why you should say for his father's sake," she said at once. "I do not suppose that Anthony's friends can have allowed a breath of this horrible story to affect them, so that their one wish must be to stand by him for his own sake."

She stopped and looked at Mr Mannering, who was silent.

"Surely," said Winifred impetuously, "Mr Pitt has not influenced you!"

"My dear," said Robert Mannering, looking out towards the low hills, and speaking with a little hesitation, "I think that Anthony had a difficult duty to perform—"

"Yes, yes, go on," said Winifred, trying to govern her voice.

"And that he shrank from it."

She could no longer laugh as she had laughed the night before. A sickening feeling came over her. Was this lie actually living, spreading, destroying? Her eyes filled with a rush of tears. She lifted her hand in mute indignation.

"You—his friend!—you believe that!"

He was silent again, and then said slowly,—

"Perhaps neither you nor I are fair judges, Winifred. You naturally think of Anthony, whom you have known all your life, and I think of Margaret Hare. Remember that her child was in all justice the heir, and remember what the poor mother has suffered."

"O, I remember!" said Winifred, recovering herself, and standing upright, with the full light of the sky in her face; "and I remember, too, who it was that spoke to old Mr Tregennas for the child. It is only I who recollect at all, I think. And it seems to me that there is little use in knowing people all one's life long, as you say, if that knowledge falls away into doubt the instant our trust in them is tried. If you believe this story, Mr Mannering, pray let me be the person to tell him. I may meet him now; at any rate, I am sure to have an opportunity."

"As you like," Mr Robert said, gravely. "Good by, my dear. I am afraid there is pain in store for us all."

But, although he was the first to say good by, it was Winifred who left him standing by the gate watching her, as she went resolutely along with a quickened step, and the light still on her face.

"True woman, true woman, she will not fail him," said Mr Robert to himself, shaking his head sadly. "Poor boy, I can't think of him without being sorry from the bottom of my heart, and yet it was an evil thing to do to Margaret Hare's child. I wish Pitt had not told us—I wish—"

And then he turned and went back again.

Winifred walked swiftly on for about half a mile, slackening her pace as she became aware that she was going too fast, and trying to lose the consciousness that she had come here to meet Anthony Miles, for it was only when the pitiful feeling was very strong in her heart that it overcame a secret repugnance, and every now and then this last grew into a kind of startled shyness.

Presently she heard wheels, and saw the pony-carriage coming towards her with Anthony driving. Her first impulse was to nod and smile, and pass on as if the meeting were accidental, but the next moment she was ashamed of its prompting, and stood still bravely. Ah, how strange it was that she should need any bravery where Anthony was concerned! It evidently pleased him that she should have stopped, for it was with a radiant countenance that he drew up and jumped out, and asked what had brought her so far from Thorpe.

"He should not have asked," thought poor Winifred. Then she found he was preparing to send oh James with the carriage, and to walk back with her.

"If you will let me?" he said questioningly.

"I should like it," Winifred said, so eagerly that he brightened still more. It struck both of them with a pleasant sense of warmth that they two should be walking alone together through the lanes. It was winter, but Anthony thought there was plenty of colour and brightness, and perhaps Winifred's red cloak had something to do with it. As for her, after the gleam of those few delicious moments, the dull weight of what she had to say came back with depressing heaviness. Anthony's good-humour and lightness of heart added a hundredfold to the difficulty of her task; yet, time was passing, and she felt with terror that each step brought them nearer to Thorpe. She was always deficient in the feminine art of doubling upon her subject, and in this hour of need it seemed as if she were duller than ever. Anthony, however, knowing nothing of her inward strife, was quite content with Winifred's softness and kindness; he talked gayly—more gayly than he had talked since the Vicar's death—of what he had been doing in London.

"I think I see my way to some satisfactory work at last," he said.

"Shall you live in London, do you mean?" asked Winifred, thinking not of London, but of nearer things.

"One must, you know," Anthony said slowly. And yet, although he had been dissatisfied with Thorpe of late, he said these words with a strange reluctance in his heart. "It is necessary to be in the midst of things. This place is so far off."

"Trenance is let, is it not?" Winifred was plunging nervously into her subject.

"Yes, and, oddly enough, to a relation of old Lucas. You remember old Lucas, don't you? I wonder what this Sir Somebody Somebody is like, and whether it runs in the family to wear your hat at the back of your head."

And so he went on. It seemed to Winifred, poor child, as if he had never talked so fast or so brightly, and all the while, though, as I have said, that thing which she had to tell lay like a cruel weight upon her heart, there was also a secret joy, a delight in this return of free confidence, a feeling as though the happiness which had once seemed possible were possible again. Anthony, too, had vague thoughts stirring. He was pleased at Winifred's walking back with him, at her little concession; for of late he had declared angrily that she was cold, changed, variable. He was too much taken up with his satisfaction to see her wistful looks, or to guess how her heart ached with the thought that it was she herself who must embitter these quickly passing moments. Already she was wasting time dangerously. They had reached the gate where Winifred and Mr Robert had stood and looked across the meadows. The transient glow which had so beautified the common things was gone, a grey gloom had crept over the snowy clouds, everything lay stretched in a bare, flat level; it seemed no more than a dull land of hedges and ditches, with a few ugly poplars and insignificant hills. Anthony laughed at Winifred a little for stopping to look at them, but indeed she felt as if she needed the bar of the gate by which to hold, so strange a tremor had seized upon her. She glanced at him with the hope that he would see that something was wrong and question her, for it seemed to her as if her face must tell the tale alone; but he talked on happily, until Winifred interrupted him with sudden abruptness.

"Anthony," she said, "do you know that there is a cruel report abroad about you?"

Her heart beat so fast that she could hardly speak, and yet her voice sounded in her own ears harsh and unfeeling.

"A report?" said Anthony inquiringly. He began to wonder whether she could have heard what had been told him a few days ago, that he was engaged to Miss Milman. It might be unlike Winifred to speak in this fashion, but a man is often egotist enough to forget these impossibilities, and he folded his arms on the bar of the gate, and laughed and looked round with a pleasant anticipation of fault-finding. Winifred kept her face turned from him, and went on nervously.

"They say that Mr Tregennas wanted to have changed his will at the last, and to have left half his fortune to his granddaughter—"

Something choked her voice. Anthony looked at her and gave a little whistle of astonishment. "Then why on earth did he not?"

"They say that he wrote to you to tell you his desire, placing the matter entirely in your hands, and requesting that if you decided against it,"— she left out his father's name, fearing to seem irreverent to the dead,—"you would take no notice of the letter; and they say—"

He interrupted her here sharply.

"They! Whom do you mean by they?"

"Mr Pitt," said Winifred in a low voice, after a moment's hesitation. "Mr Pitt says that you sent Mr Tregennas no answer."

"So they believe that, do they?" he said in a jarred voice.

Winifred could not answer. Her heart was too full of pity and pain for her to speak. She held by the bar of the gate, and saw blankly lying before her the wintry fields, the tall, expressionless poplars. Anthony put another question in a moment, in the same coldly restrained tone.

"How do they account for my sharing the property with Marmaduke?"

"Anthony, do not force me to repeat such folly."

"I must hear."

"It is so absurd!" said Winifred, keenly ashamed, and trying to laugh. "They say Marmaduke discovered the secret, and to avoid its becoming known you consented to—to—"

"Let him share the spoils. I see. Has Mr Pitt returned to London?"

"I believe so. A word from you will set it right."

"It should never have been wrong," he said bitterly. "After what you have said I must get home to catch the post. Good by. You don't mind walking back alone? Indeed, it doesn't seem as if my company would do you much credit."

He was gone almost before she heard, and a cold desolation crept over her as she stood still, turning her back upon the little network of fields, and watched him striding away along the muddy lane. What a fierceness there had been in his last words! What a sense of separation he had left behind him! It had required all her resolution to take this task upon her, and it was cruel that it should thus recoil upon herself; a sense of injustice must have stirred her into indignation, had it not been for the womanly tenderness which at once turned it aside with compassionate excuses. No wonder that the very breath of such an accusation should have angered him; no wonder that his first thought should have been to hurry to refute it; no wonder, ah, no wonder, that he should forget her.

She little thought that it was wrath instead of forgetfulness which was uppermost in Anthony's mind as he splashed through little innocent pools of water with angry steps. Like most reserved men, he was exceeding impatient of reserve in others, and he wanted her to have protested her disbelief in the slander which had met him, while such a protest would have seemed a positive insult to Winifred, who had never dreamed of doubting him. Her words had given him a terrible blow, and the charge was quickly fermented by his imagination into a distorted form. Conscious that he had not sought the old man's favour, that it had been hateful to him to replace Marmaduke, that he was even now setting inquiries after Ellen Harford on foot, he was accused, nevertheless, of committing what he called a crime to gain this fortune to which he was indifferent. I am not defending his manner of receiving the accusation. If he had been a hero it would have been very different; but, so far as one sees, heroes seldom leap into the world in complete armour; they are more likely to grow out of trials and temptations, yes, out of many a slip and fall, in which they seem to be beaten down and overwhelmed. Anthony had the stuff in him which would bear the furnace, although there were little overgrowths hiding its goodness; he had a ready generosity, high imaginings, longings to better the world; but these were the very feelings upon which such an accusation came like a stream of icy water. If people ceased to believe in him, he felt as if he could believe in nothing.

As he went quickly through Thorpe, he held aloof from the people, but noticed them jealously, fancying he could read meanings in their faces of which, it is needless to say, they were guiltless. Ill report of a man flies fast, but this was not the sort of report to gain wings quickly, for if any of the people heard it, to what did it amount? To the fact that before Mr Tregennas died he put it to Mr Anthony whether or not he should change his will. "A'd ha' bin a big fule for's pains if a'd said a wudd," would have been the heaviest verdict that Anthony could have received from their lips.

But we place our own thoughts in other people's hearts, and so Anthony heard a hundred unspoken things on his way through Thorpe.

Chapter Eighteen

"Anthony Miles is gone to London," said Mr Robert Mannering, walking into the library of the Red House, on the day following that described in the last chapter.

Mr Mannering looked with a shiver at the door his brother had left open behind him. He had a cold, and a great many theories about its treatment.

"I don't know what good he can do himself by going up," added Mr Robert in a perturbed tone.

"He will be able to see Pitt," suggested Mr Mannering, drawing nearer the fire.

"I wish I could feel there was any chance of his convincing Pitt. It's a bad business, Charles."

Mr Mannering looked up with a little surprise; for although his brother frequently indulged in cynical speeches, he had never yet known him to believe in them, or take anything but a largely hopeful view of individualised human nature.

"My dear Robert—would you object to shutting the door?—"

"I beg your pardon," said Mr Robert hastily, doing as he was requested with an abstracted bang, which made Mr Mannering wince. But he went on.

"Look calmly at the matter. What do we know of the contents of that letter? How is it possible to judge of the terms in which the suggestion was made?—of the burden it may have inflicted upon Anthony?"

"That is not the question," said his brother, shaking his head. "He denies, you must remember, having received any suggestion whatever. Pooh, the thing's absurd. Besides, young Lee seems to have implied that he was aware of what had taken place."

Sometimes they are odd things which warp our judgments. Robert Mannering was an old lawyer, with a red face and short iron-grey hair, and yet it took a very little thing to turn aside his shrewd every-day sense. Only a woman's name, and a curl of brown hair out of which the living light had faded.

"I have said all I can for him to the Squire," he went on. "We shall see when he comes back. But—"

He walked to the window, and stood with his hands behind him, looking out. There was a threatening of snow in the air, and a few solitary flakes, the more dismal for their want of companionship, came fluttering down upon the empty beds. That "but" sounded like the key-note of all dreary disbelief.

"Nobody can tell," said Mr Mannering, who usually took a more desponding view of human nature than his brother. "My own opinion is that you are all deciding hastily, but with the wind where it is, I don't believe there's a man alive could give an unprejudiced judgment. As to these hot-water pipes, Jane contrives to convert them into conductors of cold air, with an ingenuity worthy of a better cause."

"The room is like a hot-house," said Mr Robert, a little shortly, and still keeping his back turned. "That fool Stokes has not had the sense to mat up the red geranium. He'll have got rid of every flower in the garden before long, that's certain. Commend me to this place for incapable idiots."

While he spoke, Mr Mannering with great care and deliberation proceeded to fold a handkerchief, and to tie it round his head, thus imparting an extraordinarily rueful expression to his face.

"Yates tells me they're going to push the Bill for connecting the two lines," he said, fastening the knot.

"So I supposed. Nothing is too fraudulent for me to discredit, and I'm quite aware that you may pick as many pockets as you please, if only you do it on a large enough scale."

"Come, come, Robert. You'll be had up for a libel."

"I dare say. There's no bigger libel than truth in these days."

And then he suddenly turned round with a laugh at himself. To do him justice, he was not often so cross, but then he was not often so sore and disappointed at heart. It was very bitter to him to think of Anthony Miles committing a dishonourable action, and it smote him again to remember the injustice to the dead. He could not get one predominant feeling, and that irritated his natural sense of orderliness.

Winifred, of whom he thought much at this time, was, perhaps, more impatient than grieved, having an unflinching faith in the triumph of right, which to such natures is as the very air they breathe. Only she had not lived long enough to know that though the triumph comes, it is not always the thing we picture to ourselves, laurel crowns, joyful music, and the people looking on and shouting. There are other triumphs besides this, wounds and tears, and a slow struggle upwards.

She believed that every shadow of blame would be swept away from Anthony as soon as he returned from seeing Mr Pitt, and though keenly sensitive to the reproaches she was forced to hear, took a pride in treating them indifferently, as stings too slight even to require defence. When Mr Robert met her one day and would have said something, she was very cool with him.

"When Anthony returns," she said, scarcely stopping, "we shall know exactly how such a mistake can have arisen."

"Anthony is come back," said Mr Robert, gravely.

She could not resist the rush of blood to her heart, which made her ask hastily, "When?"

"He came last night. I have just seen him," Mr Mannering said in the same tone.

"Well?"

"You will hear from himself, no doubt. Only, my dear, don't set your heart too strongly upon things being made straight."

Winifred had grown a little pale, but there was not one shade of doubt in her clear eyes as she looked at him.

"I do not understand you," she said quietly. "Things must be made straight, as you call it, in the end; and in the mean time, of course, no one who knows Anthony can doubt him for a moment. That such a report should have ever lived for an hour is the real hardship that we have to regret."

She was so unflinchingly steadfast, that Mr Robert, who believed there was more trouble in store for her, left his warnings alone, and went away mute. After all, she would know soon enough.

And to know enough, in this case, simply meant to know nothing. Anthony had come back as he went, with hard lines about his face, and the bitterness deepened and intensified. His first care had been to go to Mr Pitt's chambers, where he found the old lawyer polite, cold, and unshaken. "I posted the letter myself, Mr Miles. You have ascertained, I presume, that it is not to be heard of in the Dead-Letter Office?" was the text to which he returned when all had been said. He had not seen the contents, but Mr Tregennas had communicated them to him. Anthony grew exceedingly angry, and lost his temper. Although he was aware when he left him that it was absolutely imperative that he should follow Mr Pitt's suggestions, which were of a very obvious and practical nature, the manner in which they had been thrown out had raised so strong an antagonism in his blood, that he was tempted to fling them and all prudent dealing to the winds, and was, perhaps, not without a feeling of satisfaction, when they proved altogether barren of results.

It was a word, however, of Mr Pitt's about Marmaduke Lee, which gave him something approaching to a clew, at first no more than an idea that his brother-in-law might be able to assist him to grope in the darkness in which he found himself, but gradually, after he went down to Oakham, and had seen Marmaduke, growing by some instinctive power into a perception of what had actually happened. Only those who have some knowledge of the strength and weakness of a character like Anthony's can conceive what a shattering of landmarks came with this perception. All his impulses were full of indignation and contempt; he almost withered Marmaduke with an outbreak of angry scorn, and yet felt compelled, by the very intensity of this scorn to save so miserable a man from the consequences that would have crushed him. Something in the excessive meanness and cowardice of the act filled him with a loathing shame which made it impossible to proclaim it. Naturally his connection with Marion touched him more nearly with its dishonour, but without such a shield it is probable that he would have shrunk from dragging such a deed from its hiding-place, in order to shelter himself behind it. Yet, although there was a certain generosity in this attitude, there was little mercy in his heart. It enraged him to feel the helplessness of his position, the impotence with which he must submit to the world's verdict His was a nature to which injustice was the most unbearable form of persecution that could have visited him, one, also, which seemed to raise all his worst qualities in opposition, so as to sweep away with a crash the noble ideal he had set up of men and things; and such a moment in a man's life is full of danger and trial, his weakness concealing itself so deceptively that it seems to himself to be the armour which enables him to present an undaunted front.

In Marions case, it was pity which Anthony felt, and he was as anxious as Marmaduke to spare her the disclosure; but this did not prevent a hard contempt becoming visible in his manner, when she, as was daily the case, openly displayed her enthusiastic admiration for her husband. Naturally, this made her angry, and placed Anthony again in the wrong. It was, as it often is in the world, although, in spite of the repetitions of some thousand years, every experience comes to us with the sense of novelty, the man who was most heavily weighted had the least sympathy, the hardest blame, the sharpest judgments. Other people, less bound to partiality than Marion, compared Anthony's abruptness, and the strong lines which had grown round his mouth, unfavourably with Marmaduke's easy-humoured placidity by which he had become a popular neighbour. All the crooks and angles of Anthony's disposition seemed to be showing themselves, and yet the poor fellow had never so sorely wanted pity, and kindness, and patient treatment. Whether he judged rightly or not, there was something even beyond chivalry in accepting the burden of this hateful thing, to spare another a more terrible weight. There was so much cowardice and feebleness in Marmaduke's nature that to avoid the pain of disgrace he might, so Anthony believed, have fled from it at any cost,—even life itself; and though he scorned such cowardice, he had not the heart to leave it to its fate.

He left Oakham with a bitter consciousness that a gulf was dug between them, and a hot, sore feeling with the world which he was about to face without the power of clearing himself from its accusation. He would make no attempt to save anything out of the wreck; with the pride of youth, he determined that he would not stoop to offer assurances. Knowing how impossible it was that he could have done this deed,—as careless of money as those can be who have never wanted it,—it cut him to the heart that he should be suspected, and he revenged himself by a simulated indifference. Nothing could have been more repellent than his manner of meeting Mr Robert, or less satisfactory than the answers he vouchsafed. He would make no appeal for trust. Little by little, the people who wished to be friendly grew irritated, and the matter was talked of more openly and more unfavourably for Anthony when, instead of conciliating, he seemed to provoke war to the knife. When the Squire passed him with a cool bow, he retaliated by taking no notice whatever of the Squire the next time they met. Even kindness appeared to wound him. Winifred was bewildered when Anthony would lift his hat and go by as if he saw no appeal in her sad eyes. He put himself in opposition to all the world, and as a natural consequence grew hard, bitter, and mistrustful.

Perhaps our powers of endurance are never so near giving way as when we are holding them tightly strung, yet conscious of every jar and vibration in the effort; and poor Anthony, with his sensitive and affectionate temperament, went about with a dumb misery in his heart. He was rejecting friendship at the time he most needed it, and really longed to stretch out the hands with which he repelled its sweet kindness, in pitiful entreaty for some touch of fellowship which should break the cold isolation he was creating for himself.

Chapter Nineteen

"Those have most power to hurt us that we love;
We lay our sleeping lives within their arms."

Beaumont and Fletcher.

There is a curious likeness in the yesterdays and to-days of our lives, a likeness so strong that it conceals the greater differences from us until we have gone far enough to look back and compare them dispassionately. We eat and drink, talk and sleep, more or less; certain things seem to hold us in chains to which we move obediently. If it were not so, life would be unendurable, the calls upon our sympathy would harden our hearts or wear them out, joy and sorrow would jostle each other too openly in the high road. The mechanism hurts us sometimes, but it is good discipline nevertheless.

And so at Thorpe Regis the many changes were gradually covered with the old dress of routine and habit. It is almost sad how soon people become reconciled to them. A year ago it would have seemed the strangest thing in the world for anything to have broken through the daily intercourse between Hardlands and the Vicarage, and here was an alienation so great that it almost amounted to total estrangement. Not that the Squire desired it. Unused to keep a very close control over himself, he allowed his feelings to be seen, and affronted Anthony; but he would gladly have had everything as of old with Mrs Miles, and was too autocratic not to be puzzled when he found this not the case.

"It was not her fault. The girls may go to her as much as they please. The poor woman's to be pitied,—I pity her from the bottom of my heart," he would say.

Mrs Miles on her part had no very clear conception of what had happened, for she had lived in close retirement since her husband's death, and the few friends who entered that solitude were not likely to be cruelly communicative. But she was aware that unkind reports had been set afloat about the will, and, while really too sad and crushed in spirit to do more than reiterate her assurance that it would not have happened had the Vicar been alive, she was vaguely willing to take up cudgels against all the world on Anthony's behalf; in comparison with whom what was Hardlands, what was the Squire, what even were motherless Bessie and Winifred?

And so, and so, and so, — a hundred little obstacles magnified themselves indefinitely, the two sets of lives that had been so blended with each other fell apart, the little brook widened into a river. Many people thought that it would have been better if Anthony had left the neighbourhood for a time, and allowed the exaggerated reports of his conduct to settle quietly. But perhaps the idea of this sediment of black mud, only requiring a chance stone to be stirred into turbid activity, was more hateful to Anthony than the knowledge that the waters all about him were kept in constant disturbance. He made no pretence of concealing that he was unhappy, or at least no one could fail to see it in his face; and his irritation and soreness against all the world were marked so acutely that it was impossible not to foresee a reaction from so abrupt a closing of his heart. He remained at Thorpe, partly from yielding to his mothers clinging desire to do so, partly from pride which forbade flight from disagreeables, and partly from a failure in those springs of action which had hitherto urged him forward. But he could not long endure the position of solitude he had taken up, and some consciousness of this added to his discomfort.

When the thing of which he was accused had first grown into form, Winifred had reproached herself for the warm glow with which her heart assured her that Anthony would never feel her friendship fail him; but this had long ago faded away under the keen chill of his manner, keener because her generous spirit had never wavered in its faithfulness and was enduring all the pangs which he believed himself to be bearing alone. She would not suffer one throb of resentment to answer his coldness, but it cost her a daily and bitter struggle to learn her powerlessness, and to understand that he was himself making it impossible for her to put out so much as a hand to help him in his trouble.

She was in the village one day, and just turning out of it towards the Hardlands meadows when she met old Araunah Stokes and his daughter-in-law, Faith's mother. It was not very often the old man got so far from his house, and he was now walking on with a kind of feeble vigour, as if bent upon making the most of what small strength remained to him. His daughter-in-law — who had evidently been crying, and now and then wiped her eyes — gave Miss Chester to understand that it was Faith who caused their trouble by her persistence in her engagement.

"Whatever us shall do, I don't know, wi' her so contrary."

"Hold your tongue," said the old man, turning upon her with a weak, fierce voice. "The women tells and tells, till they talks the very brains out o' yer head. You'm no better than a baby when they've clacketed at ye for an hour or two without a word of sense from beginnin' to end."

"An' me niver so much as openin' my lips," said Mrs Stokes, crying meekly and holding up her hands. "An' I did think as Faith would ha' bin a comfort, me so weak, wi' no sproyle, nor nothin', and gran'father only just fit to totle about."

"It ain't much comfort you'm like to get out o' maedens," said Araunah, still bitterly. "They'm so hard to manage as a drove o' pegs. Faith shall bide where her be, though, for all her mother's setting up."

"Has she made up her mind, then, to marry this man?" asked Winifred, interested.

"He doan't give her the chance," said the grandfather angrily, striking his stick upon the ground. "Girl's a fule, that's t' long an' short o't, an' he bain't so beg a wan."

"He knows better nor to persume," said Mrs Stokes, indignant for Faith's sake. "You see, Miss Winifred, he doan't feel he've got enough to offer our maed, — I doan't know what her can be thinkin' of," continued her mother, dissolving suddenly again.

"An' her'd give up a good pleace. But her shall bide, her shall bide."

"Though it mayn't be for long, with Mr Anthony goin' to be married hisself."

Self-possession is a wonderful power. We read with a thrill of amazement of the Spartan boy, and the fox, and the hidden agony, but, after all, the heroism is repeated day by day around us. There are people getting stabs from unconscious executioners, and the life dying out of them, while they are smiling and keeping up the little ball of conversation, and betraying nothing of the pang. Winifred's voice became a little gayer than usual as she said, —

"Mr Anthony? Is he going to be married?"

"To Miss Lovell down to Under'm, haven't you heard it, miss? It's that has set Faith thinkin' more o' that Stephens."

"I woan't have it," said the old man, querulously. "I woan't have she comin' hoam to we, ating and drinking. Polly has more sense than Faith and her mother putt together."

Winifred never quite knew what she said, but she walked away with her heart suddenly hardened against Faith. Why should Faith escape?—why should she not bear her lot like other people?—why should one be set free more than another? And, O, what had Faith to endure! What grief was hers, whose lover only did not think himself worthy, or who would, perhaps, renounce his happiness for the sake of perishing souls? Grief?—why, it was an exquisite bliss. Faith stood on one side, triumphant and happy, while Winifred walked in the valley of humiliation, with sharpest thorns piercing her feet. Anthony did not love her, for he loved another. Death builds no wall of separation like this, nay, death, will break down walls,—only love itself can bar love with a hopeless fence. She fought against the bitter truth, poor soul, calling herself by hard names, and laughing drearily at her own folly; but the anguish was very acute, and she had a feeling as if, though for a little while she might keep its sharpest suffering at aim's length, it would overmaster her at last. Was it all true,—real? Was the sun shining on her, or was it rather a cruel furnace that had suddenly scorched the earth, and would burn and scorch day after day, day after day, through long years, through an endless lifetime, grey with shadows and weary with pain, and with no better hope than forgetfulness? Heaven pity those whose sorrow brings them face to face with such a thought and no further! Its very touch gave Winifred a shuddering fear of herself, and a momentary but clear perception of something that should shine through grief and overcome it, ah, even make the rugged road beautiful.

But it was difficult for her to disconnect her thoughts as yet while they were vibrating and ringing with the blow. She walked mechanically towards home, but she saw Bessie and Mr and Mrs Featherly in the garden, and feeling it impossible at this moment to join them, she stood still irresolutely, and then turned and went along the field, where a little stream was running, and a path led up through a small wood.

The day was delicately bright and hot. Across a pale moon that looked herself no more than a stationary cloud, little wilful vapours which had broken away from larger masses were sailing. Red cattle, satisfied with their rich flowery pastures, had gathered under the hedges to chew the cud and sleepily whisk away the flies. The brown water hurried along, washing long grass, and shining up at meadow-sweet and purple clusters of loosestrife. There were cool flashing lights, and tender depths of colour, and a sweet content over everything, and poor Winifred growing sadder and sadder with the sense of contrast, yet walking more slowly and looking wistfully at the long grass, with a vague longing to lie down in it, and let everything go by and away forever. It might have been this which, as she went towards a little wooden bridge crossing the stream into the wood, deafened her ears to a step until Anthony Miles himself was close to her. The instant before she had believed herself safe with the patient cattle and the water and her own sad thoughts, and it cost her a struggle to master the tumult into which her feelings were suddenly stirred. But Anthony was too much absorbed in his own thoughts to notice any disturbance, and as matters had not yet come to such a pass that they could meet in a lonely meadow and go by without greeting, he put out his hand, and said, —

"Are you going into the wood? You will find it very hot even there. A thunder-storm would be a real comfort."

"O, I like this sort of day!" said Winifred, with a hurrying desire to prove her own perfect contentment. "Everything is looking most beautiful I see Sniff is as fond as ever of the water—" She hesitated suddenly, there being a certain awkwardness quick to make itself felt in any allusion to the past, however slight; but Anthony said carelessly, —

"Sniff was due at Oakham, but as my mother seems to want him more than Marion, I shall not send him."

"Is Marion quite well?"

"Quite well, thank you."

It was all so commonplace, and the moment had given her so much strength, that Winifred made a desperate resolution.

"I have just been told something," she said, looking straight in his face and smiling. "I hear that you are going to marry Miss Lovell. Please let me congratulate you, unless it is too soon."

There was a flush on her cheek, and her words ended with an odd ring of hardness, but no one would have been likely to read these little signs. Anthony looked at her more kindly than he had yet done, and said "Thank you" gravely.

That was all. A few words, the river running through the waving grass, a woodpecker scraping the tree, flies darting here and there, Sniff dashing after a trout, Anthony, who once had been so near them all, standing by her, and answering from the other side of a great gulf. That was all. It did not seem as if Winifred could say any more except the good-by of which the air was full, and which all the little leaves in the wood rustled as she passed under them.

Anthony stood still for a moment and watched her going away. He had a very tender heart, poor fellow, though it was obstinate and proud in many things, and too angry now to be just. A remembrance of old times was sure to soften him, when once he realised that they were old and past;

and he began to think that, after all, Winifred was not, perhaps, an enemy. He watched her, and then called Sniff out of the bright brown water and walked away.

As for Winifred—well, it was on her knees that she fought her battle, into which neither you nor I need look.

Almost to all people, I suppose, there comes a time in their lives when life, not death, is the phantom they dread. One fear may be as unworthy as the other, but it is there. Only for both there is a merciful Hand stretched out, and if into that Hand we put our own it will lead us gently until we are brought face to face with our fear, and see that the dread phantom has, indeed, as it were, the face of an angel.

Chapter Twenty

"They who see more of our nature than the surface know that our interests are quite as frequently governed by our character as our character is by our interests."
Sir H. Lytton Bulwer.

Anthony walked towards Thorpe. He was going back to the cottage, and then intended to drive into Underham, and dine with the Bennetts. They evidently expected that he should spend part of each day at their house, and the arrangement was one which he did not dislike, and to which he therefore consented tacitly.

But it must be confessed that although when he thought of Ada Lovell, and the position in which he stood towards her, the remembrance was winged with a certain satisfaction, she did not occupy any large portion of his reflections. He was not thinking very much of anybody except himself, and the injustice of the world. What had he, of all men, done to be visited as he was? He was so sensitive, so conscious of his own uprightness, that the cold blight of suspicion withered him with its very first breath; and he had put on a bold front, and, as it were, exhausted his courage with an outward show of defiance, while to his inward spirit it seemed that all life and energy had died utterly away. The very foundations were shaken. For if people ceased to believe in him, with the reaction of a sanguine mind there was nothing left in which he could continue to believe. He had made himself the centre of his own theories, working them out from himself, confident in his own powers, and suddenly all had come to an end, such an end as seemed to him the end of all things, faith, hope, and charity with the rest. To his ardent nature there was no balm in conscious innocence; it mattered nothing that he knew the falseness of their suspicions, while the monstrous feet of suspicion itself remained.

Deep down in his heart, moreover, there was a touch of that insistance upon martyrdom which is more universal than we perhaps think. He thrust away compassion, feeling as if an earthquake had separated him from his former life, and as if no one were left to stand on the same side with him. This was an exaggeration of his position, for, although the world is more ready for condemnation than acquittal, there is a party for every side, and

Anthony might have seen hands stretched out if he would. But there was not a word or look to which he did not give a warp in the wrong direction. He had persistently classed Winifred with the rest of the world, and it is possible that the very consciousness that to do so cost him a pang made the martyrdom the dearer; but her reticence had told against her cruelly, for she believed in him too fully to have thought of expressing her belief, little dreaming that a more open sympathy would have better suited his mood than her intense but hidden feeling. He nursed the soreness in the same way that he nursed all things which were painful at this time, until it really seemed as if Mr Bennett's rather coarse expressions of friendliness, and Ada's assurance that she had no patience with people who talked as the Thorpe people talked, had a value which he could not find elsewhere. And then she was pretty and good-natured, trying to please him just as ardently as in the days before the cloud,—which, indeed, she thought a matter of very small consequence,—and he felt a certain gratitude towards her. There may have been something of defiance, and a disposition to run counter to opinion, for whatever was his motive in turning suddenly one day upon Ada, who was fluttering and saying foolish amiable things, it was certainly not purely that of love; but perhaps we are all sufficiently liable to act from mixed motives, to abstain from judging him too harshly.

His engagement, although Winifred heard of it for the first time that day, had really lasted a week: some question of the time struck him as he drove to the door of the Bennetts' house, and went slowly up the steps. There had been a little confusion of blue at one side of the windows, of which he had caught sight, and guessed who was waiting for him. In the short space between the door and the staircase there rose up before him her welcome, her look, the very words she would say, as if it had all been going on for a year instead of the few days which had surely offered no time for weariness. And yet a certain weariness touched him with a sting of self-reproach, and made him infuse a little more warmth into his greeting than was usual.

"You are very late, Anthony," she said, putting her hand on his arm, and shaking her long curl reprovingly. "Do you know that Aunt Henrietta fancied you were not coming at all?"

"But you did not accuse me of anything so impossible?"

"No, indeed. I don't think I should have spoken to you for a week if you had stayed away, and I suppose, though I am sure I don't know, that you would have minded that. But now that you are here, you are to tell me every single thing you have been doing."

His face darkened slightly. This small affectionate tyranny was new to him, and he was not quite in the mood for it.

"Suppose we turn the tables," he said, with a little restraint. "What have you been about to-day?"

"I? O, I have not been beyond the garden. I sat there and read and thought—"

"Thought?"

"Ah, I am not going to tell you what I was thinking of; you men are conceited enough already. O Anthony, I hear Uncle Tom. Do go and look out of that window; do, please, go!"

There seemed no particular reason for this separation, but she was so eager that Anthony obeyed. He rather dreaded Mr Bennett's ponderous jokes himself, and it was possible that Ada had not yet become used to them.

"Ah, Miles, here you are, here you are! just in time for the salmon, after all. My wife took it into her head you'd be late, but I said, 'My dear, put a salmon at one end of the line, and a man at the other, and the two must come together somehow.' Ha, ha! not bad, was it? And you'd something else to draw you besides, hadn't you? Ada,—where are you, Ada? Come, come, you'd have me believe you've never met before; perhaps you'd like to be introduced. It's never too late to mend, is it?"

"O Uncle Tom!" said Ada, smiling, and trying to blush. She looked very pretty in spite of the failure, and Anthony's face relaxed from the lines which were becoming habitual. She was pretty and affectionate, adornments on which a man sets a high value, often taking a little silliness as a natural and not much to be minded accompaniment. The room was cheerful, not furnished altogether in the best taste, but laden with a certain air of ripe and drowsy comfort which went far to atone for a few sins of colour. It was not so easy to get over Mr Bennett's prosy facetiousness, but his business kept him generally out of the way, and both he and his wife possessed a fund of that kind-heartedness which never fails to create a friendly atmosphere. If they were apt to err on the side of plenty, there was no doubt that they gave good dinners, dinners which Anthony, who was fastidious, liked, although not to the extent to which Mr Bennett credited him. Thus there were, on the whole, reasons which made the house pleasant to him, and with the morbid fret that had grown into his life—or out of his life, if you will—worrying him incessantly, it gave him a feeling of ease to find himself in the midst of a softly moving existence, where all sharp corners were rounded off, all hardness padded, and where he was made much of and gently flattered. Mrs Bennett had always sleepily thought—if thinking is not too strong an expression for the occasion—that it would be a good match for Ada, who had lived with them ever since she had been left an orphan, two years ago; and as for the absurd stories which had been spread about, it was far more agreeable to her good-natured stolidity to have no opinions on the matter. It was very likely a mistake from beginning to end, or, if not a mistake, no doubt Mr Miles had good reasons for all he had done. Her comfortable kindness, so unequivocally free from hidden doubts, was really soothing to poor Anthony, and paved the way for the step which Ada's prettiness and enthusiasm and desperate admiration brought about at last. No one could have suspected indolent Mrs Bennett of match-making, but she liked to see people happy, and had not a tinge of malice or uncharitableness in her disposition.

"It is so hot," she said, coming into the room with her soft heavy step, and sinking into an easy-chair. "One of those things they have in India—punkahs, don't they call them?—would be very nice. Does your mother feel the heat, Mr Miles? I really think it is quite a labour to have to go down to dinner."

"My dear, I can assure you it never answers to neglect the inner man," said Mr Bennett, laughing weightily at his own jokes, on his way to the dining-room. "Come, Ada, it's all very well to live upon air, but when you are as old as your aunt and I, you'll find it'll not pay. Not it, indeed. No, no; keep up the system, that has always been my maxim. By the way, Miles, I haven't seen Mannering or his brother for the last ten days. Nothing wrong, I hope?"

"I don't speak from personal knowledge," said Anthony, with the shade again on his face, "but some one in the village said that Mr Mannering was laid up with an attack of rheumatism."

"Poor fellow, poor fellow, he has wretched health, and no wonder. Any one must suffer in the end who lives upon mutton six days out of the seven. Tell him, when you see him, that he must come and dine with us as soon as he can, and try a little variety. Or you might drive out there one afternoon, my dear, and see what really is the matter. I've the greatest regard for Mannering."

"Yes, indeed," assented Mrs Bennett in the slow round voice that seemed hardly able to utter a contradiction.

"And I will go with you, Aunt Henrietta," said Ada, cheerfully. "I want to see that darling Mr Robert, and to get him to show me his flowers. It will be very nice, and you will meet us there, Anthony, won't you?"

"Mr Robert is a better showman when he is not interfered with," said Anthony, with a sharp pang of remembrance. "I'll meet you afterwards, and hear what you have seen."

"Well, I think Adas plan is not a bad one," persisted Mr Bennett, "and, dear me, you must be as free of that house as if it were your own! Say tomorrow."

"Tomorrow I am engaged."

"Well then, Wednesday."

"It will not be possible for me to go to the Red House," said Anthony in an odd, unyielding tone.

Mr Bennett gave a long "Whew!"

Ada said with a pout, "O, but you must!" and Mrs Bennett came to the rescue with the unconsciousness which constituted a real charm in Anthony's eyes.

"It will be too hot for us to drive there just yet. Ada and I must go some day when I am a little less overdone and the weather is cooler."

Mr Bennett was sufficiently shrewd to be alive both to the jar and to a perception that the subject was one which had better be allowed to drop.

"It is hot, as you say, my dear, and perhaps it would be as well to wait until Mannering is about again. Try a little of that Sauterne, Miles; capital stuff for this weather. Well, Ada, what have you been doing with yourself? Warren told me he had seen you at the station."

It was Ada's turn to look discomposed.

"The station? O yes, I remember. I walked across to see whether the Mannerses came by the four-o'clock train. I forgot that I had been out of the garden when you asked me," she said, with an elaboration of openness which was unnecessary, as Anthony had no suspicions to be allayed.

"O, he's been asking you, has he?" said Mr Bennett jocosely. "It's lucky you can explain yourself, or poor Warren would have put his foot in it."

"Mr Warren!" said Ada with scorn.

"Come, come, what has the poor man done? Upon my word, I should have thought young ladies would consider him a good-looking, agreeable young fellow. I am sure you did when you first knew him, Ada, eh?"

"I don't know what I thought once," said Ada, looking down, and smiling prettily again; "all I know is that I don't admire him now."

If Anthony wanted mollifying,—which was perhaps not the case, although this family party had not seemed to go quite as smoothly as those which had preceded it,—this little speech effected its purpose. He liked the covert homage, and, congratulating himself upon the good-humour which Mr Bennett's rather trying allusions could not ruffle, roused himself into the old brightness which only now came in occasional flashes. Ada was enchanted, shook back her long curl, and put out all her attractions; and Anthony, walking home through the quiet lanes sweet with the dewy freshness of a summer night, dreamed his new dream with a better success. Only, alas, even in dreams there are jangled notes, struggles, interruptions. People's faces come and go, and look sadly at us, changing often, just as the joy of their presence makes itself felt. Every now and then out of Ada's face other eyes looked at him; eyes that were grave and true and tender, and full of a trust that had never failed, although he had read it wrongly.

Chapter Twenty One

"While friends we were, the hot debates
That rose 'twixt you and me!
Now we are mere associates
And never disagree."

Fraser's *Magazine.*

Anthony's engagement, coming so soon after the other affair, made a little sensation in the neighbourhood. Things die out so quickly that, except in the more immediate Thorpe circle, his supposed act of injustice might have ceased to interest people; but the young man was so antagonistic, so sore, so fierce with all the world, that there was nothing for it but to take the position he insisted upon. The news of his engagement gave something pleasanter to talk about. There were a few injured mothers, but the gentlemen generally pronounced that he had shown his sense by making up his mind to marry Bennett's niece. The Bennetts were favourites, and held a thoroughly respectable place in the county; and though Anthony might have done better as to family, every one felt that a sort of cloud had just touched him, and was on the whole glad that the Bennetts should be rewarded for their hospitality and liberality and conservatism by seeing their niece well married. As for the Squire, who had been more ruffled and made uneasy by the consequences of his own coolness than he himself knew, he came into the room where Winifred and Bessie were together, chuckling and rubbing his hands.

"So there's to be a wedding to waken us all up," he said briskly. "You know all about it, girls, of course. I'm always the last in the place to hear a bit of news—but there!"

"But there!—you always know it before we've time to tell you," Bessie said saucily. "Is that what you mean, papa?"

"You'll find out what I mean one day, when you won't like it, Miss Pert," said the Squire, pulling her hair. "I must say Anthony Miles has shown greater sense than I should have expected. He's just the man to have made a fool of himself. If he'd not been so confounded touchy about that business of Pitt's, I'd have walked down and wished him joy; but I suppose that won't do,—not just at first, eh, Winifred?"

"No, indeed," said Winifred, her face flushing.

"I suppose not," said Mr Chester, regretfully. "Those young fellows fly off at such tangents, there's no knowing where to take them. One would think I'd been the one to set that report going, and I'm sure, for his fathers sake, I'd have given a hundred pounds—well, it's over and done now, and can't be helped; people do say there was no real harm in it when old Tregennas left it in his hands, but I wouldn't have believed it, I wouldn't have believed it. And then he goes and fights shy of the friends who would have stuck by him if they could."

"Papa, he never did it. How can he help being hurt with you all, when you will not trust him!"

Winifred's face had grown pale after the flush, but her voice did not tremble, and she looked at her father with clear steadfast eyes which always affected him, though, oddly enough, they often gave him a twinge of discomfort, and a little irritated him into obstinacy.

"Nonsense, Winifred," he said sharply, while he winced. "He has never so much as denied it. Women shouldn't talk of what they don't understand. And it hasn't anything to do with his getting married, has it? I wish you to tell Mrs Miles that it's given me a great deal of pleasure to hear of this match, and you and Bess had better drive into Underham and call on the Bennetts."

He was really desirous by this time to mend the breach, and perhaps a little secretly relieved that Mr Pitt's other idea about Anthony had been proved so erroneous. Before all this had happened, and while Anthony had been a poorer man, a marriage between him and Winifred, although it had never presented itself to his imagination, would have met with no opposition from him, except the fret which arose from a little personal dislike, natural enough between the two characters. But since a breath of dishonour had rested upon the young man, it would have been a bitter blow to the Squire to have been forced to give him his daughter. He could by this time make some excuses for him, for his father's sake,—indeed, now that he was not constantly meeting him, and getting irritated by his schemes, he really liked him a good deal more heartily than he had ever done before. But that would not have availed in such a trial. Therefore he now felt a certain amount of gratitude to him for removing the vague uneasiness which every now and then cropped up when he looked at Winifred or remembered shrewd Mr Pitt. He even spoke sharply to Bessie, who yawned and declared it was too hot to go to Underham.

"You'll go where your sister bids you. Winifred, don't let that child give herself airs to you. If she does, speak to me. I'll get a governess again, or pack her off to school, or something."

"I wonder who would mind that most," said Bessie, jumping up and hugging him.

"That's very fine. I know somebody who'd cry her eyes out over backboards and French exercises, and all the rest of it. Not but what I believe your mother would have had you do it," said the Squire, with a sudden wistful look at his favourite.

"She is not so bad as she seems, papa," said Winifred, rousing herself. "We read every morning, and she really works hard. Mr Anderson is quite satisfied."

"Well, mind she doesn't get her headaches again," her father said, veering round to another anxiety. "I'd rather she only knew her ABC than get headaches, and I'm not sure you're careful enough, Winifred. Do you hear, Bess? Go out for a scamper on the pony when you're tired of all this work. You're not so strong as your sister." Winifred did not answer. Something crossed her face so quickly that only the tenderest watcher could have seen it, a look which is very sad on those young faces. There is no storm or impatience in it, but a kind of weary protest. You hear it sometimes in a voice. The Squire went on with his injunctions about Underham and Miss Lovell.

"I'm ready enough to be on friendly terms," were his parting words, "only one doesn't know on which side to meet these touchy young fellows. But this marriage looks as if he were coming to his senses."

"And we are to smooth over everything," said Bessie, shutting her book and jumping up. "I don't care to smooth it now that Anthony has been so stupid. That horrid Miss Lovell! Don't you know how she walks, holding her hand out stiffly—so. You needn't look shocked, Winnie dear, for she does, and I know she is horrid."

"Don't say anything more about it, please," Winifred pleaded, with a look of pain. "I am going to order the carriage at four o'clock."

"I hate them all, and I hate going," said Bessie rebelliously. "Well?" as her sister made no answer to this downright statement.

"Well?"

"Don't you mean to scold, or at least talk me into my proper behaviour?"

"You must learn to find what you call your proper behaviour for yourself," said Winifred, trying to smile brightly, as she looked into the girl's dancing eyes. But her own suddenly filled with tears, and just as quickly Bessie's arms were round her.

"Something is the matter, I know, and you may as well tell me, Winnie, or I shall be obliged to find it out. Something is making you unhappy. Is it about Anthony?"

The hot colour flashed into Winifred's cheeks, but she was too honest to give an evasive answer, and said, holding Bessie's clasping hands, and pausing for a moment between her sentences, —

"I think it is, dear. Anthony has suffered cruelly from this wicked report. And it is so miserable between us all, when—we used to be so happy—"

She stopped. She had been speaking in a low, almost humble voice, as if her heart felt a pang of shame in its sorrow.

"Anthony doesn't care for her," said Bessie, shaking her head with a little experienced air. "He can't, because she isn't really nice. I believe he has been stupid enough to do it because he was cross."

Was it true?—this dread, that even Bessie could put into words? And if it was—O poor, poor Anthony!

The girls drove into Underham that afternoon, when the extreme heat of the day was supposed to be over. But there still remained a dry parching oppression in the air, the long weedy grasses hung listlessly one above the other, without a breeze to shake the dust from the motionless leaves, the pretty green hedges were all whitened and dead looking. Without any thought of avoiding it, it almost seemed to Winifred, as she drove along, as if the pain of the visit would be unendurable. But there was no such relief as hearing that Mrs Bennett and Miss Lovell were not at home, and the sisters were ushered into the comfortable drawing-room where Ada sat with a somewhat too apparent consciousness of being prepared to receive visitors, and quite disposed to make a little show off of the dignity she considered appropriate to the occasion.

"It was very kind of you to come in this heat. My aunt wished me to drive with her, but I really thought it too oppressive. Don't you find it very trying?"

"I do not think we thought about it," said Winifred, truly.

"Ah, then you are so strong. It must be very nice to be so strong, and not to be obliged to think so much of one's self. Now, I am obliged to be so careful, for if I were to go out in the sun, very likely I should have quite a headache."

It was so difficult to be sympathetic over this possibility, that Winifred found it hard to frame a suitable answer, and was grateful to Mrs Bennett for coming in at the moment, and presenting another outlet for conversation. Bessie was sitting upright, rigidly and girlishly contemptuous, and subjects seemed alarmingly few.

"My father begged me to leave his card for Mr Bennett," Winifred said at last. "He would have come himself if some magistrate's business had not been in the way, but he is such a dreadfully conscientious magistrate, that all our little persuasions are quite hopeless."

"I hope he is not very severe,—the poor people are so much to be pitied," said kindly Mrs Bennett. "Only think if one was starving! I am sure I should be very likely to take a joint or something."

"No, he is not very severe," Winifred said hesitating, with her thoughts wandering. "It is rather that he has such strict ideas of uprightness that he finds it hard to make excuses—"

She stopped suddenly, and the colour faded out of her face. Looking at Mrs Bennett, she had not heard the door open, nor seen Ada's rippling smiles, nor known that Anthony had come behind her, until a general movement made her look round, and then her start and change of colour gave an unlucky point to the words. Fortunately, Ada, who had longed that Anthony should come in, was triumphant, and not quick enough to read any discomfiture, claiming him at once with a show of possession.

"O Anthony, have you seen Mr Mannering? He has been here and was so nice. He has asked us all to a garden party on Saturday, on purpose to show me his flowers. He asked me what time would be best, and I said four to seven, and we promised to be there punctually. I told him I would tell you all about it, but he says he shall write a formal invitation, so you are sure to have it, though of course I answered for you. I dare say you will be there," Ada went on, with a gracious patronage of Winifred.

But Winifred was not likely to notice such small affronts, although at another, time she might not have been so meek. She was looking at Ada and wondering. Was this indeed his ideal? Could he be satisfied? There was a sort of bewilderment in recalling the fastidious Anthony of past days, which hardly allowed her to answer Ada, who, however, was too content with her position to require much. Nothing could be more delightful to her than to queen it before Winifred and Bessie, and to dwell on the party which was to be given in her honour; and, without any real ill-nature, she liked to feel that she was in possession of what she fancied was the ambition of all womankind, an acknowledged lover, and thus exalted above Miss Chester, who had always seemed to her a little unapproachable. In her turn she now felt herself placed on a serene altitude, and being there, it would have been impossible for her unimaginative nature to have conceived that adverse currents should be blowing. She went on cheerfully, when no one answered her,—

"The great thing is that it should be fine. I do so hope it will be fine, don't you, Anthony?"

"Yes—if you have set your heart upon it," he said, with a little shortness, for which he hated himself. But even to be called Anthony grated upon him at this moment, and he carefully avoided using her name.

"Of course I have, and so have you, too. Will you come here first?"

"I am sorry to say I cannot be there. I shall be in London on Thursday night."

He said it not unkindly, for it struck him sharply that it was hard upon Ada, but he made no attempt to soften the words, and turned immediately to speak to Mrs Bennett, who was talking kind little placid talk to Winifred. Ada opened her eyes for a moment's astonishment, and then laughed.

"O, London must wait, of course! Aunt Henrietta, do you hear? Anthony has the most absurd idea that we shall let him go to London before Mr Mannering's party!"

Even silken fetters can cut, and something had nettled Anthony throughout the conversation; but he kept the irritation very fairly out of his reply, only saying earnestly,—

"I am particularly sorry to do what you dislike, but there can be no question of my going. The London business has already been neglected too long."

Ada still believed in her own invincibility. "He will come,—I shall make him," she said, smiling and nodding.

There was nothing more to be said, and Winifred, who had almost against her will been garnering impressions, felt that escape was possible. Anthony had rather pointedly abstained from addressing her. She was not quite sure how much of the strain and oppression was due to her own feelings, but her heart ached under some new, sad weight as they drove away.

Chapter Twenty Two

"The fall thou darest to despise
Maybe the slackened angel hand
Hath suffered it, that he may rise
And take a firmer, surer stand;
Or, trusting less to earthly things,
May henceforth learn to use his wings."

Adelaide Procter.

When Winifred and Bessie had stopped at the post-office and taken their letters, some little remarks passed between the postmaster and his wife, who had gone out to the door and watched the two pretty, girlish figures hurried away by their impatient little pony into the green tangle of trees and hedges which a golden sunlight was brightening. It looked as if it were a sort of enchanted land, into which no storms could follow them; but Mrs Miller, who had a face which might have been intended to protest against sunshine, shook her head solemnly and said, coming back to the counter,—

"There's trouble enough in the world, to be sure, and it's hard when the Thorpe letters, as have gone together these years, has got to part company. But there's no saying where the love of money will lead a poor human heart."

"I'm not so sure about that matter as you are, Maria," said her husband, cheerfully sorting his letters. "Young Mr Miles is too pleasant-spoken a young gentleman to do all the things they charge him with, in my opinion; and it's always the way with you women, when once a bit of mud's thrown, each of you wants to try her hand."

"It isn't to be expected you should know better," said Mrs Miller gravely. "When you're converted, you'll understand more of the depravity of the human heart. It's a bottomless pit," she concluded, shaking her head.

"Um, um, um," said her husband irreverently. "Then I ain't one that's always wanting to be poking into such places, and if I were you I'd come out for a bit into the fresh air. But," he added, lowering his voice and giving a quick sign towards an inner room, "since he's been here, you're more than ever set against the old ways."

"No," said Mrs Miller calmly, "I am not altogether satisfied that he preaches the pure gospel. It's rare to find one who does. But I am thankful not to be blind to shortcomings, like some. And I'm sorry for Mr Miles, but what could be expected from one who was so given over to the world?"

Her voice had been carefully lowered in tone, but David Stephens heard the first part of the conversation with vivid distinctness. Every word sank into his consciousness, not as something new,—for the subject was rarely absent from his thoughts,—but because they seemed to offer him a new opportunity for arguing the case, and for proving to himself yet again and again that he had done well in keeping silence about the letter. A strange complication existed in his mind. The self-deception which ensnared him was not that self-deception which conceals itself under false colours, for when he formed his resolution it was with the feeling that he was forever bidding farewell to his own peace of mind,—the voluntary acceptance of a crushing burden. It is difficult to conceive such a state, but there is no doubt that it existed in him,—whether the result of a too self-reliant creed, or owing to a stronger impulse of resistance than obedience, or to other of those secret springs which move men's actions. In his struggle with Anthony Miles, his opponent had become a very embodiment of all the powers that league themselves against good, especially the good of other men's souls. He had first heard him spoken of slightingly, without remembering the answer to the reproach which he might have afforded; but directly it flashed upon him he opened a pocket-book, in which were placed the few and tiny atoms of paper which he had preserved with the intention of examining, and had since forgotten. And then began the contest. Here in his hands he held, as he acknowledged, the means of clearing Anthony so as to re-establish him completely in the eyes of other men. But Anthony, triumphant and successful, represented a great antagonistic force to what David held to be his mission, and to forward which he would have thankfully endured even to the point of martyrdom. Anthony, on the contrary, with the suspicion of a dishonourable deed clinging to him, lost half his power, would cease to influence, and might no longer succeed in impressing his opinions upon Maddox, whose newly stirred fears inclined him to turn to Stephens, while an old feeling of respect yet bound him strongly to the Church, personified by the Vicar's family. He was conscious of weighing a sin in himself against what seemed the advantage of feeble, starving souls, and he shrank from the burden with a cry of anguish, which—blame him as you will—had in it no creeping taint of hypocrisy. Only at rare times could he accept the excuses offered to his conscience,—that it was no crime of which Anthony was accused, that his interference would prove useless,—the truth generally stood out in keen cold outlines, and he would acknowledge to himself that he had done an accursed thing. Yet he would have held it a worse sin to have cast it from him. It was to save others. He might suffer; he might have lost his own soul,—he acknowledged it,—but it was that others might go in at the gate which he closed against himself. What could Anthony's burden seem beside his own? The system in which his religious thought had been moulded had developed in Davids character both an extraordinary greatness and an extraordinary littleness; for while he longed with an ardent and intense love to save the souls about him, longed so that he would sacrifice his dearest hopes, his peace, his very integrity,—he yet appeared to himself to be fighting single-handed, to be alone in the tremendous struggle, sometimes as if our God himself were regarding it passively without stretching forth his hand to save. And this blank and awful solitude opened out before him, as the path in which he must walk, with bleeding feet, and now with the hateful companionship of a sin bound to him by a voluntary acceptance forever.

Chapter Twenty Three

Thorpe was a little excited over Mr Mannering's garden party. To be sure it could boast of much the same amount of hospitality annually offered as the other little country-places in the neighbourhood, but, on the other hand, these hospitalities generally took the form of dinner-parties, and people came in closed carriages or flies, instead of driving in gayly with their pretty bright colours flashing out for the benefit of the women who stood on the door-steps, or the children who were all agape. Besides, owing to the Vicars death, there had been fewer gayeties than usual, and another sort of gloom had gathered about the village after the rumour of Anthony's deed made a break in the old cordial intercourse. Robert Mannering was sorely perplexed and grieved. Faithfulness to his old love made him quick to resent for Margaret Hare any injustice done to her daughter, and yet the estrangement from Anthony was very painful to him. He had tried to prevent it, but he could not show that there was perfect trust in his mind, and Anthony was keenly offended. Throughout his boyhood and bright youth the young fellow had been full of sanguine ardour, flushed with dreams and visions of great things to be done, where he was always the champion and deliverer, and would go forth, single-handed if need were, to fight against wrong. Suddenly, in a shape of which he had never dreamed, wrong had leaped upon him, and smitten all his weapons out of his hand, so that where nothing had seemed impossible was there now anything possible except weariness and bitterness to the end? Such a mood, if he had belonged to another creed, might have driven him to become a Trappist, not from any deepening of religion, but rather from repulsion of the life he had hitherto lived, which had so instantaneously changed colour. One would speak reverently of the workings of a man's soul in a crisis of his life, knowing that there is at times a strangeness, a madness, a wilfulness, at war with what is highest and noblest, making strife terrible, and asking from us prayer rather than judgment. Anthony chafed so hotly against the injustice of society, that he was conscious of a longing to outrage it, but the strong, tender force of associations, the purity of a father's memory, are safeguards for which many a one is in after years thankful; only his pride revenged itself by holding aloof from his former friends. He would have gone to extremes with the Mannerings if Mr Robert had permitted it; but he was blind to all avoidance, took no notice of cold treatment, went to see Mrs Miles as usual, and though the announcement of the engagement gave his kind heart a pang for Winifred, he believed it to be for the best, — considering the Squires vehemence, — and was glad to make it a kind of opportunity for reconciliation. Personally, too, he liked Ada, who was a favourite with most of the gentlemen round, and he saw no reason why she should not enjoy her little innocent triumph. Therefore Anthony's refusal to come to his house vexed him not a little.

"If that foolish fellow is going to walk about on stilts all his days, there will be no living in the place with him," he said, pacing up and down the study with the short, heavy steps which always produced an air of endurance in his brother. "What do you say to it, Charles? O, I see, you don't like my moving about! Why didn't you stop me?"

"My dear Robert, I might as well stop a watch that is wound up."

"That's nonsense. Of course, I recollect it if you'll only speak. It's merely that sitting down in this heat gives me the fidgets, and you can't stand another open window. What were we talking about? — O, Anthony! Here's his note. Did you ever in your life read such a shut-me-up epistle?"

Mr Mannering read the letter, and shrugged his shoulders.

"It must be one thing or the other with him."

"It's a pity it should always be the wrong thing," said Mr Robert, mechanically resuming his march. "The matter has blown over, and there's an end of it. A pretty girl, and a fresh start, and not one of us but is ready to shake hands. What on earth can he expect more?"

"You must have patience," said Mr Mannering. "The lad is sore and unhappy, he may be looking at the matter from an entirely different point of view to yours, and at any rate he is not one to shake off either accusation or act readily."

"Well," said his brother, with a little wonder, "you have been his best friend throughout, even to disbelieving plain facts."

"You should read more classic poetry, Robert."

"Pooh! Why?"

"You would get rid of that terribly prosaic estimation of facts. They may be as deceptive as other many-sided things."

"Well, as Anthony insists upon drawing his sword and holding us all at arm's length, I wish the fact that half a hundred women are coming to trample down my turf were deceptive. What a difference there would have been a year ago!" added Mr Robert, with a sigh of regret. "That boy would hare been up here twenty times a day, planning and contriving, and worrying us out of our senses. It is not right of him, Charles, whatever you may say; it's not right for the poor girl."

"Will you be so good as to close that window, Robert?" said his brother, shivering. "When your guests come I shall be doubled up with rheumatism. To drag me into society is really an act of cruelty, for I am quite unfit for it, and as useless as a log."

Mr Robert stopped his march, and looked at his brother with a comically grave expression of sympathy. The same little comedy was acted again and again, Mr Mannering protesting against the society in which he delighted, and a victim to aches and pains until the guests arrived, when he became the perfect host, only occasionally indulging himself with an allusion to his sufferings, and full of the social presence of mind invaluable under the circumstances.

Ada had been as much offended at Anthony's desertion as it was possible for one of her nature to be, but it could not seriously ruffle her temper. All her life had been spent in a kindly appreciative atmosphere, and a certain placid self-satisfaction seems irrepressibly to radiate from such lives. No doubts were likely to trouble her. She was too serenely comfortable to be conscious of the little stings and darts which torment some people every day. She was haunted by no sense of short-coming. There looked out at her from the glass a pretty smiling face, her uncle and aunt petted her, the days were full of easy enjoyment,—all of us have been sometimes puzzled with these lives, which irritate us at the very moment of our half-envy of a placidity which seems so far beyond our reach. And now, although Anthony's absence caused her a prick of mortification, she had no intention of resigning, in consequence, any of the honours which the occasion might bring to her feet, nor even the attendance of an admirer, for she had persuaded good-natured Mrs Bennett—always readily moved to anything in the shape of a kindness, and especially of one which affected the bodily comfort of her acquaintances—to offer a seat in the carriage to Mr Warren, a young would-be lawyer who was working under Mr Bennett, and who would otherwise have had to tramp out along the dusty road, instead of, as now, appearing in the freshest of attire, ready to be Ada's very obedient servant, and not at all ill-pleased to stand, if only for a day, in what should have been Anthony's place.

It gave Winifred a start to come upon the two walking towards the green-houses; Ada with much the same little air of prettiness and self-consciousness which she had displayed towards Anthony on the day of the sisters' visit, Mr Warren certainly more attentive and lover-like than the real lover had been. And Ada was not in the least discomposed by the look of astonishment in Winifred's clear eyes. There was, on the contrary, a triumphant tone in her voice.

"We are going to see Mr Mannering's ferns. It is such a delightful day. I do think it was so charming of Mr Mannering to give this party, but then he is charming, and I was just telling Mr Warren that I had lost my heart to him."

It is strange how from some lips praise of those we like becomes much more unbearable than its reverse. Winifred had never felt so uncharitably towards Mr Robert.

They went on through the flickering sunshine—which the bordering espalier trees were not tall enough to shadow—talking and laughing, while Winifred looked after them with a perplexed sadness for Anthony. What was he about?—why was he not here?—did he think he could escape pain like this? She was right in concluding that his absence would not improve his position, for people who came with the intention of being gracious were thrown back upon themselves. It looked odd, they said, to see Miss Lovell there and Mr Miles absent. It left the party incomplete. The day was exquisite: a little breeze rustled through the great elms, the lights were laden with colour, there were grave sharply cut shadows on the grass, a soft fresh warmth, full of exhilaration, Mr Robert's brightest flowers sunning themselves, but—somehow or other there was a jar. Even Mrs Bennett began to look a little troubled at the speeches which reached her ears, especially when Mrs Featherly drew her chair close to her, and began what she intended for consolation.

"You and Mr Bennett should have made a point of it, you should indeed, if only in consideration of what is past," she said, shaking her head impressively. "There can be no doubt but that it was his duty to come. And it always grieves me deeply when you see people endeavouring to evade a duty."

"He has gone to London," said poor Mrs Bennett, with a feeble show of indignation. "And my husband says that ladies have no idea of what business requires."

"I flatter myself that there is nothing of Mr Featherly's business which I do not know as well as he does himself," said Mrs Featherly loftily, "and I should make it a point of principle to be acquainted with that of any one likely to become connected with our family, especially if there were a past to be considered. But of course, if Mr Bennett is satisfied—and he is, I believe, remarkable for his caution?"

It was one of Mrs Featherly's peculiarities to credit people with virtues which could not be considered strong marks in their character. Caution was so far from being Mr Bennett's prerogative, that one or two little difficulties in his profession had arisen from his lack of that lawyer-like quality. Mrs Bennett thought of moving to another part of the garden, but she was in a comfortable chair and could see no other vacant seat, so she murmured an assent and let her tormentor run on.

"One is bound at all times to hope for the best, and, of course, we feel an interest in this young man, the son of a neighbouring clergyman and all, as my husband very properly remarked. But it is most unfortunate. Poor Ada, I am really quite sorry for her, and so is Augusta. Were you thinking of moving? I know you are so active that I dare say you hardly share my relief in sitting still. With a parish like ours I assure you the responsibilities become a very heavy burden, but, as you say, there are family responsibilities which are scarcely less trying, and poor Ada not being your daughter—"

It was like a nightmare. Poor Mrs Bennett, who had not thought much of Anthony's going to London, and was conscious of all the capabilities of comfort around her, began to feel as if everything were wrong, and had no weapons with which to defend herself. Luckily for her Mr Mannering came by, and she almost caught at him as he passed.

"It is rather hot here," she said, searching about for some physical means of accounting for her discomfort. "I think I should like to move to a shadier part."

"We will both go," said Mrs Featherly, spreading out her dress. "Now that you are here, Mr Mannering, I may as well remind you of your promise of subscription to our organ. Was it you or Mr Robert?—but of course it is the same thing."

"I wish it were," said Mr Mannering, in his courteous, easy manner. "Robert is the philanthropic half of the house, and I have every desire to benefit by his good deeds. I always aid and abet them at any rate, so that, if you will allow me, I will make him over to you where he shall not escape."

"Ah, but you must assist us, too," said Mrs Featherly. "It is a most dangerous doctrine to suppose that you can avoid responsibilities. That is just what I was pointing out to our friend. Naturally she and Mr Bennett feel much anxiety with regard to their niece, and it is so unfortunate that Mr Miles did not make a point of being here to-day at all events."

There are some people in the world for whom it seems the sun never shines, the flowers never blow, the earth might be sad-coloured, for anything that it matters. Even Mrs Bennett, whom all these things affected in a material sort of way, was more influenced by them than Mrs Featherly, who shut them out of her groove with contempt.

"Here is Miss Chester," said Mr Mannering with some relief, for he did not quite know how to separate the two ladies. "Miss Winifred, I want you to be kind enough to help Mrs Featherly to find my brother. He is avoiding his debts, and must be brought to book. Mrs Bennett is tired, and I am going to take her to a shady seat."

Mr Mannerings voice was too courteous for Mrs Featherly to be able to persuade herself that she was affronted, but she certainly felt that she had not said so much as she intended to Mrs Bennett upon the subject of Anthony's delinquencies. She was not really a malicious woman, but she considered that her position gave her a right of censorship over the morals of the neighbourhood, and that it was both incumbent upon her to see that people acted up to their duties, and to speak her mind when she was of opinion that they in any degree came short of them. And as she never had any doubt as to the exact line of duty which belonged to each person, she was not likely to distrust her own power of judgment. She prepared herself to deliver a little homily to Winifred.

"My dear, I was so surprised to see Bessie here. Does your father really think it wise for so young a girl? Why, she will not come out for another year and a half."

"Bessie will be seventeen in October," said Winifred, "and she has coaxed papa into promising that she shall go to the December ball at Aunecester."

All Mrs Featherly's ribbons shook with disapproval.

"The Aunecester ball! Impossible! It would be most injudicious. Eighteen is the earliest age at which a girl should come out. Augusta was eighteen, I remember, on the twentieth of December, and the ball was on the twenty-seventh. If her birthday had not fallen until after the ball, Augusta has so much proper feeling that no consideration would have induced her to persuade me to allow her to go. She would have known it was against my principles. Eighteen. Eighteen is the earliest, and Bessie will not be eighteen for a year. I must speak to Mr Chester myself, and point out the impropriety. I must, indeed."

"My father has promised," said Winifred, smiling. "He never will call back a promise."

"He must be made to see that it is a matter of principle. The young people of the present day have the most extraordinary ideas. Now, there is Anthony Miles. Why is he not in his proper place to-day, when, in consideration of his position, and out of regard for our excellent friends, we were willing to meet him, and to let bygones be bygones?"

"Anthony need fear no bygones," said Winifred, with an indignant flush burning on her cheek.

"You must allow other people to be the best judge of that," said Mrs Featherly, drawing herself up stiffly. "Both Mr Featherly and I are of opinion that appearances are very much against him; and appearances, let me assure you, are exceedingly momentous things. At the same time, it may be the duty of society to make a point of not proceeding to extremities, and, taking into consideration the young man's position in the county as a gentleman of independent means, as the son also of your late Vicar, society in my opinion acted as it should in extending its congratulations on the approaching event, while the young man has, to say the least, been injudicious. Most injudicious."

"It is certain that he would not meet society on such terms," said Winifred, with difficulty commanding her voice.

"My dear, a young lady should not undertake a gentlemans defence so warmly."

Poor Winifred was helpless, angry, and provoked almost to tears. For though her heart was not too sore to be generous, every now and then so sharp a pang struck through it, that her only refuge seemed to lie in such hard thoughts of Anthony as should convince herself that she was indifferent. She did not want to be his defender. And yet it was unendurable to hear him suspected. Perhaps she did the best that she could when she stopped and said gravely, —

"If we talk about him any more, I might say things which you might call rude, and you are too old a friend for me to like to affront you. But I want you to understand that Anthony Miles was brought up like our brother, and I know it is as impossible for him to have done such an act as you suppose, as for my father to have done it. There is some unfortunate mistake. Please, whether you believe me or not, do not say any more about it. Did you not wish to see Mr Robert? There he is. I must go to Bessie."

So poor Winifred carried her swelling heart across the sunshine which lay warm on the soft grass, and past the blossoming roses, leaving Mrs Featherly more keenly mortified than she knew. No possibility of a last word was left to her, and she was so utterly discomfited that she even forgot the organ and Mr Robert. But as she drove home she said to her husband, —

"James, we shall pass that man Smiths, and I must beg that you will get out and tell him that I cannot allow Mary Anne to come to the Sunday school with flowers in her bonnet."

"If you wish it, my dear, of course," Mr Featherly said reluctantly. "But it might be as well not to irritate that man just as he is beginning to show signs of a better—"

"Principle is principle." Mrs Featherly had never felt so uncompromising. It was one of those odd links of life which baffle us. Here were Anthony and Winifred and Mr Mannering's garden party unconsciously playing upon big Tom Smith and poor little blue-eyed Mary Anne, who had somewhere picked up a bit of finery, and decked herself out. Mrs Featherly had received a check that day, and wanted to feel the reins again. "Principle is principle," she said unrelentingly.

Chapter Twenty Four

"The days have vanished, tone and tint,
And yet perhaps the hoarding sense
Gives out at times (he knows not whence)
A little flash, a mystic hint."

In Memoriam.

When September came, things had changed but little since the summer, except that talk had drifted into other channels, and there was less curiosity in noticing Anthony Miles's behaviour. He still kept aloof from his friends, and looked worn and haggard, while the charm which used to take the people by storm was rarely visible. The men, who had never liked him so well as the women, grumbled at his manners, and the women confessed that he had lost his pleasantness. Winifred, who now scarcely saw him, used to wonder how true it was, and what she would have found out if the old intercourse had not ceased. One day, when she and Bessie were in the High Street of Aunecester, they met the Bennetts, and Anthony with them; and as they were coming out of a shop it was impossible to avoid walking with them, though he was so cold and constrained that Winifred longed to escape. It was a keen autumnal day, the old town had put on its gayest, in honour of a visit from some learned Association or other; there were bright flags hung across the narrow street, setting off the picturesque gables and archways, and here and there decking some building black with age.

"Are you going to the concert?" asked Mrs Bennett. "Ada would be sadly disappointed if I did not take her; but, really, I have been sitting in the hall and listening to all those lecturers until I have a headache. I think it would be much nicer if they stopped now and then, and let one think about it, for I became quite confused once or twice when the heat made me doze a little, and I heard their voices going on and on about sandstones, and slate, and things that never seemed to come to an end."

"I was so glad to get out," Ada said. "I believe Anthony wanted to stay, but I really could not, it was much too learned for me. I suppose you liked it, Miss Chester?"

It seemed as if she could not resist a little impertinent ring in her voice when she spoke to Winifred, and Bessie was going to rush in with a headlong attack, when Mrs Bennett made one of her useful unconscious diversions.

"There are the Needhams," she said.

"They are going to the concert, I dare say," said Ada. "Anthony, I hope you took good seats for us?"

"I took what I was given," he said, a little shortly, and at that moment Ada spied Mr Warren, and invited him graciously to accompany them. It turned out that he had no ticket, and Anthony immediately offered his own.

"Then I shall go back to the hall," he said, "for Pelham is going to speak, and one does not often get such an opportunity."

"That will be a capital plan," said Ada. Winifred could not tell whether she were vexed or not. To her own relief they had reached the end of the street, and there was a little separation; the concert people went one way, the Chesters another, Anthony went back to his lecturing. Just as they parted Winifred asked for Marion.

"She is better, thank you," he said gravely. "She has been very ill, but we hope it will all go well now."

"I did not know she had been ill," said Winifred. She could not avoid a reproachful jar in her voice, and the feeling that her lot was harder than Anthony's, since she met distrust from him, and he only from an indifferent world. "Does he think we are made of stone?" she said, walking away with a sad heart. Perhaps she was not far wrong. For Anthony's was a nature which such a blow as he had received, anything indeed which shook his faith in himself or in others, would have a disposition to harden, and all that was about him would certainly take its colouring from himself. He was letting his sympathies dry up, almost forcing them back out of their channels, and was ceasing to believe in any broader or more genial flow in others. People are not so much to us what they are as what we see them, so that there are some for whom the world must be full of terrible companions.

And with poor Anthony the colouring he laid on at this time was cold and grey enough. Every gleam of brightness lay behind him in the old days which had suddenly grown a lifetime apart,—school, college, home, where on all sides he was the most popular, the most brilliant, the most full of life. And now—old friends had failed him, old hopes had been killed, old aims seemed unreal, old dreams foolishness. The saddest part of it all was that he was making even his dreariest fancies truth. There are few friendships that will stand the test of one dropping away from the bond: as to hopes and dreams and aims, they too become what a man makes them,—

no less and no more. He was beginning to feel with impatient weariness that his engagement was not fulfilling even the moderate amount of contentment which he had expected. He had never professed to himself any overwhelming passion of love for Ada, but he had turned to her when he was sore and wroth with all the world, and it had seemed to him as if here were a little haven of moderate calm. If he had loved her better he would have felt as if she had a right to demand more, but I doubt whether this ever troubled him. With an older man also the experiment might have succeeded better, but his life was too young, and as yet too full of mute yearnings, for a reaction not to follow. It was not that clear-sightedness was awakened in him: the girl's character was just one which the dullest woman would have fathomed, and scarcely a man have read rightly, — it was rather a cloudy dissatisfaction, a weariness, a consciousness that neither touched the other nor ever would, a sense of failure. No thought of escape was haunting him, he had a vague impression that his destiny might for a time be delayed, but meanwhile his destiny stood before him, and he knew that he was moving towards it, whether with willing or reluctant steps.

Of Winifred he thought very little. He did not choose to think of her. If ever there had been a day when it had seemed as if she might have become a part of his life, that day was gone like many another day. She and the world were against him, and if his own heart had been on that side, poor Anthony in his desperation would have fought against them, — heart and all. It would all come to an end some time, and meanwhile — Well, meanwhile he could go on towards the end.

As he walked down the old street under the flags, a sudden brightening of sunshine lit up the gay fluttering colours, a fresh breeze was blowing, the houses had irregular lines, rich bits of carving, black woodwork, — an odd sort of mediaeval life quietly kept, as it were, above the buying and selling and coming and going: now and then a narrow opening would disclose some little crooked passage, narrow, and ill-paved with stones which many a generation had worn down; while between the gables you might catch a glimpse of the soft darkness of the old Cathedral rising out of the green turf, trees from which a yellow leaf or two was sweeping softly down, a misty, tender autumnal sky, figures passing with a kind of grave busy idleness. There was a band marching up the street, and at the corner Anthony met Mr Wood, of the Grange, and at the same moment Mr Robert Mannering.

"Glad to see you," said the latter, ignoring the younger man's evident desire to hurry on. "You're the very couple I should have chosen to run my head against, for Charles never rested until he had made Pelham and Smith, and half a dozen of their like, engage to dine with us to-morrow, and they'll certainly not be content with me for a listener, so take pity, both of you, will you? Half past seven, unless they give us a terribly long-winded afternoon, and then Mrs Jones will be in a rage, and woe betide us!"

"No, no," said Mr Wood, shaking his head, and going on. "Don't expect me. I've just had a dose of Smith, and his long words frighten me. They don't seem quite tame."

"I'm sorry that I can't join you," said Anthony, putting on his impracticable look.

"Come, come. You've treated us very scurvily of late. Miss Lovell must spare you for once, Anthony."

"Thank you. It is not possible."

He said it so curtly, that Mr Robert's face grew a shade redder; but as he watched the young man walking away down the street with short, quick steps, the anger changed in a moment into a sort of kind trouble.

"He'll have none of it, and if it's shame I don't know but what I like him the better, poor boy! I know I'd give pretty nearly anything to be able to put out my hand and tell him I believe that confounded story to be a lie. But I can't, and he knows it. The mischief I've seen in my day that had money at the bottom of it! Well, I hope that pretty little girl will make him a good wife, and I shall make it up to Margaret's child by and by. There goes Sir Peter, on his way to patronise the Association, I'll be bound. He'll walk up to the front and believe they know all about him, how many pheasants he has in his covers, and what a big man he is in his own little particular valley. Why shouldn't he?—we're all alike. I caught myself thinking that Parker would be astonished if he could only see my Farleyense; and there's Charles as proud as a peacock over his Homer that he's going to display, and Mrs Jones thinking all the world will be struck with the frilling in which she'll dress up her ham, and so we go on,—one fool very much like another fool. And as the least we can do is to humour one another, and as, to judge from the shops, the Association has in it a largely devouring element, I'll go and look after Mrs Jones's lobster."

He turned down a narrow street. The Cathedral chimes were ringing, dropping down one after the other with a slow stately gravity. People were making their way across the Close to the different doors. The streets had their gay flags, and carriages, and groups in the shops, and mothers bringing little convoys from the dancing academy, and stopping to look at materials for winter frocks,—but hardly a touch of these excitements had reached the Close. It seemed as if nothing could ruffle its quiet air; as if, under the shadow of the old Cathedral, life and death itself would make no stir. The chimes ceased, the figures had gone softly in; presently there floated out dim harmonies from the organ. As Mr Mannering passed along under one of the old houses he met the Squire.

"Winifred and Bess are there," he said, nodding towards the Cathedral. "The children like to go in for the service. They're good children—mine—God bless them!" he went on, with a sudden abruptness which made Mr Robert glance in his face.

"Good? They're as good as gold."

"So I think, so I think. Bess, now. She's a spirit of her own, up in a moment, like a horse that has got a mouth worth humouring, but all over with the flash, and not a bit of sulkiness to turn sour afterwards. And Winifred, she's been a mother to her sister. She has, hasn't she, Mannering?"

"Don't harrow a poor old bachelor's feelings. You know I have lost my heart to Miss Winifred ever since she was ten years old, and she refused to marry me, even then,—point-blank."

But the Squire did not seem to be listening to his answer, or if he heard it, it blended itself with other thoughts. He said with something that seemed like a painful effort, "Pitt had a notion that Anthony Miles liked Winifred. There never was anything of the kind, but he took it into his head. I'm glad with all my heart that Pitt was mistaken, for I would not have one of my girls suffer in that way for a thousand pounds. But I've been thinking to-day,—I don't know what sets all these things running in my head, unless it is that it is my wedding-day.—My wedding-day, seven-and-twenty years ago, and little Harry was born the year after. I wasn't as good a husband as I should have been, I know, Mannering, but I used to think, if little Harry had lived—"

He stopped. He had been speaking throughout in a slow disjointed way, so unlike himself that Mr Robert felt uncomfortable while hardly knowing why.

"Come," he said cheerily. "Look at your two girls, and remember what you have just been saying about them."

The Squire shook his head.

"They're well enough," he said, "but they're not Harry. Who was I talking of—Anthony Miles, wasn't it? I've been thinking that perhaps I've been too hard on the boy. It would have broken his father's heart if he had known it, for there wasn't a more honourable man breathing; but if my Harry had grown up, though he never could have done such a thing as that, he might have got into scrapes, and then if I had been dead and gone it would have been hard for never a one to stick by the lad. I don't know how it is. I believe I've such a hasty tongue I never could keep back what comes uppermost. Many a box in the ear my poor mother has given me for it, though she always said all the same, 'Have it out, and have done with it,

Frank.' It was a low thing for him to do, sir," went on the Squire, firing up, and striking the ground with his stick by way of emphasis, "but—I don't know—I should be glad to shake hands with him again. Somehow I feel as if it couldn't be right as it is, with his father gone, and my little lad who might have grown up."

And so, across long years there came the clasp of baby fingers, and the echo of a message which was given to us for a Child's sake,—peace and good-will.

"I wish you would," Mr Mannering said heartily. "He is somewhere about in the town at this very minute; perhaps you'll meet him. Only you mustn't mind—"

He hesitated, for he did not feel sure of Anthony's manner of accepting a reconciliation, or whether, indeed, he would accept it at all, and yet he did not like to throw difficulties in the way. But the Squire understood him with unusual quickness.

"You mean the lad's a bit cranky," he said, "but that's to be expected. Perhaps he and I may fire up a little, for, as I said, I'm never sure of myself, but there's his father between us, and—well, I think we shall shake hands this time."

Not as he thought; but was it the less truly so far as he was concerned? For a minute or two Mr Robert stood and looked after him as he went along the Close, a thick, sturdy figure, with country-cut clothes, and the unmistakable air of a gentleman. The Cathedral towers rose up on one side in soft noble lines against the quiet sky, leaves fluttered gently down, a little child ran across the stones in pursuit of a puppy, and fell almost at the Squire's feet. Mr Robert saw him pick it up, brush its frock like a woman, and stop its cries with something out of his pocket. The child toddled back triumphant, the Squire walked on towards the High Street, and Mr Robert turned in the other direction. Some indefinite sense of uneasiness had touched him, though, after all, there was no form to give it. If Mr Chester's manner had been at first slightly unusual, he explained it himself by saying that he had been stirred by old recollections, and the vagueness his friend had noticed quite died away by the end of their conversation. He was walking slowly, but with no perceptible faltering.

"And a man's wedding-day must be enough to set things going in his head," Mr Robert reflected. "If matters had fallen out differently now with Margaret Hare—Well, well, so I am going to make an old fool of myself, too. I'd better get on to the carrier, and set Mrs Jones's mind easy about her lobster."

Distances are not very great in Aunecester, and it did not take long for Mr Mannering to reach the White Horse, transact his business, and go back to the principal street to wait for his brother. There was one particular bookseller's shop, to which people had parcels sent, and where they lounged away what time they had in hand, and just before he reached it Mr Mannering noticed an unusual stir and thickening of the passers-by. He concluded that the band might be playing again, or that some little event connected with the Association had attracted a crowd. It was not until he was close to one of the groups that the scattered words they let fall attracted his attention.

"An accident, did you say?" he said, stopping before a man whose face was red and heated.

"Yes, sir. A gentleman knocked down. That's the boy, and a chase I've had to catch him."

Mr Mannering began to see a horse, a policeman, and a frightened-looking lad in the midst of the crowd.

"Nothing very serious, I hope?"

"It looked serious, sir, when we picked him up. He is took into the shop, and they've sent for the doctor. Boys don't care what they ride over."

"I fancy something was wrong before the horse touched him, though," said another man, with a child in his arms. "There was time enough else for him to have got out of the way."

"Who is it?" asked Mr Mannering, with a sudden wakening of anxiety. At that moment Anthony Miles came quickly out of the shop, almost running against him in his hurry.

"Have you seen them?" he said hastily, when he saw who it was. His face was drawn and pallid, like that of a man who has received a great shock.

"Who, who?" said Mr Robert, gripping his arm. "It isn't the Squire that's hurt?"

"Yes," said Anthony impatiently. "He's in there. Somebody must find Winifred, or she'll be in the thick of it in a minute."

"She is at the Cathedral, she and Bessie," said Mr Mannering, asking no more questions, but feeling his heart sink. "They must be coming out about this time. God help them, poor children!"

Anthony was off before the words were out of his mouth. Mr Robert, his kind ugly face a shade paler than usual, turned into the shop, which was full of curious customers, and made his way to a back room to which they motioned him gravely.

It was a little dark room, lit only by a skylight, on which the blacks had rested many a day, and hung all round with heavy draperies of cloaks and other garments, which at this moment had something weird in their familiar aspect. The Squire had been laid upon chairs, hastily placed together to form a couch; the doctor and one or two of the shop-people were talking together in a low voice as Mr Robert came in, and a frightened girl, holding a bottle in her hand, stood a little behind the group.

By their faces he knew at once that there was no hope. Perhaps for the moment what came most sharply home to him was the incongruity of the Squire's fresh open-air daily life, and this strange death-room of his. He said eagerly to the doctor, —

"Can't we get him out of this?"

"Not to Thorpe," Dr Fletcher said gravely. "But we can move him to my house. I have sent for a carriage."

"Is he quite unconscious?"

"Quite. There will be no suffering."

There was no need to ask more. Death itself seems as helplessly matter of fact as the life before it. Mr Robert stood and looked down with moist eyes at the honest face that had been so full of vigour but the day before, when the Squire went through his day's shooting like a man of half his years; and then thought of him as he had seen him that very hour, on his way to make peace, comforting a little child. Those had been his last words, the kind, good heart showing itself behind its little roughnesses, and softened as it may have been—who knows?—by a dim foreshadowing.

Chapter Twenty Five

"Its silence made the tumult in my breast
More audible; its peace revealed my own unrest."

Jean Ingelow.

Anthony told everything on their way from the Cathedral to the shop, for, indeed, he did not know what might not have happened even in so short a time. But except that the crowd had pretty well dispersed, leaving only a few of the more curious idlers to hang about, all was much as he left it, outside and in. Bessie was crying and trembling, but Winifred went softly in, without looking to the right or left, and, kneeling by her father's side, clasped his hand in hers.

"We are going to take Mr Chester to my house, where he will be a good deal more comfortable," said the doctor with the cheerfulness which is at all events intended for kindness.

"Not home?" Winifred asked, without looking up.

"My dear, the long drive would be more than he could bear while he is in this condition," said Mr Robert gravely. "And now Dr Fletcher will have him altogether under his care, which is particularly desirable. The carriage is here: we only waited for you."

She rose up, showing no agitation except a tremulous shiver which she could not repress, while Bessie clung to her and sobbed convulsively. Anthony, who was greatly shocked, had fallen involuntarily into his old brotherly ways. He brought a fly, and put the two sisters into it, and when Bessie looked at him imploringly, got in by their side instead of walking round with Mr Mannering. It was like a dream, the flags, and the bustle, and the people coming down the street from the concert, and this sad cloud chilling their hearts. He saw on the other side Mrs Bennett, and Ada, and Mr Warren: Ada was staring in wonder, but he cared nothing for that or anything else except the beseeching look in Winifred's sad eyes.

By the time they reached the doctor's house, Bessie had rallied from the first terror of the shock, and Winifred was as outwardly calm as possible, ready to receive her father, quick to comprehend Dr Fletcher's directions, and so helpful and quiet that it was only now and then that Anthony knew that she turned to him with a mute appeal in the look, as if in this wave of sorrow she too had forgotten all estrangement and coldness, and gone back to the old days which both believed had passed away forever. There was a strange sort of tender pride in the way he watched her, which must have startled himself if he had been aware of it. But he was not. He was not thinking about himself, and, indeed, might have argued that the veriest stranger must have been touched and moved at such a time. When he was obliged to leave her, he could hardly bear to do so.

"I may come back in the morning, may I not?" he said, unable to avoid saying it.

"Do come," Winifred had answered with a quiet acceptance, of his help, and going on to tell him what was wanted from Hardlands. As he went out of the door he met Mr Robert coming to see if he could be of any further use.

"I have made Charles go home, for he is not fit for this sad business," said Mr Robert in an altered voice. "Poor things, poor things! It is one comfort to know he does not suffer. Fletcher says he will not recover consciousness. Good Heavens, I can't believe it now! His last words,—ah! to be sure, Anthony, he was going off after you when it happened."

And he told him what the Squire had said.

It touched Anthony inexpressibly, but it seemed also to bring back an avenging army of forgotten things, so that Mr Robert could not understand what made his face grow dark, and let his voice drop coldly as if it were a shame to waste a sacred thing on one so unforgiving, not knowing to what his words had suddenly recalled him. The past had been sweet through all its sorrow, and now it was over, and he must gather up his burden.

"The Bennetts are at Griffith's, and were inquiring for you. Good-night," said Mr Mannering shortly.

Anthony went mechanically towards the bookseller's, knowing exactly all that would be said to him, the exclamations and questions which Ada was likely to pour out seeming unutterably wearisome at this moment when Winifred's face would persistently rise before him, so brave, so patient, so womanly in its sorrow, that Ada could not stand the contrast. And yet he was to marry Ada, to become one with her, to swear to love her. He turned white when the thought struck him suddenly, as if it were a new knowledge. She was standing at the bookseller's door, waiting impatiently, and smiling a pretty show of welcome, as usual.

"I am so glad you are come, Anthony; it was such a pity you did not go to the concert. And poor old Mr Chester,—do tell us all about it I don't think I shall ever fancy Springfield's shop again."

"I don't wonder you are shocked," Anthony said, rousing himself and conscious that he owed her amends for the very agony of the last few minutes. "It seems hardly possible as yet to realise it."

"No, it is dreadful," said Ada, her looks wandering away. "Does Miss Chester feel it much? She looks as if it would take a good deal to move her. There are the Watsons,—you didn't bow." Mrs Bennett's face at the other end of the shop looked like a refuge to which he might escape. To escape,—and he was to marry her! He had not yet heard the end of the petty inquiries which fluttered down upon him, but at length he saw Mrs Bennett and Ada driving away, and Ada pointing towards Springfield's and explaining. Anthony went quickly into a back room, wrote two or three letters to the Squire's nearest relations, rode as fast as he could to Thorpe, gave Miss Chesters directions to the Hardlands servants, and then, after a moment's thought, turned his horse's head back to Aunecester.

He said to Dr Fletcher, "Do not say anything of my being here to Miss Chester; it can do no good, I know, but—we were near neighbours, and I may as well sleep to-night at the Globe, so as to be at hand if I am wanted. You'll send for me if I can do anything of any sort? And there is no change?"

"None whatever. We have, of course, had a consultation, and Dr Hill entirely takes my view of the case. I regret that I cannot tell you that he is more hopeful. I am inclined to think Mr Chester's condition not altogether attributable to the blow, but that there might have been a simultaneous attack."

There was nothing to stay for, and Anthony went, though not to the inn. He walked about the old town for more hours than he knew, thinking of many things. Those last words of the Squire had touched him acutely, and his thoughts were softened and almost tender towards the friends whose countenance he had been rejecting. But the idea which seemed to hold him with a rush of force was that he must see Winifred again; that, happen what might, it was impossible but that there should be a meeting, if not one day at least another. It did not strike him as an inconsistency that this thing which he wanted had been within his reach a hundred times when he would not avail himself of it; like most men when under the influence of a dominant feeling, he did not care to look back and trace the manner in which its dominion had gradually asserted itself, nor, indeed, to dwell upon it so far as to admit that it was a dominion at all. Was he not to marry Ada Lovell? Only pity moved him, pity that was natural enough, remembering the old familiar relations, or allowing himself to dwell upon the sweet womanly eyes which no darkness could shut out from him. For gradually the dusk had deepened into night, the Close in which he found himself was singularly deserted, now and then a figure that might have been a shadow passed him, a quiet light or two gleamed behind homely blinds, and by and by was extinguished, the trees stood black and motionless against the sky, only the great bell of the Cathedral clock now and then broke the silence, and was answered far and near by echoing tongues. Such a night was full of tender sadness, to poor Anthony perhaps dangerously soft and sweet, for he had been living of late, in spite of his engagement, in an atmosphere of cold restraint, peculiarly galling to his reserved yet affectionate nature. All Ada's pretty assurances and the pleasant amenities of the Bennetts' house had never removed the chill. They were something belonging to him, at which he looked equably, but they had never become part of himself. Alas, and yet to-day a word or two of Winifred's—Winifred whom he did not love—had pierced it.

Winifred—whom he did not love.

With one of those unaccountable flashes by which an image is suddenly brought into our memory, there started before him a remembrance of her in the old Vicarage garden, that Sunday morning when he and she had strolled together to the mulberry-tree,—the quaintly formal hollyhocks, the busy martins flashing in and out, the daisies in the grass, Winifred softly singing the old psalm tune, and laying the cool rose against her cheek. Had he forgotten one of her words that day, this Winifred whom he did not love? And then he thought of her again at a time which he had never liked to look back upon, that winter day when she had met him in the lane, a spot of warm colour amidst the faded browns and greys,—thought of the gate and the cold distant moorland, and the words which had struck a chill into his life. It had seemed to him then as if it had been she who had done it, and he had never been able to dissociate her from her tidings; so that no generous pity for the woman who had wounded him, nor any understanding that she had done it because from another it might have come with too cruel harshness, had stirred his heart, until now when another compassion had forced the door, turned his eyes from himself, and shown him what Winifred had been.

The darkness reveals many things to us, and that night other things were abroad in the darkness,—death, the unfulfilled purpose of one whom he had chosen to regard as his enemy, if, indeed, it were not rather that God had fulfilled it in his own more perfect way,—these were working upon him, however unconsciously. Yet those revelations were full of anguish, opening out mistake after mistake in a manner which to a man who has over-trusted himself becomes an intolerable reproach. The accusation which had seemed literally to blast his life stood before him in juster, soberer proportions; his manner of meeting it became more cowardly and faithless, made bitter by an almost entire forgetfulness of the Hand from which the trial came. And in the midst of his angry despair, by his own act he must deliberately add another pang to his lot, and, putting away his friends, bind himself for life to a woman for whom his strongest feeling was the fancy for a smiling face. Perhaps, as yet, he hardly knew how slight that feeling was, but even by this time he was bitterly tasting the draught his own weakness had prepared. These thoughts all came to him with a quiet significance, adding tenfold to their power, yet touched by a certain solemn gravity which gave him the sense for which he most craved just now, the old childlike trustfulness in an overruling care. As we sow, so we must reap, but even the saddest harvest may yield us good sheaves, though not the crop we longed and hoped to gather. And this night was the first hour which seemed to bring Anthony face to face with his own work.

He had been walking mechanically about the Close. Turning out of it at last, he went back to Dr Fletcher's house, and looked up at a light burning in an upper window, little thinking, however, that it was a watch by the dead, and not by the living, that it marked; for in spite of what Dr Fletcher had told him, the tidings he heard in the early morning fell like an unexpected blow. He would have gone away without a word, but that Dr Fletcher came out at the moment.

"There was never any rally or return to consciousness," he said, leading the way into the dining-room, where his breakfast was spread, "and although this naturally aggravates the shock to his daughters, they have been spared a good deal that must have been very painful, poor things! My wife is with them. Will you have a cup of coffee with me?"

"He was always supposed to have such a good constitution," said Anthony, looking stunned.

"Perhaps not so good as it seemed. He led a regular life, temperate and healthy,—I only wish there were more like him,—and he had never been tried by any severe illness. As to this, a more tenacious vitality might only have prolonged the suffering. I think you said you had written to the relations? I would have telegraphed this morning, but Miss Chester was anxious that her aunt should be spared the shock."

"My letters will bring them as soon as possible," Anthony said. "There is a sister of the Squire's, a widow, an invalid, and her step-son is quartered at Colchester. Besides them there are only cousins. Mrs Orde will start at once—But, good heavens," he went on, breaking down, and burying his face in his hands, "it is so awfully sudden! What will they do?"

Dr Fletcher made no immediate reply. He was a kind-hearted man, but his sympathies were chiefly bounded by his profession, and it was easier for him to be energetic in behalf of a suffering body, than to express anything which touched more internal springs. He was wondering whether Anthony would have the courage to face a woman's grief, and meditating on the possibility of giving up his own morning's work, when he said aloud, quietly, —

"Miss Chester will probably return to Hardlands to-day. Is there any one who can be with her and her sister?"

"My mother is their oldest friend," Anthony said, without looking up, and pushing his plate from him with a slight nervous movement. The doctor waited for some assurance to follow this assertion, but Anthony could not give it, for his mind quickly ran over the situation, and foresaw that his mother's kindness would not suffice to guide her past the little embarrassments which awaken so great throbs of pain at such a time. Finding he was silent, Dr Fletcher went on, —

"Would you wish me to inquire whether Miss Chester is ready to see you? That is, unless I can persuade you to take a little more food?"

"I am quite ready," said Anthony, getting up hastily. He dreaded the interview fully as much as the doctor had divined, and the force with which he compelled himself to meet it produced a certain hardness which, to a shallow observer, might appear like cold indifference: certainly there were hard-set lines on his face as he stood at a window waiting for Winifred. Trees, with iron railings before them, were planted in the space in front of Dr Fletcher's house; there were crimson berries on the thorn-trees, a robin or two hopping about familiarly, a grey rainy-looking sky, and now and then a warning drop on the pavement below. Winifred did not come at once, for it was difficult for her to leave Bessie, who was overwrought as much with terror as sorrow; and Anthony, having strung himself up to the meeting, lost himself again in thoughts which grew out of but did not absolutely belong to it, and did not hear her behind him when at last she entered the room.

When he turned round she was standing close by him, and put out her hand.

"I thought you would come," she said simply.

But she saw in a moment that it was she who must be the comforter, and went on without leaving a pause which should oblige him to speak. "It was all so calm and so peaceful that I cannot realise anything beyond the comfort of knowing that he had no suffering to endure. Poor Bessie's grief seems something for which I am very sorry, but in which I have no share. It must be as I have read and never quite believed, that a great shock deadens all one's perceptions."

"Yes, indeed," said Anthony, relieved by her quietness and the simple words which had nothing constrained about them. "And by and by you will be thankful that you were with him,—so close at hand—"

"O, I am thankful now!" said Winifred, with intense earnestness. "It does not seem as if one could have borne it to be otherwise; but now I have all the last looks,—the knowledge that there was nothing lost. You can think what that must be."

Twenty-four hours had put away on her side all the divisions that had existed, and taken her back to the old familiar friendship, so that if she remembered any cause of estrangement, it was that she might touch it softly, and let Anthony feel that it had only been a shadow, not affecting the true kindness of her father. With an instinctive loyalty she would have liked to clothe the dead in a hundred virtues. But Anthony himself was feeling the separation with a strength that almost maddened him. There was a gulf between them which was of his own digging. There they were, he and she, and yet he could not put out a hand, could not take her to his heart and comfort her. As she spoke he shook his head with a quick gesture, throwing it back, and turned away from her towards the window, against which the rain was now pattering gently. Winifred was surprised, and a little hurt, but as it struck her that he might dread what she was going to say, she went on with a voice that faltered for the first time,—

"Dr Fletcher told me that you would settle for me what ought to be done, but—perhaps—I believe that I can give directions—if it is painful to you—"

"That is impossible," Anthony said, almost sharply, and without looking round. "I will do it all,—why else am I here?"

She drew back almost imperceptibly, but then, as if moved by an opposite feeling, went up to him, and touched his arm.

"Anthony," she said in a low voice.

If it was to oblige him to look at her she succeeded, for he immediately glanced round, although he did not answer, and indeed she went on hurriedly,—

"I dare say you think I do not know, but Dr Fletcher explained to me that there must be an inquest. It is not so painful as you fancy,—nothing seems painful just now,—do not be afraid to tell us what is necessary. Dr Fletcher says it had better be here, he will make them come as soon as possible, and he wishes us to go back to Hardlands at once. I would rather have stayed, but I can see that it would be bad for Bessie, and—he would have liked her to be spared. Richardson is in the house, if you would tell him to go back, and bring the carriage at once—and,"—she hesitated wistfully, for it did not seem quite so easy to her to ask anything of Anthony as it had been at the beginning of their interview—"would it be possible for you to stay,—so as to be at hand,—to stay until to-morrow, or till my cousin comes? Some one must be here," she said, with a little passionate cry of sorrow, as her self-control broke down; "he shall not be left alone." She stopped again, this time for an answer, but when none came she said with an effort, "Perhaps you cannot stay,—perhaps Mr Mannering would come?"

"Of course I shall stay," Anthony said, in a bitter, half-choked voice.

He knew that she thought him cruelly hard and cold: he heard her give a little sigh as she moved away a step or two, but it was with almost a feeling of relief, anything being better than that she should know the real feelings of the moment. Winifred was not thinking of him as he imagined, but something in his manner brought to her a keen impression of the breach between the dead and the living, which she had been trying to make him forget. She stood for a moment with her hand on the door, and her head bent,—thinking. She said at last, softly and pleadingly,—

"If it has not been between you and him of late quite as it was in the old days, you will not remember that any more, will you, Anthony? If he ever did you an injustice in his thoughts, it was not willingly, only—only one of those misunderstandings which the best, the noblest, sometimes fall into. If he had lived he would have told you this himself one day, and therefore I say it to you from him," she added, lifting her eyes, and speaking with grave steadfastness, as if she were indeed delivering a message from the dead, "and I know that you will be glad to think that it is so, and to help us for his sake."

The moment she had said this she went away so quickly that Anthony's call did not even reach her ears. It was only one word, "Winifred!" but it was as well she did not hear, since one word is sometimes strong enough to carry a whole load of anguish and of yearning love.

Chapter Twenty Six

"In my own heart love had not been made wise
To trace love's faint beginnings in mankind,
To know even hate is but a mask of love's,
To see a good in evil, and a hope
In ill-success."

Paracelsus.

Ada's frame of mind at this time was one of thorough content and satisfaction. She had always taken life smoothly and with a certain ease, perhaps inherited from her aunt, and she could manage either to slip round its little angles and roughnesses, or else to exert a faculty of not perceiving or comprehending them, to a really remarkable extent. She was so well satisfied with herself that it never appeared possible that others should not share the satisfaction to the full; and this armour, call it amiability or self-complacency or what you will, made her absolutely impervious to the darts which prick and goad more thin-skinned victims. Even to good-natured Mrs Bennett it had sometimes become apparent that Anthony was not so ardent a lover as might have been expected, that he expressed no anxiety about the wedding-day, that he was often late in coming, and not infrequently stayed away when there was no reason to account for his absence; but Ada was never ruffled by such reflections. It was a matter of course that Anthony should be most happy when he was by her side, and if he were obliged to stay away, she expressed a little contented pity, and smiled, worked, and talked, with a serene absence of misgivings. Hers was not a nature to be quickened into rare moments of deep delight; Anthony was simply one of the things which had been sent to make her life what she had always expected; it was a good match, as her uncle had repeatedly assured her, they would have money, comforts, an excellent position; but she had never been troubled with any doubt that in due time all these would naturally come to her, and everything seemed only moving in the sequence that was to be expected. Of any unfulfilled dream, or sense of dissatisfaction in the relations between herself and Anthony, she was unconscious, for the reason that it never entered her mind to conceive of herself as other than she was.

Nevertheless, although her reflections could not so much as touch the possibility of discontent on her lover's part, she was aware now and then that he was both dull and moody, and it was in her eyes one of the appointed pleasures of her lot that Mr Warren should be more attentive and bent upon displaying his devotion than in the days which preceded her engagement Mr Bennett used to laugh, and declare that Miles would be jealous; but he was an honourable and unsuspicious man, more pleased at an occasion for a joke than troubled by fear of mischief-making, nor indeed had the thought of an actual preference to Anthony—Anthony, be it observed, comprising all that he could give—entered further into Ada's head than her uncle's. It was simply that Mr Warren's attentions and little compliments were agreeable to her, and she had never been accustomed to deny herself what she liked. Anthony himself was indifferent about the matter, considering young Warren an empty-pated and harmless youth, and wondering a little that Ada should make him welcome to the house, but beyond that not troubling his head. The Bennetts were so hospitable, their house so open, that it was hardly possible to conceive a shutting of doors upon any one; and if such a thing were needed, there was a natural solution in the kindly interest Mr Bennett was known to show towards the young men who worked with him. Both Mr Bennett and Anthony were ignorant of a good deal that passed, such as meetings which were certainly not the result of chance, and which Underham discussed actively. But after what has been told, Anthony Miles could scarcely have borne to have found fault with Ada, even if he had known the utmost. He was oppressed with a terrible sense of wronging her, which, though it often produced intense nervous irritation, made him the more scrupulously polite in every word and action. Moreover, he was hesitating between two courses, and rather bent upon dissection of his own motives than upon weighing Adas merits and demerits, from which, with an instinctive generosity, he recoiled at such a time. Since the discovery of his own feelings, it was impossible for him not to realise the question of right or wrong involved, that there were conflicting claims; he tried to think of it with cold words, to force himself to judge as if from the outside, but more often he felt with a blank despair that he could do nothing except let matters drift on where the current carried them. Men sometimes call that resignation which is no more than a fear of facing pain, and the deception may be so subtle that it evades discovery until too late.

There had been an idea, on Anthony Miles's part, of his spending three months of the early winter in London; for although his dreams had lost their brilliancy, there are other motive-powers besides enthusiasm, and he was feeling the need of work as a refuge from thought, and talked of seeking occupation of some sort with more determination than he had yet employed.

But the days went on and he remained at Thorpe. To a certain extent he had resumed his old position. He no longer avoided his neighbours, and if he kept up any coldness towards the brothers at the Red House, it was only now and then shown by an increase of the reserve which had grown on him. To Hardlands he went by fits and starts, sometimes finding one or another pretext for a daily visit, sometimes absenting himself for a week at a time. Mrs Orde, the Squire's sister, was for the present remaining at Hardlands, Mr Chesters will having expressed a desire to that effect; and Bessie's despair at the idea of leaving was sufficient to reconcile Winifred to the arrangement, although she herself had a longing to go away. But she was happier in Anthony's return to friendliness; of any other feelings on his part she was spared the knowledge, since her own peculiar loyalty and faithfulness prevented her from thinking such feelings possible. Unfortunately, he had caught the trick of comparing her with Ada, and there was but one end to all such comparisons, for although, had he only known the one after the other, things might have seemed different, the pang was very acute of perceiving to what he had wilfully blinded himself; and every fresh instance of Winifred's sweet nobility of nature came to him like a revelation. Perceiving his continued gloom, people began to talk curiously again. Mr Robert could not feel as kindly towards him as in the old days, yet Anthony's looks worried him; and had he not unfortunately begun by getting hold of the wrong end of the string, or had Anthony been magnanimous enough to understand and forgive the error, he might have been the young man's best counsellor. As it was, Anthony had to meet this second complication, which had grown out of the first, with a sore perplexed heart, and no friend to help him. He felt utterly humiliated as well as miserable, for although a happy love is not the one thing needful to a man, and if it is denied him there are other things worth living for, such a mistake as he had made is apt for a time at least to destroy the spring of energy and doing.

Frank Orde soon followed his step-mother to Hardlands. He had taken his long leave before Christmas, with the intention of spending it at Thorpe. Anthony had never liked the thought of this arrangement, and when he arrived there was something so attractive about him that he felt all his prejudices confirmed. It was like a breath of fresh air coming into the midst of the little household who were moving about with saddened quiet faces, and already falling into the little feminine ways which mark the absence of the more vigorous race. Captain Orde had the physical activity which made him send his luggage in the carriage, and himself walk from Underham on the day of his arrival; he had also a taste for exploring and geological theories, the enthusiasm of which roused his cousins into interest; indeed he was so full of energy, so open-hearted, and so secure of sympathy, that to withhold it was as difficult as to avoid being warmed by the sun of midsummer.

They were all at dinner one evening when the day had been so persistently rainy that only Captain Orde, to whom weather was apparently a matter of indifference, had faced it, coming in just in time to avoid breaking the punctual routine which the Squire had established at Hardlands. Mrs Orde sat with her back to the fire: a thin woman, with a plain pleasant face, high cheek-bones, rugged features, and an upper lip too long for proportion, but curving in to a well-closed mouth; there were the two girls in their black dresses, and Captain Orde, unlike them all with his dark twinkling eyes and a fresh look of unbroken health. He had been telling them, with the vivid enjoyment that characterised his talk, his adventures in the muddy lanes round Thorpe, and of the difficulties he had met with in the way of extracting information; but it was not until the old butler had left the room, and they had drawn their chairs after a pleasant old-fashioned winter custom round the fire, that he said, —

"By the way, I fell in again to-day with my friend the local Wesleyan, as he tells me he calls himself. You haven't any of you taken to him more kindly, have you?"

"Do you mean that dreadful David Stephens?" Bessie said, setting a chestnut on the bar of the grate, and holding up her hand to screen herself.

"It has been hard to do anything for him," said Winifred, thinking of Captain Orde's old words, "almost impossible, although I dare say you cannot believe it. How can one help him?"

"He would say, build him a chapel."

"Frank!" Bessie said indignantly, from her knees before the fire.

"I thought you were in earnest," said Winifred with a touch of disappointment.

"I only say that is what he would choose. I don't recommend you to do it. There is something he really wants a good deal more."

"Tell us what you mean," said Bessie, tossing a hot chestnut into his lap.

"Never mind. It is nothing you will ever give, my dear," said Frank, who was looking at Winifred, while his mother looked at him.

"I should think not, if it is for that man," said Bessie defiantly, "and the sooner he goes away the better. We were all as glad as could be when Anthony put a stop to his horrid plans."

But Winifred asked no more questions. Perhaps there had come to her already, through the patient teaching of life, perceptions of a broader, kindlier horizon than used to bound her view. Perhaps she saw dimly what once seen can no more cease to grow upon our sight than the daylight which from the first eastern flush grows into the glory of the great day, that the blessed good in our fellow-man is that which we must look for, and help, and nourish; that so best wrong may be made right, and evil conquered, and weakness strengthened.

Bessie was not satisfied. "What did he mean?" she said in the drawing-room, nestling against Mrs Orde, of whom she was fond by fits and starts. "What did Frank think that I should never give?"

"I suppose he was talking about sympathy, my dear," said Mrs Orde, dryly. She was a kind-hearted woman herself, but a little timid over other people's kind-heartedness. I am not certain that she did not consider it a dangerous doctrine, at any rate for young men.

"He had no business to say so," Bessie replied petulantly. "I am sure I am as sorry as can be when any one is ill or anything. No sympathy, indeed! What does he know about it?"

"What do you know about it," Mrs Orde said decidedly, "a young thing like you? Frank was quite right. Go and play that sonata: I don't believe you have practised it at all, and your lesson is to-morrow."

"There's a ring," Bessie announced, going slowly. "It must be Anthony, for no one else comes at this time of night."

Captain Orde had also heard the ring, and the young men met in the passage and came in together, making a contrast, more marked than usual, as they stood side by side. Frank dark, high-shouldered, keen-eyed, and Anthony with his slight, wiry, nervous build, and a face depending for all beauty upon the expression which happened to be uppermost. It was not at its best now, for he was angry with himself for coming, and therefore, by a not unusual consequence, angry with those among whom he had come. His own heart was warning him. And yet he would not listen to his heart, lest it should shut him out from this haven. Other things made it only too easy. Mrs Orde liked him. She knew nothing—having so lately arrived, and from the circumstances having entered not at all into society—of the story of the letter, which might have influenced her judgment; but she knew that he was engaged to be married, and perceiving that he was unhappy, which, indeed, he took no pains to hide from the world, she mentally put two and two together, as she said, and drew her own conclusions. Sensible, steady-going people are the most romantic of all. Mrs Orde, who never did a foolish thing, began to reflect what would be Frank's case if he were engaged to a woman who was not worthy of him,—a supposition so possible that she could only shudder, and be kinder than ever to Anthony. As for Winifred, she saw quickly enough that he was gloomy and unhappy, and had not the heart to put obstacles in the way. If anything were worrying him, it seemed only natural that he should come back to his oldest friends, and it was a sign of that reconciliation which she liked to think death had not really hindered. Her own burden was made the heavier, but a woman does not think of this. Anthony, who knew what Winifred did not, should not have come, but—he was there. And he used to get hurt and sulky with Captain Orde. That night Bessie, who was affronted with her cousin, and anxious for an ally, began in the intervals of a little idle running up and down on the keys of the piano,—

"What do you think, Anthony? Frank has struck up an acquaintance with David Stephens. He is going to help him to build a chapel, and then to hear him preach."

"Really!"

There was a good deal not very pleasant in the "really," and Frank looked up from the newspaper he was turning over as he stood before the fire, and laughed.

"Bessie's facts are indisputable," he said. "It is all true, of course. By the way, I am afraid my ally is no ally of yours?"

"I've done my best to keep him out of the place," said Anthony, with some bitterness. "The fellow is a rank dissenter to begin with, and does a great deal of underground mischief of other kinds. I say nothing against his character; I believe he deludes himself with the belief he is in the right, and I dare say makes a good enough clerk, though it's a pity he should have found an employment to keep him here. But I do not consider it advisable to listen to his talk."

Frank took no notice of Anthony's tone, which had in it an imperious touch. He said as if he were replying to a calmly conducted argument,—

"The question is scarcely whether or no one will listen. Merely as a matter of cold prudence, it is surely better policy to help a stream to find safe channels than to refuse it a passage through your land."

"That is the talk which will ruin the country," Anthony said coldly. "Every doctrine nowadays has but one basis,—expediency."

"I don't understand what you are talking about," said Bessie, who was playing, a gigue with quaint trills and turns in an undertone, "but I am quite sure that Anthony is right."

"Yes, I think he is right," said Mrs Orde, sighing. She was looking at her son, and admiring his sweet temper, but for all that she thought it was necessary to oppose his opinions, lest they should carry him too far. Winifred was glancing from one to the other, with her eyes dilating and then melting.

"Well," Frank said good-humouredly, "it sometimes requires greater courage to stick to the popular side than to go against it. If my doctrine is ruining the country, the want of it is injuring David Stephens, unless I am much mistaken."

"All the better,—if it drives him out of the place."

"O Anthony!" said Winifred, in a low tone of hurt reproach. He looked round and saw she was on the other side, and grew a little white. Frank looked at the same moment and brightened.

"It is wiser not to mix one's self up with such persons," said Mrs Orde, talking exactly contrary to what she would have done, as people often do.

"No, mother," said Captain Orde, becoming grave, "that is a very helpless receipt. I suppose you don't want me to say that I don't agree with the end to which this man's thoughts have led him? But they have surely in some measure been forced upon him, and I hold that we are to blame for it, and are responsible. I should be very glad to convince him that we have a common interest, instead of dwelling with such persistence upon our points of antagonism."

"You must excuse my doubting the wisdom of your plan," Anthony said in the tone the conversation seemed to have awakened in him. "My own conviction is that, for the sake of others, these men should be put down with a strong hand."

He was too bitter to be anything but unjust, and Winifred looked sadly at him, thinking of his own troubles, and the misjudging which she had thought might have softened him towards others. She knew nothing of that other trouble which had its grip upon his heart as he glanced round at the bright room with its warm lights, and at Winifred and Frank, thinking angrily that he had cut himself off from her, and another had come in and filled his place. Nobody knew the wild, mad thoughts that were battling with him that night. All that could be seen were four or five people smiling and chatting, the fire crackling and leaping round a log of wood, and throwing dancing shadows on the pretty chintzes, and the bits of quaint old china, and the piano where Bessie was playing soft visionary music with tears in her eyes; for the Squire had liked the dreamy chords, and the girl had gone back to him, as she did more often than they fancied. And yet to one of the number the pleasant and kindly harmony of the hour was full of sharp discords, of things that fretted and jarred him. He made up his mind that he would not come again. He looked reproachfully at Winifred.

And yet, as he walked home across the silent fields, on which the moon was casting cold silvery streaks, he felt as he had never felt before, as if he could not marry Ada Lovell.

Chapter Twenty Seven

"It was in and about the Mart'mas time
When the green leaves they were falling."

Old Ballad.

That afternoon, when Captain Orde fell in with David Stephens, the two men had walked together to within a hundred yards of the Red House. Here, for it was almost dark, Captain Orde struck into one of the fields which would take him to Hardlands, and the other, standing for a moment as if lost in thought, went on through the red mud and the quantities of fallen leaves which had dropped from the hedge-row elms by his side.

As he passed along the wall enclosing Mr Mannering's garden, a door opened, and Stokes came out, locking the door after him. David had stopped, and his peculiar figure probably marked him sufficiently even in the waning light, for the gardener said in a slow and rather injured voice, —

"That's you, is it?"

"Yes, it's me."

"And you'm going to see Faith?"

"Yes, I am," said Stephens; and the two men walked on side by side in silence.

At last Stokes began again heavily, as if he had been reflecting on the answer, —

"'Twould be a dale better if it warn't you. That's arl I've got to say, and I've said it a dale better."

There was another silence before David spoke, with a fire of purpose contrasting strangely with the other man, —

"I don't pretend that I don't know what your words mean, and I don't say they haven't got something on their side. I suffered myself to be misguided by my own stubborn heart when I spoke of love to Faith. I should have known that this is no time for marrying and giving in marriage, with souls crying out of the darkness. It was a snare of the enemy to withhold me, and I was weak and feeble, instead of plucking out the eye, and cutting off though it were the right hand. I thought much of my own love, and that maybe we were called to work together in the vineyard, never rightly taking home to myself what was the sacrifice the Lord had called on me to make—"

David stopped suddenly with a tremor in his strong voice. Stokes was always slow of speech, and for a few moments there was no sound but that of the heavy steps trampling through mud and dead leaves.

"I doan't know nowt of what ye're talking up," said the elder man at last, doggedly. "It's my Faith as I've got to think of. Nowt else."

"You've got your soul, and the souls of others, if you'd only see it," said the other. But Stokes shook his head.

"Noa, I ain't," he said, "that's the passon's business. I bain't no passon, nor yet no pracher, nor I doan't think much o' prachers as comes and takes t' bread out o' passon's mouth. I ain't nowt to do wi' souls. I goes to choorch, and a'll be buried up thyur comfor'able, and us doan't want no prachers to Thorpe."

"That's the teaching of the enemy," said Stephens, vehemently. "Don't you ever think of the sin and wickedness about you? What of Tom Andrews, and Nathaniel Wills, and that poor girl at Peters's farm? Don't you believe that if their hearts have been stirred by a faithful messenger they might have been saved from their sins?"

"Noa, I doan't," said Stokes, with a persistent force of opposition. "That thyur Tom Anders has been a bad un ever since he wor a little chap, and stealed tummerts out o' my basket before my very eyes. I told his feyther then as he'd be hanged before a'd done with un, and so a wull. And Nat Wills is another poor lot. Leave 'em aloan, and us'll soon see th' last of 'em. That's watt I says."

"Ay, what you all say, and the most any of you can do," David said bitterly. "Parson and people all alike. He sits in his arm-chair and expects those poor sinners to come up to him, and preaches fine sermons in church, when there's not one of those as wants the sermons most there to hear him. I walked twenty mile yesterday, and fetched Nat Wills home with me, and I've got him at my lodgings now; but if I hadn't gone after him, do you think he'd have come to me?"

"Then you was a fule," said Stokes, promptly. "He'll never do you no good. An' now you'll be convertin' him, and setting un up for a saent. I doan't hold by they thyur doings."

They had come into Thorpe by this time; a bright light streamed out from the blacksmith's forge at the corner, where three roads met. A man who was standing there, with his face turned towards the fiery sparks struck out with every blow upon the anvil, looked round as he heard the advancing steps.

"Be that you, Tom?" he asked, peering into the darkness.

"What's brought you in from Wesson this time o' day?" said Stokes, answering one question by another in his slow deliberate way.

"Th' old missess is tooked so bad, master fetched the doctor hisself, and sent me right off for the passon. I'm to bide hyur for un, and go back in his trap."

"So th' old woman's come to her end at last, and has sent for the passon? Hyur's Stephens been tryin' to set down passons and choorch, and arl the rest o't."

"Ay; he'd like to have it a' under his own thumb, for a' he's so smarl," said Stringer, who, like most of the people about, knew David, and had nodded to him across Stokes. He did not mean to offer any offence by his words; it was only stating facts when he alluded to the young man's personal appearance. "That's the way wi' the Methodists. My mawther wor wan, and she never gived poor feyther no quiet. But wann they'm took bad, they likes a rale minister. I take it very kindly o' Passon Brent to turn to at this time o' night."

"Yes, he'll go," said Stephens, gravely, "and flatter with smooth words. But what has he done for that old woman's life? Hasn't she a name through the country for her hard, wicked, grasping ways? Has he ever been to her, and pleaded with her, and been faithful with her sin? Do you think the Lord's Apostles were content to go and say a prayer over the poor souls that were dying?"

"Been and pladed with her?" said Stringer, at once. "You'd ha' had a kettle of boiling water over you, if you'd tried that on wi' the old missess. Noa, noa,—I doan't say as passons is bound to ran risks wi' the wommen, such as that. But they've been going on wi' their ways for a good bit, and it bain't so strange to they as't is to you dissenters, as think you've found out something new, and must go runnin' arl over the country a talking about it."

"That's it, Dannel, that's it," said the gardener, moved to a chuckling delight by his friend's acuteness. "Passon knowed arl about it before you was born," he added, turning on Stephens.

"It must be a new thing to you and me, though, before it can work on our hearts," said the young man, almost passionately. "You think it's enough for another man to know it, and to preach about it, but I tell you that you must feel its burning power in yourselves, and then it will give you no peace until you tell it out to others."

At this moment there was a sound of wheels coming along the wet road, and Mr Brent drove up in his rough dog-cart. He pulled up sharply,—he did everything sharply,—and called out in the same tone,—

"Come, Stringer, are you there? Get up behind as fast as you can. As it is, with these roads we shall be a longer time than I can spare getting to Weston. Is that you, Stokes? The master has been complaining of Samuel again. The boy's doing no good whatever at school." And without waiting for an answer, or taking any notice of Stephens, who was standing in the full light of the forge, Mr Brent drove quickly off towards the farm.

Burge the blacksmith, who had come out to the door, and stood, lifting his cap with one hand, and passing the other through his straight black hair, was the first to make a remark upon the last-comer.

"He bain't such a pleasant-spoken gentleman as old Passon Miles."

"P'raps he bain't," said Stokes, gruffly; divided between injury on behalf of the culprit Samuel, and a fear of weakening what he looked upon as his late victory over Stephens and the dissenters. "P'raps you and me shouldn't be so pleasant nayther if us had to turn out to Wesson, wann us had done our day's work, to plaze the old missess."

"Day's work!" said the blacksmith, coughing violently, and going back to his labour. "I'd give something to kep your hours. I sim, sometimes, a smith ain't got no hours. He's at everybody's call, worse luck to me."

David had not heard the other men's remarks. He was standing at the door of the smithy where he had first stopped, with his eyes fixed upon the ground, and the red glow from the forge lighting that side of his face which was nearest it. These fits of abstraction were not uncommon with him, and, as something which they did not understand, and set down as not quite right, added to the disfavour with which he was commonly regarded by the people of Thorpe. David was quite aware of this disfavour. He was in the position of a reformer attempting to benefit society against its will. Each sin of which he heard, and each neglect, smote on his excitable nature as a crime on the part of those who might have prevented it. Driven in very much upon himself and his inward communings,—for the fervour of his opinions found as little favour in the eyes of his brother Wesleyans as in those of Churchmen, and he himself shrank in disgust from all that appeared to him to savour of worldliness and self-advancement,—the one thought that was always in his mind lost its fair proportions and grew as, alas, the best within us may grow, out of shape and out of bounds. All that opposed him seemed to be the especial opposition of the Devil, a conviction leading to its corollary, that hardly any means could be thought unlawful which tended to circumvent the evil one. He regarded Anthony Miles as the chief adversary raised up against him, and the great wrong he had done him he would not have undone, though it weighed like lead upon his conscience.

When David at length lifted his eyes, and recalled his thoughts from old Mrs Mortimer's deathbed, where he had concentrated them with a powerful purpose, and a stern disbelief in the adequacy of the means now on the way to Weston for her assistance, he found himself alone. The gardener, who was not unwilling to shake off his companion, had taken advantage of his abstraction, and departed. He lacked the energy of old Araunah, and had not attempted to hinder Stephens from seeing Faith by more decided opposition than lay in surly ungraciousness; but he knew that his wife and father would expect more from him, and made up his mind to keep silence as to the meeting and David's intentions. He himself regarded the latter with a sort of contemptuous dislike, mainly, no doubt, arising from his deformity, but partly from the new-fangled opinions, which were both unpleasing to his ears and disturbing from the fact of their being presented to him when he was unprepared. His own religion consisted of Sunday services, in hearing an occasional chapter read to the old man by his wife, and less frequently in listening with astonished admiration to some glib answers in the catechism repeated by his youngest "little maed." David's passionate and fervent appeals were as confusing to his mind as it would have been to have had his meals at other times than those to which he had been accustomed always from his childhood. He therefore disliked him, but there was a certain torpidity in his most acute feelings, and he was not likely to interfere with Faith in any manner more active than by expressing his own poor opinion of her lover.

David himself, recalled to his position, went away from the blacksmith's shed and walked through the village towards Mrs Miles's cottage. It was now quite dark, and wild gusts of wind were sweeping across the fields, and up the street where thatched cottages stood back in little gardens with rows of bright chrysanthemums in flower before them. The children were safe in bed, the women, many of them, out talking or buying. Quite a little knot was gathered in the little shop which provided both groceries and clothing, and from which a cheerful light gleamed out upon the wet road. The warm brightness beckoned invitingly to the young man, who, as was not unusual with him, was both tired and hungry. He stopped for a moment to look with an almost wistful gaze at the group. The women were laughing at some jest, even the pinched features were smoothed and brightened. A little bitterness surged up in his heart as he contrasted himself with these people whom he was yearning over, spending himself for, and who would have given him, perhaps, scarcely so much as a kind word. What was he to them? And what were they to him that he should wrestle for them, ay, even give up his dearest hopes in life? There was Nat Wills's mother laughing with the rest, while David was hungry because he had shared his little with the boy whom he, and he only, had walked those weary miles to reclaim. There was a thin woman whose husband was a drunkard, there was another whose daughter had left her,—he knew all the histories of these poor sin-stained lives, and for the instant a bitter sense of injustice swept upon him. Was he forever to stay in the darkness and the cold? Must he always put from himself light and love and pleasantness for the sake of those who neither cared for nor would hearken to him? Might he not turn away and leave them to their fate?

Ah, if he, standing thus, could repel the impulse, by the might of the love which bound him to their souls, do you not think that the Greater Love which helped him in his struggle would lead him with infinite tenderness, out of his loneliness and self-deception, into the full light of the perfect truth?

Chapter Twenty Eight

Faith, when she heard the knock at the back door, knew very well who had come, and her heart leaped up, for all day she had felt as if she could scarcely longer endure the suspense in which she was placed, and had been blaming David with the unreasonableness of impatience for not coming during the hours in which he was employed at the post-office. She jumped up and stopped a younger girl who was going to answer the knock. But when she had opened the door and saw David himself, all her little reproachful speeches were forgotten.

"I don't know that you'd best come in," she said hurriedly. "Sarah would be pleased to see you, but she and Jane are both there, and there's things I want to hear."

"No, I must see you by yourself," said Stephens. "The wind's high, but it's not so sharp, and if you stand by the door you'll not feel much of it."

"You're tired," interrupted Faith.

"Ay, no doubt. A man must be tired whose work lies where mine does. They're rough paths along which one has to go to find those poor sinners, and the enemy doesn't make them more easy to those who are searching."

"Mother says you'll wear out yourself, and everybody else," Faith said, with a touch of petulance, — "going on so."

David was silent for a moment. It was often the case that in the first sweetness of being with her he lost sight of the purpose which had gradually been strengthening in his mind, but such words as these brought it back with a sudden shock. And he knew that to-night he must speak plainly, whatever it cost him.

"Your mother is right, dear Faith," he said gently. His speech was often abrupt, and rather fiery than persuasive, but he had a full and mellow voice, and it was at this moment modulated into the tenderest tones. "I've thought it over on my knees, and I know I've been over-hasty in asking you to be my wife. I didn't ought to have done it, and I can never blame myself enough. For you couldn't bear it, any more than I could bear to see it."

His voice failed him in these last words, and he held his breath tightly, waiting with an eager faint hope for Faith to make some answer which would show that she would work by his side. She understood what he meant, knowing it was the self-imposed hardships of his life to which he was alluding, and she took the most effectual method of replying by putting up her apron, and beginning to cry piteously.

Stephens made one step towards her, but then he suddenly checked himself, though the dim light that came from the kitchen showed his strong features working with agitation.

"Why should you be different from other men?" said the girl, sobbing. "There's Jane going to be married, and Mary Bates, and Elizabeth. What's to prevent you and me from settling down quiet like them?"

Ah, what? Here was the thought with which he had just done battle presenting itself in a fairer, softer shape. Why should he be the one to leave the brightness and warm glow, and content himself with cold and hunger and weariness? Not of the body only,—that seemed to him as nothing, if Faith might be by his side,—but hunger of the heart. Then, as the longing within him was to him a divine longing, and all that opposed it took the form of the evil one, a sudden anger rushed into his heart against her who was tempting him.

"Hush, Faith!" he said in a stern, sorrowful voice, "you are setting yourself against God's work. I have got my hand to the plough, and I cannot look back."

"But, David," said Faith, frightened at his tone, and forgetting all except the fear of losing him, "I wouldn't keep you back, I wouldn't, indeed. You might go to preach, you know, just the same, and when you came back I should have things comfortable for you."

"Yes, my dear, you would," he said, with the thrill again in his voice. And then he cried out passionately, so that Sarah in the kitchen wondered what was being said, "Don't make it more hard, Faith, don't! I've heard of tearing out one's heart, but I never knew before what it meant. Think what my life is. There are so many sick and suffering that I must help somehow, or their eyes would follow me to the very judgment-seat,—I must do it,—I am constrained. I have had no food to-day but a crust of bread and a glass of water. Up in my lodgings I've got that poor nigh-lost Nat Wills. I walked twenty mile yesterday to get hold of him, and there he is. By and by I'm going to his employer to see what is to be done. It's the same always. But if I had a wife I don't know that she would think it right to her that I should do it, and yet I could never dare leave it undone. I couldn't, Faith."

His voice had kept at the same high-pitched abrupt tone, as if he were speaking under the pang of some physical anguish. Faith was frightened by it, but her mother had told her to pluck up spirit, and she thought, like other women, that a show of anger might bring David to her way of thinking. So she turned half away from him, as he saw very well by the dim light, and said, throwing her apron over her arm, —

"That's all fine enough, but I don't see as how you're more bound to them than to me, after the things you've said, and the neighbours knowing and all. It would have been better if I'd minded grandfather's words, and Mis'ess told me neither she nor Mr Anthony was pleased to think of me marrying a man that sets himself up against the Church."

Faith delivered this speech with considerable energy, but there were tears in her eyes which it was well for David's resolution that he could not see. Her mention of Mr Anthony stung him sharply. He said in a compressed tone, —

"You will not listen to him? There's no man in the county has done so much against the good cause, and may God forgive him, for he needs forgiveness!"

Since he had kept silence about the letter all Anthony's deeds had grown blacker in his eyes, and he thought, with the strange self-deception which men permit themselves to weave, that the obloquy that had fallen upon the young man was but a just retribution for those acts for which he had now professed to ask forgiveness. Faith, who had been silently crying for a few moments, found her voice to continue in the same tone, which she thought had produced a little impression, —

"I've stuck to you faithful, for all I've had to bear from every one. And this is what I get—" she added, breaking down altogether into sobs at last.

"It's a heavy burden," said David, drawing a quick deep breath; "the worse for me, because I should have spared you, and ought never to have told you how I loved you. But with the light that's been given to me, I dare not follow my own weak heart, unless—unless—" he went on, in a voice that trembled as a woman's might have done.

"Well, unless—?" said Faith, looking up.

"You couldn't bear such a life as mine must be?" said David, speaking slowly, and as it were out of a strange silence. "Poverty and hardship, and men's bitter persecutions, and only me faithful by your side? You couldn't bear that, my dear, could you?"

The words were so tender, so wistful, that for an instant Faith hesitated. But her love was not strong enough either to cast an ideal light over the life he thus unfolded before her, or to enable her to face its endurance for his sake. Instead of giving him a direct answer, she said with a touch of anger,—

"And you'll be marrying another girl, I suppose?"

Stephens caught hold of her hand.

"Don't say that again, Faith, for I can't bear it. You know that to my dying day I shall never love but you," he said hoarsely.

This assurance of love was sweet to Faith. After all, he would never be able to give her up.

"You'd do well enough," she said quickly, "if you'd keep to your business, and not share your own with every idle body, which nobody's called to do. Come, David, and then we might be comfortable."

"It can't be that way," he said; and there was a direct force in his words which let her feel the uselessness of saying more.

"What shall you do, then?" she asked, in a tone that was half petulant and half tearful.

"The way isn't clear to me yet," said David slowly, "but there's one of our body has spoken to me about going out to South America as a missionary. He thinks there is a manifest call there to a faithful worker, while there are others holding that work may be done here more effectually than hitherto, though we are so cramped and fettered in its discharge. It will be made plain to me before long. You will think as kindly of me as ever you can, Faith, won't you? Words don't seem worth anything between you and me, but there's an inward speaking surer. You won't let them set you against me, my darling,—you'll forgive me—"

He stopped suddenly, speechless with rush of intense feeling. Faith's spirit failed her, the hope that had so persistently kept its place died away out of her heart, all her little persuasions seemed useless; and, touched by some vibration from his own strong emotion, with a mute gesture, pathetic in its helplessness, she turned round; flung up her arms against the wall, and pressed her face between them.

When she lifted her head to speak, David was gone.

Chapter Twenty Nine

By the time the morning came, Anthony had not made up his mind what course to take, but he had seized the idea that relief was possible, and this thought gave a buoyancy to his spirit and a new freedom to his step. His mother brightened immediately. She followed him into the garden and made her usual remarks in a happy voice, even consenting, though not without a pang, to the destruction of her favourite flower-bed, because Anthony thought the turf should have a broader sweep, and she said, with tears, that Anthony's improvements reminded her of the old Vicarage days.

The day had been fair, with a fresh and constantly changing beauty, but as the afternoon wore on, the greyness so often to be seen in late autumn came over sky and land. There was a veil of thin mist hanging about the meadows when Anthony, with Sniff at his heels, walked through the lanes to Underham. Sniff, it must be said, had a particular attraction in Underham. He was a dog with a peculiarly strong sense of humour, and in the little town it unfortunately happened that there lived another dog, the property of an old lady, and the victim of innumerable washings. Mop was a white Spitz, of a depressed and meek turn of mind, probably the result of the many torments to which his white coat condemned him; and, with a profession of gambolling friendship which it would have been impossible for Mop, even if he had possessed the spirit, to resent, it was Sniff's great delight to choose a muddy spot of road, rush at and tumble him into it. It added much to his enjoyment when, as was every now and then the case, he could see his friend, with drooping tail, caught by the cook and carried ignominiously to the tub; and his appreciation of this little comedy of his own invention was so great, that it was almost impossible to avoid taking him to Underham. Some mute signs there were which instinct enabled him to detect, and, with that walk in view, no coaxing could induce him to venture where a door might be shut upon him; and more than once Anthony, congratulating himself upon having given him the slip, had found the little Skye waiting for him at some corner of the lane, wagging his tail with the most irresistibly deprecating expression of brown eyes.

So favourite a diversion at the end of his journey made Sniff run on more cheerily than his master could follow; for, although Anthony's old sanguine disposition to some extent asserted itself, a man does not go very happily to such an interview as lay before him. As the colour died out of the sky, everything looked dull, blank, uninviting: sodden grass clothed the hedges, the air was laden with a smell of crushed apples, a few yellow leaves hung on the scraggy moss-grown trees of the orchards, the ricks caught no gleams of sunshine, the farmyards were drearily prosaic. Until now, Anthony had hardly realised how he had grown to hate the road to Underham; even now he tried to believe that the unattractiveness lay in all these outward things. He pictured to himself the Bennetts' house, Ada coming forward with her pretty smiling face,—would it change?—would she care?—could it be possible that the next day he might be journeying away from Underham, free, unfettered? He went on thinking these thoughts until Underham itself was in sight, a few white cottages, the marshes, a canal, a bridge, and to the left red houses, black wharves, and a little confusion of shipping, all lying in the grey mist. There was another road joining that from Thorpe before it crossed the bridge, and two figures coming along under the trees Anthony glanced at carelessly, until they resolved themselves into Ada and Mr Warren.

Ada looked almost frightened for a moment. She came up quickly, and laid her hand on Anthony's arm.

"We could not have the carriage to-day, and I always get a headache if I stay at home all the afternoon, so I came for a walk. Isn't it odd that I should have first met Mr Warren, and then you?"

"Very," said Anthony shortly.

"He had been for a night to Stanton, and was just coming back."

"It's a good day for a walk after the rain," said Mr Warren, in his turn.

They were awkward little explanations, or might have been, if Anthony had been bent on another errand. As it was, after a momentary wrath at the man's impudence, his strongest sensation was that of discomfort at Ada's mark of affection. That they should be walking arm in arm towards her house was not the preamble he would have chosen to that which he had to say. Otherwise, it did not seem to him that he had any right to find fault with her. And he was too generous to admit the thought that he might use her own conduct as a weapon against her in the coming interview. He did not say much, because many things were in his mind, but his silence did not arise, as Ada and Mr Warren imagined, from displeasure with them. Ada quickly recovered herself, and wished Mr Warren a careless good-by. As they passed the rectory they met Mrs Featherly coming towards them, presenting the soles of her feet very visibly as she walked.

"I understood you had a cold, Ada," she said. "I am surprised to see you out in the damp."

"Have you a cold?" asked Anthony, when they were alone.

"Yes—no—I had, but the fresh air has cured it, as I thought it would."

"Then you would not mind staying out a little longer?"

He had thought, suddenly, that it would be easier for him to speak there than in her uncles house. Ada hesitated a little. Each had their own anxieties as to what was coming, and she was divided between dread of the conversation and a wish to keep her lover in a good-humour by yielding.

"It is getting late," she said slowly.

"But it is not cold. Come to the edge of the canal, and see that Norwegian schooner unloading."

"Very well," Ada said, hoping to charm him by her acquiescence.

They went to the edge of the wharf, at a little distance from the vessel, where there were men working at cranes, and great planks of deal from northern forests lifted and dropped on shore among the coils of rope, and sailors and boys who were lounging about and looking. Sometimes one comes upon a little scene of bustle like this, which yet lies under a strange hush. For a soft greyness had veiled all colour in the distant moors, a line of cloud as soft and as grey resting at a little height above them. Between cloud and hill the sun was sinking, a mighty ball of fire, throwing out no perceptible rays, but a ruddy glory, which rose behind the greyness, spread over the western heavens, and faded in a clear bright sky, softened by vapoury lines of cloud. The light was repeated in the water of the canal with a grave, gentle solemnity; there were groups of masts, rounded lines of boats, and, slowly moving out of sight, one tawny sail on its way to the river. Nothing could break the hush of departure which rested on the water, the quiet meadows, the hills, the changing sky—Anthony, who was always quickly affected by external influences, now that he had drawn Ada to the water's brink, found it strangely difficult to enter on the subject which a few hours ago had come shaped to his thoughts in burning words; the soft melancholy of the time made it hard to say anything which should give pain, and yet how was it possible to speak without sharp pain to himself and to her? Ada, meanwhile, who knew more than he did about the meeting between herself and Mr Warren, was for once a little shaken from her self-complacency; the young fellow had said some foolish words about his return, and she had walked along the road by which she knew he might be expected, with a pretence of wonder when she saw him coming; and now she was turning in her mind what she was to say, and feeling sure that this was the reason of Anthony's abstraction. Her own silence was unusual to her, but she had a perception that, her position would be bettered by his opening the attack, and his first words unconsciously added to her impression, although he only spoke them out of that fencing with ourselves with which we try to postpone a difficult task.

"Had you been out long, Ada, when I met you with Warren?"

"No, O no," she said eagerly. "Aunt Henrietta thought as I had a headache I had better go out. She wanted some ferns, so I went towards Stanton, but it really is the worst of living near a town that one cannot escape from people. One might expect the Stanton road to be quiet, mightn't one?"

He took no notice of this appeal. He believed all that she said implicitly, and her secret uneasiness had not in the least touched his consciousness. He was looking at the sinking sun, at the water moving slowly away, at the moments, perhaps, that were passing. She became more uneasy at his silence, but it was so unlike what she had been expecting when he at last spoke, that her breath seemed to fail her.

"Ada," he said quickly, "I have behaved very ill to you."

The ring of pain in his voice was too unmistakable to admit of the possibility of a thought that he was not speaking in earnest, which would otherwise have been her first reflection. But it was an instantaneous relief that he should be blaming himself and not her.

"Have you?" she said, with a little laugh, "I dare say you have. Old White, who was my nurse, used to say one should never trust any one. But I don't know—I have not found her words altogether true as yet." And she slipped her hand into his arm with a little caressing touch which added tenfold to the difficulty of his task.

"I shall never forget your trust in me. I can never forget that when other friends were ready at once to think evil, your generous belief never wavered," he went on, speaking nervously, and not looking at her. "It is partly on that account, and because I feel it is impossible to repay that debt, that I must tell you the truth now."

She was a little startled and uneasy again at his manner. Her imagination was not quick except in matters which concerned herself; but she began to picture the possibility of Anthony having done something much more dreadful than that act of simply leaving a suggestion unnoticed, which had never seemed to her such a mighty matter. Perhaps all his money was to be taken away from him. She drew back her hand and waited. The sun was gone, the sail had passed out of sight, Anthony went on more rapidly when he no longer felt the touch upon his arm.

"I knew that I was grateful; I was conscious of the relief and comfort that Mr Bennett's house, with its kind atmosphere of welcome, never failed to give,—selfishly conscious, I am afraid. And so I asked you to be my wife."

He stopped suddenly again, and looked at her for the first time, with a troubled imploring look, as if her mind must have leaped to the understanding of what he was trying to say, and no further words were needed. But except that she was relieved from her first fear, she did not understand in the least.

"Yes, Aunt Henrietta always knows how to make a house pleasant," she was saying, smiling up at him. "I don't think that rooms ought to be quite so hot, but, except that, they really are as nice as they can be. I am so glad you like it all, Anthony."

"You are too good to me, all of you," he said, reading only in her words a care for him which stung him with new remorse. "Ada, have you never repented?—do you think you can be happy with me?"

"O, why not?"

Perhaps some remembrance of Mr Warren came across her answer, and gave it just a touch of chill. If Anthony had not immediately been aware of the shade, I think he would have failed altogether in the courage which was necessary to pursue the subject; but, although Ada smiled again after her words, he was too sensitive to let it escape him.

"Men and women have made mistakes before now, I imagine," he said with a little bitterness, "and it would be no honest means of proving my gratitude to bind you to a mistake until it becomes irrevocable. So, for pity's sake, let us speak openly to each other,—while we can, at any rate."

It flashed rapidly upon Ada that she had at last found the solution of the riddle, and that Anthony's unaccountable words sprang, as she at first supposed, from the meeting that afternoon, although it was not anger which moved him, but fear lest she should be repenting of her choice. It was not the case. That little shade which had made itself felt in her answer to his question went no deeper than a little surface regret. She had no desire to marry Mr Warren rather than him, unless some change could alter the relative position of the two men; and it was quite necessary that Anthony should clearly understand this fact, although the idea of exciting a little jealousy was not undelightful to her vanity. She lifted her face, and said reproachfully,—

"I have always made a point of speaking openly. I do not know why you talk about mistakes, unless, indeed, you feel that you have made one yourself."

This undesigned home-thrust staggered Anthony for a moment, and then helped him to his purpose.

"In one sense I have," he said in a deep voice. "It need make no change in our mutual position, but in your eyes it may do so, and at least I should put it before you. It is a poor return for all your goodness to me to say that I believed I had a whole heart to offer you, and that I was a fool, for a part of myself belongs to another, always has, and, I suppose, always will; but, Ada, would it not have been worse to have hidden it from you? I could not have done so, it must have blistered my tongue when I spoke; I could do nothing but tell you, and put my fate into your hands. Will you still marry me?—will you believe that I will do all I can to make you happy?—will you forgive me?"

As he used the words, he was not looking at her. He had a vague perception in the midst of them that he was trying to thrust his emotions away from both her and himself, and to bury them out of sight. He hated himself for speaking the words at all. They were part of that wretched mistake of his life, which he began to feel would hold him tightly in spite of his efforts. He hated himself for doing her this wrong. He could not look at her. He felt that burden of humiliation and vexed anger which will make even a generous man indignant with the woman who has caused it, although innocently. There was a blank silence which lasted some minutes, while he was even more taken up with what he had said than with what it was possible she might say, and yet when her answer came at last, it startled him.

"Are you engaged to Miss Chester?" she said coldly.

"Good Heavens!" he exclaimed, stung to the quick, and facing her angrily. "Am I engaged? Do you know what you are saying?—do you suppose that I have been acting a lie all this time?—"

The hot words died suddenly on his tongue. Had he not been acting a lie to her and to himself together? The blood rushed into his face, but his words all came to an end. Ada, however, who had been impressed with the passion in his voice, began to recover from the anger which had been the first weapon her wounded vanity had caught up in self-defence. It was so impossible for the serene self-satisfaction of her nature to conceive a preference on his part for another woman, that her mind immediately began to cast about for some ether reasons for his words. Mr Bennett had often said that Anthony was morbid. She had not troubled her head about it, but the expression came to her now with relief. He had walked away a few steps, and stood moodily looking into a boat, with his shoulders a little raised, and his hands thrust into his pockets. Ada followed him and touched his arm.

"Dear Anthony," she said softly, "why should you be angry with me? After what you said, I thought you really must have some object in saying it. Had you? Do you wish not to marry me?"

"I wish you not to marry me without knowing the truth," he said, feeling as if circumstances were against him, and as if common humanity demanded some touch of tenderness on his part towards her. "I told you that I was conscious of having behaved very ill, but you know all now, Ada."

"Then all that I know is that you are very fanciful and very foolish," she said, speaking lightly. "If you tell me that you wish our engagement to be at an end, I should wish it too; I should only think of your happiness—" and as she said these words, she allowed her voice to change and falter slightly, so that Anthony, smitten with fresh remorse, turned and caught her hand in his,—"but if you are only speaking from some scrupulous— crotchet, shall I call it?" she went on, looking up at him, and smiling, "and fancying that I am not content, don't make yourself miserable about what is really nonsense. Most people have little likings before they marry and settle down. Aunt Henrietta always says I am not like the foolish girls in novels. I am quite sure we shall be very happy."

"If only I can make you so!" said poor Anthony, touched and overcome by the manner in which she had borne what he had to say. He forced back the sinking numbness which was creeping over his heart, and made his resolve tenderly. While those two had been standing there, the glow and ruddy lights had faded away, the grey deepened into gloom, the idlers had lounged home, a little red fire burned on board the unladen vessel, and made odd shadows, at which Sniff was barking in puzzled wrath. Anthony and Ada were standing in the darkness when he stooped slowly down and kissed her.

"So you are satisfied?" she said triumphantly.

"I am glad you know," he said, in a deep voice which he used when he was moved.

Two or three men on board the Norwegian vessel, who were sitting in a dark group by the fire, began suddenly to sing one of their folk songs. It was a pathetic simple little air, without much variation in the refrain which came again and again. "Forloren, forloren," it repeated, as if the lover could find no other words for his sadness. Was it an answer to her question? Was it his own heart crying out in the darkness? As they went slowly away, the sound followed them, growing sweeter when the distance softened it, as distance and time soften all sadness.

Chapter Thirty

"Then every evil word I had spoken once,
And every evil thought I had thought of old,
And every evil deed I ever did.
Awoke and cried, 'This Quest is not for thee.'
And lifting up mine eyes, I found myself
Alone, and in a land of sand and thorns,
And I was thirsty even unto death."

The Holy Grail.

The depression of spirit which fell upon David Stephens after leaving Faith was deepened by a number of other circumstances, which seemed to choose the saddest moment of his life to cast their separate troubles at him. When he reached home it was to learn that one of the most influential members of his body, in whose hands a sum of money had been gradually accumulated by means of the most painful labour and self-denial, had gone off to a Mormon settlement, carrying the money with him. And on the following day, David, hastening back at dinner-time to the prodigal whom he was sheltering and yearning over, found the little room empty, and the boy gone. The landlady, who had been in a heat of lofty indignation since Nat Wills was first brought to her house, would give no information; and David, tired and sick at heart, sat down on his bed, forcing his mind, by the strongest coercion he could bring to bear, to travel wearily along the probable roads by which the lad was setting forth again upon his downward journey, that so he might go after him and bring him back,—no matter what it cost him.

But although his resolution was no less supported by an iron determination than it had been a few days ago on almost the same errand, the spring which had then made it comparatively easy had lost its power. His face was haggard and worn as if with a long illness. His hands moved restlessly from one thing to another. He turned with loathing from the food on the table, which, frugal as it was, was more than he would have ordered if he had not provided for the guest who had left him. Never in his life had such an unconquerable gloom seized him as that which held him now in an ever-tightening grasp.

It appeared to him and he believed that he was looking dispassionately at what he judged, that all his attempts had resulted in failure. He had prepared himself for it in some sort, but not as it had met him, lull of crushing pain, a pain which had grown into his eyes, never to leave them again, and perhaps gave them some of the strange power which people noticed when he spoke. His aim had been the highest. Blame him as you will, his faults had been the falling short of that aim, his manner of striving towards it, his wilfulness in its pursuit, not the forgetting of it, or turning aside to something lower. He had yearned for the poor souls about him, the force of his love-making every shortcoming towards them horrible in his sight, so that out of his very pitiful compassion there grew actual injustice. Then he had seemed to gain many, his burning words having in them a compelling force which frightened and attracted the souls they touched. Against pride in this success, against the pride of which some who were jealous of his eloquence accused him, he had prayed intensely and passionately. He had not sought worldly advancement, riches, or fame, the only use of these things in his sight being as means by which he might have scope for the work, the desire of which possessed his soul. Men who have such longings are apt to believe that the very purity and nobility of their aims must needs put what they want within their reach, not perceiving that it is the very height at which they grasp which causes what they call failure. For, evermore, as we toil and climb we learn our littleness, and something of the glory of that which lies beyond; until with the struggle there comes the knowledge that here is not the end, nor the crown, nor the fulfilment.

But to David at this moment the end seemed to have been within his reach and to have been missed. The power which he believed himself to have attained over some of the minds, or rather the affections of those with whom he had been brought in contact, directly it was touched by the test of self-interest, even in its basest form, failed. He told himself bitterly that if a passing emotion led them to ask how they might flee from the wrath to come, with something of the spirit which urged the Ephesians to burn their books, the Florentines to cast aside their vanities at the bidding of Savonarola,—when the emotion passed, the older selfishness reasserted its sway. As for himself, what was he to them? A humpbacked preacher, to whom novelty would attract them, but for whom not one would turn out of his way to send after him so much as a kindly word. The sense of desolation which surged up in his heart as he thought this was so terrible that great drops stood on his forehead and his limbs trembled. In spite of himself, he had never lost the hope that Faith might have faced his lot, and clung to him: but Faith had given him up; the boy for whom he had been pinching himself had run away; the man whom he called friend had crushed his last hopes of gaining what he believed absolutely necessary to the success of his work. Everything was against him. Men clung to the wreck from which he would have dragged them, hurt him with hard words, turned their faces from him; and standing there, solitary, in a room heavy with the remembrance of the boy who had shared and left it, David cried out in the anguish of his heart as though some one had smitten him a deadly blow. Yet with it all there was no faltering of his resolution, no holding back of his hand. He would go out again that evening, walk all the night if it were necessary, once more to bring back the last lost. As he passed along the street to the office, the boys jeered at him. "Thyur's another pracher for the Mormuns!"

"Wann be'm going, Jim?"

"Doan't 'ee know? Whay, wann thyur's a lot more money scraped up for to build a chapel." Although David walked along without paying any apparent regard, each word fell like a lash on his sore heart, on which the burden of the other man's deeds seemed to be heaped.

He went through his work dully and mechanically, but without failing in any point of its routine. He was, however, detained at the office until a later hour than usual, owing to a delay on the line, and he made up his mind, in the intervals during which he allowed his mind to dwell on the subject, to search for Nat Wills in Underham itself before going farther; thinking it not unlikely, from some words the boy had let drop, that he would find a hiding-place there.

When he left the office it was quite dark, and long ago the glory of the setting sun had faded out of the heavens. For an hour or two he went, as he had determined, from house to house in the black courts where vice and misery huddle together, nearer us oftener than we think in our contentedness. And even here he was scourged by the other man's sin. Women taunted him with it, every taunt carrying a fresh sting. Some of them in moments of emotion had given him their pence for the object he had at heart, and cast this in his teeth again, or reproached him with mute white faces which were more intolerable. No one could tell what it cost him to feel that the work he had believed to be in progress lay all unravelled and useless in his hand, the stone which infinite labour had pushed upwards had dropped back an inert mass. The solitude, too, of a sectarian creed was upon him. He felt alone among these people. When he came out at last into a wider street, the light from a lamp hard by falling on his face showed it intensified with a look of such pain as a man cannot endure long and live.

The purpose in his heart was, however, as strong as ever, and he moved slowly along the street towards another quarter in which it was possible that Nat might have found refuge. Just as he reached a corner Anthony Miles came round it on his way from the Bennetts'. It was not a happy time for him to meet David, after the talk of the night before, and when the evening had been such as we know. He stopped abruptly, and David stopped also.

"That's you, Stephens, is it not?"

"Yes, sir."

"Mr Bennett has been telling me of the rascally manner in which that man Higgins has made off. I should think that ought to show you the set of fellows you're getting mixed up with. But if you will run your head against a wall there's another thing I've got to say. I understand you are still trying for a bit of land in Thorpe, and you may as well know that I've not changed my mind, and that I shall fight you through thick and thin before you get it."

"I know that, sir," said David, with a concentrated forlornness in his voice of which Anthony was immediately aware. "You've done it with all your might up to now, but you won't need to trouble yourself much longer."

"Have you changed your opinions, then?" said Anthony, softened by the thought of concession.

"Have I given up my faith, do you mean?" Stephens said bitterly. "Can I put my religion on and off as easy as you your glove? No, Mr Miles, if there's no more left to me, there's that, at any rate. What I mean to say is that since the money has gone there's a further hindrance put in the way of the gospel, and that if there's any who can triumph over the working of another man's sin, they may do it now."

In spite of his irritation at the man's meaning, Anthony could not repress some sort of pity for the deep dejection with which he spoke. It was impossible to doubt his earnestness, although he had no sympathy for his efforts.

"There are different ways of preaching the gospel, Stephens," he said more kindly, "without taking other men's duties upon ourselves. Well, good-night to you. I wished to give you that warning. If I were you I should shake myself clear of the Higgins lot."

Each figure went its separate way in the darkness, little thinking how soon they were to meet again. For the first time for some weeks a fresh alarm awoke in Davids conscience, perhaps caused by the touch of change in Mr Miles's manner, perhaps by the end of those hopes which had influenced his conduct towards him. He had succeeded in persuading himself that Anthony had been a persecutor of religion, and that his own silence had been caused by no mere personal grudge; now, wounded by the scorn and disappointment of the last two days, he began to realise what he had permitted to fall on the other man. What if he, more than Anthony, had been the persecutor? What if here were a sin which he had nursed until God would have patience no longer, and had smitten him and his labour to the earth?

He groaned aloud, and stretched out his hands towards heaven and the stars which were shining softly. A woman who passed noticed a dart figure leaning against a house, and fled in terror. David never saw her. The anguish which he had carried with him all the day reached its crisis, and almost overwhelmed him. His soul, struck with a sense of its own weakness, swallowed up by a terrified horror, was crying out for help, for teaching, in a new-found passion of humility. He sank down on his knees in the road, and, taught by the spiritual experience of his life to crave for and to obey sudden impulses, had almost resolved to follow Anthony at once, and to tell him all he knew. The recollection of Nat Wills withheld him; and as if he would lose no more time in finding him, and thus becoming free to follow his design, he staggered to his feet, and hurried along towards the water.

Chapter Thirty One

"But this I know, that not even the best and first,
When all is done, can claim by desert what even to the last
and worst
Of us weak workmen, God from the depths of his infinite
mercy giveth.
These bones shall rest in peace, for I know that my
Redeemer liveth."

Owen Meredith.

The short conversation between the two men did not leave the same impression upon Anthony as it had left upon David. Other thoughts had hold of him too completely to allow of much wandering from them. Although he had made no distinct resolution to do that which he had done, and permitted himself to believe that his words had not been premeditated, but were such as grew out of the situation, the possibility that they might be spoken had in truth lived in his heart, or had, rather, been lived upon, for some time past. He was too young not to feel that suffering was intolerable, that his own wrong must be righted, deliverance come in some unknown fashion. The hope was never altogether absent even in his moments of deepest dejection, and as yet he could scarcely grasp the fact that he had used the one resource which had seemed to him at once desperate and certain, and that—it had failed him.

When he reached the bridge a bark at his heels startled him. He stood still and whittled for Sniff, and meeting no return remembered that he had left the Bennetts hurriedly, and had forgotten to ask for the dog. He turned round at once, and more from a vague feeling that some pain haunted the road by which he had reached his present point, than from any actual choice, took the path by the canal, and passed the spot from which that day he had seen the sun sink, and watched the shades gather.

The Norwegian vessel lay still against the quay, its masts rising sharply against the softer darkness of the sky, in which tremulous stars were shining. Underneath the wall there was a blackness of water, where a plank or two floated and caught the faint light. Smoke was still pouring out of the little hooded funnel where the men had their fire, and there were three or four figures on the deck, and laughter which did not sound quite friendly.

Anthony, as he came nearer, could distinguish words of broken English, and fancied that the men had been drinking and were quarrelsome. It was all shadowy and dusky, with here and there a little weird leaping light, and rough voices grating on the silence. But as he passed by the water's edge he heard another voice which he recognised as David Stephens's, and this made him look at the group with more curiosity, and wonder what the young man could be doing on board a foreign vessel. He could distinctly see him standing in the midst of the sailors, who were jeering or threatening, and presently he saw him turn away as if to jump on shore. Anthony lingered, he could scarcely tell why, when suddenly there was a cry and a splash; one of the men by accident or design had pushed violently against David, and he was in the water. The sailors, sobered in an instant, were crowding, looking, shouting, and in another moment Anthony was in the midst of them, had caught a rope, and swung himself down between the vessel and the quay. He was a good swimmer, the danger lay in the cramped space in which it was possible to move, and in the darkness which hid everything; but presently lights flashed, people were running and calling, and a gleam struck for a moment on something at which he clutched and missed, and clutched again, and dragged up at last on the slippery planks. Help came very quickly, men collected, two boats were jostling each other, and they lifted the burden from him, laid it in the boat, and rowed to the landing steps. There the men who were carrying poor David paused as if in doubt.

"Where shall us take un, sir?" asked one of the old sailors.

"It's young Stephens, the preacher!" said another who had got a lantern, and held it up to the white face.

"You may carr'n over to my place, if you'm minded," said a gruff voice out of the little throng. "It's handy, and the mis'ess wouldn't be willing for he to be drownded."

"Take him to whichever house is nearest. And, here, one of you, go off for Mr Bowles," said Anthony, recovering his breath.

They carried him very tenderly across the road to a door at which a little light was already shining. The foreign sailors were watching with alarmed faces, uncertain how far they would be held answerable for what had happened. One of them began explaining in broken English to Anthony that he had come on board to look for some boy whom he accused them of harbouring, and then the men made fun of him, not in the least intending what had happened, their spokesman declared. It was so impossible to say whether there had really been more than this, that Anthony could only listen in silence. He was a little confused himself, for it had all passed in a minute, and there was a strange flutter of unreality about the darkness and the trampling feet moving through the narrow door. A kind grave-looking woman was there, who came forward with wet eyes, and touched Davids hand gently; she had had but a moment of preparation, and yet it all seemed ready as the men came in with their dripping burden, and carried it up stairs and laid it on the bed. Her husband stopped the people who were pressing after, but a lad broke past him, ran up into the room, and fell on his knees by the bedside, crying bitterly.

"I'm Nat, David. I'll go back with you where you please," he said over and over, with a sharpness of appeal which touched them all. It seemed as if the heavy lids must lift themselves, the mouth unclose, in answer to this boyish cry; the men fell back a little, and waited in mute expectation. David had been right in tracking him to the ship. He had got one of the men to hide him for a lark, and then he had heard all the inquiries, the jerk, the sudden splash. They had some ado to keep him from flinging himself over the side, too.

But neither cries nor remorse touched the quiet of the face which lay unconscious of them all in that awful insensibility which affects us with a curious sympathy as something that one day must hold us also in thrall. They thought that he was dead, and when at last, after the doctor had tried all means of restoration, life struggled feebly back, it was so slight and so precarious that it scarcely seemed like life at all.

"I suspect some blow was received in the fall; but the poor fellow was weakly before, and the shock has proved too much for his rallying powers," said Mr Bowles, under his breath.

"Do you mean that he will die?" said Anthony, shocked.

"You had better go and change your clothes, Mr Miles," said the doctor, evading the question. "Can you find your way to my house?"

"I will go to the Bennetts', and hurry back as soon as possible. Is anything wanted?"

"A little brandy for yourself. Nothing here, thank you."

Anthony was quickly back again, and Mr Bennett with him, full of fussy good-nature. David had spoken a word or two, and the calm of his face had deepened into something that looked like happiness, as he lay with his eyes resting upon Nat Wills, who was burying his head in the bedclothes, and now and then lifting it to sob out remorseful words. But as his look turned towards Anthony, and lay there for a minute or two as if he were not sufficiently conscious to know who it was, those who were watching saw a sudden change pass over the still features. It might have been wonder, fear, even terror, which drew the muscles together and opened the eyes, but it was shown so sharply that every one turned at once to look in the same direction, and see what caused the movement.

"You may as well just slip behind, the sight of you seems to excite him," said the young doctor, a little curious like the rest. As for Anthony, the intensity of the look fairly appalled him. He had disliked and opposed Stephens, but he was one of those people to whom it is always a shock to have ill-feeling returned, especially at a moment when he was full of kindly emotion towards the man whose life he had saved.

"He wishes to say something. Keep back, good people," said Mr Bennett. "Is there anything you want, my poor fellow?"

The pale lips parted and closed again.

"He has not strength to bear questioning," said the doctor, impatiently. He would have stopped it more decidedly if that look had not remained upon the man's face, so terrible in its dumb language that it seemed as if something must be done to loosen its tension. And yet Anthony had drawn back into the shadows. After a moment's thinking, Mr Bowles motioned him forward. "You had better speak and find out what is the matter," he said in a low voice, "for something is exciting him more than he can long bear."

Side by side with Nat Wills, Anthony Miles knelt down by the bedside.

"Do you know me, David?" he said, with the gentleness that death teaches us.

Once more David tried to speak, once more the words failed him. His eyes turned away in piteous entreaty, and the doctor, passing his arm round him, got him to swallow a few drops of stimulant. Then those who were nearest heard his voice as if front far away.

"I was going to you—next—that letter—"

"The letter?" repeated Anthony in surprise. The shadow of his life was not touching him at that moment; he could not understand.

"Have you given him a letter?" asked Mr Bennett.

"The letter—- about the—will."

The blood rushed over Anthony's face. He understood at last. For an instant it was like the lifting of an iron weight, for an instant his heart leaped up. Mr Bennett came closer and began to question eagerly,—

"Do you mean the Cornish letter?—the one all the talk has been about?"

"I ought to have told—O God, have mercy!"

"Told what?—What do you mean?—Say it out, man!"

"Give him time," said the doctor, quietly.

"It did come—I saw the postmark—Polmear—I gave it myself to—"

"Hush!" said Anthony, very gravely and kindly. "You need not tell us any more, David, for I know it all."

"But—Anthony, Anthony, my dear fellow, for Heaven's sake, let us hear what he means. Our coming here I consider quite providential. Here is this abominable story on the point of being cleared up. Don't stop him for worlds."

"Mr Miles never had—it," said Stephens, speaking more strongly. "You will find the bits—I picked up—and the date in my pocket-book. He tore it up—"

"There is nothing more to be said," interrupted the young man, much moved. "If this has been on your conscience, David, I am very sorry, for I knew that the letter reached Underham, although I never saw it. Your being able to tell these gentlemen so much ought to be a good thing for me, I suppose," he went on with a touch of the old bitterness; "but as to other particulars, the way you can best repair any wrong is by keeping silence." The dying man's eyes met his once more with a mute look of anguish. Was the sin he had nursed to die with him without his being permitted to reveal it?

"I thought—you hindered the—good work," he said, lifting his feeble hands as if to ask for mercy.

"And what troubles you now is, that you feel you have wronged Mr Miles?" said the doctor, who began to understand something.

"David, listen," said Anthony, speaking in a low gentle voice. "May God forgive me as I forgive you, freely, fully. May God forgive my hard thoughts of you. He is teaching us both something, and I think I have the most to learn. I wish there was one soul could cling to me as that poor boy is clinging now to you."

David's eyes turned slowly towards Nat Wills, and softened into a look of great love.

"Nat," he said faintly,—"Nat!"

"I'll go just where you likes," said the boy, eagerly looking up.

"Then you'll go to Thorpe—to Mr Salter—Mr Miles will, maybe, help you—and you'll tell. There's nothing like telling before it's too late." His voice had grown stronger, his eye brightened.

"Do you know that it was Mr Miles who saved your life?" said Mr Bennett, who had been a good deal shocked by what he heard.

But David was still looking at the boy.

"The mist is lifting from the water," he said slowly. "Does Faith see it?—Faith told me she would—look, look!"

"He is wandering," said the doctor, softly.

What does the soul see when the cords are loosened for a moment, and it goes where our feeble pity follows, not knowing what we say? Do the mists lift indeed, and does the glory of the Day Dawn shine in its nearness? Whatever David may have beheld, something of its wonder touched his face, and brightened it with an intense joy, a joy which rested, and at which by and by they looked reverently as at something which had done with earth and its sin forever.

Chapter Thirty Two

Mr Mannering was sitting in his library the next morning, when Mr Bennett was announced. It was not yet twelve o'clock, and the Underham lawyer was generally deep in his work at that hour, so that Mr Mannering met him with a touch of wonder in his cordiality.

"The more welcome because I should as soon have expected Thorpe to receive a visit from the Mayor and Corporation as from you at this time of day. Sit down, pray. My papers are all over the place, but I believe you can find a chair."

"If I had not known better, I should have said you were still in harness, I own," said Mr Bennett, looking round upon the familiar signs of business.

"Harness? I sometimes think that for men who have passed the greater part of their lives at work there is no getting out of it. There is a review in the last Quarterly which all the world is talking about, and I can assure you I have not yet found five minutes in which to look at it. The truth is that an unlucky mortal who has neither time, money, nor health, should make up his mind to endure a great deal in this world."

"What's that, Charles?" said Mr Robert, coming in with a ruddy glow upon his face. "If you had Stokes for a gardener, you might begin to talk about endurance. Glad to see you, Bennett, this fine fresh morning. All well, I hope?"

"All my household, thank you," said Mr Bennett, settling himself to his story with great satisfaction. "But we had a sad accident in Thorpe last night. Anthony Miles had been dining with us, and had not left half an hour when back he came, and really it was fortunate that Ada had gone up stairs, or she might have been terribly alarmed to see him dripping from head to foot at that hour of the night. However, the ladies were out of the way, by a stroke of good fortune."

"Dripping! Had he tumbled into the water?"

"Not at all, not at all. It was a foolish thing to do, but it seems he saw the man fall, and jumped in after him. And then, of course, he came to me for dry clothes."

Mr Mannering was leaning forward in a trim attitude of attention, with his legs crossed, and his head a little bent. Mr Robert was fidgeting as usual under Mr Bennett's prose.

"But who was drowned or dragged out, or what was the end of it?" he said hastily. "Bless the boy, he'll be himself again, if people believe him to be a hero. Who was it, Bennett?"

"Ah, there is the extraordinary coincidence. It was such a fortunate thing that I went back with Anthony, because, although it was not the case for a formal deposition, I am ready to prove that he made a voluntary declaration."

"He—who, who?"

"The young man's name is David Stephens," said Mr Bennett in a tone of mild reproof. "He is a clerk at the post-office."

"Young Stephens, the humpback preacher! Deposition?—Do you mean there had been a quarrel or anything?"

"My dear Mr Robert, if you were to guess for a week you would never imagine what he had to say," said Mr Bennett, sitting back in his chair, and tapping one hand lightly with the other, too secure of his story to mind the little pokes and digs that were being administered. "I can assure you that in the whole course of my experience I have never met with anything I consider so strange. It just appeared the shadowy kind of accusation which is most difficult to rebut; and, although I was convinced that it might be explained in some perfectly honourable manner, it cannot be doubted that there were persons whom it did influence otherwise."

Mr Mannering looked as courteously attentive as ever, Mr Robert had sunk into a despairing silence.

"My most sanguine hopes hardly amounted to an actual acquittal, owing, as I have said, to the difficulty of proving anything in the matter—"

"You are talking about Anthony Miles," cried Mr Robert, jumping up, and becoming very red in the face. "But what on earth had that young Stephens to do with it?"

"Could you have imagined that he had in his hands this letter which made all the stir, that he gave it to a certain person, and that, it having been destroyed, Stephens was able to tell us where we might find one or two of its fragments, minute fragments I need not say, but sufficient for the purpose of identification, and such as under the circumstances may be considered conclusive."

"Conclusive?—but of what? The existence of that letter is the very fact to which we have all been trying to shut our eyes," said Mr Mannering, dubiously joining his fingers.

"The letter existed," said Mr Bennett, leaning forward and speaking emphatically,—"the letter existed, but it never reached the owner to whom it was addressed. Another person received it from Stephens, and, as I have told you, apparently destroyed it. One or two things must have excited Stephens's suspicions, for he managed to possess himself of a shred or two of the writing. I have them with me."

Nobody spoke for a moment. Mr Robert walked to the window and blew his nose violently. Mr Mannering took the tiny witnesses, and fitted them together with his long slender fingers.

"Here are four," he said at last, "one with only the word 'will,' which is valueless; another may be 'proposal' with the first letter and half of the second missing, and the remaining two are, I should say, unmistakably part of the signature. You are right, Bennett. They prove nothing, and yet under the circumstances they prove a great deal. I am heartily pleased."

"Who was the rascal?" asked his brother from the window.

Mr Bennett pursed up his lips and did not answer until Mr Robert repeated his question, and then he said,—

"That is the most unsatisfactory part of the business, I lament to say. Will you believe that Anthony Miles knew all that I have told you from the first, and would not speak, and that now he has prevented our becoming acquainted with the name of the person?"

"Whew! That complicates the matter again. How can Anthony be such a fool!"

"I have urged everything in my power," Mr Bennett went on, rather pompously. "His position in regard to my family gave me the right to do so. But he is exceedingly determined. He says the information is not new to himself, and he even requests me to keep complete silence on the subject."

"Don't pay any attention to his crotchets, Bennett," said Mr Robert, marching back from the window. "Silence?—Tell everybody, everybody!— it's the only thing to do. He has proved himself too incapable to be allowed any longer to manage his own affairs. Besides, for Miss Lovell's sake—I'm delighted, more than delighted; that business has been a load on my mind ever since I first heard of it. We'll give a dinner-party, Charles, and ask the whole neighbourhood; I'll write to that dry old Pitt, and insist that he shall come down and eat his words before he has any other dinner. Poor boy, we've treated him shamefully. But, I say, Bennett, what of Stephens? It seems to me that he comes badly enough out of it. What has he got to say for himself, eh?"

His kind, ugly face was radiant. Mr Bennett looked up nervously, for the tragedy of the night before had touched him more deeply than he knew himself.

"I don't think we had better say anything further about his part of the business, poor fellow," he answered, a little apologetically. "He is dead now, and he did his utmost at the last. Perhaps it's easier to judge than to understand."

"Dead! I thought that Anthony Miles had saved him?"

"Bowles said from what he saw and heard from a miserable boy—who, by the way, belongs to your village—that Stephens had got down to a very low ebb with want of food and want of rest, and the shock was too great. It really was very affecting, the boy's grief and all that, and this morning the house is besieged. I think the poor fellow must have had some good in him, in spite of the ugly look his silence has."

When Mr Bennett had gone, Mr Robert came back to the library, rubbing his hands.

"Well, Charles," he said.

"Well, my dear Robert."

"I am going to the cottage at once."

"I would go with you if this lumbago only left me the power of moving. But let me forewarn you not to expect a very warm reception from Anthony."

"Warm or not, I couldn't stay away an hour. I shall go on to Hardlands, and perhaps somehow or other get a lift to the Milmans or to Stanton. It seems a sin to leave that matter uncleared another day. You'll write to Pitt, Charles," added his brother, suddenly becoming grave. "I suppose we both guess who was the other person?"

"I am afraid we do."

"It was sheer folly to have sacrificed himself, but, naturally, their relationship added to his reluctance. Well, we have no right to make other people acquainted with what is simply conjecture, but I shall be surprised if others besides ourselves do not put two and two together."

"Nevertheless, remember that as the story cannot be made altogether clear, we may expect incredulity yet."

"The story is clear enough," said Mr Robert, indignantly. "Nobody can doubt it who is not wilfully malicious. Anthony's statement was that on a certain date he had received no letter. People could not prove that he had, but it was just open to doubt,—upon my word, I don't think I'll ever doubt again to my dying day,—now comes a witness who can swear that Anthony is correct, who saw the letter in other hands, and produces a portion of that letter destroyed. What on earth can be asked for more? If you are not satisfied, Charles, I shall say you are as unreasonable as Stokes."

He went away laughing and rubbing his hands. The day was warm and damp, the clouds had a uniform tint of grey, drops clung to the beautiful bare boughs, which had so much cheerful undergrowth of green that they lost their wintry aspect, as Mr Robert started on his triumphal progress, which, however, like other triumphs, was not free from disappointment. Anthony was not at the cottage, and Mrs Miles would have resented any rejoicing over a proof which it seemed to her absolutely wickedness to demand. Mr Mannering could not be sure that her son had told her anything, and the only compensation of which he dared to avail himself was praise of Anthony's courage the night before.

"Which way has he gone?" he asked, as he stood at the door.

"I think he has walked up to Hardlands. I wish he would have kept quiet to-day, after the shock and all," said Mrs Miles, proudly.

"I suspect the shock was in the right direction, in spite of my gentleman's pride," Mr Robert reflected, walking out of the gate. "It will not hurt me to trudge to the Milmans, and then he shall make his own revelations at Hardlands. If only the Squire could have seen the day!"

Chapter Thirty Three

"For Love himself took part against himself
To warn us off, and Duty loved of Love."

Tennyson.

That afternoon Winifred was at home alone, rather an unusual thing for her, but Mrs Orde had occasion to go to Aunecester, and her son and Bessie had gone with her, while Winifred was glad of some excuse for staying at home, not having yet become accustomed to the sight of the street where her eyes were constantly picturing what had happened such a little time ago. A large fire was blazing, and she opened the long window, and sat down with some pretence of work in her hand, but after a few minutes' attention her eyes wandered away to the grey familiar view before her. The firs to the left looked thin and dreary, the grass of the field which stretched beyond the lawn had grown a little coarse, no lights flashed from a mass of low heavy-lying clouds, all colours except cold greys and browns seemed to, have been drawn from the distant trees, the cottages, the little line of sea, the sad hills. Winifred's eyes filled with tears as she looked out. It would have been so natural for the Squire's strong figure to have made the foreground of the picture, his voice might so well have been heard calling the dogs, and gathering around him a little circle of cheery life, that the blank solitude smote her with desolate pain. It is, however, possible that when such a sad and unacknowledged jar has grown into a girls life as had come to Winifred, there is a certain luxury in a permitted sorrow. It seems at the time as if trouble were being heaped upon trouble, but it really takes away that hard feeling of repression which is like an iron band on a wound. Perhaps there is hardly a grief over which we mourn, but has those hidden behind it of which the world knows nothing. How imperceptibly do other memories weave themselves round the one remembrance that is so sad and yet so dear! How heavy with longing may be the thoughts which creep softly back to days not very long ago, except for that drag which makes time seem interminable! It was not only over her father's image that Winifred was crying softly when she heard a sound, and Anthony Miles came in.

It may have been that he was too preoccupied with his own feelings to notice her tears, or that he did not dare to notice them. Winifred herself rose hastily, and sat down again a little hastily too, taking care to turn her back to the light which she had before been facing. She knew that her hand was trembling, and although it might have been caused by the momentary surprise, the feeling of weakness it produced unnerved her, and she was thankful that Anthony, when he sat down, sat leaning forward with his elbow on his knee, and his face on his hand, looking straight before him through the open window at the dull greyness, as if he saw nothing on either side.

A minute before Winifred had not felt as if it were possible to speak, but it is often necessary to fly from silence and take refuge in commonplaces, and she gathered up the work which lay in her lap and said,—

"I hope you did not want to see the others, for they have driven to Aunecester."

"I did not want to see any one but you, Winifred," said Anthony, without changing his position.

The words were so unlike what she expected, that she trembled again with a thrill that was neither joy nor fear, but something more exquisitely painful. Anthony went on after a moment's pause,—"I suppose you do not know what happened last night?"

"Last night? No."

"That poor fellow of whom we were speaking the other evening, David Stephens, fell into the water, and died in a few hours."

"O poor Faith!" said Winifred, touched by an instantaneous sympathy.

"Yes," said Anthony, gravely. "We would have sent her home, but she has begged my mother to let her stay."

"Were you there?—how did you know about it?—where was it?"

"Yes, I was there. It was in Underham," said Anthony. He had spoken throughout in the same short abstracted tone, as if a fit of absence were upon him; but what he had told her was sufficient to account for it, and she had forgotten herself in its sadness, and was looking at him with compassionate eyes, when he turned round for the first time, and said slowly, "I wished to see you alone, because you may as well know that it is proved—sufficiently, I suppose, for the satisfaction of my friends—that I am not quite the rogue they made me out to be. I can't answer any questions, and it is not possible now, any more than then, to explain exactly what did take place. Therefore, there is, of course, still room for doubt. At the same time David, before he died, poor fellow, declared that the letter never reached my hand, so—you may take the evidence for what it is worth. You are the only person to whom I shall repeat it."

Passionate tears sprang into Winifred's eyes. This clearing of Anthony's honour, for which she had prayed and yearned, had all gladness frozen out of it by the coldness of his words and the want of trust they implied. Her fate crimsoned, and when she tried to speak her voice was choked. Anthony, who had expected congratulations instead of this silence, turned towards her in surprise, and met her look intensely reproachful. He started up and walked quickly to the window. That look thrilled him suddenly with a doubt that carried sweet anguish and bitter joy. Had her faith been, after all, unshaken? Had it been he who had thrust her from him?—his pride which had separated them forever? He turned round and looked at Winifred again; burning words rose to his lips, and died away: if he had found a voice I do not know what he might not have said, but for a moment it was impossible to speak, and Winifred, although she was trembling under his eyes, was bravely holding back her own emotion.

"I am so thankful," she said. "Now all that has past will lose its pain. I don't want to ask any questions, but it has been very cruel for you,—for us all," she added softly.

"Pain does not go away so easily as you believe. I think it has only just begun," said poor Anthony. "Answer me one thing, Winifred. Does this that I have told you make no difference in your thoughts of me?"

"How should it!—how should it!" she cried out with an impetuosity of rejection which startled him. "O, how could you think so! Do we not know each other?—are we not friends?—can you suppose that for one moment I ever doubted you?" She stood up and looked at him with reproachful eyes, only eager to repel the accusation. He, looking also, knew for the first time that he, not she, had failed; that the want of trust, the want of friendship, had been on his side, not hers. And yet she said that now the past would lose its pain! He turned away with something like a groan.

"What is the use of it all then?" he said.

"One thinks of other people, I suppose," said Winifred, trying to understand his mood. "So many people are ready to believe evil. If you are not glad for your own sake, you must be for those for whom you care—"

She stopped trembling, for he was facing her again, with his eyes fixed upon her, and a depth in their gaze before which her heart fluttered and leapt up. For an instant she felt as if it had met his own; for an instant the happiness that flooded her carried her on its triumphant tide; for an instant the world was full of a sweet joy, beyond either measurement or control,—

for an instant and no more. Her voice had scarcely faltered, and she might have been only completing the sentence when she said in a low tone, —

"For Miss Lovell, especially."

She was looking away from him and did not know whether he had changed his position or not, for he did not answer. There was a strange heavy silence in which she could hear a watch ticking, the sigh of the wind among the fir-trees, a scream from the distant train, the throbbing of her heart. All her strength seemed to have gone out in those four words.

"Yes," said Anthony, at last, hoarsely, "for Miss Lovell, especially."

Something in his voice or in the mechanical repetition of her words brought back Winifred's courage.

"For her sake and your mother's," she said, earnestly. "However insignificant an accusation may be, its falseness must be a grief to the friends who best know how very false it is. I hope you will not try to prevent our being glad, although I dare say the poor man's fate makes rejoicing seem heartless."

"It makes me believe that failure is the end of our best hopes, — of all that is best in us," said Anthony, standing with his back to her and speaking in a tone of deep despondency.

"Not failure, really," said Winifred, with a flush of lovely eager colour rising in her cheeks. "Surely it is not possible that what is best can fail. It may seem so even to ourselves, but it cannot be the thing itself, only our way of thinking of it. Don't you believe that failure and victory are sometimes one?" Anthony was silent. Was it so indeed? Sometimes one, triumph and defeat, death and life, the end and the beginning? Was it now—when he was ready to cry out that all was at its dreariest, with pangs of which he was tasting the most utter sharpness—now that he caught, through the clouds, a glimpse of something beyond change and beyond sorrow? He came and stood in front of Winifred, and put out his hand.

"I can't tell," he said. "It may be so, and I think you are more lively to be right than I. At all events, one has to learn how to accept failure, and perhaps—some day—one will understand better. God bless you, Winifred."

She sat where he left her; she heard doors open and shut, and, turning round, saw him presently go quickly down the little path, pass under the fir-trees, and disappear from sight. Her breath came and went rapidly, a light was in her eyes. With all her struggle, those minutes had not been so bitter to her as to him; there was a joy in knowing that he loved her, it seemed to lift a secret reproach off her heart; and though this knowledge might bring sharper sadness to her by and by, for the moment the relief was so great as to make all sadness seem endurable.

Chapter Thirty Four

Thanks in a great measure to Mr Robert's policy, the news of Anthony's clearing spread rapidly through the neighbourhood. The Milmans had a luncheon party about a week afterwards, and as Lady Milman said to her daughter beforehand, it was really quite a comfort to have something to talk about. She contrived, very skilfully, to keep the welcome topic out of the desultory conversation before luncheon, feeling that it was too valuable to be broken into fragments, as would then have been its fate. But in the first pause after they were seated in the dining-room, Mrs Featherly's voice was heard emphatically declaring, —

"A very strange and unsatisfactory story this, about Anthony Miles. Not that I ever expected the matter to be cleared up in the manner one has a right to desire, but with his father vicar and all, I often told Mr Featherly that I should make a point of hoping against hope."

"Well, I don't know about its being unsatisfactory," said Lady Milman, looking very handsome, and inclined to take a kindlier view of things. "It's odd, of course, and unlucky that we can't hear the whole affair, but so long as he did not receive the letter it is really no difference who did. I always liked Anthony Miles, and I think his jumping into the water and saving the man who had done him so much harm was a very fine thing."

"O, but it was in the dark, so he could not possibly have known. I can tell you precisely how it all occurred," said Mrs Featherly, who would have scorned to have been unable to give a precise account of anything which happened within a circuit of ten miles. "He had that minute left the Bennetts', and heard a scream and a splash, and saw some one in the water, so of course he could do nothing less than jump in. There were the steps close by, and there was no possible danger."

"Ah, it's a capital thing to be able to economise one's neighbours' virtues," said old Mr Wood of the Grange, helping himself to mayonnaise.

"Well, if Anthony Miles knew who it was," said Mrs Featherly, tartly, "he showed a very proper spirit, a dissenter and all. Dissenters are never to be trusted, and this one behaved in a most reprehensible manner, going about in my husband's parish and making himself exceedingly troublesome, — though I should be the last person to speak ill of the dead."

"It is unsatisfactory, as you say, because they can't feel it," put in Mr Wood again, in a tone of assent, which Mrs Featherly accepted as a tribute to her argument.

"I have no doubt that it is all true so far as that David Stephens acted very wrongly," she continued, "but then I do feel that if one hears part one should hear all. I should like to know, if Anthony Miles did not get the letter, who did?"

Mr Mannering had already laid down his knife and fork, and joined the tips of his fingers together, divided between a desire to speak and a fear of impoliteness.

"Excuse me," he said, in his pleasant, courteous tones, "but I cannot but feel with Lady Milman that here we open another subject. I am sure Mrs Featherly, with her usual candour, will admit that Anthony Miles's conduct may be considered blameless in the matter?"

"Indeed, I am not so presumptuous as to call any human being's conduct blameless," said Mrs Featherly aggressively, "especially that of a young man who has the snare of no profession. Not that anything seems to have any effect nowadays. There is that young Warren, good for nothing but to dance attendance upon Miss Ada Lovell. I have told Mr Featherly he really must make a point before long of speaking to Mr Bennett."

"Warren?" said Sir Thomas Milman, joining in from the end of the table. "That will be his cousin whose death was in yesterday's paper. It must have been sudden, very sudden. He only came to the title about four months ago, and now it goes, I should say, to this young fellow's father. Isn't it so, Mannering?—you're up in all this sort of thing."

"Sir Henry Warren is undoubtedly dead, and if this young man's father is his uncle, it must be as you say," said Mr Mannering, a little startled. "But I always understood theirs to be a family of great possessions. I had no idea this young Warren belonged to them."

"Well, as often as not there's a poor branch hanging on to the big stem, though they don't very often get such a puff of good luck as this to set them straight. But there's no doubt about the money."

"O, they creak of money," said Mr Wood. "Their pedigree is not long enough to have given them time to spend it as yet. They must wait for that till they get a little good blood into the family."

"I shall make a point of calling upon Mrs Bennett this afternoon," said Mrs Featherly, who had been listening in blank amazement, "so that I may learn exactly what has happened. Mr Warren the son of a baronet! Well,

I must say he has always performed his duties in an exemplary manner, and I shall be quite glad to show him a little attention, that he may see we appreciate it. It is certainly one's duty to do so. I shall make a point of it." Even Mrs Bennett had been raised to something like excitement, when her husband told her of Mr Warren's sudden prosperity.

"So much happens every day that it quite takes away my breath," she said comfortably from the soft chair in which she was sitting. "Then, my dear Tom, Mr Warren will not stay with you? Dear me, Ada, you and I shall be quite sorry to lose him, he has really always made himself so pleasant and so attentive. I hope he will come and tell us all about it. And the poor young man who is dead, how sudden for him! Only three-and-twenty, too!"

"He takes it very properly," said Mr Bennett, rubbing his hands. "Of course it puts me to a little inconvenience, and he spoke very well about it, very well. Offered to stay, and said quite the right thing. But I should not take any advantage of that sort, as you may suppose. He'll go to the University, I imagine, and probably to the bar afterwards. Odd world, Ada, my dear, isn't it?" As for Ada, the tears had rushed suddenly into her eyes. She murmured something in reply, but the weight of disappointment which she felt almost frightened herself, and when she made a faint attempt to assure herself that Mr Warren was nothing to her, it was only to become conscious that he was truly the embodiment of those things for which she most cared,—brightness, compliments, admiration, attention; and now— how much more besides! Ada was only romantic when romance did not interfere with more solid comforts, but to have all within her reach, and yet to be obliged to turn away, was a trial which touched her sorely. It seemed to develop a vein of bitterness, as opposed as possible to the petty prettinesses of her life, which made her thoroughly uncomfortable, and which she tried to dignify by the name of misery, although her feelings were at no time deep enough to admit of strong names. It added to her vexation that, so short a time ago, Anthony should himself have offered to free her from her engagement. Her vanity found so pleasant an excuse for his words in setting them down to a fear on his part that she should not be fully satisfied, that she felt no anger towards him for what he had said, but it provoked her that it should not have been later, when she might have been guided by these new circumstances. Marriage with Mr Warren had hitherto been out of the question; and now that its possibility was suddenly presented to her, Ada wept the bitterest tears of disappointment she had ever shed in her life. People with whom life has gone smoothly are not disposed to admit of any course of events whereby they are defrauded, as they think, of the good things that yet should fall to their share; the very shadow of withdrawal astonishes them in a manner which is not without its pathetic side to those who have tasted draughts out of the depths. There is, too, in these natures, often a curious power of centralisation, so that their own life becomes the point round which all others revolve, and in relation to which all others are considered. Ada would have understood the sin of another girl acting in what the world would call a heartless fashion; yet, so far as Anthony's heart was concerned, she looked at it only as made for the satisfaction of her own; so that it would not have entered her head that suffering which seemed wrong and unendurable for herself might not properly have fallen to his share, and indeed there was, perhaps, a feeling as if a balance were struck with Providence, by admitting the necessity of tribulation for other people. It was not the pain she might inflict which weighed upon her now, but a vague dissatisfied conviction that her uncle and aunt would not permit her to throw over Anthony; a kind of dim sense, it might be, of honour, growing out of an atmosphere which, if easily selfish, was not dishonourable. Marrying him, she would feel all her life long that a great injury had been done her, yet she was aware that, cruel as it was, she might be called upon to endure this wrong.

Things seemed so harshly upset that, for the first time in her life, Ada caught sight of her tear-stained face in the glass, and her pretty eyes swollen and discoloured, without any answering impulse being awakened to put aside what so greatly marred her beauty, as easily crushed as a flower by a storm. On the contrary, she was touched by a sort of despair that the prettiness of which she was wholly conscious could not, after all, give her what she had a right to expect from it. It was a curious petty turmoil, yet for one of Ada's nature it marked serious disturbance that she should have gone down stairs after only languidly pushing back her hair, without the usual marks of trim order which characterised her, and that she should have been pettish in her answers to her aunt. She was so evidently out of spirits when Anthony came in, that it was impossible for him not to remark it, but he was almost grateful for the change. Her constant flow of smiles grew at times to be full of weariness, the weariness which makes people feel conscience-stricken at the little repulsion that rises up. He looked very ill, and unlike a man from whom a heavy burden had just been lifted. Is it not so often? — what we want comes, and it is no longer what we want, — the load is taken off, but we would fain have it back again, if its weight might only be exchanged for the aching pain that has grown up elsewhere; we rail at the present, and lo, it passes away, and in its vanishing shadow we see the glory of an angel's face, and stretch out our hands with vain weeping.

Anthony Miles had come that day with a determination to press his marriage, and to take Ada away from Underham. They would settle in London, by which he knew that he should fulfil one of Ada's dreams, and there he would fling himself into work with a will, if not with much heart. Something of that shame of disappointment which scourges into fresh energy was upon him. He had resolved to be very gentle with Ada, and the change in her manner made it more easy than usual. She was sitting listlessly in an arm-chair near the fire, for her grief would never be likely to interfere with her comforts, and at this moment a sense of injury was uppermost, for which she instinctively felt compensations to be her due.

"I am afraid you have another headache," said Anthony, standing before her, and looking down, with a vague compassion in his heart.

"Nobody thinks anything about my headaches," said Ada, in a complaining voice. "When Aunt Henrietta is ill herself, she makes a great fuss about it, but she never cares about other people. This place does not agree with me; Dr Fletcher has always said so, but they will not believe him."

"Will you let me take you away from it, then?" said Anthony, speaking sadly, but kindly, and trying to put away all thoughts but care for her. "London, you know, might suit you better."

"Are you talking about our marrying?" Ada's face lit up for a moment with a vision of her wedding-dress, but dropped again into its new expression of dissatisfied listlessness. "My uncle must settle all that."

"But you do not object?"

"I don't know,—I have a headache,—there can't be any hurry."

The indifference of the tone struck him, but it was too much an echo of his own feeling to seem as if it were anything strange.

"Then I will speak to him?" he said.

"Very well," said Ada, turning away with tears in her eyes.

"Is there nothing I can do for you?" said Anthony, still touched with the feeling that it was bodily suffering she was experiencing.

"No,—nothing. I can't talk. There is a ring, who is it?"

"I think I hear Warren's voice."

He did not expect to see her jump up, and turn with a smiling face to greet the new-comer. Not a trace of her languor remained; she talked, laughed, and congratulated, all in a breath. "What does it mean?" thought Anthony, looking at her sparkling eyes in wonder. Sniff had stolen in unperceived behind Mr Warren, and crept under his master's chair; but seeing his hand hanging down could not, even at the risk of detection, refrain from a rapturous lick. Anthony got the dog's head in his hand and fondled it, while he sat and wondered mutely.

"And you are really going away?" Ada was saying. "We shall all miss you so much."

"You may be certain I shall come back again."

"O yes, you must. Still—I don't know—I am afraid there will be something different, and I dare say you will have forgotten all about us."

"I am sure I shall never forget,—how could I?" said Mr Warren, turning very red, and almost stammering in his eagerness. "I have met with so much kindness in this house, I do not believe I shall be so happy anywhere as I have been in Underham."

"O, but you will live in the country, and in such a beautiful place!" Ada said, shaking her curl, and sighing involuntarily as she thought of what her lot might have been.

"I like a sociable place like this better," said the young fellow honestly, "and as to that, it's the people—"

He stopped suddenly, with a perception that Anthony was sitting and looking grimly at him. He had a soft heart, and the idea of going away from Ada was solidifying his feelings, which had hitherto scarcely taken shape beyond the amusement of the moment, so that for the first time it gave him an actual pang to remember that the real separation lay in this engagement of Ada's. One or two discoveries were made in that moment. Anthony awakened to the perception that another mistake must be added to the list, and it was a mistake which, whatever may be a man's feelings, is sure to gall him. An apparently transparent affection, such as Ada's, had been grateful to him at a time when he was very sore with all the world, and the fact of this soreness and of his own changed position gave it an air of reality which he had never thought of questioning. Even if he had discovered that her heart held no great depths, what was there he believed to be all his own; and Mr Warren would have been the last person presented to his thoughts as a possible rival until now, when Ada's manner and sudden change from gloom to gaiety made him very wroth, with the anger not of jealousy, but of wounded pride. Nor did his own failure towards her soften him, for he satisfied himself by thinking that he had at least told her the truth, and put the matter into her own choice, while she had deliberately deceived him by liking this young idiot, and showing her preference unblushingly the instant the fellow's position was changed. Anthony's face grew blacker and blacker, and Ada, perhaps desirous of driving him to desperation, put out all her charms for Mr Warren. There was a certain comfortable prettiness about the room, about the cheerful colouring, and the big fire which looked brighter and brighter as the afternoon shortened, and in the midst of it all one of those half-absurd, half-tragic complications, which sometimes seem to get inextricably knotted round a life. Anthony jumped up at last.

"I am glad your headache is better," he said shortly.

"Are you going? Good bye, then," said Ada, in an indifferent voice.

He stood still, and looked at her for a moment, so that her eyes fell under his. But she recovered herself immediately, and glanced up as if she were waiting for him to speak. He said no more, however, but went out of the room, Sniff barking with delight the instant he found himself safely in the hall.

As he walked home, his feelings could scarcely be called enviable, the less so because, turn which way he would, there seemed no line of action which he could take. It was impossible for him to find fault with Ada, who, indeed, had done nothing against which he could bring a serious complaint; it was more manner than words, and to fall foul of manner requires a lover's quarrel, and a lover's quarrel a lover. He could no more go seriously to Ada and blame her than he could fight smoke with a sword. And after his one failure he said to himself that come what would there should be no further attempt on his part to loosen the bond which bound them to each other. But he was very miserable. For until now he had felt that, although the deepest love was wanting which happiest marriages need, something they both had towards a happiness which, if not the greatest, might serve instead,—on her part a simple unreasoning affection, on his a certain gratitude and tenderness. He had not thought of these failing until this new turn of the wheel. Now he could no longer feel the gentle kindliness to which he had trusted as the foundation of a moderate happiness; and even at that, insufficient as it once seemed, he looked back as a drowning man looks at the harsh rock from which he has been torn. He could do nothing except wait, and there was a passiveness about his future which made it seem utterly dark and hateful to poor Anthony.

As he came near the Red House, the day brightened in some degree; the faint beauty of the sun had gained strength, little cold lovelinesses were creeping into life, a poor little pool of water was shining away, and a scarlet glory of berries flamed from the hedge where a tiny wren slipped in and out, scarcely moving the grass. Mr Robert was just riding out of the gate, and pulled up to greet Anthony.

"This rainy weather has knocked poor Charles over altogether," he said, "and I'm going to fetch Bowles. He always gets moped when he can't go out. Ah, Anthony, in old days you would have been up to see us long ago."

There was a little tone of sadness in Mr Robert's cheery voice, which Anthony detected in a moment, and it may have been a proof that the young man's own troubles were no longer hardening him, that it touched him in the way it did.

"The old days—?" he said, his words almost failing him. Mr Robert looked at him in an odd, questioning way.

"My dear fellow," he said, putting out his hand and grasping Anthony's, "I'm ready to admit that I didn't stand by you as stoutly as you'd a right to expect, and I ask your pardon for it. If you knew the story of my life, for even red-faced old bachelors have stories, perhaps you'd see some sort of reason for my feeling about it. But then we none of us take what we don't see for granted." Anthony was utterly shamed and overcome. "Don't, don't!" he said, putting up his hand to his face, for he had a generous temper, quick to respond to kindness, and he felt now, somehow, as if he had been in the wrong throughout. Mr Robert went on in his kind grave voice,—

"Perhaps I'd no claim to it, but I wish you could have treated me as your friend, and let me know how matters stood exactly. You'll not be angry at my saying that I guess now what a painful position you were in. I'm not sure that you were right, mind you, but I am sure that not one man in twenty would have behaved as you did."

He wrung his hand again, and went on. The two men understood each other at last; it is sometimes a little odd to think how a few minutes and a word or two will mend or mar enough for a lifetime. Things did not seem quite so sad to Anthony after that little interview. He would try to do what was right to Ada, to everybody. The bitterness which made him refuse to accept friendship, because it had disappointed him once, was gone; for he had been too blind himself to demand that others should see perfectly, and he felt as if he owed them all amends, if only for the sake of Winifred, whom he had so misjudged.

Chapter Thirty Five

That winter dragged heavily to more than one of those whose stories I have been telling in a broken one-sided fashion enough. Anthony, one of whose failings, perhaps, was the procrastination which is often joined to a certain eager impetuosity, was going on from day to day without taking a decided step as to his marriage. The spring had been the time originally proposed; and though at one time he had been disposed to hasten matters, his wish had received a check which he had not forgotten. Ada, indeed, did not encourage him to press it. She had lost her old brightness, and the constant smiles were exchanged for a kind of listless irritability, which sometimes broke out into querulous complaint. Nothing had been heard of Mr Warren since he had left them; it seemed as if the young man were trying to forget Underham, or were ashamed of his feelings. At Hardlands life was very quiet. Mrs Orde was doing her best to act as a mother to the two girls; people said how fortunate it was that she was able to live with them, which was true enough; and yet poor Winifred sometimes wondered how many little jars and frets had grown into her life. Frank Orde, who was there again soon after Easter, sometimes wondered sadly, too. His step-mother was a true-hearted woman, full of practical common-sense, but there was a want of sympathy between her and Winifred which could not be explained. The girl was always admiring her and blaming herself for it, but it is probable that it was one of those contrarieties which could hardly have been otherwise. There are people who, quite unconsciously, seem to place us at a disadvantage. We may like them, even love them, but it is from some force of circumstances: they destroy our ease, banish our ideas, and reduce us in some strange fashion to nonentities. Winifred used to puzzle herself by trying to think how this could be. She had a strong sweet nature, to which people turned instinctively for help, but she would shrink at some little speech of her aunt's which yet was quite free from any sting of unkindness. The fear of bringing it down upon herself would often hamper her, even prevent her from doing what she longed to do. One is struck sometimes by the boundaries with which certain lives are hedged in. They seem so small, a word, an allusion,—perhaps no more than a thread, and yet the thread is as impassable as any fence. Frank Orde, who loved Winifred with all his heart, used to wonder sadly, as I have said, at the want of harmony between the two women who were to him the best and dearest in the world. Perhaps, if he had but known it, here was a little unfolding of the riddle, a touch of jealousy making the mother cold and sarcastic. It was not much, but it caused Winifred's life to be a little harder than it need have been, at a time when it was hard enough, poor child!

She and Anthony met but seldom through the winter, for after that one interview, which Winifred blamed herself for holding in tender remembrance, they knew that it was better not to see each other more than was necessary. But when the spring came, the time when all beautiful things seem possible, the burden weighed more heavily, and she longed feverishly to hear that the marriage day was fixed.

Anthony, too, felt that the delay must not last much longer. Ada could not accuse him of having given her no time in which to make her resolution, and these months of waiting seemed to be eating the heart out of more lives than one. Without coming to a determination beforehand, he one morning obeyed a sudden impulse and started for Underham to see Mr Bennett and let matters be set in train.

His mother went to the gate with him, where Nat Wills was at work, putting in some plants which Mr Robert had sent over. Anthony turned round more than once to see her nodding at him, and smiling with happy content. As he passed through the village the little gardens were bright with clumps of blue gentianellas, out of the midst of which scarlet anemones blazed. Inside the school the children were singing and marching, and stamping merrily as they marched; the rooks were hard at work, the air was full of sound: here was Anthony setting off to fix his wedding-day. They are sad hearts sometimes that go on what should be the happiest errands.

He had scarcely got out of the village, however, when, to his surprise, he saw Mr Bennett himself driving towards him. He did not notice Anthony until he was close upon him, and then pulled up suddenly.

"I was coming to Thorpe to see you, Miles," he said in an oddly constrained voice. "I suppose you are on the road to our house?"

"Yes, I am."

"Well, would you mind driving a mile towards Appleton with me instead? I've some things I must talk over with you quietly, and should be glad to feel secure from interruptions."

At any other time Anthony might have been struck with the contradiction that after he had jumped into the dog-cart, Mr Bennett, instead of plunging at once into his subject in his usual good-tempered, pompous fashion, remained silent, and seemed to have a difficulty in beginning the conversation. But Anthony was too much absorbed in his own difficulties to notice those of another, and the silence was too great a relief for him to think it strange.

It troubled his companion, however, for he did not know how to break it, and being a straightforward man, any roundabout course was very unwelcome. He looked over the hedge-rows on either side, at the fields which, owing to a wann wet winter, had lost no vividness of green, at the apple orchards nestling round the old thatched and weather-beaten farms, at the less frequent patches where the blue green of the young wheat contrasted with the red earth from which it sprang; but nothing that he saw helped him to his purpose.

"There's been too much rain for the crops," he said at last, with a sudden vigour as if this were the thought he had been maturing all the while. "At this rate everything will be washed up again. I saw Fisher at the turnpike,—you know Fisher?—and he detained me for at least fifteen minutes talking over his grievances. Otherwise I should have met you nearer home."

"Fisher talks for a dozen people besides himself. Mr Mannering is his landlord, is he not?"

"Ah, yes, yes. Mr Robert is a thoroughly upright man," said Mr Bennett, vaguely. "Never in my life saw any one so pleased as he was when I took him out news of what that poor Stephens had said,—never. Well, I was always certain something would set that matter straight."

"You at least acted as if it had never been crooked," Anthony said warmly, at once.

"Don't say anything about it," said Mr Bennett, getting red and uncomfortable. "There's another thing I'm afraid is crooked, which—which I'm ashamed to talk to you about, that's the long and short of it. I never thought I could be driven to fence and shuffle over any business as I've been shuffling now. I'd sooner bite my tongue out than tell it. But there's the thing,—past my altering, and I've the shame of it, if that's any comfort to you."

The man was speaking in short sharp sentences, as unlike as possible to his usual genial rather over-familiar manner. Some presentiment seemed to seize Anthony, and his face grew hard.

"Well, what is it?" he said in the deep tone he sometimes used.

"I wouldn't have had this to tell you for half a years income."

"If it has to be told I can't see that any good can be caused by delay."

Certainly Anthony's manner was not encouraging. "I only hope you will exonerate me and her aunt," said Mr Bennett, nervously.

"Then it's about Ada?" said Anthony, after a moment's pause.

"I'm ashamed to say it is."

"Well?"

"It's anything but well. Though I am her uncle, I do say she has behaved disgracefully. She says she did not know her own mind when she accepted you, and that she has discovered she always cared for Adolphus Warren. His going away, she declares, opened her eyes—"

"You should give effects their right causes," said Anthony, in a low bitter voice. "Say the change in his position."

"I'm half afraid of it," said Mr Bennett, whipping the old grey in his perturbation. "What can I say? Nothing can be worse. It has cut us both to the heart. I utterly declined at first to tell you, I was so ashamed; but she's had one fit of hysterics after another, until her aunt is quite worn out; and, unpleasant as it was, I felt you ought to be kept in ignorance no longer. I've always thought she was so amenable to what was right, but I'm really afraid nothing will move her."

"You need not fear my making the attempt," said Anthony, still in the same tone.

"You've a right to hold her to her promise," said Mr Bennett, unheeding. "Of course you've a right, and so I told her. But women are such irrational beings, that I really believe sometimes their minds can't grasp the obligation of a right. You might bring an action against her, for the matter of that. I should not oppose it. Any possible reparation—"

"Do you suppose that would console me?" said Anthony, grimly. "But I'll tell you the whole truth, for you have behaved just as every one in the neighbourhood would have expected from you. It isn't pleasant for a man to be kicked over at any time, but I had begun to think, from one or two reasons with which I need not trouble you, that we had made a mutual mistake. I went so far one day as to tell Miss Lovell something of the sort—"

"You did!" said Mr Bennett, facing round in wonder.

"And if she had known her own mind,—it was not so long ago as to make that impossible,—it would have saved some unpleasantness."

"You don't feel it so much, then?" said Mr Bennett, not quite sure whether he liked this or not.

"I imagine you would hardly begrudge me that alleviation?"

"O, certainly not, certainly not! I'm exceedingly relieved to find the blow not so heavy as we feared it might be. Then I presume the unfortunate affair may be allowed to drop as quietly as we can arrange between us?"

"I shall not call out Warren, nor begin a lawsuit, if that is what you mean. As to the quietness, I have no doubt that by this time all Underham knows that Miss Lovell has thrown me over."

"Confound Mrs Featherly!" muttered Mr Bennett, under his breath.

"Don't be uneasy. In these cases it is always the rejected who is the object of scorn. Besides, is not Warren the heir to a baronetcy?"

"I don't know what you mean. It was none of my seeking," said Mr Bennett, hotly.

"Well, well, you should allow for a man's grimacing a little when he finds himself in such an unexpected position. Now, as the news has been broken to me, and we are not on the way for anywhere so far as I am concerned, I will jump out, and wish you good by."

Mr Bennett reined up the old grey so suddenly that he almost threw her on her haunches.

"Good heavens, what am I about!" he said apologetically. "This business has quite upset me. And I honestly tell you, Miles, I don't understand your way of taking it. In my days, if my wife had treated me so, I—I should have cut my throat—though I'm sure I don't want you to do anything so rash. Still—"

Anthony had sprung into the road, and now was leaning over the wheel with his arm against the dog-cart. He said in a changed voice, "I can't wonder that it should puzzle you. I have been a puzzle to myself for a long time past. I doubt whether ever any one has managed to make so many mistakes as I. Don't blame Ada too much, I have been at least as much in fault as she, and yet I want both you and Mrs Bennett to think as kindly of me as you can. Nothing can ever touch the remembrance of your goodness."

He spoke with a strong feeling which brought Mr Bennett back to his side in a moment. He caught Anthony's hand, and began shaking it vehemently.

"My dear fellow, you've behaved—I can't tell you how I think you've behaved," he said, stopping only to begin again. It was the greatest possible relief to him that he might go home and tell his wife that matters were all comfortably settled, and that they need not be angry with Ada any more.

"Do you think so?" said Anthony, oddly. He shook hands again to satisfy Mr Bennett, and then drew back from the dog-cart. The old grey, a little affronted at her unaccustomed treatment, started off with a snort. Mr Bennett was looking back, and waving farewells so long as the road kept Anthony in sight. Overhead the clouds were parting, a yellow sun shone out and struck the young glistening leaves, a blackbird was whistling with clear beautiful notes; a great heap of weeds was burning in a field close by where some boys were shouting. Anthony found himself noting everything, wondering idly, and shutting his mind's door by that sort of compulsion which we have all of us in some measure in our power. When he could no longer do this, he set off, and walked for half a mile as quickly as if he were walking a match.

That Ada should have treated him in this manner was the utmost humiliation his pride could have endured, the more so because she had bestowed upon him so many gentle flatteries, had been so soft and yielding, so free from even the small reproaches for which he acknowledged she might at times have had an excuse. And the humiliation became greater as he began to recollect past trifles which had been forgotten, but which floated up to his remembrance now, as the flood which sweeps away boundaries will bring to the surface little in significant straws. He recalled words and actions of Ada's throughout their engagement; the manner in which she had quoted Mr Warren, who had been too small a figure to make an impression on Anthony; the readiness with which she accepted his society; he recollected that evening when he had made his appeal to Ada, and had seen two dim figures coming towards him under the trees, and her quick excuses. He turned from himself with a sick disgust as he realised how completely he had taken the false for the true, the true for the false. There was a terrible satire in his life, or so it seemed to him when he thought of his old self-reliance, and the end of it all.

Yet it must be allowed that, although this sting of humiliation was the first dominant feeling in his mind, it quickly began to yield before the relief with which he felt as if a long strain had suddenly relaxed. He stood still and stretched himself, flinging back his arms with a longing to express this joy of freedom by some bodily action. There was a gate close by him which had fallen off its hinges; he set to work to put it up again, labouring with a fire and vigour which was like an old inheritance renewed, and afterwards leaning over it and looking from the high ground on which he stood to the wooded fields below. Where the hedge dipped he could see the Thorpe cottages lying in rich brown patches, the Hardlands' firs, white smote curling up from the house. Ada and Mr Warren began to fade out of his mind like some blurred unpleasant dream; Winifred grew into life, brown-haired Winifred looking into his face with kind fearless eyes. He stood irresolute, an impulse which was as strong as it was sudden urging him. How could he so dishonour Winifred as to go to her at once, when but an hour ago he was the accepted, lover of another woman!—and yet, how could he not go? Even now he might be too late. Something had been said of Frank Orde in his hearing, against which his heart had leaped up with mute rage, but now it was a whirl of fear which shook him. It seemed as if all the emotions he had been holding in check were ready instantaneously to assert themselves, as if he could not endure another of those moments which up to this hour had stretched themselves out before him in long dull succession. His looks went yearningly down to that spot from which the smoke was curling easily upwards, and at last he jumped over the gate, and went with long strides down the field towards Hardlands.

Chapter Thirty Six

"Comes a little cloudlet 'twixt ourselves and heaven,
And from all the river fades the silver track;
Put thine arms around me, whisper low, Forgiven,
See how on the river starlight settles back!"

Lord Lytton.

When Anthony was looking down upon the fir-trees, there were two people standing under them, and talking earnestly. One of them was putting out her hand and saying in a voice which was very sad and kind, —

"I believe I am a hundred years older than you, Frank. Do people's hearts go on getting older and older at this rate, I wonder? I don't seem to feel as if all that you are saying could be so. Perhaps I am beginning not to feel anything any more."

"Don't disbelieve me," Frank said eagerly. "That is all I ask you, Winifred. Only try to believe how dearly I love you, and trust me, or let me have time to show you."

She did not turn away from him, she did not even take away her hand which he had clasped, and yet nothing in her attitude or in her eyes seemed to have grown nearer to him during that moment in which they stood so close to each other under the fir-trees, a little hidden from the soft, warm sun. Winifred stood as if she were thinking, but it might have been of something outside herself, and with which she was only concerned as a looker-on. Her face was tenderly grave, but Frank sought in vain for any glow which should answer his. She was silent so long, however, that at last he could bear it no longer, and said in a voice which was all uneven and broken, —

"What do you say, Winifred? You will not refuse me that one little promise?"

She said immediately, looking into his face with unshrinking eyes, —

"Ah, Frank, it is because it is so little that I feel I dare not give it. Dear Frank, what are you offering me?— do you think I do not know its worth?— and for all your heart you ask no more than just a little dead sufferance. You want to give everything, and to have nothing back again."

"What you call nothing—" began Frank, flushing, but she interrupted him quickly, with a new tone of pain in her voice.

"No, no,—why do we go on talking?—let us try to forget it all, let us try to be dear friends always, but do not ask me to do you a wrong which would make me hate myself."

Winifred might have been impetuously thrusting back something. Perhaps she was: perhaps she had a little secret, impatient longing to escape somehow, anyhow, from the associations which imprisoned her. Frank, who knew all her little story, and knew no more than she who was coming at that moment with swift steps across the dewy grass, looked at her, and felt his heart sink, though he had not lost all hope. He could wait a lifetime, he thought, and patient waiting must gain her at last. Just then the little iron gate clicked as Anthony came through: he saw them standing with clasped hands, saw Winifred look up, and turn away quickly to the house. Was his secret misgiving true?—was it too late, after all? He half stopped; but Frank had seen him, and was strolling towards him.

The two men did not meet very cordially, but they went through the usual conventionalities.

"So you're not off?" said Anthony.

Captain Orde, whose face was white, and whose hand was not quite so steady as usual, took out his fusee-box and struck a light.

"No, I'm not off till to-morrow," he said, lighting his cigar slowly. "Will you have a cigar? I shall make one push for it to Colchester. Do you ever come that way?"

"Not nowadays. Though I don't know where I shall find myself next. Sometimes I think of travelling for a year or two."

"You don't mean just knocking about Europe?"

"No, I should go farther afield."

Captain Orde gave him a quick, rather questioning glance, and walked on silently.

"How will that agree with your other prospects?" he said at last.

"I have no particular prospects, as you call them," said Anthony, shortly. "If you mean the engagement in which I had the honour to be concerned, it has come to an end."

"Does Winifred know this?" Frank was asking very gravely in a moment.

"How should she?" said Anthony, angrily. He was intending to speak without excitement, but that little scene under the fir-trees danced up and down before his eyes. "You need not think that I shall tell her," he went on in hot tumult, "for probably at this time Miss Chester is too much taken up with her own affairs to have thought to bestow upon those of other people."

"Miss Chester is not going to marry me, if that is what you mean," said Captain Orde, quietly. "I have asked her—more than once—and now for the last time."

He spoke in a dull strained voice. For him there was neither charm nor glory, only a dreary pain, a grey colourless sky. Anthony was not worthy of Winifred, but, alas, did he not know that she cared for him; that she was at this very moment, perhaps, weeping for the helplessness, the sadness of her love; that he, whose path must not touch hers any more, might send her the light and joy for which she longed? He did not hear much of what Anthony was saying, until he found that he had left him, and was making his way towards the house with quick, hopeful steps. Frank, who was going up to the clump, stood still and watched. It is a little hard to run for a prize, and see it carried off by some one who has never seemed to set his heart upon it. When a man has struggled neck and neck with you, it is easier to yield than to another who has loitered carelessly, and yet comes up, and sweeps by with triumphant ease. Anthony was going to his victory, while Frank was left out in the cold. Yet, if there are failures out of which grow success, so also there are defeats which bring rejoicing songs, though we do not hear them yet, and all that reaches us is the sadness of sighing and the weariness of tears.

Winifred was crossing the hall as Anthony Miles came in. Mrs Orde had caught her for some consultation about Bessie's masters, and she had been obliged for a little while to make and answer indifferent remarks while every nerve was on the strain, until she could bear it no longer, and, escaping from the room, was, as I have said, just crossing the hall when Anthony Miles came in.

There must be a world of subtle influences in the midst of which we live, and which is not the least wonderful part of our existence. As he, seeing her, stood for a moment with the door in his hand, the pretty lights and shades and trembling sunshine behind him, and his face so much in shadow that it was impossible for her hasty, tearful glance to read its expression, what strange joy sent a new thrill into her heart, and quickened it with intensest life? What swift movement of pity, tender and womanly, went out to Frank with the touch of wondering compassion for sorrows past so long ago, that since she had known of them night had turned into day, winter into spring, perplexity into contentment? It all only lasted for a moment, but why had it been? Anthony's own glow of eagerness died out of his heart as he came upon her in that sudden fashion, looked at her standing in the delicate light, and felt as if he could not say a word. To them both that instant seemed endless, and yet it was only an instant.

For then they came back to—realities, shall we say? Anthony left the sunshine and sparkling greens behind him, and walked into the hall where Winifred was waiting and putting out her hand calmly.

"How is Mrs Miles?" she said, "Bessie was going to take the club books to her this afternoon, for I am ashamed to say that we have kept them two or three days beyond our time."

"What will Mrs Featherly do to you?" said Anthony, holding her hand in his.

I do not think they were either of them conscious of what he was about. Perhaps it is part of the mystery of that strange world of which I have been speaking that there are states of feeling in which things that would thrill us at other times come and go quite unnoticed, and both Winifred and Anthony believed that they were cool and self-possessed, and did not think that he had her hand in his. Sniff, who had been in wild pursuit of a rabbit, dashed in at this moment, and flung himself down panting in a dark corner.

"Were you coming into the garden?" said Anthony. "Will you come?"

Winifred remembered Frank, and flushed and withdrew her hand.

"I don't think I can," she said, shaking her head. "I owe so many letters that it quite frightens me to think about it."

"One day can make very little difference," urged Anthony. "Pray come; I have something to tell you."

She looked at him, and that first flash of conviction had so faded away that her heart swelled with the thought, "He is come to tell me of their marriage." It did not cause her any surprise, but it made her hand tremble as she took down her garden hat and went slowly out into the sunshine. Once there, she began to walk quickly, so that Anthony became a little vexed by the idea that she wished to avoid listening to him. The path was so narrow that he could not walk by her side, until presently it led to a wider part where were some horse-chestnuts bursting into leaf, and Winifred stood still and leaned over the iron railings to coax an old pet pony of the Squire's. It was one of those soft bright growing days which are the most perfect in the world. Things were thrusting themselves out, calling, answering. Broken lights fell tenderly on the delicate tints. Sheets of pure blossoms swelled round the farms; the air was full of young, hopeful scents, of dancing insects; the grass was starred with innumerable daisies; a little troop of lambs came rushing up from, the end of the field, and leaped away again at sight of Sniff. Does Arcadia come sometimes?—Have we all felt it? It was Anthony on whom it was smiling now while he looked at Winifred, at her cheek a little turned from him, at the pretty curve of her arm as she held out some leaves for the old pony to nibble. As for her, she was thinking of an Arcadia for him and for another. And Frank, who had got up to the clump by this time, and could just see the two figures below him in the midst of all this peaceful greenery, thought that Arcadia had already begun for them. It looks like fairy-land to those that are shut out, and still its loveliness is not enough to satisfy us, little as we believe it. There are sweeter countries yet, though no outward beauty makes us long for them, and we see the dusty feet of the pilgrims, and the sadness of the journey, while the smile upon their hearts is hidden from us for a time. Arcadia may lie on the road, but it is not the end, and we may pass through other and harsher ways, and yet meet those we love. And up there under the trees were the sweet breezes, and the sunshine, and the larks singing overhead. Do not fear. There is no desolation in God's earth.

"You have not heard what I came to tell you," said Anthony, doubtfully.

The old pony's head was close to Winifred, and she was twisting his white forelock round her fingers. The words did not come easily with which she wanted to assure him that she had guessed his errand, and at last she spoke hastily, though with no disturbance in her voice.

"Is it that your marriage day is fixed? If so you must let us wish you joy."

"No, it is not that. It is just the reverse," he said, with an unreasonable feeling that Winifred ought to know and understand all at once. She looked round at him with quick surprise, but she did not answer in any other manner, and he was obliged to go on. "Miss Lovell has changed her mind, and prefers marrying some one else."

"You are laughing!" said Winifred, flushing angrily. "And it is not kind. You may suppose we care about it."

"But I am not laughing," said Anthony, in a low voice. When she looked at him, and saw that he was very grave, her hand began to tremble a little. He had become suddenly despairing with the conviction that it was an impossible thing to say, "I was engaged this morning to another woman, and yet I have always loved you;" he felt as if he dared not treat her so, and yet that he could not leave her.

"I don't understand it," Winifred began to say slowly. "Do you mean that she has been so heartless and cruel? O, I don't think so, it is a mistake; you fancy things sometimes which people do not intend in the least! Have you been to Underham? Have you seen Miss Lovell yourself?"

"I have seen Mr Bennett. I assure you it was put in the plainest possible English. Young Warren is the lucky fellow."

Perhaps her anger was useful, as it occasionally is, in keeping off other emotions. She threw back her head, with a gesture she sometimes used, a flush was on her cheek, and her eyes sparkled.

"How can you speak like that!" she said passionately. "I hate that people should pretend not to care for what hurts them. Why can't you let us be sorry for you?"

"Because I am not sorry for myself, Winifred," he said in a changed, deep tone. He took her hand in his, and held it close, and looked down into her eyes. "Because I have known for some time that the maddest mistake I ever made in my life was when I asked Ada Lovell to marry me. Because I feel as if a weight were lifted off my heart. Because I can breathe now, and live,—yes, and love,—I must say it, Winifred, my darling—"

For she had caught back her hand, and was standing, drawn to her full height, with her breath coming quickly, and no softening in her eyes. The words fell away from his lips. He, too, stood still and silent, looking at her with a dreary sinking of his heart. So this was the end.

"You are right," he said, quietly, in another moment. "I ought to have known better. Well,—at least you will say good by? Things don't straighten themselves in the way we are fools enough to dream they will. Good by, Winifred. Come, you'll say good bye?"

He stood still for another minute, waiting, and a lark that had been singing jubilantly overhead dropped swiftly down in a hush of tender silence. Winifred scarcely dared move, Anthony's tone heaped pain upon her heart, tears rushed into her eyes, but she said "Good bye," putting out her hand, at which he caught.

"No, it is not good by," he said suddenly. "Why should I be sent away?"

There was a quick change in his voice which set a hundred conflicting strings vibrating in her heart. How dared he speak in such a tone, and yet how dear it was! His strong feeling was carrying her with it, but she still found voice to say,—

"How can I know what you mean? How can you be one thing one day and another the next?" But Anthony disregarded the reproach. He said eagerly, "If you don't love me, at least we are old friends; let us go back to what we were, and begin again. Don't you think if you were to try very hard you might learn to like me a little bit, just a little bit?"

"I cannot learn to like you," said Winifred, simply, "because we have always liked each other, and there can be no beginning again." She said this very quietly, and then suddenly broke down. "O Anthony, Anthony," she said, covering her face with her hands, "you have made it so difficult!"

And then she was in his arms. She had never consented, and yet he held her close to him. "My darling," he said under his breath, "can you forgive me?"

Forgive him? Ah, yes, she loved him, and love will lavish forgiveness with a free hand, and a sweet joy in the bounty of its giving. If it were not so, how would it be with any of us? Was there ever such a moment, — so rich, so tender? And yet there must be better things, or Frank would not have been up there under the clump alone, there would not be so many sad hearts in the world, David Stephens would not have been lying under the grass.

Well, we shall know it all one day.

Very little has been said of late touching Marmaduke and his wife, the truth being that there is very little to say. They lived what must be called a prosperous life; at least, if there were any signs of disturbance in the midst of it, they were not such as became apparent to their neighbours. It was sometimes said that Mrs Lee was cold and distant, even with her husband, and that her looks had changed since her marriage, but her ill health was supposed to account satisfactorily for this, and nothing ever reached the ears of the outer world which could make it suppose that they were not a happy couple. Miss Philippa lived with them, by Mrs Lee's especial request, and there could be no doubt of her happiness. But no children were born, and rumour declared, how truly it is impossible to say, that, after Mr and Mrs Lee died, their money would be bequeathed to a great London charity.

Anthony's first attempt to find Margaret Hare's husband and child had been checked by the despondency with which he had been visited when his world had lost its faith in him; but under a new spring of energy, he and Mr Robert were soon able to track the wanderers in Australia. Some of the circumstances were communicated to the father; he, however, utterly rejected all old Mr Tregennas's intentions as a too late atonement. He was wealthy, and there was but one girl, and the certain hard determination which had carried him up in the struggle for existence now made him obstinately resolute against accepting his father-in-law's money.

Anthony, Winifred, and their children live in London, but are often in Thorpe, where there are both living and dead to draw them, besides its own quiet and tender beauty. Anthony's life was, perhaps, too soon filled with the things it wanted to admit of its ever becoming great in the manner in which people talk of greatness. But it is an exceedingly active and useful life, in the course of which he has made war upon more than one hydra-headed monster, and that with a success of which he often said his wife ought to share half the praise. She used to smile when she heard this, thinking of the many things which had helped her champion, besides her happy love. And, indeed, the influences that mould our lives are often scarcely known to ourselves, and come from as many sides as the winds that sweep the earth.